'Cracks like a Highveld thunderstorm, hiss of a sniper's bullet, rage of a hunted behemoth; exposing real-life crime, corruption and conspiracy at the highest level.'

Ronnie Kasrils, former ANC underground chief and Cabinet minister

'Fascinating, riveting, authentic about the fight to preserve wildlife under siege from corruption and crime. Well done, again, Peter.'

Luthando Dziba, leading South African wildlife conservationist

'Tense, unflinching, and viscerally evocative. Seeps with lived experience, redolent with the spellbinding qualities of Nature herself.'

Sarah Sultoon, *The Source, The Shot*

'A gripping page-turner transporting the reader into the secretive, suspicious, perilous world of armed "dissident" Irish Republicanism.'

Marisa McGlinchey, author of *Unfinished Business*

THE ELEPHANT CONSPIRACY

corruption, assassination, extinction

Peter Hain

Sequel to *The Rhino Conspiracy*

**MUSWELL
PRESS**

First published by Muswell Press in 2022
Typeset by M Rules
Copyright © Peter Hain 2022

ISBN: 9781739966058
eISBN: 9781739879464

Peter Hain has asserted his right
to be identified as the author of this work in accordance
with the Copyright, Designs and Patents Act, 1988

A CIP catalogue record for this book
is available from the British Library

Muswell Press
London N6 5HQ
www.muswell-press.co.uk

Printed and bound by CPI Group (UK) Ltd, Croydon CR0 4YY

'Little did we suspect that our own people, when they got a chance, would be as corrupt as the apartheid regime. That is one of the things that has really hurt us.'

NELSON MANDELA, 2001

'The question is, are we happy to suppose that our grandchildren may never be able to see an elephant except in a picture book?'

SIR DAVID ATTENBOROUGH

'If you are neutral in situations of injustice, you have chosen the side of the oppressor. If an elephant has its foot on the tail of a mouse, and you say that you are neutral, the mouse will not appreciate your neutrality.'

ARCHBISHOP DESMOND TUTU

For my grandchildren, Harry, Seren, Holly, Tesni,
Cassian, Freya and Zachary Hain

PROLOGUE

He awoke instantly.

Rather like the wildlife in his care, Isaac Mkhize slept deeply when he felt safe – but the slightest danger jerked him immediately alert.

Never disturbed by normal sounds like traffic outside their apartment, or wind howling, or rain spattering, or even the whiffles of his wife, Thandi, lying peacefully beside him, sheet pulled down in the KwaZulu-Natal humidity, shimmering in the nightlight.

But this was an alien sound.

A rasp? A scrape? What was it?

Mkhize, his powerful bare torso tense, slipped silently out of their bed, pulled up his boxer shorts lying on the floor and listened. Another scrape, then movement – coming, he thought, from the living room of their compact two-bedroom second-floor flat – must have been the window, for it wasn't the front door: that was securely locked as well as bolted inside.

He crept forward, crouching on his bulging thighs and muscled calves. More rustling, somebody moving almost as silently as him – he was sure now that was the strange sound. Creeping round their bedroom door he saw the rear of a man in the dark peering into the other bedroom that Thandi (and occasionally he) used as an office.

Just as the man was about to turn, Mkhize hit him hard in the base of his back, aiming for his solar plexus.

The man doubled up, shrieking with pain, turning in confusion, a stainless-steel knife glinting as it clattered to the floor, only for Mkhize to kick him in his testicles. Agony shooting through him, the man tumbled down in snarling shock.

Mkhize lunged forward, fist raised as if to smash him in the face, feeling as if possessed by something else, cold and resolute, ready to pulverise him. No man messed with his Thandi, certainly not this cowering thug.

The man bellowed, 'No! No!' still writhing, doubled up, and thrusting his hands up from his groin to protect his face in terror.

Then his eyes switched to stare, even more terrified, straight over Mkhize's shoulder.

Thandi was standing there, stark in the dark, arms straight out, gripping in both hands the Makarov pistol the Veteran had given her – the way she'd been taught by him.

Woken by the commotion, she'd grabbed the gun from the bedside cupboard, hurriedly tried to snatch a tee-shirt but couldn't find it, had crept forward.

'*Don't!*' the man screamed, 'He will send others!'

'Who is "*he*"?' Thandi shouted. 'Who is "*he*"?'

The man shook his head. 'No way will I tell you,' repeating several times in Zulu, 'No way will I tell you – he will kill me.'

'I will kill you before he does – *now*!' Thandi shouted.

The man shook his head, starting to sob.

Mkhize punched him again – this time on the chin, not too hard, not to knock him out, just to threaten him.

The man kept sobbing, shaking his head, muttering miserably, 'He'll kill me', making Mkhize almost sorry for the thug, almost disgusted with himself for the violence he'd unleashed to protect his loved one: what sort of man had he become?

But Thandi, quivering – for she too had never done anything like this before – was absolutely fixated.

'Tell me who he is, or I shoot,' she said, the Makarov, to her utter surprise, steady as she pointed it at him, her finger on the trigger.

The man didn't know if she was serious – and, in truth, she didn't either.

Indeed, threatening to shoot a man with a gun, she wasn't sure any more what sort of woman she had become.

It was as uncanny as it was moving. Without fail, each and every year.

Each and every year now for a while, at the same time, on the same day, the anniversary of her late husband's sudden death, Elise would sit on her verandah overlooking Zama Zama Game Reserve to welcome them.

And they would always come, slowly and nobly, the mourning

2

procession, paying their respects to the Owner, the one who had befriended them when they were raging, when they had arrived abused, their numbers callously reduced by poachers, ready to take on the world, to vent their fury at all and sundry.

The one who had cherished them, had slept in his tent in the bush alongside them, showed respect, showed that not all human beings were destroyers, not all human beings were cruel, not all human beings were heartless.

And then he had been taken from them – suddenly, shockingly, almost in the way they too had been slain, their family attacked. Out of the blue one day, their tranquil life ripped apart, several of their number assassinated.

So they always came at the allotted time to stand the other side of her garden fence and pay homage before Elise, the widow of their friend. The Matriarch would always lead them – she seemed suddenly frail this year for the first time, Elise noticed, concerned.

Imperious, dignified, gentle, respectful – yet ferocious if crossed – the Matriarch would tutor the young ones, swish them back into line if they shuffled friskily, teach them about the importance of the moment, that they probably wouldn't have been there without the friendship of the Owner, that they needed to honour his memory too on this day of remembrance.

The tears ran down Elise's finely shaped face, her blonde hair with encroaching silver streaks combed back smartly, hands folded on her knees over the smart dress, always the same one she would retrieve from its place in her wardrobe, hung there to be worn only for this occasion.

A mark of respect too for her to show to them.

And then, after a decent interval, the elephant herd would turn. Elise always searched for that moment when the Matriarch indicated to the others that their remembrance service was over, but could never spot it. They would move silently, even the babies for once obedient, and begin their slow, silent retreat behind the regal Matriarch, the constant din of the birds and cicadas for once eerily absent too.

'Irish' walked, steady and strong, his Armalite rifle ready as he searched for the target ahead.

The nickname 'Irish' had been Pádraig Murphy's for as long as he could remember. Or at least since his teenager days in Crossmaglen in

South Armagh in the far corner of Northern Ireland, the Irish border very near to both the west and the south of the small village.

Cool, damp South Armagh was dubbed 'bandit country' during 'the Troubles' – the decades of horror, of terrorist attacks and police and army counter-attacks, of assassinations, knee-cappings, bombings and shootings from the early 1970s.

He'd been born a few years earlier, and had grown up in a Republican family, in a community hating the Royal Ulster Constabulary and the British Army.

'Irish' suited him, he'd always thought, because that was what he was: 'Irish', not 'Northern Irish', not some little part of the United Kingdom, but Irish, part of Ireland. Not the 'island of Ireland' as the British Secretary of State always called it, carefully navigating the treacherous waters of language between Unionists and Republicans. But straightforward, unadulterated Ireland.

When he left school aged seventeen, having dropped out, to the disappointment of his teacher, who reckoned the youngster had university promise, there were no jobs beyond the most menial. Also, he was angry about the belligerent behaviour of British soldiers on the streets towards teenagers like him – they seemed to think they owned the place. And other grievances festered, like family and friends being arrested, their houses raided. So he drifted into the Provisional IRA – the 'Provos' – who ran everything in Crossmaglen. Everything.

And Irish was soon part of that: the attacks on the security forces, bombings, killings, smuggling across the border, post-office robberies – the lot, everything Republican paramilitaries undertook to keep their fight going: to drive the Brits right out of Northern Ireland.

Then he left the Provos, resigned from the 1st Battalion of the IRA's South Armagh Brigade, disgusted by what he felt was its 'sell-out' to participate in Northern Ireland's new inclusive self-government that followed the 1998 Good Friday Peace Agreement negotiated by Prime Minister Tony Blair.

The 1st Battalion, covering Crossmaglen, Bessbrook, Forkhill and Camlough, had been one of the IRA's most deadly, to the fore of the IRA campaign from the very beginning of the Troubles.

It wasn't easy for him to resign – he left comradeship forged in crossfire – and instead joined an IRA splinter group with other dissidents. Suddenly, people he'd had known for years walked past, blanking him in

4

the street. Local shopkeepers weren't much better. He'd became an out-
sider, 'one of them dissidents'. It made him even more determined, taking
even more comfort from the beleaguered solidarity of his new 'dissident'
network – not that hard, because most had been with him in the Provos.

Although nominally still living with his parents, he increasingly slept
elsewhere, slipping out of alleys or farmyards through back doors into
strange beds and sliding off again before light, sometimes never to meet
his hosts. And never needing to worry any more about the six military
watchtowers astride the mountain peaks from where the Brits had tried to
spy on everything human that moved below, but now dismantled under
the 'peace process' he despised.

In his heyday, Irish was known as 'One Shot' for his lethal sniper
prowess, targeting Brit soldiers from their Crossmaglen barracks on foot
patrols searching for Semtex or radio-controlled bombs in cowsheds,
under bales of hay, in milk churns or wheelie bins, behind dry-stone
walls, in ditches or gorse bushes.

But now he was on a very different mission, in a very different place,
hot and dry, trudging forward, cradling his Armalite set on firing mode.

CHAPTER 1

After the new president had phoned inviting her to become one of his MPs, Thandi Matjeke spent a sleepless night, tossing and turning as she tried to make up her mind.

He had asked her to become an African National Congress Member of Parliament. *Her?* The *President* had specifically called to ask *her*? The reason, he had explained, was her courage and values demonstrated in exposing the Former President's rhino conspiracy.

She'd called the Veteran, her mentor and former prominent ANC freedom fighter, for advice. But he'd insisted it was her choice, her decision. He couldn't make it for her.

Neither could her husband, Isaac Mkhize. Her radio-production job was part-time, her activism all-consuming, his ranger job in the nearby Zama Zama Game Reserve taking him away for weeks at a time. Would they manage to make their young marriage work if she became an MP?

Did she really want to be one anyway?

Thandi had risen at five in the morning, fed up at being unable to sleep, still wrestling with her decision.

She was proud of being chosen by the President, and couldn't help feeling flattered.

As the kettle boiled for her cup of tea, she had a small glass of pure aloe juice – always her first liquid of the morning, for its maximum health boost. Then she began preparing a bowl of Maltabella porridge; her mom, a big fan, explained to her that when she was a little girl, Maltabella, made from malted sorghum grain, was 'like a warm hug in the morning'.

Thandi smiled at the memory, then jerked herself back to ponder. She

7

knew she had a habit – no, a fault – of allowing her mind to flit when she really should be concentrating.

Being an MP would give her the prestige and the platform to push her ideas, maybe even be a route into government.

But she worried she would be beholden to the Party top brass, who chose the list of candidates and, critically, in what order: the higher, the better chance of being elected.

Which meant MPs were accountable to their *party* and not to their constituency *voters*.

And what if the President who wanted her was succeeded by a corrupt one who didn't? Where would *that* leave her?

She was also repelled by the ANC's milking of state coffers, its practice of eliciting a 'donation' from each state-owned enterprise, almost as if it was their patriotic duty. Taxpayers were effectively subsidising the ruling party and paying the salaries of its full-time officials.

That also fuelled factionalism in the ANC, as different groups in the Party competed not for politics but for salaried party positions to enrich themselves.

Some countries, Thandi had read, state-funded all parties according to their voting support – Britain did a bit, Germany quite a lot, Scandinavian countries even more. But their taxpayers contributed to all the major parties, not only one.

Under a quarter of a century of ANC rule, the lines between state and party had become blurred, and the professional integrity and independence of the civil service undermined.

Yet surely the ANC was different from South Africa's other parties? It had led the transformation from tyranny to democracy, striven to unite a bitterly divided nation – to create a new country almost from scratch. Yes, it had become corrupt, but it also retained a noble mission.

Pondering all this, Thandi sipped her tea and ate her porridge, worrying and waiting for the President's call.

She was still not finally decided.

Recently appointed head ranger, Isaac Mkhize established a new routine in Zama Zama. First job of the morning for the rangers not allocated to dawn bush walks was to hunt for snares. All the elaborate blood-ivory intrigues, all the cunning poacher plots, and yet snares were most regularly the biggest threat.

It was simple and quick for poachers to slide in, set a snare, retreat, find an elephant and sneak out again with a tusk bloodily hacked off. They hung wire nooses in wildlife corridors where unsuspecting elephants passing through the bush suddenly found their trunk or neck passing through the loop, and the more they twisted and turned to free themselves, the more the noose tightened, with escape rare, death slow. Snares were cheap and easy to fix, easy to plan. If the elephants were 'lucky' the snare might only catch an ear, and tear off a bit, or even wrench the whole ear right out.

No animal was safe from a snare. Small elephants were especially vulnerable to a concealed wire loop, one end usually fastened to the base of a stout tree. As the elephants struggled to free themselves, the snare tightened. If they managed to rip the end of the snare from its base, maybe assisted by their mother, that very act of freeing themselves tightened the snare tight around their necks, the ugly red wounds gaping and going septic, which for baby elephants could be life-threatening.

Most heart-wrenching were the three snared elephant calves Mkhize had once found, each under two years old and dependent upon their mothers for milk. The baby, barely nine months old, had a snare cutting deep into her neck and jaws, her trachea almost severed. The second, a bit older, had his neck encircled and his jaws somehow trapped. The third, getting on for two years, had a snare both cutting into her neck and one front leg. It meant that for all three even being nursed by the rangers, encouraged to drink or walk, was agonising – and complicated by their protective mums refusing to abandon them, hampering the treatment on the one hand but comforting the confused babies on the other.

Although his role in the anti-apartheid struggle had been modest, the Apparatchik was fond of exaggerating it, talking up how in his late teens the Soweto school students' uprising in 1976 had first sparked his political interest, had led him to identify with the ANC, though so finding that its illegality made it difficult for him to join.

He claimed to be a founding member of the militant Congress of South African Students, though none of the actual founders could recall him.

His dashing anecdotes of James Bond-type behaviour, bigging-up his role in the ANC's underground wing, uMkhonto we Sizwe, or 'MK', were derided by contemporaries. Much the same was true for his claims to have been a founder in the Free State region of the main resistance

9

movement of the 1980s, the United Democratic Front. 'He was nowhere to be seen,' said one founder.

But his former comrades did recall one trait: a skill at pocketing a share of funds from donations to the ANC, invariably coming in cash because it was still an illegal organisation at the time and these couldn't easily be made through bank accounts.

Nevertheless, impressive skills at football earned him his nickname 'Star', bringing him a charisma that he made the most of as he clambered energetically up the ANC ladder.

Star hailed from a small town called Vryburg ([free town)] in the then Orange Free State, or Vrystaat, as it was also known – the old Afrikaner heartland and former Boer republic situated between the Orange and the Vaal rivers. His home town had grid-patterned broad streets, still surrounded by flat, fertile farmland, with cows wandering on its pavements and a sign advertising '*die beste biltong in die Vrystaat*'.

As a boy, his preoccupation was getting enough to eat. His family came from the Basotho chiefdom, and he'd been subjected to the familiar myriad apartheid restrictions – from travelling on buses for blacks only to being banned from voting.

But the character flaws of exaggeration, self-promotion and slipperiness were to stand him in good stead as he advanced up a greasy political ladder to become provincial premier of what under him became known as a 'gangster state'.

The new Security Minister, Major Yasmin Essop, was at a loss to know where on earth to begin in the mission with which the new President had entrusted her – to clean up and professionalise all branches of policing, security and intelligence, including her old fiefdom, military intelligence.

She had walked into a shambles: police officers committing crimes and others being sidelined for investigating those very crimes from the time when, ten years before, the Former President had appointed a new head of crime intelligence to do his bidding. Secret-service accounts were plundered to line pockets, and exploited to support crony politicians and their election campaigns.

Yasmin immediately appointed a new director-general after the old one had been exposed for receiving kickbacks from security contracts. She quickly ordered the arrest of the former head of crime intelligence on multiple charges, including murder, kidnapping, intimidation, fraud and perverting the course of justice.

She had uncovered evidence of illicit funding of private trips to China and Singapore, and home property conversions, as well as secret-service account looting. Procurement had also been corrupted through irregular and inflated costs of personal protective equipment. At one point, an acting head of crime intelligence had been plucked from among the Former President's cronies on his personal protection team.

As was her habit, Yasmin spent a long time staring into space as she sat at her official desk, her new PA having quickly learned not to disturb her.

Yasmin never did anything on the spur of the moment. She calculated all the angles, she drilled down into all the details, as she plotted her path forward, computing who to pick off first in her corruption-riddled security services, operatives who would be the least able to mobilise pressure from the Former President's still-powerful cronies determined to thwart the new president.

Inside the security services she had only a trusted few, including her loyal aide, the Corporal. Outside there was her freedom-struggle comrade from the 1980s, the Veteran, with his small band of activists: his protégé Thandi, the Sniper, who had played such an important role in the rhino conspiracy, and his British friend, Bob Richards.

Thandi continued fretting until the President finally called.

'Good morning, how are you?' His warm, friendly greeting made her feel even more embarrassed and defensive.

'Good morning, sir, thank you for calling,' she stammered.

'Having slept on it, are you willing to join us? I certainly hope so!'

Thandi had worked out her response. She wouldn't say yes or no until he'd answered her questions.

'I am very honoured,' she began. 'In fact I am still astounded you called me in the first place, Mr President!'

He chuckled. 'Not at all. You are a talented, brave young woman, Comrade Matjeke. We need you.' His choice of 'comrade' was deliberate, to make her feel part of his ANC family.

'Thank you, but can I ask a few questions, please?'

The President wasn't sure whether to be irritated or impressed – probably both, he thought.

'Of course,' he replied.

11

'Am I right that as an MP, my primary loyalty will be to the Party, not to the voters – and therefore if your successor as president doesn't like me, or your corrupt opponents get total control of the ANC, then I'm finished, aren't I?'

'But the more people like you I can recruit, the less likely that will happen, Thandi,' the President replied, sidestepping her question.

Although she had made up her mind, she didn't want to offend him, still less to burn her bridges.

'Mr President, I want to support you. I want all the corruption in the ANC to be rooted out, and I want you to succeed. Of course I do. But I have thought long and hard, and I think I can do that better from outside Parliament, where I am free from the clutches of corrupt ANC bosses.'

The President was taken aback. He wasn't used to being refused. But although peeved, he also had to admit privately to a grudging admiration; he'd never come across anyone quite like this impressive young woman.

Before he could say anything, Thandi quickly followed up: 'Can I please have a direct phone number in case I need to make contact if there is an emergency, so I can keep fighting for you outside the system?'

The President's mind was already turning to his next of many tasks and duties. 'I am very disappointed, Thandi. But of course, my political secretary, who is listening in on this call. will ring you right away with the numbers and emails you need. Meanwhile, go well, Thandi, and be careful about your personal security, because there are bad people out there.'

He rang off and Thandi put down her phone, pondering his last, rather ominous reference to her security.

Then she started shaking.

She had turned down the opportunity of a lifetime.

She'd said 'no' to the President!

And she couldn't quite believe what she'd done.

Except that she felt an odd sense of relief.

The darkness was slowly fading and the dawn stealthily creeping up as Isaac Mkhize, rifle at his side, led half a dozen bleary-eyed visitors out of the lodge for their bush walk in the Zama Zama Game Reserve.

These ventures required full concentration, as the group was vulnerable to any predators and other wildlife they might stumble across. His colleague Steve Brown formed up the rear, keeping the excited visitors disciplined in line.

Mkhize had chatted to them over coffee and rusks beforehand, most half-awake, but one woman full of questions after her caffeine hit.

'After all the international agreements, all the anti-poaching fortifications, are elephants still facing extinction?' she'd asked.

'Sadly, yes,' Mkhize replied gravely. 'Not so long ago, ivory-seeking poachers killed ten thousand elephants in Africa in just three years. During 2011 alone, about one of every twelve on the continent was murdered. Despite international bans on the trade, black-market prices are still extortionate. It's heart-breaking: humans are such appalling killers.'

Bob Richards MP, not for the first time, was criticised for sticking his neck out.

London's City Airport had been blockaded and Parliament Square jammed up by Extinction Rebellion protesters gluing themselves to pavements, roads and planes. Central London had almost been brought to a standstill.

Despite over 1,000 arrests, one MP attacked the police for being too soft. 'I ate in a restaurant last night where there was only one occupied table. Normally the place is full, but people didn't feel safe, so stayed away,' he moaned.

Another was especially piqued at having 'to step over' XR protesters to get into her ministerial office.

Others fulminated about 'a lawless mob' causing chaos.

But to Richards, all this sounded like a scratchy old gramophone record, and he said so in a speech in the Commons, loudly heckled by several Tory MPs, to silence from his own front bench.

'Give way!' shouted several Tories as one rose to challenge Richards. He happily gave way, the clock timing his speech limited to five minutes – because so many MPs wanted to contribute to the debate – stopping at the intervention.

'So the Honourable Member is advocating law-breaking! He's a law-breaker!' The MP looked around at his cheering colleagues on the government benches who chanted: 'Law-breaker! Law-breaker!'

There was a resounding noise from the bellowing chants in the chamber, and the Speaker rose from his chair to shout: 'Order! Order! The Honourable Member has a right to be heard!'

The chanting stopped, the Tory MPs giggling among themselves.

'Mr Bob Richards!' the Speaker called, gesturing to him.

Richards rose, but another Conservative MP immediately leapt to his feet.

'Give way! Give way!' his colleagues shouted again, sneaking a glance at the Speaker, just in case another reprimand was coming.

But Richards again willingly gave way, now angry but also content and determined to stay calm, thinking: he had them rattled.

The MP bellowed above the din: 'Is the Labour front bench in lock-step with the Honourable Member's law-breaking advocacy? Is this Labour's new official policy? Is Labour now the "law-breakers' party"?'

Tories gestured at the Labour front-bench spokeswoman, bellowing, cupping their hands, gesticulating, urging her to get to her feet and answer.

But she blanked them.

Richards stood, smiling now, which infuriated his opponents even more. They pointed and shouted at him as they looked anxiously at the Speaker.

Instead, Richards held his hands up, shooing them to be quiet, looking around for nearly twenty seconds until the din had subsided, before continuing, the clock ticking again.

'A hundred years ago, exactly the same sort of outrage by male MPs and Lords was levelled at the suffragettes, who chained themselves to Parliament's railings and caused all sorts of pandemonium. When Emily Wilding Davison died under the King's horse at the 1913 Derby, racegoers in top hats were furious that their afternoon had been spoiled by her desperate protest for women to have the vote.

'Two hundred years ago, the Tolpuddle Martyrs were arrested, tried and deported to Australia for the offence of forming a friendly society to provide help when they were poorly. The Martyrs were denounced as treasonable, lawless traitors, threatening the very future of England's "Green and Pleasant Land".

'But workers then had no rights, weren't allowed to join a trade union or strike.

'Fifty years ago there was similar outraged condemnation when demonstrators invaded rugby and cricket pitches and to stop all-white South African sports tours at Twickenham, Lord's and other grounds across Britain. "Civilisation was in mortal danger," their critics cried.

'But each of these groups shares an honourable heritage with Extinction Rebellion demonstrators.

'A just cause, such as votes for women, better wages and conditions for workers, and the fundamental sporting principle that teams should be chosen on merit not on skin colour.

'All were causes deploying tactics angrily denounced at the time in the newspapers, by politicians and judges. All were also causes only won after struggle and protest, sometimes bitter and confrontational.

'But today the idea of denying women the vote is preposterous. The suffragettes are saluted. The Springbok captain is Siya Kolisi – a black man who would have been banned from representing his country under apartheid.

'When I went to join Extinction Rebellion protesters occupying Whitehall outside 10 Downing Street, I found mothers and fathers, grandmothers and grandfathers, singing about saving the planet, their numbers swelled by thousands of youngsters.

'Far from being a "threat to civilisation", they want to save human civilisation by demanding our government triggers action to combat the climate-change emergency now.

'Of course none of us like it if we're inconvenienced, but so long as governments like ours right across the world mouth platitudes instead of taking the radical action needed to halt and reverse climate change, we deserve to have our daily routines disrupted by the Extinction Rebels. Like most of us, I'm no climate-change angel – but I salute them.'

Richards sat down to harrumphs from his parliamentary opponents, who included (albeit silently) a few from his own party unhappy that he had given government ministers an opportunity, which they duly took, to denounce him for 'advocating law-breaking' and sundry other charges, instead of having to defend their decidedly underwhelming record on confronting climate change.

Although he'd been keeping a low profile since the rhino conspiracy, poacher-ringleader and former apartheid mercenary Piet van der Merwe still raged against the night.

The country was going to the dogs, he ranted.

The district municipality for the small town of Vryburg had admitted that a third of its wastewater treatment works were dysfunctional, and it now faced criminal charges after ignoring warnings, directives and notices to stop letting raw sewage flow into local streams and rivers.

Although aged infrastructure coupled with population growth had affected these sewer treatment works, Van der Merwe knew the real culprits were Star's incompetent or corrupt cronies, appointed for their loyalty, with no expertise in running a water system.

Perpetual sewage spills in many of the rivers were causing a calamitous risk for agriculture, tourism and the people who lived in the area.

A series of Department of Water and Sanitation directives to fix their wastewater treatment works had been ignored; so had legal injunctions issued by local residents and businesses in the area.

The primary sewage pond in the town was overflowing, full of sludge and spilling raw sewage into the nearby river and its tributaries, causing them to become overgrown with green algae.

Sewage had also been pouring into the town's natural wetlands with the stench unbearable. Some houses were surrounded by sewage, bits even bubbling through wooden floors. Local farmers complained about their dams going green, finding dead cows where they had drunk from them. There were worries that the systematic contamination of the area's rivers would shut down the export fruit market.

Because of lack of maintenance, the wastewater works were in a continuous state of disrepair. Elementary duties, such as cleaning the screens designed to catch sanitary pads, nappies and other foreign objects in the sewers, were not done regularly, leading to the pumps burning out. Companies obtaining contracts to fix the pumps never delivered, simply pocketing the money, all paying a cut to Star's fiefdom.

But faced with a tirade of complaints, he merely called an ANC rally to face down his critics, feted by his loyal party members, Van der Merwe shaking his head in disbelief.

That his paymaster had recently become the self-same Apparatchik quite passed him by.

Piet van der Merwe compartmentalised his life, and his thinking. A man had to earn a living. Yet a man still had a right to his own views.

An intriguing foursome, Bob Richards thought, joining the strictly private video conference initiated by Security Minister Yasmin Essop.

The Veteran – of course. The Sniper, present for his IT expertise and who mysteriously wasn't named or introduced properly to Richards. Where should South Africa position itself on robotic weapons, Yasmin had asked. It was a topic Richards had become increasingly concerned about in respect of British policy.

16

'Lots of key people are now saying that the future will be dominated by artificial intelligence, with serious worries about its military uses,' the Sniper began.

He paused, having learned to allow lay people time to understand the issues underlying his world of fast-moving technology.

'The heart of the problem is the introduction of AI into weapons. The whole point about having weapons is deterrence, not to fight wars but to deter others, because potential enemies know you have the capability to badly damage or even destroy them.'

The Sniper paused again.

'But weaponising AI could even things up. How would we really know what our enemy is capable of if we all have access, as we surely will, and even do now, to AI-controlled weapons? Will our military strategists even have the ability to out-think or out-predict robotic weapons? And remember, wars sometimes have originated from mistrust and miscalculation.'

'I'm not sure I fully understand what you're getting at,' the Veteran interjected. He'd never been afraid to ask a question even if it might signal ignorance. It was a sign of confidence to do so, not weakness – yet most people stayed silent, in case they might be embarrassed.

The Sniper pondered for a moment. 'Remember the new Google program of a year or so ago that taught itself to play chess in a few hours? It was able to beat all previous programs and all human chess players. The point is that it was able to *itself* invent new chess strategies unknown in two thousand years of the game. Now apply that sort of AI power, if you like non-human logic, to weapons and we are in a whole new and menacing world.'

The Veteran, trying to understand fully, asked: 'Wasn't it a few years ago that top scientists like Stephen Hawking argued that AI was now the biggest threat facing humankind, maybe even bigger than climate change, and one that could finish us?'

'Yes, exactly,' the Sniper observed pointedly.

Yasmin interjected: 'But the United Nations Secretary-General has urged states to prohibit weapons systems that could, all by themselves, target and attack human beings. He called them "morally repugnant and politically unacceptable".'

'Yes,' agreed Richards. 'We should press for killer robots to be banned by a new global treaty like the ones that prohibited antipersonnel

17

landmines in 1997 and cluster munitions in 2008. Have a look at the film *Slaughterbots*. There's a scene where killer robots swarm into a classroom, flooding in through windows and vents, students inside screaming as they are relentlessly killed.'

'But,' Yasmin interjected, 'China, Israel, Russia, South Korea, the United Kingdom and the United States have been developing different autonomous weapons systems, as well as other countries. Can South Africa afford to get left behind in a killer-robot race?'

Richards bristled. 'Since 2013, thirty countries have called for a ban on fully autonomous weapons: from Argentina to Austria, Brazil to Ghana. So quite a spread. Also the Non-Aligned Movement of over a hundred and twenty member states has called for international prohibitions.'

The Sniper explained: 'Drones have been made that not only identify human targets but decide for themselves whether to attack. The technology already exists to combine AI with facial recognition, so drones can target a particular person, or even type of person like an ethnic group. Fighter planes piloted by AI could soon outperform human pilots. Like it or not, we are in a race that no country wants to lose, to build robotic weapons that are far superior to human-controlled ones.'

Yasmin was growing weary. She'd had enough of all this chat. 'Remember the Soviet radar operator who spotted a sign of US nuclear missiles being launched in 1983 but did not alert his superiors because he wasn't absolutely sure. Just as well, because the "launches" he'd spotted turned out to be rare reflections of the sun on clouds. It was a very narrow escape from triggering a nuclear war. Just imagine what a fully automated warning system might have triggered.'

'Yes,' Richards, said, 'but there's big resistance from the global military powers to any new treaty stopping AI weapons. They don't want to risk being left behind. Others say AI systems can even save lives. The UK has said that because intelligent weapons are more accurate, there will be lower casualties, especially among civilians caught in the crossfire. The trouble is, we are heading for defence systems based on a hair-trigger controlled by each country's own AI – and where will that end?'

The Veteran hadn't said much, just listened intently, and now intervened: 'You cannot expect countries to unilaterally give up on AI weapons when every other aspect of our lives, from medical treatments to manufacturing, are starting to use AI more and more. Surely we need an urgent global agreement at least to prevent AI operating nuclear arsenals?

That's the absolute minimum surely? This is not about science fiction any more. Russia's leader Vladimir Putin has stated: "Who leads in AI will rule the world."'

Yasmin nodded, making a special note among her scribbled points from the exchange.

'Thanks, guys,' she summed up drily. 'Lots of food for thought when I brief the President, as he's asked me to do.'

Star had honed his factional party skills ruthlessly.

His ANC organisational motto was simple: 'If you control sufficient local branches, you can control a region. If you can control sufficient regions, you can control a province. If you can control sufficient provinces, you can control the national party.'

In the Free State, various irregularities were deployed by his acolytes, such as convening ANC branch meetings at short notice or at secretive locations, or ensuring members did not appear on branch registers, so were unable to participate. Rogue behaviour and vote rigging became the norm. Not surprisingly, Star's grip tightened remorselessly.

But his party machinations had one purpose only: not to offer a different policy agenda to assist local citizens, instead to get control of the provincial coffers and loot them.

When he was put in charge of the Free State's department of tourism, auditors brought in by the provincial premier found irregular loans and gross overpayment for goods, fraud and dodgy contracts. Then President Nelson Mandela tried to adjudicate and resolve from afar the intra-party infighting Star was pursuing to grab total power. Eventually, the ANC leadership dissolved the Free State executive and Star was first cast into the wilderness, then reinstated and shoehorned in as an MP.

But, kicking his heels in Cape Town as an obscure backbencher in Parliament, Star was all the time plotting to return to his province, where he succeeded in winning and holding the Party chairpersonship for a decade. The door was opened to his prize: the provincial premiership, where he quickly established an iron grip.

Soon its purpose became transparent. Heists of meat and vegetables through the Free State department of agriculture became commonplace when he was MEC (member of the executive council) for agriculture. There were also kickbacks from property developers and public contracts. Star used government resources to buy people and build his provincial empire just as he had built his party empire to get his hands on power.

But to keep that iron grip and its gateway into wholesale looting of provincial coffers, anybody in his way was threatened with demotion or suspension. There were suspicious deaths too.

The Scorpions – the crack security unit established to replace a crooked apartheid police system, which had been geared more to crushing political opponents than to catching criminals – tried to arrest him for corrupt sale of land. But before the Scorpions could execute their arrest warrant, Star's close ally, the Former President, had conveniently ordered the unit be disbanded in 2009, substituting the ineffectual Hawks headed by his cronies.

Star's circle was protected as serious crime soared.

She chuckled wistfully, her voice getting fainter at the effort of talking to her granddaughter Thandi, for her health had been deteriorating.

'I remember back in the early 1963 when I again opened the door to be confronted by the same two large security police officers who had arrested the mother activist – two sergeants in the Special Branch, big fat men, one we called "banana fingers" because he had such huge, spongy hands. They gave the mother activist a banning order for five years.'

'What was it like being "banned", Granny?' Thandi asked the old lady, who was slumped in her chair in the small sitting room.

'It was thousands on words of paper: I didn't understand it all, my reading wasn't that good. But it stopped her meeting more than one person at a time. She couldn't leave Pretoria and it stopped her from going to all sorts of places like black townships or courts, which she often visited for her anti-apartheid work. She couldn't even go into her children's schools to talk to their teachers – they had to come and stand outside on the pavement. And of course she was banned from taking part in politics, and had to step down as a local leader in the resistance.'

'So what did she do then?' Thandi asked, always in awe of the women who had joined the anti-apartheid struggle, been banned, jailed or, like Nelson Mandela's wife, Winnie, banished to faraway places.

'Aah, now Thandi,' the old lady wheezed, short of breath. 'The mother activist was a clever one. She found all sorts of ways to remain active secretly. She kept in daily contact with her successor as the local party branch secretary. He would call her from a phone box on the street with

20

a coded message. Like "how is your dog?" When she didn't even have one!' The old lady cackled, then caught herself as she started to cough, before continuing. 'That would be the signal for her to jump in the car and drive to a prearranged meeting point.'

'Didn't she ever get found out?'

'Never. She ran rings around the Special Branch. We just called them "the Branch". Once she suddenly asked me to go home in the middle of the week – very unusual because I normally only went home for week-ends. When I returned, it was obvious someone had slept in my little bedroom by the garage. But I didn't ask her about it. Not because she didn't trust me, but best not to know.'

Old Mrs Matjeke winked, a small, conspiratorial smile on her creased, weathered face.

'Did you ever find out why, Granny?'

'Yes, but only a year later when the same thing happened. A political prisoner had escaped and asked her for help. She smuggled him into my room over the back of the kopje and drove him out in her car, squeezed into the boot, past the Special Branch parked on the roadside outside. Very brave, because if they had found the prisoner, she would have been put in jail.'

'I suppose it must have been sort of exciting and horrifying all at once, this struggle activism, Granny?' Thandi asked

'Yes, exactly that. But I wouldn't have missed it.'

The old lady was tiring now and Thandi helped her to her bed to sleep, quietly letting herself out of the small square brick house, locking up and pushing the key back through the letter slot in the door so her granny was safe.

Thinking back to that time – over ten years ago, when she was in her mid-teens – Thandi wondered what her granny would have made of yet more evidence of corrupt incompetence, this time of imploding health provision in the Eastern Cape, with one of the highest death rates in the world – more than 500 per 100,000.

Six newborn babies had died in a few days, specialist services for children with cancer were collapsing, and the Eastern Cape health depart-ment was about to run out of money.

Because of hospital-acquired infections in a shockingly overcrowded neonatal unit, one nurse sometimes had to look after twenty-eight babies. Another hospital was only able to provide four intensive-care beds and

21

did not have enough doctors or money to provide twenty-four-hour medical care.

A paediatric oncology unit was facing closure because dire staff shortages made it unsafe to treat children there. Doctors warned that public hospitals were running on empty, with crippling staff shortages of nurses, doctors and specialists, and there were outbreaks of infections with multi-antibiotic-resistant organisms.

'Wherever you look,' Thandi complained to her husband, Isaac, 'you find the horrible results of all the looting and cronyism under the Former President.'

Star quickly saw the Free State's housing budget as an ideal source through which his friends and associates could get the most lucrative housing contracts, often cutting standards, with companies added to the approved database without national home-builder registration.

They all stuffed their pockets. He also put his cronies into the province's spending departments to ensure billions of rands in national government grants were splurged on favoured cronies who gave him kickbacks.

Free State MECs were peremptorily sacked if they strayed from Star's gravy train or had the temerity to challenge him. At a national level, senior ANC figures were sacked by the Former President if they threatened to expose Star.

When the Special Investigating Unit referred its findings to the National Prosecuting Authority (NPA), which in turn referred matters on to the ineffectual Hawks, a mountain of cases piled up with no resolution.

The Auditor General had identified billions of irregular payments in Star's Free State, but nothing was ever done about it, and no politician or official was ever held to account for what amounted to a housing rip-off.

Star bulldozed through laws, procedures, checks and balances, always carrying wads of cash on him to dish out rewards. Any businessman who won contracts from his administration was obliged to make donations to the Free State ANC – except that many of these disappeared into favoured pockets rather than into party coffers.

Local media was also captured. Any journalists digging about were threatened and intimidated. Those carrying pro-Star stories were rewarded, so too were crony columnists – especially those who attacked his critics. Millions were channelled via Free State administration adverts to compliant media, nothing to critical media. When the former finance minister tried to pursue a Treasury investigation, he was blocked by the Former President, who was witnessed consorting with Star at regular parties and annual Diwali celebrations staged by the Former President's fellow conspirators, the Business Brothers.

Star's closest aides also racked up huge bills in hotels and restaurants, allegedly for official business but in fact for jollies. Meanwhile, young women associates, known as 'Star's girls', set up consultancies that provided services to the Free State government as well as decidedly non-consultancy services to him, his wife pretending not to know as she lavishly decorated their home, entertained her friends with champagne and outside caterers, and focused on their grandchildren.

Pádraig Murphy's New IRA – by then the largest of the breakaway Irish Republican 'dissident' groups – had become pretty promiscuous with its alliances.

Not so much for political objectives, but out of expediency, including for acquiring arms, mortars, assault rifles and bomb-making equipment. Hezbollah and other radical organisations in the Middle East, for instance, had provided the New IRA with weapons and financial support, not out of any ideological affinity but on the familiar basis that 'my enemy's enemy is my friend'.

That was in contrast to its 'parent', the principal Republican para-military force of the twentieth century and into the twenty-first, the Provisional IRA, which forged alliances on a political basis. Before it laid down its arms in 2005 as part of peace-process negotiations, the Provos linked up with Spain's Basque paramilitary group ETA and the Palestine Liberation Organization. And, from the 1990s onwards, with the ANC for insights on a peace and negotiating strategy to replace bombs and bullets.

ANC leaders such as Cyril Ramaphosa and Ronnie Kasrils had worked with Sinn Féin and leaders of the IRA to encourage its rank and file to embrace peace because inclusive negotiations had been offered by Britain for the first time, especially under Tony Blair's government from 1997.

Which is where Murphy had first bumped into the Apparatchik on the periphery of an event, and struck up a friendship which, a couple of decades later, got called in.

By then, around twenty years after the 1998 Good Friday Agreement,

Murphy had long left the mainstream Provisional IRA in disgust at what he and others felt was a 'sell-out' of Republican principles.

The final straw was when Sinn Féin, with the support of the IRA leadership, signed up to support policing and the rule of law as a prelude to an agreement with their bitter old Unionist enemies to share power on a self-governing basis for Northern Ireland.

The Sinn Féin leadership argued that, since policing and justice would be devolved and would no longer be under the supervision of the Brits but their own new self-government, it would not be run by the British state and it was therefore no longer tenable for Republicans to oppose it.

At a meeting in early 2007 in West Belfast's Clonard Monastery, there were heated exchanges, with Pádraig Murphy and his cohort standing at the back of the church shouting 'traitor' at the Sinn Féin politicians speaking from the altar, one woman walking out muttering at them, 'My son didn't die for this.'

For Murphy it was the end. He joined the small breakaway New IRA, finding himself and his colleagues on the receiving end of that very toxic label used by Sinn Féin leaders, who denounced him and his ilk as 'traitors to the island of Ireland' after the New IRA had killed a Catholic police constable.

It was a watershed moment, revealing the vicious divide within modern Republicanism, and signified Pádraig Murphy's final self-banishment from mainstream Republicanism into the cold of the marginalised fringe.

When she focused on a subject – and she was known for flitting about, her attention wandering between all the many subjects catching her interest – Thandi could be relentless.

She'd pulled his leg, always did, accusing him of loving his elephants more than her.

'Come on, Isaac,' Thandi chided, 'tell me why – why you worship elephants so much.'

'What do you mean?' he bristled, only for show, rather enjoying her banter with a purpose.

'Well, like their intelligence for instance, and why they are so important to you – to all of us.'

'Okay,' Mkhize paused, thinking what information would best help for her latest mission.

'First of all, African elephants have an incredible sensitivity – much,

much better than humans. Even from many kilometres away, they can smell food. They also hear sounds, far below human ear range, for long-distance communication, and read earth vibrations transmitted over very long distances. If they feel or hear seismic activity caused by humans – like building new roads or drilling for minerals – they will flee.'

'How does this happen?' asked Thandi.

'Some scientists think they receive vibrations through bones in their legs transmitted to their inner ears. Others believe they have pressure sensors in their feet. They may be able to detect other elephants, thunderstorms and human-made noises from very far away through sounds that are inaudible to humans.'

'Elephants are also eco-animals. When they feed, forest elephants open up gaps in vegetation allowing new plants to grow and also pathways for smaller animals, and their piles of dung are full of seeds from the plants they eat, boosting local diversity of grass, bush and trees.'

'And poachers are their biggest enemy?'

'Yes. But the threat to elephants is not only from poachers. Humans are crowding them out of their traditional habitats, through housing, farming, roads, railways and pipelines. Which means elephants then start to attack farmers' crops and compete with people and livestock for land and grass.'

'Trees are really important to elephants, not just for food but for shade, and they rest there during the heat of the day, trying to keep cool. Because they are so enormous, they can get really hot, and African elephants flap their large ears, which are full of blood vessels to cool themselves too.'

'So are they really heading for extinction?' Thandi asked.

'Yes,' Mkhize replied gloomily. 'Their ivory gets very high prices, especially in East Asian countries, where it is a big status symbol.'

CHAPTER 2

The local Vryburg councillor laid down his knife and fork and rose from the kitchen table in the cramped box-like house as his wife expressed irritation, having just dished out the food she'd cooked.

The eldest of their three young daughters had asked: 'Who's that knocking, Dad?'

It was dark outside, but locals frequently bothered him about this or that – any time of the day, any day of the week. He didn't mind, saw it as part his duty.

The door was stiff, and scraped sharply as he dragged it open, peering into the night.

A balaclava-clad figure stood menacingly before him.

Before the stunned councillor could say anything, the figure raised his arm and levelled a pistol.

In the kitchen they heard two shots, which seemed almost to lift their tiny home off its concrete base as it shuddered with the impact.

Pandemonium.

The eldest girl ran towards the front door shouting, 'Dad! Dad!', her terrified mother screaming, 'Come back! Come back!'

She found her father slumped, shrieking piercingly, clutching both his thighs, as silent Balaclava Man walked away, not even looking back, unfazed as to whether any of the neighbours saw him, a henchman protected.

Job done. Another nuisance dealt with. Instructions carried out to the letter. Not to kill, instead to hurt.

Anybody who got in Star's way faced a blunt choice: either to back off or to be disposed of, for he brooked absolutely no alternative. So it proved for the local councillor, who had begun asking questions about a large fenced-off area spanning fifty square kilometres outside Vryburg. Who was behind the new company 'Vryburg Enterprises', which had been awarded the central government contract to run a new business promising desperately needed new jobs to local people? Agricultural workers, the word was. But exactly what experience did its directors and executives have of turning such a large area beside the Vaal River into something productive? And so on.

All normal questions, normally easily answered.

But not this time. Maybe not ever – for the local councillor certainly wasn't going to ask anything like that ever again.

As for the local police, they shrugged, disinterested. In their 'gangster state' they knew who was in charge. And who never to cross.

Except that, as the councillor, writhing in pain, was lifted into an ambulance to be rushed to hospital, he called his wife over, whispering to her: 'Call my dad – tell him what happened; tell him to call his old comrade from the freedom-struggle days.'

Distraught and hardly able to think straight, she did exactly that.

And Star couldn't have known that the local councillor's father, Jacob Kubeka, had kept loosely in touch with someone with whom he had formed a bond during the ANC's guerrilla war against the armed might of the apartheid state.

And that man, known these days as 'the Veteran', had helped strike a mortal blow against Star's mafia-like godfather, the Former President, barely a year before.

Had he been aware, even Star would have flinched. Instead, he was blissfully enjoying the report that another busybody had been dealt with.

On her way to work in Richards Bay, Thandi crammed into one of the ubiquitous African minibuses serving as taxis, long ago colloquially labelled 'Zola Budds' after the 1980s bare-footed South African sprinter.

While the other passengers chatted among themselves, she was silent, daunted by the sense of heaviness that had descended upon her young shoulders.

'Hey sister! Cheer up! You could come with me for a nice time!'

One of the youths in the taxi leered at her, his mates urging him on.

'Go for it, bro!'

'She's so miserable she needs a cool dude to snuggle up to!'

27

Thandi blanked the lot of them, though everyone was jammed in so tight the youths were hard to ignore.

The taunts continued, the jibes got more raucous, the cackling louder, the mood uglier.

Thandi tensed, knowing from her past that a confrontation was now inevitable because she would never submit to them.

'She's a bitch!'

'No, she's a dyke!'

'Nah, man, she's a virgin!'

'She's never enjoyed a real man!'

They were winding each other up, and Thandi, by a supreme act of self-discipline – which she subsequently found astonishing – managed to curb her temper and refused to react, instead staring ahead.

Then one of the young blokes winked at his mates. 'Let's see what her privates feel like!'

She braced herself, readying to kick, jab and punch – anything to defend herself in the cramped space of the jam-packed minibus.

But suddenly it pulled up at a stop, and she jumped straight out. The most obnoxious youth made as if to follow her, but the rest pulled him back, loudly calling: 'Waste of time, dude. She's shit, you want a NICE girl.'

The taxi pulled off and Thandi, shaking with both fury and fright, decided to walk the rest of her journey, reflecting soberly that she'd railed against sexual harassment, sexual abuse, rape and domestic violence – all rampant in the country – but had so far escaped most of it herself.

The latest assessments of the plight of African elephants were pretty damning, Mkhize told Thandi.

Both the forest elephant and savanna elephant were threatened with extinction. The number of forest elephants had collapsed by nearly 90 per cent over the previous three decades, and savanna elephants by around 60 per cent over the past half-century. Apparently, they had split from each other 5 to 6 million years ago – around the same time humans separated from chimpanzees. Forest elephants were smaller, with more oval-shaped ears and straighter tusks, while savanna elephants lived in larger family groups, with bigger ears and different-shaped skulls.

Around 400,000 elephants remained in Africa: most forest elephants in the Congo Basin in Gabon, most savanna elephants in Botswana.

The former congregated in tropical rainforests, the latter in grasslands and savannas.

Almost as worrying as the collapsing numbers were the reasons for it: not only poaching but habitat fragmentation and habitat loss, triggering conflicts between elephants and people in which elephants were killed.

But underlying the poaching epidemic was, as always, money. In China, a pair of ivory chopsticks could still be worth over US$1,000 and carved tusks could sell for hundreds of thousands of dollars – which was why the historic ban on the processing and sale of ivory products announced by China on 31 December 2016 was so important. The United States had also implemented a near-total ban on elephant ivory trade that year, and the United Kingdom, Singapore, Hong Kong and other elephant ivory markets had followed suit.

But still the poaching continued, ivory wars too, especially in Central Africa, where ivory poaching and sales were driven by terrorist groups to finance their activities.

Then there was the latest threat to tens of thousands of African elephants from plans for a huge new oilfield stretching across Namibia and Botswana. Scientists, environmentalists and local communities maintained the project jeopardised crucial water supplies, not least for the Okavango Delta, a World Heritage Site where Mkhize had spent enjoyable months working in his early ranger career, the region a wondrous wildlife wilderness.

Noise and vibrations from exploratory drilling and building new roads threatened to drive elephants away from ancient migratory routes, nearer to villages and agricultural communities, leading to more human–elephant conflict, and also devastating local ecosystems, farming and fishing.

Oil project bosses insisted that the project would bring jobs and huge economic benefits, including funding local wildlife and ecological conservation, but environmentalists countered that the consequent rise in emissions would add to problems in the region, already hit by droughts and hyper-heatwaves, with rising numbers of 'climate refugees' desperate for food and work.

For Mkhize this was a *wildlife* issue; for Thandi it was a *political* issue: the dichotomy of their young marital relationship.

The virulent social media attacks on Bob Richards MP came thick and fast.

Although not a Twitter devotee – he didn't constantly scan the

29

platform like many of his younger parliamentary colleagues and even younger aides – he did use it regularly to put across his standpoint on issues he felt strongly about.

Often his tweets were retweeted, always a good sign that they were making an impact.

But on two subjects he had obviously touched sensitive points. When he'd spoken out against poaching and South African presidential corruption under parliamentary privilege, he had been subject to a tirade of abuse from the Former President's gravy-train allies. And these continued, albeit at a lower ebb, well after the Former President had been forced from office.

Richards was a 'colonial puppet', or an agent of 'white monopoly capital', or a 'self-seeking, self-promoting media junkie'. And those were among the politer smears.

The second string of attacks came from allies of his party leader, whom Richards had challenged over his failure to tackle virulent anti-Semitism by some of his supporters during one of the regular Monday-evening closed meetings of the Parliamentary Labour Party.

'Closed' in the sense that it was meant to be private. But a huddle of journalists waiting outside Committee Room 14 – where the PLP always met on Monday evenings at six o'clock – were regularly briefed about who said what, either by party press officers or others present with an axe to grind or an angle to promote.

Richards had deliberately chosen that 'private' forum to tell the leader he wasn't doing anything like enough to stamp out the problem, which had turned the once Labour-sympathetic British Jewish community into open hostility to the Party.

Before sitting down to muted applause and to some heckling from the bitterly divided factions in the Party, Richards had reminded his leader that they shared a common heritage of anti-apartheid and anti-racist campaigning, as well as for Palestinian rights.

But he hadn't joined the queue of MPs criticising him in public.

Yet the media pack reported his strong line that the Party 'could not win a general election' in the face of near-universal antagonism from such an important community of British citizens, with the echoes of the Holocaust, historical pogroms and discrimination still very much alive in its cultural hinterland.

And, as if a water pipe had suddenly burst, there was a torrent of tweets attacking him. A few of his local constituency party members, who had only recently joined, called for him to be deselected and barred from standing at the next election.

No matter that he had been to the fore of activism in the Anti-Nazi League, fighting fascism and racism in Britain. No matter his record in the anti-apartheid struggle. No matter his long and vocal support for Palestinians, and criticisms of Israeli state assaults on Palestinian rights.

Richards had had the temerity to question his Great Leader and needed to be politically defenestrated.

For the leader's fanatics he had crossed a line. He was a 'traitor', a 'right-wing conspirator', an 'apologist' for Israeli international crimes against the Palestinians or discrimination against its own Arab citizens.

Funny, he thought, how both sets of quite separate antagonists – South African gravy-trainers and British hard-left fundamentalists – turned the truth upside down in their frantic tirades.

Tweets from outright liars and abusers he simply blocked. Others he doggedly tried to let wash over him – until the next wave arrived and the cycle repeated itself.

But for a moment his thoughts were elsewhere: his comrade and underground chief from the freedom-struggle days, the Veteran, had messaged to request a covert call.

The Veteran, frustrated and fretting, cursed his new life of disability.

It wasn't that bad, just that he had to use a stick as a prop to walk or rest, couldn't lift things, had to chug around his local village, Kalk Bay, on his beloved Cape Peninsula, on a mobility scooter sticking out like a sore thumb, he moaned.

He'd been an action-man all his life, from the days of flitting incognito between London and the ANC camps in Zambia or Tanzania in the 1970s and 1980s, to his 'retirement' years of relentless speaking engagements and book launches, flying not just within South Africa but to London, Berlin, Rome, Bethlehem – indeed, pretty well everywhere.

But there was one very important way his life had taken an infinite turn for the better. Her name was Komal Khan.

And – albeit in a very different manner from his protégée Thandi Matjeke – Komal was to become crucial to the Veteran.

Serene where he was effervescent, Komal had gained a reputation for free-spiritedness from an early age (much to the annoyance of her devout Muslim father).

She was the Khan family vet, nursing injured birds, helping family cats when they had kittens, becoming a handy little helper to her father, who was in the St John Ambulance brigade, where he rendered first aid at big sports events, and she enjoyed marching along with the St John brass band.

Although her name, Komal, meant 'tender, sweet and innocent', for some reason she was attracted to guns at a very early age and managed to smuggle her father's revolver out of the house, proudly boasting that she could shoot the imam they were visiting. Her shocked and horrified mother insisted that her husband get rid of the gun.

Instead she found an air rifle to play with, managing to shoot a neighbourhood boy in the leg. Only much later did she regularise her unusual hobby by undertaking target shooting, gaining a competency certificate that she regularly renewed and kept current.

She was born in Cape Town's Walmer Estate, on the lower slopes of Devil's Peak and Table Mountain, a mixed-race area at the time, even during apartheid. Her father was a carpenter by trade, having emigrated from India, her mother a machinist and former model for her employer in a clothing factory.

But her grandmother was Dutch-Indonesian, so like others in her neighbourhood, her family background was Malay/Indonesian. This caused racial category complications and absurdities. Under apartheid, part of the family, including Komal, were classified 'Malay', or 'Cape Malay', two brothers were classified Indian, and another brother was classified white.

Prayers were strictly observed, especially at sunset, as well as fasting during Ramadan. Eid was celebrated – yet Christmas too. Her father believed he was wasting his money sending a girl child to school, and Komal rebelled by resisting prayers when she wanted to play and watching the spectacular sunsets over Table Bay, gaining a rebellious reputation in her wider family.

That also began to be translated into politics. With a full view from her bedroom window of Robben Island, she was reminded of the political prisoners toiling in the stone quarries. She also joined her schoolmates in 'occupying' the nearby whites-only Rhodes Park, because they had better swings and merry-go-round equipment, bullying some white children out of 'their' park, to fierce reprimands from the park attendant.

As a teenager, Komal gathered her girlfriends to use whites-only building entrances and occupy whites-only beaches. With bus seating segregated, her light skin confused black passengers, who complained she was taking one of their seats – so she promptly found a seat in the white section of the bus, provoking complaints there too.

Graduating to clandestine resistance against apartheid as a courier carrying secret messages between those unable to move freely inside the country, as well as to neighbouring areas such as Swaziland, Mozambique, Botswana and Zambia, she was eventually forced to flee the country with the security police hot on her heels.

On her return from exile, she had used her journalistic training and experience to help transform the SABC, the state broadcaster, from an apartheid propaganda machine to one more in keeping with the new country. She first met the Veteran during protest marches against the Former President's proposed law to limit press freedom, dubbed the 'secrecy Bill'.

Within a few years they decided to get married, but had trouble organising it, with the Veteran travelling extensively to speak and Komal's journalism work meaning she was also always on the road. Finally they settled on a date and a Cape Peninsula venue. But he could only arrive the day before the ceremony, which was to be held in St James, just along the beach from Kalk Bay, where he lived. So Komal had to fix all the arrangements for the event from Johannesburg, where she worked.

They had a Muslim wedding ceremony – the Veteran (Jewish by birth, though not a practising one) choosing a Muslim name – attended by family and friends, activists and several former ANC ministerial colleagues. The bride threw her stocking garter, but her family's boys were too shy to respond, so she kept trying and by the third throw a Jewish guest managed to catch it.

Marriage vows were done in Arabic and English, Komal's sister making a speech, all unusual and new in her family's male-dominated culture. And then another celebration across the road in the Jewish tradition, prayer in Hebrew and the smashing of the glass, for the good and the bad times. A few days later they had a more conventional wedding, with celebratory song and dance, a passing sangoma (female witch doctor) in Xhosa dress joining the dancing too.

Savvy from her days of militancy, Komal always answered the house phone warily. But this time, she could sense immediately, was different. The man at the other end seemed diffident, uncertain, stammering a request to speak to the Veteran, who was clattering away as usual on his computer, writing yet another book, a memoir from his Johannesburg childhood during the 1940s and 1950s.

'Can I take your cellphone and name please?' she asked carefully, 'I'll get him to call you back.'

The man sounded disappointed. 'Tell him Jacob Kubeka phoned, and it is very urgent, please.'

Life had settled down for the Sniper.

His regular visits to the Zama Zama Game Reserve carried no stress any more. No more of the tense shootings of poachers he had carried out. They seemed to have been spooked by the relentless deaths of anybody who tried to down one of the reserve's rhinos and hack off its horns. Local men who had guided the criminal poaching gangs a year or two earlier wouldn't go anywhere near the game reserve for it was rumoured a sangoma had put a hex on any alien intruders.

Nevertheless, he flew from home and work in Johannesburg down to nearby Richards Bay for most weekends, to carry out regular IT upgrades and repairs – and to stay with Elise, the new owner, gradually asserting her leadership after the untimely shock of losing her husband, founder of the reserve.

Theirs was a platonic relationship, although he wished it could be more intimate, and he respected her self-containment, still grieving and readjusting but enjoying having him around for help and company.

The amount of time he put in on IT work at the expense of his IT business made his accountant ask acidly if he had converted it into a charity.

But the Sniper didn't care; he was a contented man again, for the first time since his wife had abruptly told him to leave their family home – shocking him to the core because he hadn't the faintest idea their relationship for her had reached rock bottom. It had forced him into a profound rethink about his whole inner self.

Pádraig Murphy's most testing mission to date had been in the Costa del Sol – the sun-drenched Spanish paradise west of Málaga.

One of the New IRA supporters had a home outside Estepona, a pretty seaside town, its centre off the beach promenade full of winding little streets and hanging baskets of attractive flowers fixed to the small houses; unspoilt by the Costa's overbuilt standards, outside the town, under an hour's drive from the airport, was where he was offered a bed to stay.

But nearby Marbella, a city of 150,000, was Murphy's real target. That was where the guns would be, in a sprawling city of two halves. One comprised luxurious villas for Gulf sheikhs, who made use of local escort girls, and wealthy expats from Britain, the Netherlands and Germany – and, increasingly, jet-setters from Russia too. It was a place of tranquillity with a quaint old town centre, and, for local residents, safe too.

The other half was a centre for organised crime. Over breakfast there would be locals eating toast and drinking coffee or a *carajillo*, oblivious that only twenty-four hours earlier, a man had had holes drilled through his toes in a kidnapping, a settling of scores between criminal gangs.

In nearby Puerto Banús, playground for wealthy men and trendy tanned women in white dresses and sunglasses, a young British criminal clutching several mobile phones strolled out of a Gucci shop and was abducted by a hulking squad of young Maghrebis hailing from the Marseille crime scene, his Rolls-Royce standing abandoned nearby. Naples mafiosi took note and resolved to deal with these young trespassers into their territory.

In the 1960s, under General Franco's dictatorship, the criminals had been invited to bring in their money – as long as they caused no trouble for the locals. There were now, Murphy was briefed, over a hundred criminal groups representing sixty different nationalities in residence. Puerto Banús was barely an hour's drive from one of Europe's main entry points for cocaine, Algeciras port, just across from the British overseas territory of Gibraltar, itself a tax and smuggling haven where 10,000 Spanish citizens crossed the isthmus daily to work, some bringing marijuana from the Málaga and Granada mountains.

For decades there had been a kind of equilibrium in Marbella, but then the young mobsters started strutting their stuff along the streets, armed and dangerous. The old gangsters, settled with their families behind gated walls, complained that these incomers didn't recognise the old codes, didn't have any respect, walking about with their black Calvin Klein bum bags, serving their bosses in Dubai.

Albanians competed for a piece of the action with Romanians, Serbians, Moroccans and Colombian drug traffickers with a Kalashnikov tattooed on their foreheads, breaking into homes, robbing and assaulting, with a rise in violent clashes between gangs the result. The old-timers bemoaned the disruption to their way of life, which combined ruthlessness in private

35

and courtesy in public, especially toward legitimate neighbours and café or restaurant customers.

Police reported that the local residents and European expats, enjoying perhaps the best climate and lifestyle in the world, had no idea what was going on around them, no idea that in certain local clubs frequented by the flash *banditos*, table reservations cost £5,000, with champagne or bottles of vodka or tequila included. Outside, valets parked their Ferrari and Lamborghinis, while inside USB flash drives were exchanged containing millions in cryptocurrency for money laundering.

The Irish had their own local pubs on the Costa, and it was to one of these that Murphy headed. Although a cold Guinness would be very welcome out of the heat, it was not drink he wanted but guns. He nudged the door open warily, scanning the dark air-conditioned interior for the face who would lead him to the military consignment he had come to collect.

Since puberty, when her girlhood morphed into womanhood, Thandi Matjeke had always carried herself very differently from her peers.

Where her school friends were preoccupied with their smartphones, the latest fashion in lipstick and wearing wigs with shoulder-length smooth, dark hair to cover their naturally short, crinkled hair, Thandi was proud of who she was. Proud of her wavy hair. Proud of her blackness. Proud of her indigenous African heritage.

That's what her mom and her granny had encouraged: *Don't try to be what you aren't*, they had advised. Despite seductive adverts on Facebook or YouTube imploring you to do so, resist the pressure to try to look like some white Americanised pop celebrity – a Britney Spears or a Taylor Swift.

She didn't think of herself as beautiful, though others certainly did. Men ogled her when she wasn't looking (if she was, they got the Thandi stare, which quickly put them back in their boxes). Women envied her trim figure, the sweetness of her smile and the elegance of her face uncluttered with make-up, only a touch of cream to keep her skin fresh.

Thandi attracted resentment from women of her generation, not because she was at all arrogant but because she could be aloof – aloof from their mindless chatter about their clothes, their appearance, their dates, the parties they'd attended, the ups and downs of their love lives. Aloof from all that ephemera she so despised.

Different also because they didn't seem to know about – or still worse,

36

care about – their history. Didn't know about Oliver Tambo's brave leadership of the international anti-apartheid struggle after going into exile in London in 1961, while Mandela went underground until he was arrested and despatched to Robben Island to begin his twenty-seven years in prison.

Didn't know of Tambo's simultaneously suave-suited diplomacy in the international corridors of power and bush commander in fatigues leading the guerrilla armed struggle from camps in Zambia or Tanzania.

Didn't know that Tambo had commissioned leading ANC activist Albie Sachs, a lawyer, to begin drafting a new post-apartheid constitution a few years before Mandela walked free in 1990.

And certainly didn't know of the great women of the freedom struggle, those Thandi idolised, especially Adelaide Tambo and Albertina Sisulu: the history books were mainly about their husbands, but Thandi knew of their heroic contributions too.

Old Granny Matjeke, ailing in her last year, had tutored the bright-eyed teenage Thandi, who soaked up her history like a sponge but found she was the only girl in her class, the only one of her school circle, who seemed at all interested in where she had come from, why she had her rights protected under the Tambo-conceived constitution – rights denied to her mother and her granny, and yet taken for granted by the 'born frees' like her.

'Born free': that had been a label worn proudly by the post-apartheid generation like her, until it started being questioned by young radicals with whom Thandi sympathised. How could they be 'born free' when youth unemployment still stood at 60 per cent in many parts of the country? How could they be 'born free' when the 2019 Rugby World Cup-winning Springbok captain Siya Kolisi had to be given an elite-school scholarship to be rescued from abject poverty, his main obsession as a rugby-mad kid getting one meal a day to sate his constant hunger, not kicking a ball like his well-fed white teammates?

'Jacob Kubeka?'

Komal had interrupted the Veteran's train of thought on the memoir taking shape on the screen of his chaotic study, papers strewn across his desk.

He searched his memory, for he wasn't as good with names as he once had been in his razor-sharp freedom-struggle days.

Then it clicked: he could visualise the lithe Free State ANC cadre, low-key, dedicated, trustworthy and efficient, one to whom he could safely delegate but doubtless a paunchy 'greybeard' like himself these days.

Memories, memories. Of getting Kubeka to build hidden compartments for carrying arms and ammunition in a safari vehicle taking oblivious tourists across the Mozambique border and into South Africa. Of how Kubeka would readily undertake cross-border missions himself, carrying messages from the Veteran to fighters operating clandestinely in South African cities, and how these were always undertaken efficiently, without fuss or ego. A comrade he could rely on, someone for the struggle, not for himself.

But then the Veteran recalled the pain inflicted upon Kubeka by the ANC itself, and his own shame. Having spent years in MK, the ANC's military wing, in Angola and Europe, it was decided Kubeka should be deployed home clandestinely and fight from the inside.

He was in an MK unit of five in July 1987, which the Veteran had commanded to cross from Botswana to Bophuthatswana on its way to the Transkei, only to be captured at the Makgobistad border post.

It was devastating. They had left an ANC base in Zambia and surmounted a variety of obstacles, including a freezing cold night crossing the Zambezi River with a rubber dinghy, moving through the Hwange National Park, being arrested by the Zimbabwean police in Bulawayo, and being detained at Mzilikazi police station as illegal immigrants.

After the ANC had successfully negotiated their release, and having crossed the Zimbabwean border illegally on foot into Botswana, the unit was met by his former training instructor from an ANC camp in Angola, and taken to a hotel for the next two days.

There Kubeka became deeply unsettled because others in the hotel seemed to know far too much about from where his unit had come, and to where it was heading: far too relaxed for the front line. Not comfortable about pressing ahead, Kubeka feared being branded a coward, ridiculed and sent back to MK camps in bad odour.

So he was up early, ready to leave, only to be told they would be going the following day instead. By then he was restless to the point of being paranoid, noticing plenty of strange movements in and out of the hotel, hardly able to sleep that night.

Their five-strong unit decided to split up. Three were relatively unknown, Kubeka and his Free State friend Billy the two most easily identifiable because of the years they'd spent in ANC camps as instructors: they might be recognised by 'askaris' – ANC cadres 'turned' by the apartheid Special Branch into informers or state agents against their former comrades.

In the early hours of 27 July 1987, Kubeka and Billy were collected by one of the training commissars in Caculama and driven in a bakkie, a small pick-up truck, towards the Botswana/Bophuthatswana border fence, given alibis as students from the Transkei en route to Botswana for university educational opportunities. The bakkie having left them nearby, they were shown the road leading to the Makgobistad border post to have their Transkei travel documents endorsed.

Kubeka was worried, having opposed this very procedure when briefed by the Veteran, who had changed the guidance as a result. Obviously it had been ignored. He and Billy took off the blue work coveralls they had been wearing so that their clothes wouldn't be damaged by the bush, and proceeded on foot to the border gate, assuming it would be abuzz with movements of people and vehicles, as they had been briefed, so they wouldn't be noticed.

Instead they were the only ones intending to cross, and spotted an observation post in a tree with a South African Defence Force soldier carrying a pair of binoculars. An SADF patrol vehicle pulled up, and the immigration officer summoned a policeman to assist him.

'How did you two arrive here?'

'From a white bakkie in the village,' Kubeka grunted, pointing back along the dirt road.

The immigration officer began singing 'Who's Fooling Who?', a Xhosa security officer (an askari, Kubeka surmised) visibly angry, pacing up and down until he began the interrogation himself, quickly exposing Kubeka's alias.

One shouted: 'TPA 3441 positive!' – a reference to Kubeka's number in the official Terrorist Photo Album (TPA).

His heart sank, all his fears justified. The album had photos of everyone, from ANC President OR Tambo to the most recent recruit in exile.

The two were dragged inside, stripped naked and thoroughly searched. Their operational funds were seized, and they were blindfolded, handcuffed and put in leg-irons. A helicopter arrived and they were thrown inside, soldiers resting their feet on top, pinning them to the floor.

The helicopter flew off to intelligence headquarters in Mmabatho,

39

Bophuthatswana (a 'self-governing' puppet statelet), where the two of them were separated, stripped naked, handcuffed and beaten, questions raining down.

Immediately, it was clear to Kubeka that South African security officers were expecting him.

'Why did you come today, because we were waiting for you yesterday?' they barked.

'Where are the others?'

'What is your mission?'

'Who and where are your contacts? Where are your weapons?'

'Why did you come through Bophuthatswana and not Lesotho like others, because it is nearer the Transkei?'

'Who is your commander?'

Then a senior military intelligence officer from Pretoria arrived and took the lead, the torture as brutal as the stories Kubeka had heard before. But neither of them gave in, trusting in each other and ignoring jibes from interrogators that the other had started talking.

When they were finally put together, they could hardly recognise each other under their swollen faces. They'd had no water, no food, no sleep. Desperate, Kubeka asked to go to the toilet. But because there was no sink, he had to slurp up what water he could as he flushed it, the stink from the filth in the bowl making him nauseous. He shuddered in disgust.

In their cells, there was a steel ring cemented to the floor, to which one of their leg irons was locked, like a dog on a leash in the yard.

Then the interrogation continued, this time both of them together, the askaris joined by some former Rhodesian Selous Scouts, also notorious for their brutality, the purpose now very different: to recruit Kubeka and Billy. The interrogators knew everything about Kubeka's MK unit, except key information known only to him, Billy and the Veteran, concerning their intended targets, weapons to be used and contacts.

'We've already sent information to the ANC that you've sold out,' they sneered.

Kubeka felt utterly bereft: their MK comrades would believe they had betrayed the ANC, when in fact they were still bruised and battered under torture in an enemy dungeon defending the ANC. Who were the real traitors high in the movement? How compromised was MK, he wondered?

But still the interrogators relentlessly persisted, promising to kill them if they didn't turn into askaris and work for the apartheid security forces, now that their reputation had been trashed within the ANC.

Somehow, they survived that day and the months that followed. And then came a lucky break. One of the Bophuthatswana intelligence officers agreed to post a letter to Kubeka's family, who took it to lawyers sympathetic to the resistance.

They demanded Kubeka's appearance in court, leading to him and Billy being transferred from Bophuthatswana to a prison in East London on South Africa's eastern Cape coast, where they spent more than a year in solitary confinement, incommunicado under Section 29 of the Internal Security Act, before being sentenced to ten years' imprisonment.

They were finally freed following the release of the Robben Island leadership from late in 1989 and eventually absolved within the ANC. Kubeka ending up working as MK chief Chris Hani's personal aide, and his friend Billy in Oliver Tambo's personal protection unit.

Kubeka would never forget spending his twenty-first birthday in Bophuthatswana nursing his bruises in shackles, serving the same ANC which, under Star in the Free State thirty years later, had turned sour on him again.

The Veteran immediately called the number his wife had handed over as she returned to her own computer to carry on with her work running training courses for journalists.

'Jacob! How are you, my comrade?'

'Not so good, sorry. My son Edwin has been shot and I need some help, please.'

He explained what had happened to the Vrydorp councillor, his agony and the seeming impunity in the bearing of Balaclava Man.

'But *why*?' the Veteran asked.

He had been asking questions about a new public contract on a vast area of land, Kubeka explained.

The two men talked for half an hour to explore the problem, the Veteran probing, analysing and assessing what he might be able to do.

Then they hatched the rudiments of a plan.

And, before they ended the call with some nostalgic reminiscences, they established a much more secure method of communication – never again on their house phones, though this single time was probably safe enough in the fresh era where the bad guys in intelligence no longer ruled as supreme as they once had.

Thandi's secure phone bleeped with the Veteran's number, just as she had finished the washing-up to prepare for the next day as a producer on a morning radio programme covering the Richards Bay area of KwaZulu-Natal.

She felt a rush of adrenaline: although her job helped pay their household bills as newlyweds, her buzz came from politics – and the Veteran only ever called her on her secure phone if it was important.

They talked for around twenty minutes, and afterwards Thandi began making her plans, briefing Isaac, who was supportive, but in a worried way.

Her first call was to the retired business friend of the Veteran, very comfortably off and living in Constantia on the Cape Peninsula, his house, set in spacious, shady gardens with an ample, sparkling turquoise swimming pool. The man, now reaching eighty, had funded the costs of Thandi's special missions before. He happily offered to cover fresh costs, including booking internal flights for her.

It seemed there might be another conspiracy to crack.

Pádraig Murphy's rendezvous in the low-lit Marbella Irish pub began smoothly enough.

His contact, a Donegal expat, had recognised Murphy's introductory code, given the expected one in reply, and slipped him a small note with an address in nearby San Pedro, as they both sipped Guinness and nibbled at a small bowl of *anchoa*s – tasty olives with anchovy bits in middle.

'Drive straight there when you leave, but switch off your mobile phone before you do so. We don't want any trace. You'll find the double garage faces straight on to the street, and its door will be unlocked. It will be open especially for you, so drive straight in.'

San Pedro lay along the N-340 coastal road between Marbella and Estepona, and he found the address easily enough, down towards the beach in a street with houses set behind high white walls, manicured lawns with automatic sprinklers, leafy trees for shade from the African-type heat, and adorned with blooming burgundy bougainvillea, so much brighter than at home. The neighbourhood seemed pleasant, exuding comfort and modest wealth, not flash or bling like some of the bits of Marbella he'd glimpsed.

Murphy's Kia SUV had a false compartment inserted under the floor of the boot – enough space for twenty-five Armalites and ammunition, and he edged gingerly into the garage, having ensured his Beretta 92 pistol was cocked, with its grip upward in the driver's door-shelf, should he need it quickly.

The exchange was straightforward, however. Euros in cash for the cases of arms, ammunition and Semtex, which he opened carefully and inspected. All seemed in order, Murphy reassured that the man handling the trade was also Irish, not one of the young mobsters he'd been warned were now ubiquitous on the Costa.

They chatted amiably about the 'war against the Brits' before Murphy backed out of the garage and drove off, relieved that the first part of his mission had been accomplished, scouring the street for any surveillance and clocking his rear- and side-view mirrors constantly for any tails as he pulled out.

As if from nowhere, a black SUV veered out in front of him, engine roaring.

Murphy squealed to a halt, grabbing the still-cocked Beretta, ice-cold, as if he was back in South Armagh confronting the Brits.

As he did so, he slammed the automatic into reverse, tyres screeching as he backed away, holding the steering wheel with his left hand and leaning out of the electric window he'd lowered to shoot through the head the man who had climbed out of the passenger seat and was levelling a machine gun at him.

The man slumped as Murphy slowed, pumping bullets into both front tyres of the SUV.

He turned, racing past the stricken vehicle and – looking constantly in his rear-view mirror for any pursuers – headed up via a roundabout and onto the N-340 towards Estepona.

A narrow escape. But where was the leak, he worried.

Still scouring his mirrors, he turned right seventeen kilometres later off the *cambio de sentido* shortly before the Kempinski Hotel, looming up on the left.

But, instead of turning right to drive up Calle Alberdina to reach the *finca* in the Padron area, where his expat retired paramilitary lived, he turned left underneath the dual carriageway, straight over and into a car park overlooking the beach, turning the vehicle swiftly around to face the underpass through which he'd just driven.

43

There he waited for a few minutes, double-checking nobody had him under surveillance.

Finally satisfied, Murphy set off again, looking forward to a swim in his contact's pristine blue pool, followed by a promised mid-afternoon lunch at Chiringuito Torre Velerín, said to be the best along that stretch of the beach, not least for its excellent service. The sumptuous fish, barbecued – *espeto* – for customers to see, had been freshly caught that morning and brought in at Estepona port. The wine flowed, the chat about Republican politics was good, and Murphy began to relax.

Then it was off to an early bed for an even earlier rise to begin the 1,000-kilometre drive north, straight to the port of Santander, where he was booked on the *Pont-Aven*, operated by Brittany Ferries, to Plymouth.

It was quite a journey all in one go, but the two-litre petrol Kia was powerful, the motorway-standard roads excellent and relatively traffic-free that time of the year, so he felt confident he'd be well in time for the sailing at eight that night.

Like the journey down, it revealed a Spain he knew nothing of – the wide-open brown-grassed plains of Extremadura, the spectacular mountain passes and glimpses of walled old towns he flashed by, their mixed Muslim-Christian heritage still very evident in the old buildings, cathedrals built on top of mosques, ancient castles and forts high astride hills, isolated old *casita*s and *cortijos*, many sadly crumbling and lonely, relics of sole farmers long gone.

Several days later, via an Irish ferry from Fishguard to Rosslare, and Murphy was back in his own comfort zone, nevertheless worried that at least a couple of the Marbella mobsters had clocked his visit and tried to muscle in on it.

There had obviously been a leak somewhere and he briefed his quartermaster accordingly. Paranoia over leaks in their tight circle was extreme.

However, his stock in the New IRA rose even higher: mission satisfactorily accomplished.

Although her decision to turn down the President's flattering invitation to become an ANC MP occasionally gnawed at her – was it right or wrong? – everything Thandi had learned since seemed to reinforce her judgement.

A tainted senior Cabinet minister dismissed by the President was first redeployed by the ruling party to the most powerful position in Parliament – Speaker of the National Assembly. Then the Joint Standing Committee on his ministerial portfolio hastily dropped an inquiry into his conduct. Clearly, she thought, Parliament remained under the control of the senior ANC figures profoundly implicated in 'state capture' – the decade of prolific looting organised from the very top of the government.

As the majority party, the ANC was able to block accountability and reinforce its authority, overriding Parliament's duty to scrutinise and hold accountable abuses of power.

Influential and lucrative parliamentary roles, such as the Speaker and committee chairs, were clearly being exploited, Thandi felt, to provide soft landings for corruption-contaminated or incompetent politicians, undermining Parliament's oversight responsibilities: rather than being punished, they were being rewarded.

State capture suspects who had been ministers were returned to Parliament as ordinary MPs and then became chairs of key portfolio committees.

ANC MPs who had pushed for greater accountability and better oversight during the fifth Parliament had been deprived by party leaders from standing again in the election for the sixth Parliament, as factional power struggles were played out, blocking accountability of government spending and activities – the price the country paid for the ANC keeping peace between its warring factions.

Parliament was being manipulated by the very executive it was constitutionally mandated to hold to account – and Thandi wanted none of that, believing she was well out of it, though acknowledging, as the Veteran gently chided her, that unless there were also MPs inside the system to press for change, that change might never happen.

Even with his extensive ranger experience, Mkhize had never seen anything like it ever before.

On the other side of the river, right at its edge, he caught sight of a convulsion: a thrashing of foam, a sight familiar for crocodiles catching and killing prey.

But, amazingly, this was the precise opposite. He stared wide-eyed as a male leopard in its prime plunged into the river, grabbed a medium-to-large sized croc in its jaws and was trying to pull it out. The leopard managed somehow to get up on its haunches, digging into the river-bank as the resisting crocodile tried to pull him back. For a moment they seemed locked in time: two predators in a gladiatorial struggle to the death.

Only one outcome was inevitable, Mkhize thought.

Then, disbelieving, he realised he was plain wrong. With a titanic effort the leopard had started to jerk the twisting, whirling croc up the steep riverbank. Now the reptile was almost clear of the water, its neck clamped in the leopard's powerful jaws. But still it resisted.

Gradually, the leopard climbed backwards up towards and into the overhanging bush. Eventually the crocodile's corrugated tail disappeared, leaving his guests excited but Mkhize stunned and transfixed.

Leopard, of course, regularly dragged antelope right up into a tree, with their strength legendary. But never before had he believed that what he had just witnessed was possible.

The telltale signs of a new development outside Vryburg were all there. The entrance was closed, with a fresh sign stating, 'Private – Entry Strictly Forbidden'.

From time to time, bored security guards drove aimlessly around the fenced-off perimeter where it was accessible to nearby villages or tracks; where it wasn't (most of the length), they didn't bother.

Occasionally, the gates would be unlocked and trucks would drive through, usually returning quickly, leaving gates to be padlocked again, the security guards brooding in the heat, fiddling on their phones to keep awake as they mooched in their drivers' seats. Usually the place wasn't even guarded.

Locals, like Councillor Edwin Kubeka, wondered what was planned inside, whether there might be jobs for them. But unlike him, they never asked, for they'd heard what had happened when he did.

This cycle went on for months.

Then, as rumours spread, finally an announcement from the premier's office. The government had made a R500-million grant available to Vryburg Enterprises to create a new 'Vryburg Regeneration Park', as it would be titled. To what purpose or how the regeneration might occur wasn't clear, but at least all the jobs would go to local unemployed people – which meant pretty well everyone locally was eligible, because jobs were scarce to non-existent in this part of the Free State.

Meanwhile everyone waited – and waited – for work to start onsite and jobs to be advertised.

On the journey to the Free State, Thandi seethed over a new report showing one in four women and girls around the world had been physically or sexually assaulted by a husband or male partner.

Actual rates would be far higher if other types of abuse were included, such as online abuse and sexual harassment.

Sub-Saharan Africa, Thandi was struck, had some of the highest rates of intimate partner violence against women and girls – around half of women were abused by a partner at least once.

In her own country, around 1,000 children were murdered every year – nearly three a day. One brutal killing of a six-year-old girl was by someone she trusted, someone her mother trusted – her mother's boyfriend, who also drugged the innocent little child, beat her and sexually abused her.

What is it with men? Thandi wondered, as her mind turned to the mission ahead.

Major Yasmin Essop had inherited a real dog's breakfast in her new role as security minister. She found the state's different intelligence agencies more at war with each other than with the country's enemies, and a State Security Agency (SSA) so dysfunctional that it couldn't perform its constitutional duties.

She uncovered a world of unlawful telephone taps, an absence of credible intelligence, obsolete IT equipment incapable of confronting cybersecurity threats and pots of money disappearing from allocated budgets. Briefings in closed sessions of Parliament's oversight Joint Standing Committee on Intelligence were plain embarrassing, a mixture of bumbling obfuscation and incompetence.

The President had certainly given her a hospital pass in plucking her out of her senior role in military intelligence to join the Cabinet as security minister with a remit to clean up the intelligence services perverted by his predecessor.

How much simpler the world had seemed back in the 1980s when she had been recruited by the Veteran to work covertly during the resistance to apartheid, carrying messages between the United Democratic Front and the ANC's military wing, MK. Although her role then was vital, she wasn't one to seek the limelight, her position barely acknowledged except by those like the Veteran who knew of her vital missions.

The battle lines were also clear then: for or against apartheid, with the struggle or sitting on the sidelines. Lives of sacrifice for the cause, tragedies to confront – from assassination to torture – stories of great courage, ideals to the fore, values to cherish, comrades to admire, solidarity to experience. Now there were enemies in your own midst, once-heroic figures turned bad, ANC cadres on the make and ministers who set up friends or relatives to cream off state largesse. Yet there were also people of integrity sticking to decent principles and good behaviour.

The question for her was who to trust – indeed, who *could* she trust? And often the only way to find out was through experience.

One of those she had absolutely no doubt about – and never had – was the Veteran.

He'd just texted her on her private unlisted phone, wanting help. It was a relief to call him after the bureaucratic morass that confronted her daily.

The Zama Zama Land Cruiser drove up slowly to view the elephant herd emerging from dense bush onto the track, and stopped in a clearing.

It was a peaceful scene, but the guests were nevertheless awed to be so close to these majestic wild animals as they walked slowly about, the babies between the mothers' legs under the stomach, occasionally darting out to frolic and being swept back by the mothers' trunks.

'Aren't they amazing?' Mkhize remarked. 'You know, without the menace of humankind, elephants – particularly females within the safety of their herd – could even live up to a hundred years.'

'They are so enormous close up like this,' said one guest.

'Yes, a mature bull can be over four metres tall and six tonnes in weight,' observed Mkhize, 'and moving that huge bulk needs a complicated structure, with strong bones and muscles. Their feet are fascinating: bones on top are arranged so that an elephant almost tiptoes, the foot cushioned below by a thick fatty pad inside its sole.

'That may seem odd, but actually it is very clever. Their feet act as a cushion to soften the blow of the enormous weight on every step. It's like a shock-absorbing pad, a sort of sponge able to expand or contract, depending on whether the weight above is raised or lowered.'

'It's also pretty adaptable if the ground is uneven, or if there are steep slopes or rocks. And their feet are very sensitive. I was sleeping in a bush tent once, and listened to elephants navigating our guy ropes, worrying one might stumble, bulldozing me underneath. But instead they were picking their way about carefully, not disturbing anything at all.'

His ranger partner Steve Brown interjected: 'The big ears of African elephants are vital to keep cool – they're like huge fans, their flapping cooling the blood in them, regulating blood temperature.'

'What about their trunks?' another guest asked. 'They seem to do a hell of a lot of different things.'

'They do!' Mkhize smiled. 'Their trunks are amazing, like a fifth limb, but with no bones, really flexible, with a combined nose and lip. They pluck high-up leaves or low-down grass, and stuff these into their fleshy mouths below the base of the trunk. They also suck up gallons of water to squirt into their throats. And their trunks are their noses, the nostrils are at the very top and run right back up the trunk, allowing the elephant to sniff the air for threats or scents – extremely useful because elephant eyesight is very poor.

'The trunk is for extra cooling too, for losing their body heat and for spraying water showers over themselves. When they swim, their trunks are like snorkels. They also use them to spray dust over their bodies when troubled by flies or insects. Their trunks are powerful, handy for wrapping around fallen trees to haul them out of the way or pulling trees down.'

Mkhize paused to let all the information digest, then continued.

'You'll also see elephants showing affection by caressing each other with their trunks or entwining them. And they recognise each other by putting trunk tips just inside mouths. Their trunks also help them to be like a water diviner, able to sense water even to a depth of sixty metres.

'If they sense danger, elephants sound the alarm by screaming or trumpeting. Their young immediately scamper to the centre of the herd while the largest position to themselves on the side of the danger, forming a solid barrier, even against the largest predators like lions.'

The guests were spellbound as Mkhize turned around from the front passenger seat to talk to them, snatching glances over his shoulders to keep an eye on the herd bustling about.

He warmed to his theme. 'Their tusks are important too, for defending or attacking, for fighting or digging or bark stripping, and they usually keep growing. Older ones can have tusks over a hundred kilograms each, three metres long.'

'They seem to eat all the time!' interjected a man sitting to the rear of the Cruiser.

Mkhize nodded, chuckling. 'They eat a massive amount of food, chomping away almost sixteen hours daily. And because the leaves and grass they eat is often poor quality, and their digestive systems are very inefficient, they constantly drop heaps of dung. An adult bull will consume three hundred kilograms daily, two-thirds of which they shit – around one hundred and sixty kilograms of dung each day.'

Then he paused, turning back around, concerned. One of the females had suddenly began rumbling up towards their idling vehicle. 'Don't move, and stay silent,' Mkhize instructed quietly. 'She doesn't seem angry, more curious I think – but you can never be certain.'

She towered above the vehicle, casting a shadow, her trunk swaying up and down, sideways too.

Then she suddenly made a beeline for one guest, a British woman called Holly sitting right next to the vehicle's edge, and came up close to tower over her, trunk less than half a metre from her face. Almost as if checking out Holly, who sat frozen, the female's trunk whooshed in a circle, then she turned and trotted off as if satisfied, the remaining guests part terrified, part awestruck.

Afterwards, Holly, who adored elephants and found the experience 'magical', explained how the trunk seemingly sniffed her, making small sucking sounds, as if introducing her to a friend.

'Why me?' asked Holly.

'I think the female somehow sensed your elephant love,' Mkhize said quietly. 'They have great intuition.'

Attending Cabinet meetings for the first time and immersing herself in the work of the Ministry of State Security, Yasmin Essop had become fully aware not only of a completely dysfunctional and corrupt, crony-ridden set of police and security forces under her watch, but the extent of the financial abyss the country faced.

A decade of looting from the public purse under the Former President had left the country near-bankrupt. State-owned enterprises — there were around 900 of them, covering all sorts of economic sectors, including mining, which had nothing at all to do with the essential provisions of government — had become a drain on the taxpayer.

An astonishing 70 per cent of tax revenues were going to service the national debt and pay public wages — which kept rising while private-sector ones remained static or falling. Yasmin was no economist, but that seemed completely unsustainable.

What to do about it, however?

She had more than enough on her plate just sorting out the mess she'd inherited. And she was in any case too far down the pecking order to have much influence on those macro questions.

It troubled her however that the President — a Mandela protégé — seemed bogged down, both trapped by the competing factions in the ANC and hemmed in by some party-powerful Cabinet ministers — ones who had delivered the votes that got him elected but remained corruption-tainted themselves.

For all the President's good intentions, the government of which she was a loyal part seemed gripped by a paralysing sclerosis. Policy papers were produced, task forces set up, good intentions announced. But nothing seemed to happen on the ground.

Among her Cabinet colleagues also were a bevy known as 'the percentage' ministers: those with a record of requiring a share of the public contracts they handed out to go to close relatives or their closest appointees, including some departmental director-generals.

Since incoming ministers appointed their own top senior civil servants, this both opened opportunities for corruption and cronyism, and closed off proficiency and merit.

Even in the new presidential era, private greed continued to triumph over what had been bred into the ANC by the Tambo–Mandela-era leadership — serving the people, not oneself.

And because she was now in charge of the intelligence services, Yasmin knew that some of the bad guys and girls in the Cabinet, hang-overs from the previous president, whom the new one could not shift, were deeply suspicious of her.

As they should be, Yasmin smiled to herself, the perpetual frown she wore these days lifting for a moment.

*

Pádraig Murphy lurked in the shadows of the housing estate outside Newry near the border between Northern Ireland and the Republic of Ireland, waiting for the police constable to arrive home from work.

He'd seen that happening the last couple of nights – to greet his two young children, both less than ten years old, in time to bath and put them to bed.

The PC was one of the relatively new recruits to the Police Service of Northern Ireland (PSNI), for he was a Catholic. During the Troubles and for generations going back the old Royal Ulster Constabulary was Protestant almost to a man, and had a reputation for brutality towards Nationalists and Republicans. But that was before the Good Friday Agreement and the peace process. And the replacement PSNI actively encouraged recruits from the Catholic community.

They were seen as traitors by Murphy and his New IRA cohort. Which is why he was now ready to try and kill this young dad with his Armalite.

Like all Irish Republicans, for Pádraig Murphy the Armalite AR-15 rifle was iconic, and he wistfully recalled graffiti in working-class Republican communities proclaiming, 'God created the Irish. The Armalite made us equal!'

A compact gas-operated assault rifle with a small folding stock, the Armalite was easy to conceal and could be fired rapidly with high-velocity rounds of great stopping power. Prior to its adoption of the Armalite in the 1970s, the IRA – relying on old, cumbersome weapons, such as the Thompson sub-machine gun – was repeatedly outgunned by British soldiers and police.

But the Armalite turned the tables. It was a weapon perfectly suited to urban guerrilla warfare, in Belfast especially, easy to handle and required little training or maintenance.

'My Little Armalite' was an Irish Republican song by the Irish Brigade, an Irish 'rebel band' from County Tyrone, which began performing in the early 1980s. And the weapon became memorably part of the IRA's twin-track 'Armalite and ballot box' strategy, a phrase describing how it both fought elections through its political party, Sinn Féin, and fought British security forces.

Often supplied to IRA combatants by Irish-American sympathisers in Boston and New York, with a long history of funding the IRA using the slogan 'give a dollar and kill a British soldier', Armalites were purchased through black-market arms dealers.

The wind whispered almost straight through him, the cold wet drizzle freezing his nose, his ears poking out of the black balaclava and the tips of his fingers jabbing through his special thermal gloves.

His position at the edge of a thin line of trees around the perimeter of the housing estate had been carefully chosen. Good for a clear shot, good for a quick getaway too. He'd seen the kids arrive back from school with their mum, a teacher herself, and he'd blanked them out because he couldn't afford to be distracted by sentimentality. Their shouts and laughter as they scampered indoors bothered him only momentarily. The young woman, tousled blonde and slim, was another distraction he dismissed.

Murphy was angered by accusations of being a 'terrorist'. He saw himself as being in a long line of Irish freedom fighters. Those – especially those from his own community – who betrayed the struggle, like this police officer did, were enemies in a war. Not dads or husbands, not sons or brothers, not loved ones: enemies, pure and simple.

He had waited for over two hours, but his concentration was total, his car parked the other side of the trees, his Armalite cocked.

Murphy had accomplished this kind of shooting many times. He was clinical and cool, respected within his ranks for his cold efficiency, for assuming a different persona away from the ribaldry of the bar or the respectful but very discreet visits he paid to his parents when it was safe for him to do so – which wasn't that often these days.

First he heard the sound of the engine, then saw the modest saloon pulling up, the automatic garage door opening and it driving inside, followed by the constable walking back out, pressing a remote to close the door and walking round towards the front door.

Now. He readied to fire a burst of bullets into the back of his target.

But then he hesitated as the front door burst open and the two kids tumbled through, arms held out, shouting joyously for their dad.

Not even Irish – a legendary assassin in the ranks – could bring himself to squeeze the trigger this time. But there would be others. There always were.

CHAPTER 3

It was a hot, dusty afternoon, the temperature 31°, when Thandi stepped off the plane at Bloemfontein's Bram Fischer International Airport, named after the renowned Afrikaner lawyer and SA communist party leader who had defended Nelson Mandela and his comrades during the Rivonia Trial in 1963–1964.

Bloemfontein, straddling the Highveld and Karoo regions, had a semi-arid climate, with hot summers and cold, dry winters and sunshine aplenty: near scorching in midsummer and near freezing in mid-winter.

She had never been there before, and was apprehensive, wondering if anyone might have clocked her. She looked about continuously: apparently not, though she couldn't be sure. She had once shot into the headlines but had not been in the media since, so she hoped few, if anybody, would notice her.

The Security Minister, Major Yasmin Essop, whom Thandi had got to know well a year before, had told her to be careful all the time in the gangster state and to keep in touch via their mutually undeclared cellphones.

Although things had improved since the days of the Former President, when the security services were his personal mafia, there were a lot of the previous regime still about – especially in the Free State, where Star ruled.

She walked gingerly out of the airport, carrying a small bag with essentials for her short stay, looking for Jacob Kubeka, an elderly man whom the Veteran had arranged for her to meet by the information desk in the arrivals hall.

Thandi had his photo in her phone and she spotted him standing there – grey beard, lined face, a battered panama-style hat perched on his head enhancing his air of venerable wisdom.

Kubeka gave her a grandfatherly greeting, insisting on carrying her bag – which Thandi would not normally have allowed, but to please him happily did so. Counterintuitively to anybody who knew how feistily independent Thandi could be, complying with these old-world courtesies of that generation rather appealed to her.

The Sniper – a techno-enthusiast – was fascinated by an advanced drone system being used in Libya's civil war to kill targets using artificial intelligence. Fitted with facial-recognition technology, these drones were able to operate even out of their controller's range. Although drones controlled remotely by pilots, often located the other side of world, had been deployed in warfare for more than a decade, this was a new development, raising enormous ethical issues about remote warfare.

He'd also learned that Britain's security service, MI5, had been involved in a secret project using drones to charge up listening devices it had inserted in properties under surveillance.

Requiring MI5 operatives to not only covertly install these bugs but also ensure they remained charged over months or years posed obvious logistical risks. But piloting a small drone to recharge and extract data from bugs using wireless sensors could be straightforward, especially under cover of darkness.

Maybe the Zama Zama drones he oversaw could be deployed in that way to maintain new sensors he could install on regular poacher routes into the safari park?

'But how could the ANC in the Free State have been so badly manipulated?' Thandi asked Jacob Kubeka.

The councillor's father had parked his scruffy, dented old Nissan Micra under a large orange tree off the road outside Bloemfontein on the way to Vryburg. They opened the front doors, the stifling heat just about bearable as the tepid breeze meandered through the car.

'Remember that the Supreme Court of Appeal ruled that the last Free State provincial conference of the ANC, as well as the election of the provincial leadership at this conference, was unlawful and unconstitutional.'

Thandi nodded, though she couldn't recall the details.

So Kubeka explained: 'Under the ANC constitution, national party leaders are elected at a national conference, by about five thousand delegates, ninety per cent of whom are, in turn, chosen by "properly constituted branch general meetings". Much the same applies for the election of ANC provincial party leaders at a provincial conferences.'

Thandi nodded again.

'But the integrity of this process is damaged by factions manipulating the system to favour delegates from their own camp, allowing party bosses to control who is chosen to be a delegate,' Kubeka continued.

'Although the courts try not to be dragged into internal party matters, on the sensible basis that political parties should regulate themselves, the Supreme Court of Appeal ruled that "every political party has a duty to act lawfully and in accordance with its own constitution", and it nullified the ANC's Free State provincial conference on several occasions, holding that the voting delegates who attended did not accurately reflect the views of ANC members in the province.

'In 2011, the then Secretary-General of the ANC, Gwede Mantashe, condemned what he called "gate-keeping", where provincial power brokers blocked people who supported their opponents from joining the Party.

'But Star's camp found a much easier way of getting around these legal rulings: to manipulate leadership elections by creating phantom members and branches. They paid the membership fees of hundreds – in some cases thousands – of branch members, so corruptly boosting numbers that supported their own favoured candidates. That was an alternative to vote-buying, where delegates were paid to back their favoured sons and daughters.

'Robert McBride, who you'll remember well from his stalwart role in the struggle, also demonstrated that money from South African Police Service contracts at inflated prices went towards buying votes for the Former President's favoured candidates at the ANC national conference in 2017, who also got votes from "ghost" members.

'With others higher up the ANC's leadership ladder than him, Star ensured that crime intelligence operatives were all over the ANC's fifty-third elective conference in the Free State town of Mangaung in 2012, their mandate transparent: to ensure that the Former President's faction won at all costs. And something similar was organised for the next conference in 2017: taxpayers' money being siphoned off to fund a bunch of crime intelligence agents and moonlighters from military intelligence.'

Kubeka grimaced, then contrived a smile: 'So now you know how Star maintains an iron grip.'

'He acts as if he was impervious to the rule of law. Despite being arrested for criminal misuse of his office – through payments his firm received from another company, which he was unwilling to explain – subjected to prosecution and allowed out on bail, he remained in post, both in the Free State and as a senior ANC office holder. He also enjoyed a local groundswell of support from ANC party members,' Kubeka explained.

'Was he aiming for a presidential bid?' Thandi interjected.

'Well, the ANC is divided between our President trying to save the country from corruption and his opponents, like Star, determined to get aboard the gravy train again. So even him winning the presidency certainly cannot be ruled out.

'But what if the prosecution succeeds and the courts impose a sentence?' Thandi asked.

'The problem,' Kubeka explained, 'is that, in parallel to those legal proceedings, his ruthless programme to fix ANC branches and manipulate votes could have been accomplished in time for the forthcoming national elective ANC conference. In which case the President would have to step aside and a victorious Star would be able to give himself a presidential pardon. Star would then have control over national state entities to plunder taxpayer resources as he has done so successfully for years in the Free State.'

Thandi was angry – as usual – at anything or anybody like Star who reeked of her bête noire, corruption.

Kubeka looked sombre. 'But you must meet my son Edwin. He's the one they shot. He's why you are here.'

The Veteran fretted and brooded.

'Thandi will be fine,' Komal soothed, 'absolutely fine. You trust her fully; she's been blooded already in the fight you led against the Former President. She's bright, sophisticated and brave.'

'Yes. Yes,' the Veteran retorted impatiently, 'but she's out of her comfort zone in a gangster state. If they spot her, they will clock her immediately from when she was on TV helping me.'

'Stop trying to micro-manage everything! You're a control freak!' she teased.

The Veteran felt helpless in his disabled condition, even with Komal, so able and experienced from her struggle days in sniffing out and combating danger.

Maybe if Thandi needed help, Komal could be the person to send, he mused.

Mkhize couldn't get out of his mind the dramatic change of policy from neighbouring Botswana under its current President.

Indeed, he felt tortured by the switch, wondering what the impact on his own South Africa might be.

For the Zama Zama ranger, Botswana had become a model state under a previous President, Ian Khama, with his signature policies banning wildlife hunting and instituting a shoot-to-kill for poachers.

But that had been abandoned by the new government. A worried Mkhize discussed the change with his sidekick, Steve Brown.

'Botswana has the most elephants in the world and the new policy has provoked a backlash from conservationists – rightly, in my view. In recent times, it has often been praised for its wildlife-management policies, promoting tourism, second only to diamonds in importance to its economy,' Mkhize said.

'Yes, but the new President complains that he is being misrepresented, and critics are ignoring the plight of rural communities who take the hits of living alongside elephants encroaching on their crops and villages in search of food,' said Brown.

'Okay,' countered Mkhize, 'but see where this leads. Botswana is now opposing bans on the ivory trade and supporting trophy hunting again from the US and Europe. Hunters are paying tens of thousands of dollars to come to Botswana to hunt large male elephants in the bush, so they can show off a tusked trophy mounted in their homes.'

'Ja, you have a point,' Brown responded. 'But if elephant herds breed too vigorously, they need extra space occupied by nearby villagers, and can go on the rampage in search of more foliage, with rising numbers of people killed across Botswana.'

Mkhize nodded. 'Of course, but legalising hunting and lifting the ban on wildlife trade plays right into the hands of the crime syndicates. They don't care about wildlife. For them, elephant, rhino, pangolin are not precious species vital to ecosystems, just money-making targets. I simply don't trust the politicians in charge: for me, Botswana's previous policy under former President Ian Khama was the correct one.'

*

58

Star's personal smartphone vibrated during the meeting at his air-conditioned office in OR Tambo House, Bloemfontein. He recognised the number and immediately excused himself, stepping into the corridor.

'Ja?' he barked, listening.

'So *she's* in town?' he exclaimed. '*Where* and doing *what* exactly?'

He listened again, then cut the caller short. 'Keep a watch. Grab her if you can. But be discreet. Very discreet. And be careful: this one's a hot potato, has too many friends in high places.'

Councillor Edwin Kubeka sat awkwardly on a chair in the small back yard of their squat two-bedroom home, his legs splayed out, crutches propped up.

Thandi felt guilty: the man was obviously still in considerable pain. 'Sorry to trouble you,' she said.

'No problem. I want you to know. If these bastards attack me again, so what? I am already an invalid for life, though the doctors say I will be able to walk without sticks again.'

'Okay,' she sighed. 'Mind if I record what you are saying on my cellphone?'

'Not at all.'

'Please give me some practical examples of what's been happening,' she asked gently.

The councillor frowned, pausing to think, then started talking.

'Well, we have lots of examples of Free State MECs lining their own pockets. So the Finance and Economic MEC used the state-owned Development Finance Corporation to obtain a loan of twelve million rands for his wife to buy a farm. The Health MEC granted a loan of two million rands to a media company owned by his family to promote the province's health programme.'

The councillor shifted awkwardly in his chair, grimacing as he did so, before continuing.

'Although Star's speeches and public comments are full of pledges for multimillion-rand new projects to deliver better housing, health care and social services, most of them either flopped completely or remained half-finished, with taxpayers' money mysteriously disappearing.

'So, for instance, instead of over two hundred houses he pledged south of Bloemfontein, the land stood derelict, many plots empty, homes only semi-built and unfilled or vandalised, with a hundred million rands of the one-hundred-and-twenty-million-rand budget allocated to the project having vanished, though actually recorded as "already spent".

'Then there's the old apartheid prison in Bloemfontein, which was due to be converted. But it lies in ruins, partly demolished but unable to be completed because the funding allocated has "disappeared".'

Kubeka stopped, noticing Thandi scribbling the odd note as a guide to the recording. 'Is this too quick for you?'

She shook her head. 'No, it's just what I need – please, keep going.'

He winced, the pain from his legs excruciating at times. 'Another example,' Kubeka continued. 'Multimillion-rand mobile medical bus-clinics never materialised, despite being paid for. Hospitals commissioned for construction remained half-built despite long waiting lists for operations. Several mobile X-ray units, each costing two and a half million rands, stand idle – but most of them never appeared, despite invoices being paid to the company of which Star's nephew was chief executive, even though his only known qualification was as a football referee. The province's radiology department, once world-class, has almost disintegrated, to the utter despair of highly qualified clinicians.

'A few years ago there was a plan to build community residential units, but just eleven million rands of the one-hundred-and-twenty-four-million-rand budget was spent and just eighteen units out of the estimated five hundred and twenty-six constructed. Three years after the estimated date of completion, the great bulk of the budget allocated to construction companies could not be found.

'The list goes on and on, Thandi! Just forty million rands were spent on a new taxi rank budgeted for four hundred million rands. It's unusable by taxi drivers, the rest of the money again disappearing to building contractors said to be linked to Star.

'When I challenged members of the Free State Executive Council about all this, the premier's spokesperson was unable to explain. She kept replying that "all the relevant information is still being gathered from the various departmental units". These non-replies went on for over a year until I gave up. It was pointless.'

'So nothing happened? Despite all the stories in the *Daily Maverick*? Despite the fuss from opposition politicians in Parliament?'

'Nothing at all. He's Teflon Man. But that's history. What really worries me is this new project I asked questions about and they shot me to warn me off.'

'Please explain,' Thandi said gently, remembering how the Veteran had perfected the art of saying little, just giving people a nudge, letting them tell all in their own way and in their own time.

For this was what she had really come about.

Justice Samuel Makojaene, dapper in his crisply pressed dark suit, gleaming white shirt and anonymously shaded tie, sat at his desk on the first floor of the Constitutional Court building in Johannesburg's Braamfontein suburb.

Before him was an affidavit in the name of several wildlife charities seeking a ruling on whether South African traders were illegally selling thousands of endangered wild animals threatened with extinction under the guise of legal exports to China.

The evidence seemed pretty clear-cut, on the face of it. Live animals, such as lions, leopards, cheetahs, rhinos and elephants, together with monkeys, had been stolen from wildlife parks and trafficked to Chinese zoos, circuses and theme parks. Well over 5,000 live wild animals were exported to China over several years, including large numbers of giraffe, its meat apparently a delicacy served on the tables of China's rich elite.

Makojaene recalled with distaste how he had helped uncover the rhino conspiracy over the grotesque, illegal trade in rhino horn to be ground down into powder for the sexual and drug fetishes of affluent Chinese and Vietnamese.

According to the affidavit, some of the South African traders had links to international organised crime syndicates, and used fake permits to export the animals to China, notorious for its non-existent welfare standards for captive animals. Arriving there, they couldn't be traced and mostly disappeared, after being killed to eat or sold on.

Makojaene also noted that, chillingly, the trade was apparently expanding, with wildlife treated as a mere commodity for farming and culling, and its raw meat sold in open-air meat markets, risking human health from cross-over diseases. The report referenced as an example evidence that HIV-AIDs had originated from African gorillas, and that Ebola and SARS-type viruses had developed out of humans invading wild animal spaces, cramping them and triggering diseases into leaping both ways.

The kernel of the problem Makojaene was required to adjudicate upon was tricky because of the manner in which the legal and illegal trades in wildlife had become so interwoven as to be impossible to distinguish and therefore to police. The legalised trade with China in South Africa's live wild animals was now full of gaping loopholes, and so was wide open to exploitation by illegal wildlife traffickers.

Some destinations listed as zoos for animals caught from the wild, for instance, had turned out to be entirely fictional. Permits were mostly fraudulent and there was virtually no effective process of verification. Regulation had become a farce. Therefore, the affidavit argued, most wild animal exports in the years examined were almost certainly illegal, and that once the animals had left South Africa, there was no way to track where they ended up, except probably dead.

The nub of the issue, it appeared to Makojaene, was that the wildlife trade, often conducted in the name of promoting conservation, had in practice become an instrument for undermining conservation.

Yet it also appeared that demand in China for products made from all types of wildlife was insatiable, from tiger wine to rhino-horn powder, lion bones and elephant-ivory trinkets — so much so, Makojaene was surprised to learn, that there were now more tigers in captivity in the world than in the wild.

It seemed like the South African government was trying to please everyone and ending up satisfying nobody.

Although ministers insisted that lion breeding in South Africa and trade in their bones should stop, the country remained a lucrative destination for hunting. As well as lion, the country contained some of the world's most important populations of endangered animals such as elephant, leopard and rhinoceros. South Africa's trophy-hunting industry generated about R5 billion (over US$300 million) annually, attracting sport hunters, mainly from the US.

The captive lion industry, responsible for management, breeding, hunting and trade, always lobbied hard to protect its income and the jobs affected, South Africa being the top exporter of lion trophies in the world. Like private rhino owners — who owned most of the country's rhinos — they also insisted that legal trade helped fund the huge costs of anti-poaching measures in game reserves.

At the same time, there was a big market in East Asia for the breeding of lions for hunting and the sale of their bones for luxury medicines, often as a substitute for tiger bones now rare in the wild.

The submission before Makojaene further insisted that the presence of a legal trade both normalised consumption and triggered a demand for wild animals for commercial exploitation by criminal syndicates.

Meanwhile, UK-based Environmental Investigation Agency (EIA) undercover investigations in Hong Kong and China had demonstrated that the latest legal sale of stockpiled ivory from Botswana, Namibia, South Africa and Zimbabwe to China and Japan in 2008 had clearly failed to either reduce the price of ivory or curb the illegal trade.

Illegal killing of elephants in many parts of Central Africa had jumped, and Tanzania, Kenya, Mozambique, Zambia and Zimbabwe were all experiencing increased poaching.

Makojaene was noted in higher judicial echelons for a prodigious ability to devour, sift and distil massive amounts of data and information. Elephant-ivory products, he discovered, had become financial products to be traded, increasingly promoted for their perceived investment value by collection websites, auction houses, arts and crafts outlets and other speciality purveyors. Shrinking returns on traditional investments, such as stocks and real estate, had driven rich Chinese investors to buy elephant ivory, rhino horn and tiger-bone wine valued in the millions of dollars.

Makojaene reclined in his black leather chair and reflected, his mind wandering back decades to his time on Robben Island from his mid-teens, the abuse he had suffered, how Mandela had been such a father figure, how he had studied law, how the experience had made him stronger.

If he ruled in favour of the submission, there would be cries of anguish from safari parks desperate for income from what they believed to be a legitimate trade in the interests of conservation. If he ruled against, the crime syndicates would make hay.

The choices before the Constitutional Court always displeased somebody but had always to be in the public interest. The question was how that was defined.

He would reflect further, consider the arguments inside out, meet his fellow justices in their regular conclave, and make his recommendation.

They seemed a perfect, pragmatic fit.

Of similar age in their sixties, Peggy Oosthuizen's husband had died of cancer a few years before, Piet van der Merwe's wife, Sarie, of Alzheimer's more recently.

After bumping into each other at a mutual friend's party, Peggy and Piet had agreed to meet up again, and it wasn't long before their friendship developed. To call it giddily romantic would be rather a stretch but being together banished their loneliness. The sex was welcome, and it made financial sense for Van der Merwe to rent his Johannesburg house and move into her one in Roseville, one of Pretoria's western suburbs, and begin their new existence together.

There was a new zest in their lives. They went on holiday to the coast, on regular outings, watched TV, had friends round for braais and settled down in comfort.

Until one day when Peggy was out, there was a knock on the door and Van der Merwe opened it to find Jo-Jo, the Zimbabwean carer for his former wife Sarie, and with whom he'd slept regularly while Sarie was just down the corridor, peacefully somnolent in her distant dementia world.

Seeing Jo-Jo again could have been a pleasant surprise. But instead he was stunned. Although friendly enough, she was carrying a toddler. A little boy. Mixed race. And, Jo-Jo proudly explained, *his* son.

Looking at his watch and checking their white neighbours weren't being nosey, he hustled the two into the living room, sitting her down. The tiny boy gurgled away happily, and Van der Merwe was rather taken with him.

'He smiles like you,' said Jo-Jo. 'I only found your new address from your tenants the other day.'

Then she took a deep breath. 'I have come because I am very short of money and when he goes to school, I will need the fees for him. Can you pay me a monthly amount to bring him up properly, please?' she pleaded.

Van der Merwe's mind was in a whirl. On the one hand – and even more than a quarter of a century after apartheid had been expunged under President Mandela – to admit to his circle that he had fathered a child with a black woman was impossible. Absolutely, totally out of the question.

Some might cut him dead. As for Peggy, what would *she* say? Kick him out?

On the other hand, the baby was his flesh and blood. Or *was* it?

'How do you know he's mine?' he asked – not sharply, just that he had to know.

'Because I kept strands of your hair from one of the combs you gave me. I had a test done and he's got your DNA,' Jo-Jo replied. 'I was pretty sure myself, but the test confirmed.'

Van der Merwe took a deep breath. He still had lingering feelings for

Jo-Jo. They'd had something special, even if, as he knew all along, transient. He couldn't leave her in the lurch. Even more, he couldn't abandon his son — his *only* son, for Sarie had been unable to have the kids they'd both pined for.

The boy might be the wrong colour but could almost pass for white — albeit a sun-tanned, darkish sort of white. But as he grew older his small, baldish crown would enlarge and grow crinkly hair — inevitably. And there was no way of hiding that. The son until now he never knew existed, would probably be seen as a 'Coloured', the apartheid nomenclature for people of mixed race whose ancestors dated back centuries to the early European settlers in the Cape.

Yes, Van der Merwe was in his bones still an old apartheider. But he wasn't a bastard. He felt empathy for Jo-Jo, and he felt a bond with the boy whom he now cuddled.

'I will not abandon him,' he promised, looking intently at her. 'Bank and cellphone numbers still the same?'

Jo-Jo nodded.

'Okay, I will be in touch. But now please go before my new partner, Peggy, returns.'

As he went online to get her an Uber, he tickled the toddler, who gurgled happily, and he touched Jo-Jo whimsically on her arm before showing them out; she turned, smiling affectionately as her ride pulled up.

Then he closed the door, wondering: *What the hell am I going to do now? Will Peggy kick me out? Should I even tell her?*

Not much seemed to be happening around the planned Vryburg Regeneration Park, locals noted.

There were comings and goings. Occasionally lorries drove in and out, or around the perimeter checking that the fence was secure. But there was no sign of local jobs or any plans for opening the venture. Hope began to ebb. Too many people were surviving on the edge. They had no patience because they couldn't keep waiting forever to put food on their family tables.

Thandi, meanwhile, had returned home to her radio job and the apartment where she and Mkhize now lived. She was aching to catch up, but he was on ranger duty, so instead she called the Veteran and updated him on her visit to the Free State.

But an even more urgent issue had been forced upon her. The tiny radio news team in which she worked was abuzz with the story that the chief manager of a local minerals company had been assassinated: shot dead while driving to work when more than twenty high-calibre bullets were sprayed into his vehicle on a street corner.

The company, owned by an international conglomerate, produced from titanium dioxide a range of industrial items such as paint and toothpaste, but had been targeted by community protests of the kind that had been regularly hitting South Africa's mining industry. Some of this was a hangover from the apartheid poverty and exploitation surrounding mining, but most of the unrest arose from fights either within or between communities over the jobs and rewards at stake. A few months earlier, a director and trade-union leader at one of the company's mines had been killed in a shooting – triggering protests and a shutdown of the mine.

All of this was a deterrent to much-needed foreign investment, and politicians piled in to condemn the latest shooting. But, Thandi immediately insisted to her news colleagues, this had to be reported as another result of inter-party and intra-ANC violence in KwaZulu-Natal. The Inkatha Freedom Party was battling with the ANC for local power, and factions within the ANC were battling each other for positions, and the access to incomes and jobs that often came with these.

She argued that there was a growing and disturbing pattern of criminal attacks on the company to eliminate and intimidate its management, with the objective of local criminals replacing them and grabbing hold of the company's largesse.

One investigator reported the emergence of a 'procurement mafia' gunning for a slice of the lucrative action. The problem, she gloomily, asserted, was that politics, power and criminality had become intertwined in modern-day South Africa, with a large number of armed attacks on precious-metals facilities by heavily armed gangs.

How the leaders of the freedom struggle whom she had studied and worshipped would now be turning in their graves. It was up to activists like her and the Veteran to confront the malaise. 'It's a betrayal of their values of always putting the people, and never themselves, first,' she insisted.

Her colleagues nodded absentmindedly, thinking to themselves, *'Thandi on her soap box again.'*

*

66

Security Minister Yasmin called in the Sniper to pick his brains after being briefed about a hugely successful international sting operation coordinated by the FBI, using an encrypted platform similar to WhatsApp or Signal, to target organised crime, drug trafficking and money laundering.

'Tell me about it. Could we replicate it?' she asked.

'Well, first of all, US police investigators closed down two platforms they discovered were providing customised end-to-end encrypted devices to organised crime networks. The FBI had meanwhile set up their own secure encrypted messaging app called An0m, which these criminals then flocked to, thinking it would be an ideal replacement for them.

'In fact, the FBI were harvesting blind copies of every message posted – millions of them across thousands of devices in lots of different languages, by criminal groups involved in drug trafficking, money laundering and murder,' he explained.

'But how did it actually work? Where did these criminals get into the system?' Yasmin asked.

'The An0m network was originally cracked by an Australian police technical expert who developed a sort of "Trojan horse app" that was able to decrypt messages and read them in real time,' the Sniper explained.

'In Australia, for example, an underworld figure started handing out Android phones loaded with the An0m app to his associates. They all believed these would be secure because the phones had been customised to remove all their capabilities, such as making calls, sending emails, voice and camera functions, apart from on An0m. So they thought it was special, and made no attempt to conceal or code the details of the messages, allowing police to read or translate them.'

'So could you help us do something similar here in South Africa?' she asked.

The Sniper paused, wondering if he had the capacity to do that all on his own – which was probably what she was getting at. 'In principle I could do that for you, but only if you can first put me in touch with your oppos in the FBI or the Australian police. Also, you'd need a small unit to monitor the messages 24/7: that I couldn't manage on my own.'

Yasmin pondered for a while, as was her style, thinking through all the angles, the silence hanging between them, before eventually replying: 'That should be manageable, though the operatives involved would have to be hand-picked, because I still have layers of bad guys throughout the intelligence services installed by the previous president.'

Then she added, almost as an afterthought: 'What happened to that Australian underworld figure, then?'

The Sniper smiled. 'Apparently he absconded, because he had unknowingly set up his own colleagues, who made him a marked man. He had better turn himself in and get a new identity before they find and disembowel him.'

Thandi cuddled Mkhize as, tears in his eyes, he described how Zama Zama had lost their elephant Matriarch.

'She was part of our daily lives as rangers,' he explained. 'Matriarchs like her are the leaders in elephant society, directing when and where their herd feeds, sleeps and travels. Her duty is to maintain its unity, to ensure each member acts in the common good of all the herd. She sorts out any tensions or conflicts, and she protects them from danger. She promotes harmony and a civilised way of settling disagreements. It is really moving to watch.'

'Elephants have a matriarchal society.' Mkhize paused, smiling at her. 'You'll like that, Thandi! Younger females learn their behaviour from matriarchs, imbibing the wisdom and knowledge needed to succeed when the time comes.'

He explained that rangers had noticed the first signs the Zama Zama Matriarch had become ill a year before she died, because she was no longer as feisty or bold. 'Then the whole herd visited the main house, with another senior female leading the herd, and no sign of the Matriarch.

'We searched for her and eventually discovered her alone, having left the herd, and we brought in our vet, who diagnosed serious liver damage. Our vet injected her with booster vitamins and antibiotics, and Elise made up special meals of horse pellets, fruits and vegetables, all mixed with her medication.

'But these couldn't save her, and our anti-poaching patrol found her dead, alone in a hidden spot. We later discovered that the herd had also found the carcass, and came to mourn her passing. She was such a character, mischievous, with a temper. We will miss her.'

CHAPTER 4

Jayne Joseph was terrified.

She was sure they were closing in on her. Everything pointed that way after the balloon had gone up. She had been called in by her line manager and grilled as if she was a criminal. Despite her robust denials, other, even more senior managers had threatened her, demanding a confession.

Not because she had done anything wrong; indeed, precisely because she had done everything right.

Responsible for foreign-transaction compliance in BSBC Bank's Johannesburg branch, she had triggered an alert over what she considered to be a suspicious transaction.

For Jayne it was a routine step for the conscientious bank executive she considered herself to be. But on this occasion the roof fell in on her.

After being pilloried for a week, she alerted the bank's London office to the fact that Johannesburg was not acting as it should have done. She felt that was important because otherwise London could have been embroiled in what she suspected was a serious money-laundering operation, with stiff penalties there under stringent UK legislation.

But instead of her managers' acknowledging that she had simply discharged her duty, she was suspended without explanation. Sworn to maintain strict confidence, forced to sign a non-disclosure agreement and sent home on full pay. Then the harassment really began. Heavy-breathing phone calls on her personal mobile. Stones thrown through her front window. And, she feared, almost certainly the sack loomed.

Jayne tossed and turned in bed, spending sleepless nights, unable to talk to her friends or her worried parents, who were at a loss to understand why their bubbly daughter had suddenly become so reclusive, stuck on her own, miserable and frightened.

She thought all the time of her relative, the leading anti-apartheid activist Helen Joseph – who in 1962 became the first person to be placed under apartheid's latest restriction of 'house arrest' – and who was her personal inspiration.

After serving in the Women's Auxiliary Air Force during the Second World War, Helen had become an active trade unionist and was one of those chosen to read out the clauses of the Freedom Charter at the Congress of the People in Kliptown, Soweto, in 1955. She was also one of the main organisers of the 1956 Women's March demanding an end to apartheid. Successively arrested for 'high treason' then banned in 1957, she survived several assassination attempts. Bullets were fired through her bedroom window late one night and a bomb was wired to her front gate as she continued to be persecuted.

Although too young to have met her, Jayne knew all these details and was moved and stirred by them.

But never, ever had she considered she might find herself in a similar position decades after apartheid had been demolished.

Minister Yasmin was intrigued by the sophisticated spyware technology she'd heard of. Apparently – but only in specific circumstances – this spyware could be inserted into someone's phone without their having a clue.

It meant an attacker could utilise the spyware to take over a device, and have complete access to all its calls, messages and contacts. It was even capable of taking over a phone's camera and its microphone for eavesdropping. China, Russia and various private companies were selling such spyware technology around the world.

She resolved to ask the Sniper about how she could access and exploit it.

Even worse than the internal irregularities she had discovered and which had triggered her suspension from work, Jayne Joseph had also stumbled upon what she thought might be the real scandal.

Scrutinising bank transactions, it seemed to her that a very substantial part of the national government grant of R500 million received by the Free State provincial administration had within weeks been transferred to what appeared to be a local outfit called 'Vryburg Enterprises'.

So far so good: presumably in a worthy cause, for she knew it was a very poor part of the country.

But what then startled her as she scrolled down her computer was an international transfer from the Vryburg Enterprises account, through BSBC's Johannesburg branch where she worked, to the BSBC branch in Dubai. And although the amount transferred was a little less than that received from the national government, the great bulk had left South African jurisdiction. What on earth could this all mean, she wondered.

To date, Jayne Joseph's professional career had been exemplary and she had risen unobtrusively through the bank's ranks. But now she faced the prospect of becoming a whistle-blower – not something she had ever imagined.

And that prospect was daunting, for whistle-blowers lived an increasingly precarious life in South Africa, just as in Putin's Russia or other parts of the world.

The latest case concerned a respected senior health official shot outside her home in Johannesburg minutes after dropping off her child at school. She died in hospital hours later. She had been a witness in police investigations into multimillion-rand corrupt procurement deals in Gauteng.

The Ahmed Kathrada Foundation – which the official had contacted in desperation – had revealed she had been the victim of trumped-up misconduct charges when she had previously tried to expose the corruption, then was demoted. 'Every few years, we have a different team of people who come in and loot, and the funds seem to be a bottomless pit,' she had said in an affidavit.

And much good that had all done her, Jayne reflected morosely.

To clear her mind, she decided to go for a run in her local park, frequented by joggers throughout the day and therefore considered safe, even for a young woman like her, and even in a city where personal safety was constantly endangered.

As she changed into her running gear, her mind whirled. What had she got herself into? What did it all mean? Something fishy was going on – that was pretty obvious. A small rural town like Vryburg with financial links to Dubai? That didn't add up.

She locked her apartment door and darted across from her gated estate to the park, unaware of a nearby car pulling out from its parking spot and continuing to drive slowly, as if keeping her in view, while she ran around the park.

'Always be prepared for the unexpected,' was Mkhize's habitual advice to safari guests. The bush was full of surprises – sometimes captivating, sometimes brutally arresting.

He pointed to a herd of buffalo strolling along the riverbank, a few stragglers behind – a normal scene on a normal day in the game reserve.

Then suddenly there was a commotion, as if out of nowhere. His guests were not sure whether to be horrified or gripped by what played out as they watched from a small boat with a canvas cover shielding them from the burning sun.

The straggling buffalo started to run, and the guests realised that five chasing lionesses had suddenly appeared, swerving to focus upon a young buffalo that had begun to lag. The lionesses cornered it as it slipped, resisting, into the river.

Four lionesses plunged right in, sinking their teeth into its throat or wherever they could. But then two crocodiles appeared dramatically on the river's surface, and began tugging the buffalo into the water, with the lionesses straining to pull it back out. A real tug-of-war, the guests excitedly exclaiming that the crocs would win. But the lionesses triumphed and dragged it right out, beginning to bite greedily into the flesh.

'The lions have won!' screamed one of the guests.

But it was not over yet.

The whole buffalo herd returned to claim back its limp youngster, grunting and threatening the lionesses with their lethal horns.

But the lionesses kept lying on the ground, eating. Then a large male buffalo ran up and kicked out viciously at one lioness, driving it back from the kill, and chasing it away.

Soon the herd, now over a hundred strong, surrounded the remaining lionesses still on the ground, determined to eat their fill despite the threat.

The river was just behind them, the buffalo pack in front.

They were trapped.

An enormous buffalo ran full tilt at one of the lionesses, tossing her up with its horns, and chasing her right away, the rest of the herd advancing on the three remaining lionesses still hacking at the small buffalo, forcing them to rise reluctantly up.

The buffalo bristled and the lionesses backed away. The guests shouted:

'Look! The small one is standing!' Then, excitedly: 'They've got him back! They've got him back!'

The wounded youngster somehow staggered to safety and disappeared into the midst of the herd.

A giant buffalo hooked one of the lionesses right up, others chasing the rest, roaring, heads down, horns jutting.

But the lionesses – desperate to eat and feed their young even as they risked their very own lives – kept returning to try and grab their stricken prey, now in the middle of the herd, as some of the buffalo still charged.

One foolhardy young lioness repeatedly foraged back until eventually she too slunk away. The guests were spellbound, wondering whether the youngster might miraculously survive with chunks bitten out of it, as it was somehow hustled away in the middle of the herd.

'Never underestimate the capacity of nature to shock and surprise,' Mkhize told them ruefully.

Both those in the well of the courtroom and those in the public gallery rose as Justice Makojaene entered, then resumed their seats expectantly. Piet van der Merwe was among them. He'd been dabbling in the wildlife trophy-hunting business to see whether it might prove a fruitful source of revenue.

Makojaene began by summarising the case both sides had made for legalising or banning the restricted hunting and trade of wild animals. He noted especially the precious income received by safari parks permitting limited hunting.

At this early stage of his judgement, neither side waiting anxiously for his ruling – knowing the money at stake, also the consequences for wildlife – had any idea which way he might go. The tension rose as he methodically rehearsed all the arguments advanced over the four days of hearings.

He noted that both sides used different studies to support their arguments. A 2015 study, backed by a US-based pro-hunting group, estimated that hunters in eight countries – Botswana, Ethiopia, Mozambique, Namibia, South Africa, Tanzania, Zambia and Zimbabwe – contributed an average of US$426 million to combined GDP annually and created over 50,000 jobs. Another study, funded by anti-hunters, claimed that hunting contributed less than US$130 million per year and created only 15,000 jobs.

Hunting backers claimed the practice actually benefited the species targeted. If well managed, they argued, rich hunters' money could be reinvested into species conservation to ensure that local communities shared in the benefits, leaving animals better protected from poachers and habitat loss. Even the World Wildlife Fund conceded that in certain 'rigorously controlled cases, scientific evidence has shown that trophy hunting can be an effective conservation tool as part of a broad mix of strategies'. They also argued that hunting targets the older males that have ceased breeding, but was completely unacceptable to many conservationists and nature lovers, who cannot accept the brutal intentional killing of these elephants simply because of their big tusks.

Namibia, it seemed, had ensured that local communities in remote destinations not visited by tourists benefited from the jobs and income generated by the hunting. By contrast, in Zimbabwe, once hailed a success story with its CAMPFIRE programme, local people in hunting areas had never seen any of the money supposedly earmarked for them, due to rampant corruption.

Makojaene also noted that Gabon seemed to have conserved its forest elephants relatively well, so that half of all African forest elephants were now found in the country. 'The Gabon government has adopted what it terms a "zero tolerance" strategy towards ivory trafficking, ensuring that people committing wildlife crimes will automatically be prosecuted and imprisoned for up to ten years by a specialised wildlife-crime court. It also has plans for the first wildlife DNA forensics laboratory in Central Africa to enable DNA analysis of seized ivory in order to gather evidence vital for successful prosecutions, and to help identify poaching hotspots,' he said approvingly.

Makojaene spoke for sixty-three minutes, then paused, raised his head and looked out over the hushed and expectant court. 'I now come to my conclusion,' he said.

'I have noted that countries in Europe have recently banned the import of hunting trophies for precious species threatened with extinction. The court has also heard evidence that the wildlife sector and its associated government officials are riddled with corruption, and over-exploitation and lack of transparency. Although I recognise cases of well-managed trophy-hunting concessions, the sector shows little determination to self-regulate and to weed out bad apples and their unsavoury practices.

'Of course, the court fully understands that protecting elephants and rhinos, as well as other species endangered by poaching, costs money. But surely tourism rather than trophy hunting is the answer? Tourism brings money that helps to conserve wild spaces and wild animals. Without tourism, the organisations tasked with keeping elephants and rhinos safe cannot fund the resources that they need to do so.

'I am also conscious of the link to the national economy: it has struggled because of corruption in recent years and as more people find themselves in poverty, so new generations of potential poachers are created.

'Despite a far-reaching international ivory-trade ban, elephant poaching and ivory trafficking have reached record levels. It is estimated that between twenty thousand and thirty thousand African elephants are poached every year. Elephant populations continue to be threatened due to illegal killing, driven by continuing demand for ivory in some regions of the world. This has led to the depletion of many elephant populations in Africa, also due to an increased involvement of transnational criminal networks in illegal trade.

'The court notes also that the International Union for Conservation of Nature has changed its classification of African elephants from "vulnerable", to "critically endangered" – a category for species that have declined over eighty per cent within three generations.

'Although more countries are banning both trophy hunting and the trade in ivory, the court is also concerned about the loophole relating to legalising trade in "ancient ivory", which appears to drive a coach and horses through bans and regulations.

'I am especially persuaded by the case made by the EMS Foundation and Ban Animal Trading, together with South African-based NGOs, that we must stop thinking of wild animals in colonial terms as "resources" and "game", and see them as sentient beings that deserve our wonder and respect. Wild animals in and from protected areas in South Africa are not simply government property or a "natural resource" to do with as bureaucrats please. I have also noted the strong case made by conservation groups, who see wildlife as resources able to be sustainably harvested if properly managed.

'What has most concerned the court is that wildlife trade, ostensibly promoted to assist funding conservation, has actually developed into a vehicle for undermining conservation.

'I therefore rule in favour of the wildlife charities. It is clear that South African traders are illegally selling thousands of endangered wild animals threatened with extinction, pretending these are legal exports when they are nothing of the kind.'

In the public gallery, Van der Merwe stood as the court rose while Justice Makojaene walked out. It seemed to him like an opportunity for cashing in on trophy hunting had been decisively shut.

Still, he thought, you never knew – and there was always poaching . . .

Jayne was buried in her thoughts as she pounded the park, its formerly well-tended grass tatty and neglected and the once-pristine benches peeling and buckled.

Another reflection of the public squalor that had spread through the country, a consequence of corrupt and dysfunctional government under which self-seeking cronyism, not administrative diligence, had become the norm.

Slender and perspiring, in a world of her own, oblivious to the passing leer of the odd wheezing male jogger or the catcalls of young men, she wrestled with the images of the digital financial kaleidoscope that had unfolded on her screens.

Although she had been sent on 'gardening leave', they had overlooked the bank's secure PC terminal at her home, which still allowed access to work from there. Her immediate line manager had given her a knowing wink when she checked it would still be operable.

He had always been supportive – might even have fancied her, she thought – and, as she had grabbed her stuff, glanced at her desk and shut down her PC, he had slipped her a note with only a mobile phone number and name on it: 'Komal. Never call her from your own phone,' he had whispered.

She had stared uncomprehendingly back at him over her shoulder as, humiliated, her colleagues wide-eyed and staring, she had exited her office, wondering when or if she might ever be back.

Still consumed with worry and questions, and on autopilot, she scampered back over the road towards her apartment, glancing up to hear the guttural revving of a car bearing down fast upon her.

It had seemed to come from nowhere.

South Armagh lies along the Irish border, the different jurisdictions often only evident when road signs changed from miles on the northern side to kilometres on the southern.

Out on its marshy, pebbly fields, often wet, or traversing its winding, dipping lanes with the wind whistling through, was where Pádraig Murphy felt happiest.

Before the 1998 Good Friday Agreement, and even for years afterwards, much of his home territory was a virtual no-go area for police unless under heavy military escort. Until they were taken down in 2005, after the IRA had ended its armed campaign, huge army watchtowers, gaunt and high up on the hills, spied on everything and everyone.

Or so they thought, Irish smirked. Although an irritation and a hindrance to the IRA, the watchtowers didn't dent the impact of the Provos' armed campaign, didn't prevent much of the smuggling.

Before his defection from the Provos, Irish had worked with the legendary Thomas 'Slab' Murphy, chief of staff of the Provisional IRA and a distant relative, who had a farm right on the border, which made petrol and diesel smuggling a doddle.

Slab Murphy developed a profitable million-pound cross-border smuggling trade, first with pigs and cattle and then with fuel and oil. He had large buildings in both jurisdictions, County Armagh in Northern Ireland and County Louth in the Republic, some of these premises having the border running right through them.

Irish had volunteered to help maintain two of Slab's underground storage tanks on the northern side containing petrol. These had interconnecting pipes that led to a pig shed several metres south of the border, with concealed fuel-dispensing machines. The tanks also had a large flexible hose attached, long enough to enable petrol or diesel to be dispensed into a tanker parked in a shed north of the border.

During the Troubles, the entire Irish border became a smugglers' paradise, with lawless back lanes along the southern frontier from Irish's home in South Armagh eastwards to North Louth, up and along the Fermanagh frontier with Donegal in the west. The South Armagh Brigade of the Provisional IRA also globalised the smuggling from the farms and undulating hills of the Irish borderlands to England, continental Europe and well beyond.

But that was all years ago. Now Irish walked the fields and drove the lanes only at night, away from the prying eyes of both Provo supporters and the security forces. Occasionally he slipped into the bed of a woman he loved, always entering by a back door in a back lane, never mentioning her to anyone, even members of his own New IRA cell.

There he sought comfort, though she often wondered what on earth was in it for *her*. Utterly loyal, she would never have betrayed him. But she still yearned for normality, for the clatter of kids around and the warmth of their own family before a TV set, playing in the garden or sharing meals. Instead she worked as a nurse in a local hospital and afterwards returned to her tiny empty flat thinking of the years passing her by, all in the name of a cause she felt was slipping away into the mists of time – but she would never tell him that.

The mother pushing the pram probably saved Jayne's life, she reflected, numb and bruised, afterwards.

Pandemonium, car screeching, brakes smoking, a woman screaming. Jayne had bounced off the vehicle's front offside fender and glimpsed the stricken woman, stiff and half-cradling her baby after snatching it from the buckled pram.

The car backed off and sped quickly away, leaving the two women to console each other. 'It seemed to be aiming for you, and we got in the way,' the mother tearfully shouted as Jayne retreated into the safety of her apartment.

She tried to gather her thoughts, finding it hard to focus. Huddling and shuddering in her shower for far longer than usual, warm water gushing, she resolved while soaping herself down to call 'Komal' – whoever she was, and whatever the cryptic message meant.

But she would only do so from the phone of a friendly neighbour in an apartment two doors away. If they had tried to ram her, they might be listening to her as well.

Thandi, only half asleep, was entranced by memories of sitting eating *stywe pap* with her grandmother as the old lady, now nearing ninety, reminisced.

She'd once called the white anti-apartheid couple for whom she had worked from a phone box to report that the roof was being ripped right off her house in the Lady Selborne area of Pretoria. Blacks like her living in the township were being forced to move out to make space for whites. She was distraught because she and her three children – one Thandi's dad – had nowhere else to live.

As she was kicked out, a white official supervising the clearance of local families barked that she had been put on a list for a house in

Atteridgeville, several kilometres away. How long would it be before she could move in, her grandmother had asked. As she managed her shrieking young children while desperately retrieving her furniture where it had been dumped off the back of a lorry, Thandi's grandmother explained she had to search for somewhere to live, meanwhile staying temporarily with friends.

'We were part of the forced removals under apartheid's Group Areas Act,' her grandmother explained, tears in her eyes.

Often the old lady would wander off into the past, her stories coming thick and fast, captivating the teenage Thandi.

'I remember when the family I worked for moved house from central Pretoria out to a spot on the side of a kopje – all built over now, but not then. The Special Branch were caught by surprise, and for some weeks the family was free of the cars parked outside watching them. In the new house their telephone hadn't been connected, so the Branch couldn't trace them that way either.

'Then one day, I answered the front door to a man who asked the name of my *baas*. I used to have a routine with white strangers of pretending to know nothing and understanding even less.

'Which wasn't difficult, Thandi,' the old lady chuckled, 'because most whites thought we were all stupid anyway.'

'But when, to my relief, the visitor began turning away, the young mother-activist came up behind me to see what was happening. The man saw her, turned away and said that he was looking for a house that he'd heard was for sale.

'I was furious with the mother. "He is Special Branch," I hissed at her. "Now they'll know where we live." And I was right. Soon afterwards the usual security-police cars were parked up outside, the phone was quickly connected and the tapping started all over again. Also the police raids and the harassment that never seemed to stop.'

Their sheer chutzpah, their devilish ingenuity, always amazed Mkhize, though he had got used to being amazed over and over again.

This time his discovery was accidental and the bleary-eyed safari guests walking at dawn in line behind him hardly registered the danger before it was over.

Mkhize had been as meticulously careful as always on these walks out in the bush, rifle on his shoulder, guests implored not to stray between him and Brown bringing up the rear of the straggle, rifle also to hand. But the cacophony of excited bird chirps brought him up fast.

A predator? Or maybe even a human? Mkhize lifted his gun, cocking it, indicating with a hand gesture back over his shoulder for Brown to do the same.

Amidst the bird sound he thought he detected a scuffle. The perennial problem with safari walks was you could stumble upon wildlife – sometimes volatile wildlife, such as buffalo – without any warning at all. And cornering them was the worst thing imaginable because that was when the maximum danger occurred, when they were surprised and felt threatened.

Mkhize listened intently, creeping a few paces forward, glancing behind at the half-dozen guests, finger to his lips, pleading silence. The tension grew. Mkhize levelled the rifle, Brown too. The guests froze: in awe or terror? Probably both.

The rest happened so quickly that for the guests it was a blur. Mkhize crouched, and there, suddenly appearing round a bush, were what seemed like three poachers. One fired his AK–47 assault rifle in shock, but the bullets went wildly into the trees. Mkhize calmly pumped two bullets into the gunman, fatally wounding him as he slumped to the soil, blood seeping. The startled other two first froze, dropping their pangas in fright, then scampered back and away.

Mkhize was in full alert-ranger mode, a quite different zone from his normal genial self, full of stories for the guests. Checking that the last breath was expiring from the dead man, Mkhize crept forward, looking around, spotting another rifle, ammunition and poaching gadgets protruding from a backpack on the ground nearby.

Then he turned towards the dead poacher, stunned to the core at the pair of shoes sticking up from the now lifeless body. He'd never seen *that* before: antelope hooves were fixed under the main's soles, so that rangers on the lookout for familiar poacher tracks would not notice his footsteps.

CHAPTER 5

The rioting began getting out of hand as Pádraig Murphy crouched low, Armalite in hand, in Londonderry/Derry's Creggan estate.

It was April 2019 and teenagers associated with his paramilitary group, the New IRA, were throwing petrol bombs and burning two vehicles, the violence triggered after police raids on New IRA members in the area to seize arms ahead of commemorative Republican parades.

The disturbances were centred on the Fanad Drive area, where acclaimed 29-year-old journalist Lyra McKee was observing rioting after arriving to report.

She was standing near an armoured police vehicle with other observers when twelve shots were fired, some hitting her in the head. A masked man was captured in a mobile-phone video picking up the spent bullet cases.

Flashing lights and the sirens of a police vehicle rushed her limp figure through a burning barricade to hospital – but it was too late to save her.

In a statement afterwards, using a recognised codeword, the New IRA admitted it was responsible for the attack, and offered its 'full and sincere apologies to the partner, family and friends of Lyra McKee for her death'. But the group also accused police of provoking the rioting that preceded her killing.

Afterwards Murphy blamed 'an incursion on the Creggan by heavily armed British Crown forces, which provoked rioting'. But he was also angry with his fellow New IRA volunteers, especially the teenagers who lacked any sense of politics, he felt. Assassinating a young woman journalist did their cause no good at all.

At the same time, he was contemptuous of a local journalist who wrote: 'The people rioting on the night Lyra was shot were young themselves.

They were born after the Good Friday Agreement brought Northern Ireland into peace. They know nothing of the brutality and barbarity of our Troubles and how we are still suffering from its aftermath even today. Yet they want to drag us back to that place, to bring violence back on to our streets, to make murder commonplace again.'

For Pádraig Murphy, the Good Friday Agreement was the real betrayal – not the reckless exuberance of the New IRA's young cohort.

Isaac Mkhize had almost become a missionary over climate change, Thandi had remarked approvingly.

Although pleased at this accolade from his feistily political wife, he didn't let on, merely basking privately in her praise.

But he was also worried about the catastrophic impact of climate change on elephants, such as the poisoning of more than 300 of them in Botswana. This incident was initially treated with suspicion as a possible human poisoning for ivory, but the tusks were found intact in the carcasses.

As Mkhize explained gloomily to Thandi, 'Wildlife conservationists later discovered it came from a toxic combination of natural factors linked to climate change, such as droughts, warm temperatures at water holes and the formation of algae that release toxins into the drinking water. This was certainly not a one-off. Probably a dress rehearsal for calamitous events to come. Frequent droughts associated with climate change are threatening elephant conservation as well as that of other wildlife.'

They stared silently at each other, Thandi absorbing the full implications of what her husband had just explained before he continued.

'Scores of succulent species in the Northern Cape, especially large plants like aloes, are endangered, with the climate emergency and poaching the main culprits,' he explained to Thandi.

'These are in areas once known as a botanist's paradise, the most biologically diverse deserts in the world. One expert conservationist insists that plant poaching might even be more lucrative than rhino poaching. The more endangered species are a speciality. They fetch the highest prices on the black market. Because many succulents grow from shoots, rich kids can also plant these as prestigious gifts for their friends.

'Meanwhile, the hotter the weather, the more water plants need to survive,' explained Mkhize, 'and lower rainfall means less water in the soil. Also, stormy coastal winds make things much worse, blowing millions of tonnes of dust, vital topsoil and seeds into the sea.

'With more droughts increasing and becoming more serious, succulent plants won't be able to bounce back normally, if at all. Game reserves like ours will experience climate-change annihilation of wild animals. Ecosystems stable for millions of years are being destroyed,' he said.

'The whole world is interconnected. There's been a drastic drop in caribou herds and shorebirds in the Arctic, seven million square kilometres of it, because it's warming at twice the rate of the rest of the world. So southerly species are moving northward, as the Arctic gets greener, with shrubs replacing mosses and lichens.'

Thandi listened intently as Mkhize continued: 'Warmer temperatures have also led to new pathogens and bacteria previously unknown in the Arctic, along with migrant red foxes that kill Arctic foxes, and brown bears that kill musk-ox calves. Extreme events thousands of kilometres away in the world – like storms in the USA, raging wildfires in Australia or ferocious locust outbreaks in Africa – are dramatically changing the Arctic.'

She interjected: 'I read somewhere that a tenth of the world's mountain-glacier ice will have melted by the middle of this century. Equivalent to over ten million Ellis Park Stadiums – affecting densely populated river deltas, wildlife habitats and sea levels, causing flooding along coastal regions and rivers, with island nations most at risk.'

'Absolutely,' replied Mkhize. 'For instance, Alpine glaciers help regulate water supplies through storage in winter and releases in summer. But once they melt, whole regions lurch between water booms and busts, between torrential floods and harsh droughts.

'And there's another thing,' he added, conscious he'd captured Thandi's total attention – not always easy – 'over the last fifty years or so, almost four hundred lakes, mainly American or European, have had serious declines in oxygen levels, threatening trout and other freshwater wildlife, as well as drinking water. The problem is, once you start losing oxygen, you start losing species.'

'Ja,' Thandi said, 'I read more than five million people are dying each year globally because of extreme heat or extreme cold. It's depressing – there seems to be no end to an ecological catastrophe.'

Mkhize nodded. 'But perhaps not all is lost. Forest fires over the past ten years have destroyed nearly two million acres of forest in Spain because of climate change, rural depopulation and a drop in grazing sheep, which clear undergrowth. Some have suggested reintroducing

European bison. They became extinct in Spain ten thousand years ago, but these bison open up dense parts of the forest – letting in light, which promotes grass growth and lowers fire risk – by eating masses of vegetation such as wood fibre, shoots and leaves.'

'But isn't it risky reintroducing large animals like bison when there are no predators or competitors?' Thandi asked.

'Yes,' Mkhize replied, delighted at her engagement, 'but it is a risk worth taking because the alternative is worse.'

He went on, Thandi relishing his passion and clarity: 'Just look at what's happening. Like searing summer heat in America and Canada, melting vehicle number plates and destroying one billion marine animals off the Canadian coast alone. Weather records have been annihilated. Heat spikes in northwest America and Australia are much worse, and are happening much earlier – decades earlier – than scientists predicted. I think we are trapped in a spiral of violent heatwaves, then bitter cold, or long droughts then torrential rains, fierce winds and vicious hurricanes. One disaster after another.'

'Not so much global warming as global weirding,' Thandi remarked. She had developed a penchant for a soundbite.

Star had also been briefed about a new surveillance device for mobile phones. Pegasus used technology supplied by Israel's NSO Group, and was sold to governments, ostensibly for use against terrorists and organised criminals.

However, Star noted with approval, the Israeli police had also deployed it to conduct intercepts of Israeli citizens, including politicians and activists, despite its government's assurances that this would not happen.

Pegasus software had the power to take control of somebody's phone remotely, enabling secret monitoring and downloading of data, as well as clandestinely turning on the microphone to record nearby conversations.

Once a phone was infected, Pegasus could direct command-and-control messages to the hacked device from a remote server. It was an extremely potent piece of spyware, able to worm its way on to a phone unnoticed so that it became a twenty-four-hour surveillance device over its owner.

It could copy messages sent or received, harvest photos, record calls, even secretly film the owner through the phone camera, record conversations by activating the microphone and pinpoint locations and people met. Pegasus could harvest files, SMS messages, contacts, call history, calendars, emails and internet browsing history.

Even the supposedly encrypted WhatsApp messaging and calling by WhatsApp could be infected, along with Apple's iMessage software.

In other words, Star concluded, utilising Pegasus could help him disrupt opponents. He ordered his security chief to purchase it if they could – airily waving away protestations about its expense.

No matter that Free State citizens lacked decent health care, decent schools, decent housing or decent jobs. Nothing should get in the way of his ascent to the very summit of government – the presidency itself.

Komal, cheerfully independent in spirit and career herself, had almost become a telephone operator for her dependent new husband, the Veteran.

Although she didn't resent the role, she pulled his leg about being 'his little office girl', embarrassing his pretensions to being feminist of mind.

Sometimes the calls were from friends for a catch-up, but usually they were important – like this one. The woman sounded distraught, rather confused, as if not knowing quite why she was calling.

Komal swiftly cut her short, asked for a number to ring right back, and hurriedly passed it to the Veteran.

On his secure mobile phone – the one he used to communicate with trusted activists like Thandi – the Veteran called immediately.

'I don't know who I am speaking to or why,' Jayne stuttered, feeling silly. 'All I was told was to call Komal if I needed help.'

'No worries,' the Veteran replied sympathetically, checking which phone she was speaking from.

Reassured it wasn't her own, he asked who she was, about her job, why she was worried.

Jayne gave the bare details, feeling already as if a great burden was being lifted off her tense, knotted shoulders, casually mentioning she still had use of a computer linked to the bank's intranet.

'We need to meet in person,' the Veteran interrupted, thinking rapidly. 'But that could be dangerous, as they are obviously keeping an eye on you. How many apartments are there in your little estate?'

'Couple of dozen,' Jayne replied. Then she had a sudden thought. 'But my friend from where I am talking lives in the next small block of apartments like mine. And hers, like mine, has a back door onto an enclosed garden inside and common to all our blocks. So you could be visiting her and still come round the back way, unnoticed, to visit me.'

Thandi asked the Kubekas to drive her.

The large, locked gates were forbidding: 'PRIVATE – NO ENTRY'. The fencing was secure and seemingly ubiquitous, the appearance giving no clue as to what was inside or what was intended to be there in the future.

'Can we go down there?' she asked, pointing to a dusty track running into the distance and parallel to the fencing.

The Kubekas looked at each other uneasily. 'I don't want to hang about,' Edwin said to his father. 'Please drop me home and then you two can do what you want.'

Jacob drove off down the main road, passing a parked van with two men wearing pitch-black sunglasses sitting in the front.

The Veteran had pondered long and hard after the phone call with Jayne.

That he didn't know her at all was worrying. Her being a distant relative of his revered old struggle comrade Helen Joseph was no comfort at all; for every year that rolled by, the ties to the anti-apartheid fight became more frayed, the values more betrayed.

At the same time, Jayne had sounded credible, though confused and frightened. She clearly didn't know what she had got herself into, and nor, for that matter, did he.

Now he was lying down under a blanket on the back seat of their modest Hyundai sedan as Komal – having checked as carefully as she could that there was nobody watching the front gates of Jayne's estate – drove in and parked near her neighbour. It was at night, nobody was about and the Veteran, feeling bruised, especially around his neck and upper back where he had been badly injured the previous year, unfolded himself to be helped out of the car by Komal.

As he struggled upright, she handed him his walking stick and held his arm as he limped awkwardly into the friend's block and straight out the back door and around to Jayne's apartment.

The BSBC executive, looking strained, welcomed them nervously, showing them into her open-plan kitchen-diner living room. Startled at how stressed the Veteran looked as she shepherded him to sit heavily down on a chair, Jayne offered tea and they began to talk.

She had a vague recollection of the dramatic TV news items of the injured Veteran wheeled in before the cameras by a striking young black woman, and she knew also about his prominence in the ANC's underground campaign. He was, after all, well known to informed members of the public like her.

So she listened intently as he briefed her about his mission, Komal prodding him constantly to clarify and explain all the background, as well as the roles of Thandi Matjeke and Isaac Mkhize. But of the Sniper or his role there was no mention at all.

Jacob Kubeka dropped off his nervy son Edwin and drove on to the airport, Thandi watching the rear-view mirror for the car remorselessly following, as they hatched a new plan.

She climbed out and ostentatiously waved him goodbye, walking through the entrance and heading for the departures area, noting the sunglasses parked up nearby. Inside, and concealed from view, Thandi watched everyone coming into the airport: she could spot no morose characters in sunglasses posing as travellers.

Meanwhile, Kubeka drove off, noting the car peeling off in the opposite direction. *So far so good*, he thought, pulling into a suburban side street, where he waited for thirty minutes before returning to the airport, this time stopping well short of the drop-off and pick-up area.

He looked around. There was nothing untoward that he could see, and he waited for another hour, idly watching the flow of people in and out of the airport.

Inside, Thandi took her time, relieved that she wasn't as stressed as she thought she might be, trying to follow the Veteran's patient guidance on disguises and checking for surveillance.

She had a rooibos tea at a café and then slowly made her way to a cubicle in the women's toilets, where from her backpack she retrieved flamboyantly large sunglasses, changed her anonymous white blouse for a loud red one, replaced her tight denim jeans for a flowery skirt, put on a large lopsided hat and – eyeing herself in the mirror as she washed her hands – headed out looking a completely different, if rather zany, woman.

No ominously brooding security appeared to be in sight as she sauntered casually towards cars parked up away from the busy comings and goings, startling a dozing Jacob Kubeka as she tapped on the passenger door.

They set off for the boarded-up site fifteen kilometres away, the engine of the battered sedan wheezing.

No tailing van this time, Thandi was relieved to note, scanning the mirrors all the way to make absolutely sure.

Mkhize could hardly hold back the tears, even as he described to guests the latest poacher behaviour towards elephants.

They were always a target, even in Zama Zama, where poaching had almost come to a standstill following the safari park's rhino conspiracy encounters.

'Typically, the carcass of the mutilated elephant will lie for days abandoned by poachers, twisted and limp on its side, its legs splayed out, two on the ground, two horizontally in the air,' he explained.

'Have a look here,' he pointed to the reserve's iPad and the image he had found online. 'Its severed trunk, brutally hacked off with a chainsaw, has been flung to one side several metres from the main body. Look at this grotesquely disfigured and dismembered inside of its head.'

The guests recoiled from the photo of a large, gaping, bloodied cavity of mangled flesh, completely unrecognisable from the animal's normally magisterial presence.

It had been shot with a Kalashnikov, only hurting but not killing immediately, and once it had collapsed on the ground, the poachers cut its tendons to immobilise it – prompting a horribly long and excruciating death, compounded by chopping off its trunk to drain off its blood more rapidly.

'This is elephant genocide,' a passionate Mkhize explained. 'In 1800, there may have been around twenty-five million elephants in Africa alone, roaming across the continent from the Cape to the Mediterranean.

'By the turn of the twentieth century, the number had fallen to several million. Today the number has plunged to around four hundred thousand. African elephants will be extinct by 2040 if nothing is done to put a halt to poaching.'

'But why?' asked one guest, the others looking at him in surprise, thinking everyone knew about the value of ivory.

'Because ivory commands such high prices; it has been described by the United Nations as a significant form of transnational organised crime, alongside drugs, people trafficking and terrorism,' Mkhize patiently explained.

'China is the biggest importer, the US second and Japan not far behind. In China, ivory is often used in both art and religious sculpture by the country's rich new elite.'

Mkhize paused. He had learned not to bombard guests with too much information, but they seemed thirsty for more.

'Ivory is so valuable that elephant tusks have become a big factor in conflict zones in Africa, like Uganda, South Sudan and the Democratic Republic of Congo. Armed men come across the border from Sudan or from Somalia into Kenya to kill elephants and smuggle out the ivory.

'And it's not just that elephants are being massacred. It has a big impact on the surrounding ecosystem. Elephants are key to the balance between grass and woodland in the savanna, and they also affect water for other animals. In some areas where elephants have almost been wiped out, you see a growth of woody vegetation, which leads to grazing species like antelope disappearing. And when they disappear, so also do predators like lion, leopard and cheetah.

'Unless elephant poaching is halted, nearly all of Central Africa's forests, Africa's lungs of the earth, will experience dramatic changes in their tree species. Also, elephants eat fruits and spread seeds that other animals are too small to digest, travelling huge distances and dispersing those seeds in dung droppings, with some trees entirely dependent upon elephants for seed dispersal.

'Another benefit is that their dung contains vital nutrients, including nitrogen, in short supply in Central Africa's vast forests. So fewer elephants means stunting future tree growth. Foraging forest elephants also open up gaps in vegetation, enabling different plants to grow and making fresh pathways for smaller animals.'

Reluctant to ask the Veteran to step into her untidy makeshift office in the guest bedroom, Jayne nevertheless reckoned it was important for him to see on her computer screen what she had discovered.

While Komal hovered anxiously, the Veteran slumped down on her personal office computer chair while she grabbed a couple of table chairs.

However, he couldn't make much sense of the bank statements flickering across the screen as she scrolled continuously, briefing him on what they meant.

'You see here, instead of investing this five hundred million rands of government money through Vryburg Enterprises' account in whatever the project is, most of the money has been transferred to a company in the United Arab Emirates called Frontway Limited, registered in Ras al-Khaimah, one of seven emirates making up the UAE and a highly secretive offshore company jurisdiction. However, Frontway also has an account with our bank, BSBC.'

'Okay so far?' Jayne paused, glancing quizzically at the Veteran who nodded, fully absorbed, concentrating hard to blank out the searing pain in his neck and upper back.

'Now,' she said, 'look carefully at what happens next. Once the funds were in Dubai, it looks to me like there was a classic money-laundering manoeuvre, which transformed that illicitly grabbed money from Vryburg into ostensibly legitimate assets.'

She pointed at the screen. 'See here,' she said moving the cursor. 'They then transferred over four hundred and eighty million rands of the Vryburg money in two separate tranches through another two shell companies, ultimately consolidating it in another BSBC account for another UAE-based company called Precise Investments. Then they transmitted this money into an entity called Broadway Trading in the State Bank of India, and thereafter back into South Africa.'

The Veteran rocked back in his chair, fascinated but rather star-struck by this glimpse into an alien financial world, pausing and thinking as Jayne and Komal studied him closely.

After a minute he asked casually: 'So who are the *they* performing all these sophisticated money manoeuvres?'

'That I don't know, I'm afraid,' replied Jayne, 'but I can tell you this: the names listed in these various companies – Frontway, Precise Investments, Broadway Trading – are identical. The question is, who is really behind them?'

'That I can possibly discover,' the Veteran smiled for the first time since he had greeted her, 'but I will need you to write this all down for me and print it out, together with those bank statements, please.'

'Easy enough to do,' Jayne said, relaxing, 'but by when?'

'Right now, please,' the Veteran replied firmly. 'A big ask, but we can wait. I would also like you to give me a memory stick with it all on if you have a spare one, please.'

Mkhize regaled the latest animated safari guests with magical but authentic tales from the bush.

90

Of how he had once spotted an oxpecker resting on a rhino's horn after sharpening its beak on the surface, while the regal animal munched vegetation as if unaware.

And of a safari scene of tranquil normality – or so it seemed.

A pair of elephants drank in the river's shallows, their trunks swinging to and fro, then curling up and into their mouths to gulp dollops of water, several guests videoing from a small covered boat.

To the fore, probably only thirty metres away from the elephants, who took absolutely no notice, an egret sailed silently by, elegantly perched with both legs standing on the back of a crocodile, its snout and eyes menacingly visible on the river surface.

The Veteran knew a former ANC MP who had resigned over the complicity of senior party figures in a corrupt arms deal, basing himself in London, where he established an anti-corruption investigative unit.

Murray Bergstein, compact and terrier-like, fearlessly and forensically authoritative, enthusiastically accepted the list of the shell companies the Veteran had given him from Jayne Joseph to check out.

'See if you can trace the big names behind the front ones, please,' the Veteran beseeched him, adding, 'As soon as you can.'

He also explained that the aim was to ask Bob Richards MP to expose it in the House of Commons as he had done before. So the information had to be watertight.

'No problem,' Bergstein replied ending their brusque WhatsApp call.

When Kubeka's car approached the site, it seemed to be deserted: no visible security near the locked gates, no patrolling vehicles in sight – the guards must be having a break. Thandi noticed, though, that there were CCTV cameras around the perimeter.

Asking Kubeka to drive on without pausing, like any passing vehicle, Thandi peered about, pointing to a track down one side and directing him to take it.

They bumped along in the dust, a billowing cloud behind them, the perimeter fence sturdy and apparently electrified, rather like the one around Zama Zama, she thought. As far as she could see – which wasn't that much – the land inside seemed bare, even bleak, with few clumps of trees, sparse bushes and untidy, rocky scrub.

Kubeka concentrated on the road, grimacing at his groaning suspension and worrying it might mean an expensive repair he could ill afford, keeping an edgy eye on his petrol gauge, reassured only by the excruciatingly slow speed needed to navigate the rutted surface.

He thought back nostalgically to similar journeys escaping the Special Branch along back roads over the border to Botswana, once to rendezvous secretly with the Veteran and collect some arms, and then to drive back in, worried all the time in case he was stopped and searched. A black man driving on his own always attracted police suspicion; one driving a white master never did. This had been one of Nelson Mandela's ruses, disguised as a chauffeur, white owner sitting on the back seat, for the nearly two years he was underground before finally being captured near Howick Falls outside Durban in 1962.

Those times were tough but also invigorating, Kubeka recalled. Times of intense comradeship and deep bonds, of immense danger but immense daring too. Times long gone and consumed by much more complicated contemporary currents, where hope and resilience seemed to expire after too many people started helping themselves instead of helping each other.

They drove for nearly two hours, circling the perimeter, getting bored and increasingly fed up at not spotting anything revealing. It was a vast area, with nothing visible going on inside, yet considerable investment had been made to secure the outside.

What on earth was it? Thandi and Kubeka had no idea. It was especially frustrating for her because it seemed to have been a wasted journey. Except, except . . . maybe not, for the very fact that it remained a mystery meant something suspicious – although perhaps that went without saying in the 'gangster state'.

The afternoon sun was subsiding and the coolness sliding in as they returned once more to Bram Fischer airport. Thandi asked to be dropped off well away from the terminal, thanking Kubeka profusely and insisting on handing him R5,000 (it was left over from the donor money she'd been given in case she had to stay over in a hotel and incur unexpected costs). 'In case the car needs fixing,' she insisted, brushing aside his embarrassment, and giving him a peck on the cheek.

Thandi walked jauntily to the entrance, as befitted her eye-catchingly lurid attire – which she quickly packed back into her bag in a toilet cubicle, just in time to catch the last flight to OR Tambo International Airport.

As she was boarding, Star received a cryptic WhatsApp message from his security detail: a car had been spotted on the cameras encircling the Park's perimeter, and it belonged to Kubeka senior.

'You know exactly what to do,' he messaged back.

Before queuing at the boarding gate, Thandi called the Veteran to report back. Komal answered his phone.

'He's been having an early-evening power nap,' she said. 'I'll rouse him, otherwise he won't sleep properly tonight.'

When the Veteran rang her back, the two chatted for a while. 'Do have a read of this article from a few years ago by a respected analyst,' the Veteran said, pinging the link over to Thandi. 'It gives a bit more texture to the corruption problem.'

Before takeoff, she opened the article and read that an ANC survey carried out in Gauteng province back in 2006 had revealed that over 40 per cent of the Party's ordinary members and a nearly a third of local Party officers were unemployed, many saying that they experienced periods when they were forced to go hungry.

But although these ANC members weren't able to access opportunities for higher incomes through black economic empowerment (BEE) into the business sector, they did have some access to opportunities in local provincial and national government, and even some state enterprises.

'While this wasn't necessarily always an openly corrupt relationship, the networks of patronage underlay the hollowing out of democracy in the movement, and mobilisation of members to support certain slates, in return for access to a share of the goodies,' the analyst reported. A position in a local council sometimes conferred the ability to put food on the family table. The stakes could therefore be so high that violence and even assassination could spill over.

Over time, values were corrupted and a culture of legitimising and justifying shady or even corrupt practices began to take root. Even more so when the ANC leadership was seen to be spearheading these predatory practices.

A culture of nepotism, patronage and outright corruption was being tolerated, big time at the top, or small scale at the bottom. But it was no good just insisting upon ethical politics and government: there had to be a route out of poverty, and legitimate paths for ordinary citizens to earn greater wealth.

Thandi pondered the implications as she closed her eyes, semi–dozing until the plane touched down in Joburg before her connecting flight to Richards Bay.

Jacob Kubeka was watching a DVD with some relatives at home in the Bloemfontein suburb of Hillsboro. His wife had collected a takeaway chicken from a nearby Nando's outlet, and they settled down to relax, the men with some beers.

Then they paused the DVD so his cousin could use the toilet.

'There's a car in your front driveway,' the cousin returned to announce. 'Couple of guys sitting inside, I think.'

Wary after what had happened to Edwin, Kubeka inched the front door open and peered outside.

The next thing the guests heard was two gunshots, followed by a pause, then two more. Rushing up, the party found Kubeka slumped in the open doorway, lying face down as if he had turned to escape back inside.

He was bleeding profusely as they rushed him to a local Mediclinic, where surgeons found one of the bullets had pierced his aorta. There was nothing they could do.

The car had disappeared, and the police weren't interested. Just another unsolved assassination in Star's empire.

Weeks earlier, alarms had been triggered in the Free State Tourism and Parks Agency. All the indicators showed that the province's admired biodiversity, protected by South African governments for more than a century, was deteriorating rapidly.

Tourists were dribbling away. But the provincial government wasn't doing anything about it. Instead, the agency was embroiled in a scandal. Senior staff members were accused of serious fraud and misconduct, and above them were much more senior figures, threatening other staff members should they spill the beans.

But the CEO stood upright and honourable above all this malevolence and sleaze – and for that reason was probably living on borrowed time in a province notorious for corruption.

However, there was one person she had heard of through the South African National Parks (SANParks) bush telegraph who might assist. A ranger who had done wonders for SANParks in the Kruger but above all in a private KwaZulu-Natal reserve. She couldn't remember his name but was determined to find it.

94

Which is how Mkhize got a phone call and why Elise reluctantly agreed to let him take special leave to help out for a few days. But a few days only, she insisted. Zama Zama's resources were scarce enough with him, let alone without him.

Thandi, he was sure, would be enthusiastic – and intrigued.

Instead, when she returned home late that night, she was distraught. While driving from Richards Bay airport, she had learned from the Veteran the shocking news about Jacob Kubeka.

'I killed him, I killed him,' she sobbed.

'What do you mean you killed him? Mkhize asked.

She explained what had happened that day as he consoled her, bothered now about their own safety but insisting that she must not blame herself.

When, over the following weeks, Major Yasmin had the incident investigated, it was soon clear her enquiries would lead nowhere. She was informed that the murder weapon had been thrown into Saulspoort Dam and the getaway car had been disposed of. The hitman had melted right away; instead of pursuing him, the local police arrested Kubeka's brother and cousin and tried to frame them, plunging the whole extended family into a an even more horrific nightmare.

Star, meanwhile, confided to friends that he was worried about being arrested for conspiracy to murder. About what, he never explained.

They were even more mystified. Why would he be worried anyway, they asked themselves, when he controlled the local police?

CHAPTER 6

The Veteran decided it was time to make a new plan.

First he called his Constantia benefactor for yet another favour.

'I am sorry,' the Veteran began. 'The only time we speak is for me to ask for funds.'

'No problem, that's what I'm here for, to help because I can – and because I believe in what you are trying to do – as I did under apartheid,' came the immediate reply.

The two men chatted amiably about their shared passion for English football, and the latest news from the Premier League. Chelsea, the Veteran's team, had a new manager – yet again. Liverpool, his friend's team, had just won the European Champions League – resurrected to their past glory under their manager of several years, Jürgen Klopp.

'For you the shock therapy of constant change at the top has brought lots of trophies; for us the stability is a much more sustainable basis for football success,' the friend deduced.

'Maybe, but you haven't won much for years, including the Premier League,' the Veteran retorted, 'and during that time we've won it five times!'

Then they got down to business. The funds needed were to cover the living costs of the Veteran's protégé, Thandi – though she didn't know it yet.

As the Sniper sat in her office, Minister Yasmin quizzed him about his recommendations for activating the secret IT logistics plan he had advocated.

They already had Star's personal mobile phone number; the question was how to trace any burner phone he used – because there would almost certainly be at least one.

'Mr Bob Richards!'

The Speaker's loud command was the signal for the MP to move his amendment during the committee stage of the Trade Bill going through the House of Commons in preparation for Brexit. It was to keep an entirely open Irish border.

Richards had been banging on about the dangers to the peace process on the island of Ireland for several years since the 2016 referendum campaign on Britain's membership of the European Union.

But very few seemed to be listening, some accusing him of exaggerating because he was a 'Remoaner', as an active member of the 2016 Remain campaign.

Now, as the negotiations to complete Brexit staggered from crisis to crisis, it was abundantly clear to everyone that the Irish border was indeed the Achilles heel of a 'hard Brexit' – the Brexit version abandoning European trade rules that Ireland and the UK had shared since they joined Europe together in 1973.

As a result, MPs had started taking Richards more seriously, and the government was worried he might have cross-party backing for his amendment, which would in effect keep the UK aligned with European rules to maintain an open border.

As ministers came off their rhetorical pedestals about 'taking back control' and got down to the complex detail of the negotiations with Brussels, it was obvious they had no answers.

Richards muttered, 'Thank you, Mr Speaker' – a courtesy he never much cared for, because he was entitled to speak, but nevertheless respected.

He began: 'Named "bandit country" at the height of the Troubles, the mountains and fields of South Armagh, marking the border between Northern Ireland and the Republic, echo Yeats: "a terrible beauty".

'Even with army watch watchtowers high on the skyline, border posts and constant soldier patrols, it was impossible to police.

'But over ten years on since bitter blood enemies Ian Paisley and Martin McGuinness took power to govern together in 2007, Brexit threatens to reawaken the iconic border divisions stretching back decades. All because the border could become the customs frontier of the European Union.

'Along the entire three-hundred-mile Irish border, it is estimated that there are up to hundred thousand major and minor crossings, with five thousand people crossing each day.

'It's as if the border no longer matters. Citizens resident on either side can and do take advantage of the health and educational services nearest to where they live on a cross-border basis. People cross the border freely to work, play and socialise. Northern Ireland businesses invest without hindrance in the Republic and the same occurs for businesses in reverse. The two economies are being steadily aligned.

'For Irish Republicans and Nationalists, an entirely open border of the kind that has operated without security or hindrance of any kind for many years now is politically totemic, an everyday reality that progress has been made towards their aspirations for a united Ireland.

'But a united Ireland under the 1998 Good Friday Agreement, would properly require endorsement by referendum – important to Unionists, since there can be no such change without voter consent, theirs included.

'The Good Friday Agreement brought an end to the tragic bombings and bloodshed of the Troubles. It's been successful because it addressed the toxic identity question in a society divided down the middle between Protestants and Catholics. It made the border between the two parts of the island of Ireland virtually uncontentious. For Nationalists, it meant the Irish border had to be completely open. For Unionists, it meant any constitutional change in Northern Ireland's status could only occur by democratic consent through a referendum.

'But to keep the border open, Northern Ireland needs to remain inside both the EU single market and its customs union, so Brexit threw not so much a spanner as a great big forklift in the peace works.

'One wheeze, apparently emanating from the government, is to grant Northern Ireland exceptional status, justified by its turbulent history, within both the UK *and* the EU. That might mean a customs border across the Irish Sea, between Northern Ireland, Wales, Scotland and England – understandably toxic to Unionists.

'But just imagine what the impact of a hard border across the island would be for dairy farmers. It could decimate the Irish milk-processing sector, because milk tankers cross the Irish border all the time. Nearly a third of Northern Ireland's milk is processed in the Republic. Milk and dairy products move in both directions, sometimes several times.

'Nearly all of the wheat grown in the Republic is sent to Northern

Ireland for milling, and then reimported back. A big chunk of Northern Irish lamb is processed in the Republic, while a significant volume of its pigs and cattle are processed in Northern Ireland.

'The Irish border is, therefore, no ordinary state border. It is both invisible and ever-present, both unremarkable and deeply contested.'

His speech concluded, he sat down, the chamber noticeably quiet.

It was a good sign, for it meant MPs on all sides had been listening, including an evidently sombre minister who would have to reply to the debate later and was pondering what on earth to say: just reading out the turgid civil service draft which said nothing at great length was usually the safest thing to do.

Thandi was entranced – as she always was when alone with the Veteran – listening intently as he reminisced, not self-indulgently, more instructively.

She was staying for a few nights in Johannesburg at the new home to which the Veteran and Komal had just moved from Kalk Bay on the Cape Peninsula.

'To get away from the cold Cape winters,' he had explained, 'and to be near the buzz and easy connections of the big city.'

Komal brought them both glasses of her favourite guava juice, pulling his leg and telling him to behave himself alone in his study with an attractive young woman as she winked at Thandi.

'Isn't he past all that?' Thandi said impishly.

The Veteran pretended to bristle: 'Just because I'm in a wheelchair doesn't mean there's no life in the old dog yet!'

'I can confirm that's only too true. He's a very badly behaved old man – thank goodness!' Komal called from the corridor, laughing as she walked away.

The Veteran threw up his hands, his shoulders heaving as he laughed, hiding a grimace at a twinge of pain, a relic of his entanglement with rhino poachers. 'What do I say to *that*?'

'As little as possible. Better stay schtum while you are ahead is my advice,' Thandi retorted sharply.

He shook his head, smiling broadly. 'Now, where was I before I was so badly interrupted by you impossible women?'

He paused. 'Aah, of course, I was talking about the fight against sports apartheid. You know, when I read a book recently about the Olympics staged in Berlin under Hitler in 1936, it was uncanny to learn how the Nazis used almost exactly the same specious arguments to exclude Jews from their sports teams as apartheiders did over blacks.

'It was almost as if the Nazis foreshadowed the ridiculous contortions used by apartheid ministers decades later. And of course you'll remember that apartheid leaders, like John Vorster, were interned during the Second World War for sabotage against the Allies.'

'Ja, I heard about *that*,' Thandi replied, 'but not about the sports stuff, especially the Olympics.'

The Veteran nodded, continuing: 'At the time, Hitler was eyeing up invading or intervening in Austria, Czechoslovakia and the Spanish Civil War. So he suspended his Jew-baiting, vilification and oppression, and staged an extravaganza to woo visitors, the media and diplomats. And it was supremely effective: the Olympics became a propaganda exercise for Hitler.

'But what's also fascinating is the Nazis saw sport and physical exercise as a way of boosting Aryan prowess. So much so that members of Hitler's murderous SS security elite were only allowed to marry women with Reich sports medals because only they could be relied upon to breed elite, pure Aryan babies.

'Previously, the Nazis had disbanded almost all Jewish sports organisations and, like apartheid did for blacks, banned Jewish teams from competing with Aryan teams. Non-Aryans could not be lifeguards and some ski resorts had signs stating "Jews forbidden". Jews were also banned from using swimming baths, gyms, youth clubs and other places for training, allowing Nazi leaders to claim to Olympic bosses that Jews were being excluded from German teams on merit only.'

'Was there pressure for a boycott like under apartheid?' Thandi asked.

'Yes, absolutely,' said the Veteran, warming to his theme. 'After left-wing and Jewish groups urged a boycott, one of the Olympic bosses, America's Avery Brundage, actually said: "Certain Jews must now understand that they cannot use these Games as a weapon in their boycott against the Nazis." You couldn't make it up!'

Thandi cupped her hands high and raised her eyebrows, as if in 'what can I say to *that*?' incredulity.

'Other international sports officials actually accused "Jews of bringing politics into sport" — exactly the same nonsense used against anti-apartheid campaigners pressing for whites-only South African sports teams to be excluded from all international competition.

'Under apartheid, white sports officials justified racism in sport on the most spurious basis, some almost word for word the kind of thing that Hitler and his fellow Nazis used to exclude Jews.'

The Veteran burrowed among one of the many piles of papers on his desk. 'You would be amazed at some of the things they used to say to justify apartheid segregation in sport. I have them printed out here.'

'In March 1967, the minister of sport, said: "If whites and non-whites start competing against each other, there will be viciousness as has never been seen before."

'The mouthpiece of the apartheid government, *Die Transvaler*, in 1965, insisted that whites had maintained their domination because there had been no racial intermarriage, which in turn was because there was no social mixing between white and non-white. Its editorial added: "In South Africa the races do not mix on the sports field. If they mix on the sports field, then the road to other forms of social mixing is wide open ... With an eye to upholding the white race and its civilisation, not one single compromise can be entered into — not even when it comes to a visiting rugby team."'

The Veteran reached for another sheet of paper but was interrupted.

'Come on,' called Komal, 'time for dinner — and Thandi is busy first thing tomorrow.'

Thandi offered to help the Veteran to wash his hands and eat, but he was insistent on using his walking stick, limping and muttering that he had to keep walking. 'I walk round and round the garden several times daily,' he said pointedly.

He then proceeded to open a bottle of Meerlust Rubicon, which didn't last that long between the three of them, though the Veteran easily out-drank the others — so he opened another.

Early the next morning Thandi's fresh mission began in earnest, the Veteran having given her a preliminary briefing.

Komal drove her to meet Jayne Joseph for the first time, the three women conferring for an hour before Komal left, promising to return and collect Thandi when she was ready.

Having been fully updated by Jayne, Thandi briefed her on fresh news from Murray Bergstein, quarrying away in London through his research network. Bergstein had discovered something else: at least two of the front companies were involved in a money-laundering operation used by

101

international drug cartels, as well as by terrorist groups such as al-Qaeda and Islamic State.

'It was like "spider's web", Bergstein reported. 'Vryburg Enterprises is a typical "laundry platform", a local front company to which the state grant is paid as part of a much wider state-capture programme for multiple payments. It's akin to a "local laundromat" with links into an "international laundromat": a network to repeatedly launder money through other front entities and their myriad of accounts until it can be cashed in.

'Star, it seems, has been utilising criminal networks based mainly in Hong Kong, China and Dubai, the sophisticated nature of which made it extremely difficult, if not impossible, to track the end point where the funds would be ultimately received.

'When the Business Brothers were engaged in state capture with the Former President,' Bergstein added, 'there were nearly 4,000 transactions to transfer R5 billion (£250 million) offshore in a massive international laundry operation. And that was just a fraction of their state-capture looting, estimated at over R50 billion (£2.5 billion).

'But,' Bergstein ominously reported, 'the real problem is that, although these transactions left a "digital footprint", the bank, lawyers and auditors enabling all this (and receiving fat fees in the process), showed no inclination whatsoever to cooperate with investigations to identify that footprint. They were all as culpable in the looting.'

Van der Merwe was given fresh instructions for a new mission through a familiar intermediary from his old apartheid days of clandestine dealings in the military and intelligence.

He'd never met Star before but knew full well who he was and the ruthless reign he exercised. The money would be very useful: it would pay for a cruise from Cape Town to Maputo and back for him and his new love – and leave him more comfortably able to pay Jo-Jo for the care of his illicit son.

He began to ponder. Who could carry out the mission for him?

Inevitably his mind turned to trusted associates from the old Buffalo Battalion days. They had been ruthlessly efficient in eliminating apartheid's opponents under the radar – and he certainly needed the same stroke of pitiless proficiency now.

That triggered an idea: what about his old friends in the South African Institute for Maritime Research? Its neutral label belied a history of apartheid-era dirty tricks, including supplying weapons to those plotting an uprising in the early 1990s to thwart Mandela's impending rise to power.

At the time, Van der Merwe had flirted with that notion himself but concluded it was far too reckless. He had an uncanny knack of steering clear of personal trouble, instead orchestrating others.

The problem, however, was the Maritime Research guys were rather old, so he thought further.

He also had contacts from the apartheid era in the private security firm Precision Security Services (PSS), some of whose executives had participated in attacks on residents, including schoolchildren, in Soweto and other former apartheid townships.

The PSS, explained one of Van der Merwe's mates, was a company run on the same system that the apartheid police used to work on – running parallel police investigations, and operating a parallel police network.

It had worked for a global British tobacco corporate, sabotaging competitors, infiltrating law enforcement agencies, paying bribes and carrying out illegal surveillance. The UK company hired PSS to conduct on-the-ground spying campaigns that stretched from factory-floor informants to high-level professionals in competitor companies. It also gained access to the Johannesburg police's CCTV network, and had unlawful access to the state automatic number-plate recognition system, enabling its agents – many of them former police officers – to place tracking devices on vehicles.

Could be very useful, Van der Merwe thought. But, again, his contacts in PSS were of a certain age, and he needed someone honed for action – a killer, not an investigator or a spy.

Then he had an even better idea. Someone who'd been headquartered on a one-hundred-hectare farm nestling in the hills twenty kilometres west of Pretoria on the Hennops River.

Piet van der Merwe had known it well, and in fact had been on the periphery of its notorious activities, but had never been directly involved. He was always too careful for that.

Vlakplaas – 'shallow farm'. Even its name still sent shivers down his spine, because he knew exactly what had gone on there, despite invariably feigning ignorance when it suited him.

Van der Merwe was familiar with the single-storey building, with two large metal water tanks towering over it, a corrugated-iron roof sloping down over a verandah, and plenty of rooms inside, including even one for playing snooker, which the security police officers operating there used for relaxation.

Relaxation – from the torture, the murder and the beatings carried out at Vlakplaas, headquarters of the secret South African Police counterinsurgency unit C10 (later called C1). That was its official designation. In practice, it was a paramilitary hit squad to fight the anti-apartheid guerrillas of MK and APLA.

The unit was established in 1979 by security police captain Dirk Coetzee, who headed Vlakplaas's fifteen-member death squad. This was a group of elite assassins who, at the end of long days, enjoyed binge-drinking sessions and *braaivleis* outside the building.

A lawless operation, both inside and outside South Africa, it captured those designated as enemies of the apartheid government, took them to the Vlakplaas farm, and either 'turned' (converted) them into askaris or executed them. More than a thousand died in this way, the exact number never established, so wanton, callous, secretive and unaccountable was it.

Many abducted and taken to Vlakplaas never left it, their remains buried somewhere – in an enlarged warthog hole, anywhere that could be found to prevent discovery – burned or even blown up, the aim being to leave no trace whatsoever. People simply 'disappeared'.

Van der Merwe helped with logistics, supplying everything Vlakplaas needed, from food and drink to bedding and other furniture. He would procure the supplies and drive them there himself as a trusted part of its outer circle, on friendly terms with Coetzee or his successor as commander from 1982, Colonel Eugene de Kock. But he had never been present in the inner sanctum. Never to witness, only to hear, the harrowing, haunting screams and to drive quickly away.

Yet he had still winced when he watched, on live television in 1999, Eugene de Kock's confessions before the Truth and Reconciliation Commission. Presided over by Archbishop Desmond Tutu, the commission had been established to uncover the truth about apartheid-era brutality in return for amnesty. De Kock admitted to committing more than 100 atrocities – torture, extortion and murder – on behalf of the Vlakplaas unit.

Eight years later, in a radio interview, De Kock also accused South Africa's last apartheid president, FW de Klerk, of having hands 'soaked in blood' in ordering specific killings by Vlakplaas hit squads – allegations fastidiously denied by De Klerk, a Nobel Peace Prize winner with Nelson Mandela, who never explained how the shadowy state units like Vlakplaas and other 'third force' exercises operated on his watch.

During the four years between Nelson Mandela walking out from prison in February 1990 and becoming president in May 1994, more people were killed than at any time under apartheid. It was as if De Klerk's regime wanted it both ways: praise for first releasing Mandela and his fellow ANC leaders and then negotiating a transition with them, but still trying to cling on to power by murdering their grass-roots followers.

Contemplating further, Van der Merwe remembered one of the youngest Vlakplaas operatives, who was hardly out of his teens when the farm was closed down. Although that was a quarter of a century ago, he might be just the man.

Van der Merwe resolved to track him down.

Veronica Selepe, the new recruit to the Zama Zama ranger team, wore her peaked cap jauntily, and soon became 'one of the boys' in the previously all-male cohort.

She settled in quickly, having plenty of expertise from her studies and safari-park placements but limited experience of escorting in the wild. With guests around the lodge fire in the evening, she soon became popular, the wives and girlfriends especially pleased to have a woman to relate to.

She had been allocated a room in the small row of lodgings where Mkhize slept, away from the lodge. After the guests had sloped off to sleep, they drove the short distance to their rooms. On the way, Veronica had been swinging a spotlight back and forth, looking for the denizens of the night. Mkhize tutored her to methodically scrutinise trees, gaps in the bushes, any hiding spot for a nocturnal creature concealed. Not for them as such but for their eye-shines, which, like beacons, could reveal the presence of an animal sometimes hundreds of metres away.

He could often even tell, from the height of the eyes and their width apart, what animal it was. Eye-shine, they both knew, was a kind of iridescence, so some animals' eyes shone in different colours, allowing expert trackers and rangers to distinguish between species of concealed animals.

105

He suddenly stopped the Land Cruiser. To their left, drooped over a tree branch, was a leopard, with what seemed to be a bushbuck it had pulled up to eat.

They drove on and drew up inside the gate of their lodgings, Veronica flushed with excitement at what they had seen, and they soon got chatting, sitting out on camp chairs as they wound down.

The minutes became an hour and the chatter between them was non-stop.

'Have you read about this new study by scientists that humankind is now responsible for a sixth mass extinction event in our planet's history?' Mkhize asked.

'They remind us that there have been five "mass extinction events" in history – all caused by dramatic natural phenomena. But this one we are living through right now is caused by humans. We are the only species able to manipulate the Earth on such a massive scale,' he added.

'I saw something about that online, but haven't other studies disagreed?' replied Veronica.

'Ja – but these guys have looked at an invertebrate family that includes snails, clams and slugs. They reckon that as many as a quarter of a million of all known species have already gone extinct, mostly on land, though also in the seas. Human activity is so bloody destructive, we have created a biodiversity crisis so gigantic that it seems unstoppable.'

Mkhize was enjoying himself until he noticed the time. God! After midnight – and he had to be up and fresh and early at five to prepare for a bushwalk.

He rose and made to bid her goodnight.

'Can I join you?' she asked appealingly, that twinkle in her eyes almost effervescent with the moon high.

Mkhize, aroused, was sorely tempted. He stood up as she moved towards him.

Then he thought of Thandi, hundreds of kilometres away in Johannesburg on one of her missions. 'Sorry, I'm married,' he muttered sheepishly, turning away.

'That doesn't matter,' she said, her fingers stroking his arm, 'only for a bit of fun!'

Mkhize gazed at her. 'It does matter to me,' he said gently. 'You are a very attractive woman, but I am spoken for.'

They turned reluctantly away from each other, Veronica only a few rooms along, and Mkhize, tossing and turning in his bed, reflecting upon the temptation of Veronica versus his love for Thandi.

How much he missed her, wondering about the separated lives of their new marriage, eventually falling deeply asleep for a few hours in time to be jerked awake by the alarm for his dawn duties.

'Explain this to me simply, please?' Thandi pleaded.

'Look, I don't know exactly what is going on,' Jayne replied, 'but it's certainly something fishy, and Murray Bergstein reckons it concerns front or shell companies, where the real owner or owners are hidden but which can get a contract from the government.'

'If you look at the transactions, you see here the government grant is paid into Vryburg Enterprises. But it looks to me like only some of it is actually spent, and most of it was quickly sent to Dubai. There it was spread between several entities, including Frontway Limited, Precise Investments and Broadway Trading.'

'Vryburg Enterprises itself seems to me to be little more than a shell company controlled by an individual called Kamal Vakram. I cannot find out much at all about him – can you help, please? Who he might be fronting for?' Jayne asked Thandi.

'I will follow up,' Thandi promised, thinking this was probably one for Minister Yasmin.

'But what seems also to have happened – and may still be happening – is that some of this money in Dubai has been moved back into South Africa. Murray Bergstein's investigations suggest that much of what is circulating back into Johannesburg is invoiced against bogus contracts. From what I can see, hundreds of millions of rands have been returning into South Africa in this way.' Jayne explained.

'So that I understand properly,' Thandi said slowly, trying to get her head around the mysteries of Jayne's financial world, 'you are telling me that a company gets a government grant or contract to do something specific, like in the Free State, but instead spends only some of it on that task, transfers it to Dubai, distributes it between these shell companies, which then transfer it back into South Africa to be spent on something else entirely?'

'Exactly,' said Jayne smiling, 'that's what Murray and I think is happening.'

'But you are still not a hundred per cent sure?'

107

'Not yet, no,' Jayne replied. 'Also, I have been tracking back over recent years too and I found a very similar pattern involving the Business Brothers, who you will remember only too well – the crooked cronies of the Former President.'

'I do indeed!' Thandi grimaced. 'But how can they be connected to this? They fled the country, didn't they?'

'Yes, but they bought property in Dubai with their looted billions, and still operate from there, as well as from India. Some of the same front companies they used, and probably set up, are involved in the latest financial manoeuvres I have been showing you here.' Jayne pointed at her computer monitor.

She continued. 'You may remember these Dubai shell entities were vital for the Business Brothers. When they got more than seven billion rands in kickbacks from contracts with China to supply new locomotives to the rail operator Transnet, they had it laundered through a couple of companies controlled by other companies they also controlled and part-owned, one of which was a scrap-metal company in India. Again, a lot of it was eventually repatriated back into South Africa via their Dubai operations.'

Thandi was starting to comprehend the complex whirl of looted money being laundered round and round – first out of South Africa through Dubai and also Hong Kong, then part of it back in to be spent on all sorts of nefarious purposes and ventures, including lavish shindigs for cronies, an extravagant wedding in Sun City and luxury items like jewellery.

'Murray Bergstein has also said that there were more than a dozen of these "laundry" entities. So they used one of them, then quickly moved on to another one in case someone spotted what was happening, as I think happened after the South African Reserve Bank became suspicious in one case,' Jayne clarified.

'After receiving the funds from South Africa, it seems like each of these "laundries" paid them into intermediate companies, which were also just conduits: they did nothing useful except act as channels for the looted billions. In other words, they weren't trading in anything; they weren't making or selling or offering any services.'

Thandi rolled her eyes, as Jayne continued: 'Each intermediate company then passed it on to what Murray calls "an onshore-offshore bridge".'

'What the f***?!' Thandi exclaimed. 'Now you have lost me entirely!'

108

'Sorry,' Jayne looked sheepish. 'I'd never heard of this label before, but Murray says onshore-offshore bridges are companies that receive and then aggregate funds from different sources before transferring them offshore, mostly through Hong Kong/China but also to Dubai. Anyway, they are designed to obfuscate even people like me who are supposed to know about these things.'

'Well, that's a bit of a relief, because it's pretty well bamboozled me!' Thandi responded, looking glum. 'Also, doesn't the use of these complex laundries mean it is impossible to trace the looted funds to where it finally ends up?'

'Yes and no,' Jayne replied carefully. 'It is very difficult to follow the money. But Murray Bergstein has shown examples of how to do so. His investigative unit based in London showed how the Business Brothers and their cronies used the same money-laundering networks as serious violent organised crime, as well as drug traffickers, the Taliban and terrorists like al-Qaeda and al-Shabaab.'

'And you suspect the same kind of thing is happening again in the Free State?' Thandi mused.

'Yes I do, maybe using exactly the same channels.'

'Something else,' Jayne added almost as an afterthought. 'Bergstein also showed that they used half a dozen individuals, yet none of them had a clue these payments had been made and accounts had been opened in their names.'

'What?' Thandi exclaimed. 'Are you saying that their identities had all been stolen?'

Jayne nodded. 'In the case of Transnet, Bergstein's investigations showed Chinese rail companies paid hundreds of millions of dollars in kickbacks for the orders of locomotives into the HSBC accounts of companies based in Hong Kong but controlled by the Business Brothers. Once the Chinese rail kickbacks were in these accounts, they were moved in thousands of transactions into a range of Chinese and Hong Kong companies that didn't do any trading but were simply bought off the shelf in Hong Kong – so yet more front companies, used often as channels for money to be moved back into South Africa.'

'Pretty ingenious,' Thandi remarked, still trying to absorb what it all meant.

'Yes, and Bergstein also showed that these very Hong Kong front companies were part of a much larger global money laundry. HSBC admitted as much after an internal investigation in April 2017, which revealed its massive complicity in the corruption of the Business Brothers who used it. The bank had covered up the money-laundering exploits of the Business Brothers, involving around ninety accounts in Hong Kong, which received over four billion dollars in payments. Standard Chartered and Baroda banks were similar money-laundering conduits.'

'Okay,' said Thandi slowly, her brain whirring, 'but now we have to find out what on earth is happening in Vryburg and who is behind it – though I could have a pretty good guess.'

It was almost an accident, she reflected later.

Yasmin Essop had stumbled upon what she assessed might possibly be a conspiracy to oust the President.

His corrupt opponents – despite losing office a few years earlier – still had close associates who were agents within the SSA, which she was supposed to be in charge of as security minister. These were the very same people irregularly recruited, appointed and armed by the previous presidential regime.

They constituted a discreet and private force, hand-picked by the former head of the SSA's Special Operations Unit and accountable only to the Former President. And, it seemed to her, this unit had not been decommissioned.

An armed militia, still unknowingly funded by taxpayers, was still operational. Effectively, its agents with their automatic weapons and other arms remained outside the control and authority of the new, more accountable state under her boss, the new President.

The SSA, Yasmin concluded, was a hangover from twelve years of mismanagement and corruption, and a redirection of resources away from serving the public to servicing narrow and private interests.

She had discovered that billions of rands, either in cash or assets, could not be accounted for by the SSA. Massive amounts of cash had simply been removed from the SSA's Pretoria headquarters just as the Former President was losing the battle to maintain his dynasty through a chosen family successor. Law enforcement agencies had been captured, damaging their capacity and trashing their accountability.

Her job was both to sort out the mess and re-establish the rule of law with a system of state security that could command the confidence of the public, protect national interests and no longer be an instrument for shielding the looters.

But meanwhile, who was behind the plot against her president?

She had a lot on her mind. Scurrying out of her office to be in time to see her youngest daughter, now in her last year at Pretoria Girls' High, play water polo, she worried about her eldest daughter, who'd won a prestigious Fulbright Scholarship and was now living under the vagaries of Trump-ruled America. She worried about her husband, always out of their bed before dawn, crouched over his computer, working on yet another book, with no time to exercise, overweight, his back a mess. She had no time to worry about how she could fit in the eye operation she needed, or properly manage her chronic asthma.

Minister Yasmin had the cares of the world on her shoulders.

From the moment he walked through arrivals at Bram Fischer airport Mkhize knew something was wrong.

He'd recognised the Tourism Parks CEO he'd spoken to on Skype, but she looked tense, flanked by two slouching men in sunglasses.

She stepped forward and they shook hands, the men standing sullenly, immediately behind her.

'They are from security,' she muttered, 'they will drive you.'

'Sorry,' she whispered, 'they turned up unannounced this morning from the premier's personal security, told me I must follow their orders, told me not to come with you.'

'What the hell's going on, then?' he asked.

She shrugged. 'I honestly don't know. The premier seems to want a safari park built, but has not allocated the full resources it would need. I have a plan, which is why I invited you, but now ... I'm not sure any more. Sorry, I hope you haven't wasted your time coming.'

She waved goodbye, walking away, looking morose.

Mkhize did not know what to say. Although worried, he didn't know what else to do, except go with the flow.

He had followed Thandi's advice about the journey from Richards Bay, leaving early, the connecting flights to Bloemfontein booked for him by SANParks, for he'd never been to the Free State.

It was hot but without KwaZulu-Natal's humidity, clouds drifting over the blue sky, as they walked out of the compact terminal and over to a black Mercedes van in the open car park.

111

Mkhize sensed nobody was up for small talk, the two security men brusquely ushering him into the windowless back, gesturing for him to sit on a roughly upholstered bench. The door was banged shut, the security duo jumped in the front, and the van lurched off.

They drove for about twenty minutes before the van stopped, its engine idling. There were a few shouted instructions and answers in Sesotho, the main indigenous language of the province, which he didn't really understand. What sounded like a gate was being inched squeakily open, then the van drove off for a few minutes along bumpy terrain with few concessions to those in the back. It was as if they were cargo, not passengers.

When it pulled up, the door was opened by one of the sunglasses who gestured him to get out.

Mkhize blinked into the brightness, looking around.

Instead of 100,000 hectares of derelict farmland that could be proudly restored to its near original wilderness of fresh-flowing rivers, profuse flora and free-running game, electrified fencing and barking dogs confronted him.

He walked away from the van, the men leaning up against it.

Mkhize, frustrated, blurted out: 'I need to see all the terrain, otherwise it is a waste of time.'

They nodded. 'There,' one pointed to a scratched, dusty Toyota Aygo, 'you can use that to drive about.'

Mkhize squeezed his bulky, muscled frame into the small vehicle, pulling the driver's seat back but leaving his legs still cramped. This was getting even more bizarre, he thought, looking about.

He knew well that the essential foundation of flourishing species was the extent of suitable habitat for them. Building sustainable game reserves meant expanding diversity of species, as declining reserves had declining diversity.

To recreate a wilderness suitable for wildlife required great plant diversity, from aloe-dominated kopjes to acacias in woodlands and an abundance of rich grasses were needed for grazing herbivores, something damaged by staple herds of cattle, which had been on this land for decades, but now even those farms were closed.

Only with such grasslands, and dense vegetation and trees, might it be sustainable to introduce animals appropriate for a new wilderness, such as buffalo, leopard, white rhino and elephant. Even then, grading of tourist roads had to follow the natural contours of the land, the rivers, valleys and mountains. All expensive.

One conservationist in the Free State had stumbled across San rock art in a cave below a jutting lump of granite, using the animals depicted by these ancient preservationists as a guide to which antelope to reintroduce there, including zebra, blesbok, blue wildebeest, mountain reedbuck, oribi, red hartebeest, waterbuck and sable.

Mkhize also knew that predators needed to be stocked in areas big enough to support them, and that when this was the case they too became important ecologists by killing sick or wounded animals. But if the reserves of antelope were too small, the introduction of carnivores could destabilise an area, including provoking attacks on domestic livestock and humans in surrounding communities. So nature's in-built equilibrium needed to be recreated and then nurtured.

On the other hand, carnivores could attract other species. Mkhize recalled reading about how, in a remote natural park in the USA, humans exterminating wolves had invited a rise in antelope, which browsed on young willow shoots, triggering in turn the disappearance of the very plants that beavers needed to survive. Reintroducing wolf packs, which reduced numbers of their prey, antelope, indirectly promoted new beaver colonies. The beavers, in turn, built ponds and dams that radically improved rivers and created cold water suitable for fish life.

He thought about the introduction of lions to constrain both the density and behaviour of their prey, opening up 'room' to enrich the local biodiversity. As well as being a magnet for tourists and the vital income they brought, of course.

Along with elephants and the rest of the Big Five there was the potential for a very successful tourist destination here, Mkhize thought as he looked about.

At the same time, he was acutely aware that what scientists representing more than thirty nations described as 'collapseology' – ever-increasing exploitation of the planet's resources, with relentless population growth, industrialisation, pollution, food production and resource depletion – was leading to societal collapse. The decimation of species by humans – for instance, Africa's elephant population plunging from 20 million to 400,000 in less than two centuries – was torpedoing the earth's natural biosphere, rapidly becoming life-threatening.

There'd also been a terrifying collapse of white rhino in the Kruger

National Park, which had by far the biggest number on the African continent – down from 12,000 to 3,000 over the past decade. Numbers in private parks were rising, but cumulatively in the hundreds, not the thousands necessary to reverse inexorable decline.

Here for Mkhize was the possibility to help arrest that ecological decay with a new safari park that recreated primaeval African bush – and maybe to link up with Thandi, who had also been involved in the province. But would that be at all possible with the mysterious, baleful security enveloping his mission?

Irish threaded his way through George Best Belfast City Airport to board the short flight to Cardiff.

From there he flew, also on a false passport under a new identity retrieved from a dead Belfast resident, on Qatar Airways via Doha to Johannesburg, connecting directly to Bloemfontein. His departure and booked flight connections were logged by MI5, which – unknown to Irish – had searched his hold suitcase in Belfast, finding a dismantled Armalite rifle nestling in a compact case to travel in the aircraft hold. Alongside it was his Beretta pistol.

The MI5 officers decided to leave them there, wondering what on earth he was up to. They alerted their sister service, MI6, at London's Vauxhall Cross, which in turn informed its station in Pretoria.

Irish was crystal clear about his mission: to earn the £100,000 (R2 million) promised for his services by Star to the New IRA, which was desperate for the funds.

How long it would take and what exactly would be required of him was unclear: he had an open return ticket and no flights home had yet been booked.

Normally, he prepared meticulously for any IRA mission, and was known for being ultra-careful, never just jumping in – which attracted some scorn from fresh young recruits restless for action.

If it was an assassination, he would study the target, his or her patterns of behaviour, plan for the unexpected, scout a suitable venue and always fastidiously map out an escape route. His rule was the target must die, not him.

There was no glory in risking his own life, no Islamist baloney about one hundred virgins awaiting in the afterlife; he considered himself a practising Catholic but had always been doubtful about being elevated into life after death.

114

If it was a bombing, he would be equally cautious. He'd sometimes made bombs from nitrobenzene and fertiliser, either large ones designed to blow up buildings or smaller devices intended to be thrown at British security forces. In his service as an IRA volunteer, he'd also made nail bombs to inflict high casualties, even what the IRA labelled a 'drogue bomb' or 'stick bomb', a grenade to attack vehicles consisting of explosive packed into a large tin can attached to a throwing handle.

As a young Provisional IRA volunteer, he'd learned of bombs utilising a condom as a fuse-delay device by filling it with sulphuric acid: the time the acid took to dissolve the rubber creating the delay mechanism. Once dissolved, the acid reacted with the incendiary material and exploded.

However, although novel and original, such devices were very dangerous to the operator. Resistance came from individuals usually willing to store caches of ordnance in their homes. They refused in this case because condoms were proscribed by the Catholic Church at that time.

Murphy had been chosen for the South African mission because of his versatility with arms. Earlier in his IRA career he'd gained a reputation for his proficiency in the application of quite advanced technologies to build bombs, mines and other devices.

But 'fastidious' was almost his middle name, and what made him profoundly uneasy about this latest mission was its unknown nature, making it almost impossible to prepare in the way he normally did. Still, his New IRA was extremely short of funds, the leadership needed the money urgently, and he was the one to earn it.

So he flew out with little to no knowledge of the terrain into which he might be deployed, or the circumstances. Didn't know whether he'd be in urban situations or rural ones. Knew nothing about the local wildlife or even whether he'd be operating in the wild at all. Catching a series of wildlife scenes on YouTube was hardly what he called preparation, though he did that anyway.

During the long flights in a cramped economy seat – broken only by wandering around Qatar's Hamad International Airport terminal while waiting for his connecting flight to Joburg – Murphy worried all the way. He wasn't by nature a worrier, instead priding himself on his professionalism, but this time he was going in largely unsighted.

Still, duty called, and he took pride in being a soldier of Ireland, bound by army discipline.

*

Yasmin Essop realised that, post-1994, building an entirely new, professional, non-partisan police service from the old apartheid police and security apparatus was always going to be a tall order, including integrating former liberation fighters.

But these problems were eclipsed under the Former President. He had appointed an acting commissioner who Yasmin helped ensure was now facing criminal charges.

The Former President also made a series of flagrantly improper appointments to senior positions of political cronies, friends and members of the uMkhonto we Sizwe Military Veterans' Association (MKMVA) – some even criminals.

There were massive procurement irregularities and other financial crimes. Police crime intelligence officers were repurposed to target not criminals, but political enemies, some receiving specialist training in Russia.

The police were also remilitarised, as they had always been under apartheid – something that had been deliberately expunged under Mandela from 1994. And that encouraged brutality, notoriously when police massacred defenceless striking miners at Marikana in 2012.

Another abuse Yasmin had uncovered was the rapid promotion of cronies into well-paid but superfluous roles. The police became top-heavy with incompetent generals and brigadiers rather than proficient community police officers.

She had inherited a police service riven with factions and infiltrated by criminal networks. But trying to get rid of them would lead to time-consuming, employment-law procedures, doubtless with many challenges.

She also discovered that Star had many allies in the police service, including in the ANC-aligned Police and Prisons Civil Rights Union, which had initially played a valuable role after 1994 but had then become enmeshed in corruption itself.

As serious as anything was her discovery that crime intelligence officers in KwaZulu-Natal had been involved in the murder of a corruption whistle-blower, apparently as part of an authorised project to assassinate politicians in the province who were hostile to Star and the Former President. State security agencies were also implicated in these political killings – there seemed no end to the Pandora's box Yasmin had opened.

*

116

At the same time, Mkhize was explaining the wonders of elephants to the six safari guests.

'They are capable of complex mental operations and feelings, and so are not as different from humans as people think.'

With Steve Brown, he had set up a picnic table in the bush under some yellowwood trees, providing shade from the fierce sun. It was a treat for the guests to be served as if in the wild, the table and chairs efficiently unfolded, even a crisp white linen tablecloth too, cold beers and wine offered, serviettes and cutlery neatly set out, all in five minutes. Thandi would have been proud of him, Mkhize thought to himself – though she'd probably observe tartly that if he could do that in the bush, then he might do it more often at home.

As the two rangers began serving sumptuous cold salads, Mkhize continued with his description of the social prowess of the elephant species.

'They can recognise each other from as far away as two kilometres through very low-frequency sounds. Adult females can know the voices of up to a hundred others, and remember them for years. Daughters remain close by their mother until she dies. And when she does, daughters are distraught, grieving by guarding the body silently or covering it with leaves.

'Elephants show great empathy – they are loyal and sociable, forming close friendship bonds. In one case, circus elephants who had been separated for over twenty years recognised each other immediately and even knocked down a fence to get close, and were then inseparable until one died years later.

'They are bright too, able to recognise themselves in a mirror, and can form close bonds with humans. A ranger I know returned to a safari reserve twelve years after moving to work elsewhere and was reunited with a wild African elephant, which he called out to. The elephant immediately recognised his voice and walked up close to the vehicle, nuzzling him affectionately with his trunk.'

'But surely they can be dangerous too?' asked a guest.

'Yes, of course. They can kill humans who invade their space, mostly over battles for habitat. But, frankly, these incidents are very rare compared to the numbers of elephants humans kill all the time.'

Van der Merwe had found his man, a Vlakplaas veteran, though barely out of his teens when he had operated at the farm.

117

Even since then, Hennie Strijdom had worked in the shadows, earning a living as a mercenary in other African states – where there was plenty of demand for someone with his skills. He was a 'khaki criminal', the label given to white operatives behind much of the poaching in southern Africa, who rarely got caught or killed in shoot-outs, instead hiring poverty-stricken local black villagers to do their dirty work. But sometimes they undertook special wildlife missions themselves, and Van der Merwe had just such a one to offer.

Strijdom had married young and divorced young, amidst allegations of domestic abuse towards his wife, allegations he vehemently denied – after all, he had loved her, friends and in-laws noticing his courtesy and almost proprietorial concern for her. He played with their kids, was keen on sport, especially rugby. He always did the gardening, washing-up and DIY. He helped assiduously with the housework, always brought her a morning cup of coffee when she awoke, seemed visibly proud of her talent for drama teaching and her popularity among her students.

But she had found his personal predilection for aggressively sadomasochistic sex unbearable, though there were rarely, if ever, any telltale signs of abuse. This made his relatives and friends sceptical about her stories – whinging, whining, some said of her, would never be satisfied, should be lucky to have married such a sought-after, handsome, fit man.

Privately she was desolate, often in pain, with blood seeping between her thighs after one of their sessions, during which he seemed possessed by the demons he never displayed in public with friends and family. It reached the point where she first moved into her own bedroom, then refused him sex, and that caused a hell of a row.

Since then his relationships with women had always been short-term, promising to start with, sour to end. He never left them, they always left him, as he moved on to another eligible partner with his stories, his caustic wit, fitness, financial generosity over outings and Casanova-like charm.

Each was surprised to discover he was nearly fifty; he seemed lean and young of mind and body, his muscles toned. He had no beer gut, and his greying blond hair was a mark of distinction rather than age, felt most of the women he dated.

The agreement with Van der Merwe was specific and concerned a development outside a small place in the Free State called Vryburg, which he had never heard of. But no matter: the mission didn't seem very arduous and the fee he demanded was high – as always. It was certainly enough to support his second home, an apartment in Cape Town's prestigious Sea Point, overlooking the beach next to the Atlantic Ocean – and a big attraction for would-be girlfriends.

Mkhize shook his head in sadness. A raging battle between two dominant elephant bulls, each four decades in age, had left one dead, prone on the ground, fatally wounded in the head, its tusks fully two metres long.

For once he didn't feel like responding to guest questions, felt just emptiness. Why didn't these elephants – super-intelligent in so many ways – comprehend the danger of their extinction from humans and prioritise their own safety among their own species? A pointless question, he knew, because the laws of the wild always took precedence.

But still he wished he could converse with them. Tell them about the ivory wars, tell them why the threat was so huge. Tell them about human greed, human fetishes for their ivory, scream out loud into the bush in grim warning. He had an instinctive, intuitive bond with the Zama Zama herd, but still he couldn't get through to them that key warning.

He had been kicking his heels for over a week now, watching SuperSport channels on his hotel-room TV – just about every English Premier League match was covered, which grated with him. Authentic Republicans had a disdain for English football, much preferring Gaelic football, but he watched it anyway out of sheer boredom.

He went on daily runs, pumped iron in the gym, drank too much in the bar, spurning the odd glance from women perched and inviting trade.

Pádraig Murphy longed for his homeland, for where he felt most at ease, amidst its lush green fields with blackthorn hedges and rugged slopes overlooking wide plains.

South Armagh sat in one of Northern Ireland's six counties, occupying around 300 square kilometres. To its east was the A1, the main Belfast-to-Dublin highway, to the south and east was the Irish border, and to the north was Mountnorris and Keady. A columnist in the *Irish Times* once caricatured it as 'a place, depending on whose version you accept, of virtuous freedom fighters struggling to save Ireland's soul from the Brits or a place full of cattle-smuggling gunmen who'd shoot you for the price of a pint'.

But for most of its 25,000 residents and tourists it was more a land of poets, folk songs and storytelling, and of the burial cairns and chambers of inhabitants thousands of years back. The splendid forest park of Slieve Gullion, with its natural walkways, had on top a mountain lake and a Neolithic passage tomb said to predate even the pyramids. A tradition of lacemaking went back to the 1830s and was said to be one of the few, perhaps only, ways women could get an independent income back in those days.

Why was he out here in this godforsaken place? Hadn't been told yet. Just that his Armalite skills were in demand. Not to what purpose. Not in what cause.

If indeed there *was* a cause at all, and looking at the TV news channels, South Africa, once the darling of the world, seemed to have lost its way. Allegations after allegations of corruption, top politicians arrested, new scandals every day.

Murphy squirmed as he watched. What exactly was he getting himself into? His whole life was as a soldier in a cause. Here he seemed a mere mercenary for hire.

A new bunch of tourists to Zama Zama, a new bunch of questions for Mkhize, always new questions, testing his wildlife expertise but never testing his patience. He loved passing on his knowledge.

Their Land Cruiser had come upon a herd of giraffe, browsing quietly, tails swishing. These gentle giants of the bush could be a nightmare if trapped in a snare, with a vicious kick in a frightened state.

The previous evening they had gone with Mkhize to witness the intricate way in which a badly snared giraffe could be saved. Unsnaring elephants was difficult enough – coaxing them away from protective herds with the mothers especially protective over babies, then trying to dart them with a tranquilliser. But that was easy compared with a giraffe.

First it had to be tranquillised – but only mildly. If fully tranquillised, the giraffe's long legs, long neck and weighty head meant a fall could easily be fatal. Then, once it was dopey, ropes were flung lasso–like around its neck and legs. Finally, it was completely anaesthetised, Mkhize and his ranger colleagues gently supporting it to subside and lie on the ground.

They had to work quickly to unfasten the coiled snare, vet at hand, Mkhize supervising, constantly alert in case the animal regained consciousness: it would rise in seconds, could kick out and kill or maim unintentionally.

Fortunately, they managed it in time for the giraffe to stagger up and set off groggily. As the spellbound guests watched, a much-relieved Mkhize climbed back into the passenger seat, turning around to explain his worries about Africa's collapsing giraffe population.

'They are in real trouble, numbers nearly halving over the last three decades on the African continent to under a hundred thousand because of human encroachment into their habitats, unsustainable harvesting, disease, poaching and trophy hunting. Scientists say giraffes face a "silent extinction" because there aren't the same campaigns as there are to save elephants, rhinos, lions or tigers.'

He paused. 'But there is one thing which helps their survival, and that is close friendship bonds between female giraffes. Not only to help them reduce harassment from males and warn each other about predators, which means that their chances of survival are much better than solitary females, but also because forming social friendships with other females also helps them cooperate in caring for their young.'

CHAPTER 7

Moving the elephants to the Free State from the herd's traditional grazing area in Limpopo province had to be done carefully with expert and experienced help, and Star was content to finance that.

Specially constructed steel crates were sourced from a local company, and the elephants were encouraged to get used to them standing out in the open. The five-tonne slumbering giants were then sedated by firing anaesthetising darts from a helicopter. The darts, which punctured their thick skin, contained a drug capable of killing a human in seconds and took about four minutes to knock out an elephant.

As that short interval ticked by, different elephants stumbled about, some even running, the rangers following to ensure none fell on their chests, which could crush their lungs. Having fully lost consciousness, each one was carefully laid out to avoid injury, and a twig propped into each trunk opening to ensure their airways stayed open. Their ears were also flipped forward to protect their eyes from the burning sun.

They were then hoisted by specially made cranes into the crates, constructed with solid metal and hardwood frames, their hinged doors secured with a series of metal bars across the front. These were lifted by ropes tied around their leg bottoms and loaded onto the backs of low-loader trucks to be driven the nine-hour journey to Vryburg. Given an antidote to awaken them from their tranquillised state, the elephants remained subdued but aware of the journey.

When the convoy stopped to fill up with petrol, it was obvious that some of the herd were stirring, so it was decided to sedate them with a syringe fixed to the end of a pole. One of the minders climbed onto the roof of the low-loader lorry, spotting a ventilation gap through which he could accomplish his task.

But then a trunk lashed at him through the gap, catching him on his ankles, almost dragging him through. He managed to jump back, avoiding an ugly death yanked inside among the angry herd, fearful about what was happening to them.

Getting the animals out of the trucks was not straightforward either. They had to be coaxed, because they were so big and the only animals unable to jump. So, on arrival they were allowed to wake fully, then cajoled down special ramps into a ten-acre boma, a securely enclosed area, surrounded with electric fencing, where they were encouraged to familiarise and habituate themselves to their new surroundings.

But the escorting rangers knew full well that there had been examples of elephants unhappy with their new surroundings breaking out of their bomas. In one case, two large elephants working as a team had crashed down a massive tree straight on top of the electric fence, breaking through it and cutting the electricity, and had surged out to freedom.

In another case, the elephants had ingeniously discovered the transformer that powered the fence. Although it was just a small, unremarkable metal unit hidden in thick bush well away from the fence, they had nevertheless somehow discovered its purpose and destroyed it completely, trampling it into a crumpled wreck, then easily moving off to push down the now harmless fence intended to incarcerate them for a week or two.

In this case, however, the elephant herd seemed to settle down, the matriarch encouraging acceptance rather than defiance, even the young restless bulls grudgingly toeing her line, until the gate to the boma was opened and she led them out into what they hoped was their new freedom.

The Free State SANParks senior figures were frustrated.

They had supervised the procurement and transport of the elephant herd in a complex, tricky operation. They had built a suitable boma for the transition, then monitored the adjustment of the herd before letting them out.

The next stage would have been to keep a careful eye, to ensure the herd didn't suddenly take off, break out and try to head back to its ancestral habitat in Limpopo, far to the north. For that had happened often before, causing chaos, elephants marauding destructively through villages and farms, causing confrontations, destroying or gobbling up shrubs and crops, pulling down trees, barging over buildings.

In at least one case it took a courageous and expert helicopter pilot to wear down a marching herd by repeatedly flying close, skimming over treetops, the thunderous rotors intimidating the elephants. After an hour in which they defiantly lifted their trunks and roared at the chopper, he finally wore them down and the matriarch turned back to head for the wildlife park from which they had escaped through primaeval forest.

But instead of allowing the expert SANParks team to do its job of care, Star's office unaccountably ordered them to pull out.

There was only one option left for the conscientious Tourism Parks CEO: send for Mkhize. At least he could have a look and report back. There was not much he could do on his own, but they couldn't refuse him entry, because to do that would cause ripples outside the gangster state. Attracting unwanted attention would add to the swirling local speculation about what on earth was happening behind the closed gates, with locals hearing and seeing the thunderous arrival of large transporter lorries, tantalisingly unable to catch a glimpse of what was inside them – or what on earth was going on behind the secure perimeter.

Months earlier, there had been a local buzz of a different kind.

Around a hundred residents were informed that they were going to be made shareholders in, and get jobs at, the Regeneration Park. To do what, and for what purpose exactly, they weren't told. Instead they were instructed to bring their IDs to the municipal office, and to sign papers there.

This they had duly done, but they had heard nothing since.

Jayne Joseph continued to burrow away, her salary still being paid, but spurned by her office. Although she remained in a curious career limbo, she had found a new purpose and, she discovered too, a new sort of fulfilment.

For how long she would remain on gardening leave, she had no idea, but better to make the most of it. Anxious still about her safety, she had also felt more at ease having met the Veteran and engaged with Komal, Thandi and, from London, Murray Bergstein.

It was an illusion, of course, to imagine they could offer her any real security, and she still felt very lonely. But at least she was no longer on her own, had a new support network, as she pored over her computer through long hours, researching away, trying to get to the bottom of the conundrum confronting her.

She knew full well that electronic banking was the simplest and fastest means of transferring funds between people and across borders. It allowed for legitimate transactions of course, but also enabled criminals to move their money to jurisdictions known for turning a blind eye through deliberately light regulations. And she knew that through such means stolen money was 'cleaned' by mingling it with other funds and obscuring its source, thereby making it much easier to invest or spend.

She knew especially that during the decade when the Business Brothers had reigned supreme, they had used several international banks – household, supposedly reputable, names such as her own BSBC, as well as HSBC, Standard Chartered and Bank of Baroda – to transfer money, conceal payments and camouflage the source of their funds.

These banks all freely assisted with opening bank accounts in Johannesburg and thereby granted the Business Brothers access to the global banking network to transfer illicit funds out of South Africa and then back in.

As she delved into it all, she marvelled at how these suspicious activities hadn't been spotted much sooner, or immediately. Maybe she too had been inadvertently culpable? What had gone so badly *wrong* with the banking culture in which she worked? After all, some of the dodgy activity was pretty obvious when she examined it now, sadly in retrospect.

There were secretive transactions to obscure the ownership of the accounts. There were unexplained payments to and from third parties with no obvious connection at all to the underlying transaction. There were funds transferred to and between shell companies that didn't trade and hid the people in charge of them. There were also unexplained connections with, and movement of large funds between, different countries. All just waved through, no questions asked, no apparent checks made into this now demonstrably illegal activity.

Yet banks were supposed to have access to all the customer data, all the transaction data, for all accounts they permitted to be opened and all the transfers they facilitated. They were supposed to be statutorily regulated, surrounded by red tape, which strangled the average honest citizen while giving the green light to rampant money laundering by master criminals. International money laundering, she was horrified to discover, now totalled well over US$2 trillion – yes $2 trillion, she paused to note – each and every year.

But still. She checked herself from getting carried away. She still hadn't got to the bottom of what was really happening in the Free State. Thandi was relying upon her to do so. No pressure then, she contemplated, smiling at the thought of the bright, witty but intense young woman, wondering whether her relative Helen Joseph had been like that in her anti-apartheid youth. And feeling an umbilical link to the legendary activist singled out for praise by Nelson Mandela, the relative she'd never known but now more than ever wished she had, a lump formed in her throat, her eyes moistening.

Jayne got up from her computer chair and resolved to go for a run to clear her mind, this time constantly on the look-out for threats from any lurking vehicles or lounging men.

His Zama Zama guests, huddled in the Land Cruiser, couldn't believe what they were seeing on the opposite riverbank.

Despite their reputation as the gentle giants of the animal kingdom, elephants can become extremely aggressive if their children are threatened. Which is precisely what one crocodile had discovered when it tried to grab a baby elephant drinking from the river.

Immediately, the mother elephant turned on the croc, hammering it violently on the head with her trunk, at one point wrapping her trunk right around and tossing it up toward the sky. Then she systematically stamped all over the massive reptile, pressing all life from its writhing body, only its teeth still jutting from its crushed mouth a reminder of its once-hideous menace.

'But,' Mkhize explained, 'although elephants may be the world's largest land mammals, they hardly ever attack crocodiles. Too dangerous for them. It's usually only when their young are in danger.

'And they have to be very careful of protecting their trunks, because crocs always go for those. Damage to trunks can be fatal for elephants, stopping them from foraging, drinking or breathing. They can sometimes survive with mutilated trunks, but it isn't at all easy for them.'

'Any similar sightings of elephants attacking other big, dangerous animals?' one guest asked.

'Yes,' Mkhize replied, 'but not very often. There have been witnessed cases of elephants stabbing and killing buffalos with their tusks and even flipping a hippo right up and over. Incredible stuff.'

Another matter was bugging Minister Yasmin – the mega-nuclear deal with Russia, pushed hard by the deposed Former President, who was widely believed to be helping himself to a multimillion-rand kickback, a nice nest-egg for his family in retirement.

This had been kicked into the long grass by the new president but was still in the ether. It was widely felt to be terrible idea for South Africa, a hyper-expensive drain on taxpayers when the country was near bankrupt and had abundant cheaper renewable energy resources anyway.

But she hadn't been able to find out what the Deputy President – not at all reliable, even though he had ensured his considerable provincial votes went for the President, so defeating the old one's dynasty – was really up to during an extended five-week leave of absence in Russia.

What was he doing? She knew Star was plotting to topple the President, but was the Deputy President, supposedly loyal, up to no good as well, with Putin's people hoping for to get back on the inside of the presidency again?

She'd also had unconfirmed reports of training sessions on insurrection and sabotage for Star's coterie in Russia. It was very disturbing.

She'd better find out, though without alerting any of the bad guys from the previous regime still infesting the security and military intelligence services she was supposedly in charge of and had been entrusted by the President to get a grip of.

For Van der Merwe, the task brought back memories.

Of how the African ivory trade today had been initially established through past civil wars, some between colonial powers and African independence movements, going back to the 1950s. And in the 1960s when, for example, South Africa's apartheid rulers and army chiefs had secretly traded weapons for elephant tusks with Jonas Savimbi's homicidal National Union for the Total Independence of Angola (UNITA) forces in Angola.

Apparently, Savimbi was so appreciative he had once even given an apartheid president a full-size ivory replica of an AK-47. What a black African leader was doing in cahoots with a white tyrant suppressing other black Africans, Van der Merwe could only wonder.

Southern Africa had become awash with weapons, and poachers now had the firepower to drive elephant poaching to new levels. Van der Merwe had been on the fringes of the trade in the 1970s and 1980s, when modern poaching of elephant and rhino reached epidemic levels.

Jayne Joseph returned, out of puff, perspiring from her run. Though physically tired, she felt renewed with a fresh spirit after a shower.

She checked over her carefully drafted text, based upon meticulous research, and handed it on a memory stick to Komal for her and the Veteran to redraft and get it ready for the revelations in London.

For Hennie Strijdom, the task seemed pretty straightforward: find the elephants in the Vryburg Regeneration Park and deal with them.

It hadn't taken him all that long; he had spent most of the morning driving about, looking for their huge footprints fresh on the sand, also for fresh droppings, little mountains defecated as they walked, all leaving traces, signs, amounting to a trail, their progress able to be followed quite easily by someone schooled like him.

Nevertheless, when he had come upon them, it was quite sudden – as was often the way with elephant herds. They were so large, so visible, it was incredible how they could appear as if out of nowhere, from within a clump of trees, tails swinging and sweeping off flies, eyes swivelling, their trunks swaying, chomping, sniffing. Could be threatening if they had babies, could be placid if they were shown enough room and respect.

Strijdom gave them both as he pulled up, just above the herd, a good vantage point for his assignment.

He wasn't conflicted about it. Admired the stately giants, resplendent in the early afternoon sunshine. Enjoyed the scene of wildlife tranquillity. But he had a job to do and he would do it regardless. He had insisted upon being paid in advance and in cash – always did. It was accepted by the paymasters, even if sometimes grudgingly, for they knew that he always delivered. He'd been paid, as usual, using cash loaded onto a Travelex card, a type of prepayment card used by drug cartels and terrorists in order to ensure payments could not be detected.

Strijdom carried out his tasks methodically, efficiently and – for him – safely. One straight after another, with as little time as possible for the herd to rally, as one by one they were all felled. Immediately afterwards each elephant ran giddily, screaming, some round in circles, then slumped to the ground. Until the whole herd was felled.

Strijdom drove out, didn't look back, didn't reflect; didn't want to – wasn't proud or satisfied. Just task completed, for the cash he would soon access.

At the steel gates, he nodded to the guys with the keys who locked up, called Piet van der Merwe to report crisply, and set off for the long drive home to Joburg.

Never flew on these operations, never wanted to leave a name trace in a flight, never wanted his ID card to be shown or checked.

In. Out. Job done. And on to the next one. No regrets. Never allowed himself the slightest space for any such sentimentality.

Bob Richards was soon on his feet again in the Commons, the green benches in front and alongside, packed and feverish during Prime Minister's Questions on a Wednesday, now almost empty. No matter. His audience was the government, UK opinion-formers and the South African media.

His intention was to pin down the government and reveal the extent to which global corporations – most household names – were up to their necks in assisting, knowingly or otherwise, the state-capture corruption that had poisoned South Africa's politics and its public administration.

After the usual formalities, such as thanking the chair, Bob Richards launched straight into a passionate speech about international complicity in South Africa's money-laundering and corruption scandals.

'Without complicit fee-clutching global corporates and turn-a-blind-eye governments – from London and Washington to Dubai, Delhi and Beijing – the decade of prodigious looting and money laundering could not have happened.

'Robbing South African taxpayers of billions of rands (hundreds of millions of pounds) and contributing to a catastrophic loss of GDP of around a fifth under the Former President, was ultimately the fault of international actors. They helped the Business Brothers move their ill-gotten gains out of South Africa, and then sometimes back in, undetected.

'It was international actors who helped the Business Brothers and their associates create complex corporate structures disguising the true ownership of funds and complicating the tracing and repatriation of stolen funds while earning huge fees out of the looting.

129

'It was international actors who provided refuge to corrupt individuals and the means to continue their activities through less-regulated "open" economies such as Dubai and Hong Kong.

'It was international banks – many of them household names, such as HSBC, Standard Chartered and Bank of Baroda – that enabled them to transfer money, disguise payments and hide the source of their illicit funds.

'These banks should have spotted this suspicious or illegal activity by the Business Brothers much sooner, especially as much of this occurred when South African media outlets were exposing corruption under the Former President and identifying the Business Brothers' key role.

'None of these three banks stopped these transactions, despite the fact that government funds were leaving the South African jurisdiction to a company beneficially owned by the Business Brothers with no material explanation provided for the suspicious payment structure.

'It is totally unacceptable that senior directors of HSBC and Standard Chartered – who cited "client confidentiality" – would not cooperate. When specifically asked to trace and track the money laundered by the Business Brothers. Bank of Baroda bosses, they brazenly denied any culpability.

'Then there are the "professional enablers" – lawyers, consultants, auditors, accountants and estate agents – who "clean" the money for a fee. Their role is to disguise the source, location and ownership of funds.

'Lawyers assisted the Business Brothers to set up complex shell companies enabling money to be moved from one country to another country where there is low transparency.

'Accountants audited incorrectly, leaving suspicious transactions hidden in the accounts. Estate agents received laundered money into Business Brothers-controlled accounts during property purchases.

'Well known corporates such as KPMG, Bain & Co. and Hogan Lovells assisted the Business Brothers in their looting from the South African people. They all profited while the Business Brothers hid stolen funds that could otherwise have been spent on essential public services and on helping to repair the colossal damage caused by apartheid.

'Firms such as Bain and KPMG have access to client data, and it is high time they established robust compliance policies and procedures to spot and prevent money laundering.

'Meanwhile consultants SAP and McKinsey nefariously brokered deals with evidently corrupt government officials and associates, also earning enormous fees.

'Globalisation has made it easier for criminals to dissipate tainted funds to countries unconnected to the underlying crime. Without cooperation and coordination between states, criminals are able to dodge the rule of law by relocating themselves and their stolen funds to less regulated jurisdictions where it is easier to hide funds.

'The UK and South Africa, for example, both have strict anti-money-laundering regulations, but the Business Brothers nevertheless easily managed to evade this legislation with the assistance of South African public officials and London-headquartered or -located banks and professional enablers.

'The ruler of Dubai, a steadfast ally of the US and UK, allowed the Business Brothers to safeguard their stolen wealth and buy a luxury home. Hong Kong took no public action against the Business Brothers for funnelling laundered funds and receiving kickbacks. India (their country of birth, where they also reside) claims to have investigated the Business Brothers, but has taken no enforcement action, nor repatriated funds to South Africa.

'Investigative agencies (such as the Serious Fraud Office, National Crime Agency and Financial Conduct Authority in the UK, and the Directorate for Priority Crime Investigation within the South African Police Service and the NPA and the Special Investigations Unit in South Africa) require proper resourcing.

'Yet in neither country has that been the case. In the UK in 2019 the head of the National Crime Agency requested an additional £2.7 billion pounds in funding for that agency alone – not granted.

'Banks and professional enablers should be on the front line in combatting financial crime, and it should be a source of shame for the world's leading economies that the banks and other corporates responsible for facilitating corrupt practices in foreign countries are headquartered in their jurisdictions (London, New York, Delhi and Shanghai, for instance).'

Richards paused and sipped from a glass of water before continuing.

'How can it be right that the average, honest citizen on a modest or medium income is subject to all manner of frustrating and time-consuming bureaucratic procedures and requirements to open a bank account or legitimately move money, but somehow banks wave through global crime, such as that perpetrated by the Business Brothers, their cronies and allies, on a gargantuan scale?

'Funds moved across the world today leave a digital footprint. Banks especially possess the technological and financial clout needed to force change, and that power should be harnessed to assist – not hinder or obstruct – regulators to target their limited resources.

'Although some sharing of information already occurs, it is paltry and ineffective, and banks should stop hiding behind client confidentiality and work collaboratively and proactively to share useful data and intelligence on a confidential basis with regulators and enforcement agencies.

'Banks and professional enablers should face additional sanctions at both an organisational and an individual level. Licences should be immediately stripped from banks if they consistently fail to meet anti-money-laundering standards. A "senior managers' regime" should be introduced to ensure personal responsibility. This should include disbarment for money-laundering and corruption failures such as over South Africa's state-capture scandal.

'Looted billions were siphoned from the South African offices of Standard Chartered, HSBC and Bank of Baroda through their international digital pipelines. Their Johannesburg managers cannot be allowed to get away with saying, "Nothing to do with me, guv."

'And on top of all this, the governments – especially of India, Hong Kong and China, Dubai, the UK and the US – must lead the fight against global money laundering and corruption not just pay lip service.

'Without such cross-border cooperation, no country will be emancipated from financial crime, estimated by the United Nations Office on Drugs and Crime to be worth around five per cent of global GDP, or two trillion dollars, each and every year.'

He ended with a flourish: 'Isn't it high time this government acted instead of wringing its hands over international money laundering and corruption?'

Unusually, Richards had sent a copy of his speech to the Minister's office a few days in advance. He wanted a proper response from the government, and was half encouraged. Instead of the proverbial bland ministerial reply, he received a reflective one. Non-committal – that didn't surprise him one little bit – but opening the door to a policy shift, maybe microscopic, but still progress of a sort, he ruefully supposed. He hoped Thandi, Komal, Jayne and the Veteran were satisfied that all their hard work had been worthwhile.

Mkhize froze.

He'd been invited again to advise SANParks in the Free State – though again he was curiously abandoned on his own, shepherded by some heavies, not the wildlife curators who'd invited him back a second time, oddly prevented from performing the roles themselves.

He'd sensed from the uncanny silence of the bush that there was mourning in the atmosphere: no excitable bird tweets, no movement of what wildlife existed. He'd felt an ominous dread settling in his bushcraft bones.

He'd thought that maybe he would find the elephants lying splayed on the ground with great gaping holes on both sides of what remained of their grotesquely disfigured skulls, their trunks having been cut right off – often a poacher practice.

Instead, something quite different, something not so shocking in one way but even more shocking in quite another.

The elephants were indeed lying grotesquely splayed out on the ground near each other, the carcasses fresh.

But their tusks hadn't been bloodily ripped out. The giant creatures had each been poisoned with cyanide mineral licks, probably staggering around for little more than fifty metres before they collapsed, Mkhize estimated.

The great advantage for the poachers of this method was its silence and its convenience – no ricocheting thunder of gunshots, no messy hacking out of the tusks, which involved mutilating the faces into bloodied gaping chasms.

Instead, this modern method of elephant killing involved the use of cyanide-tipped arrows, completely incapacitating the elephants and causing a slow, excruciating death.

And since the bodies decomposed quickly, the tusks could be pulled out of their sockets without effort.

Because the poison turned the meat putrid, scavengers were discouraged until the meat detoxified. But that happened pretty quickly, after which there was little if any collateral damage to wildlife, including animals that picked at the once regal hulks.

Then the vultures, followed by the hyenas and jackals, would start tearing into their flesh. Within a week these imperial specimens, the largest animals on earth, would be little more than heaps of bones on the hot dry reddish-brown sand.

Isaac Mkhize squatted on the ground and found himself crying. Not the behaviour of a muscled hulk of a man like him, but he couldn't stop himself . . .

Then his wailing misery, tears running down his cheeks like rivulets, turned to anger. What would Thandi do? She would calculate, then act, and that he resolved was what he must do.

So he methodically took photographs with his smartphone. Took photographs – lots of them – of the once-mighty elephant herd now reduced to a stinking afterlife of rotting and crawling with vermin.

He tried to WhatsApp the photos to Thandi, but reception was so poor it wouldn't send even one. He stabbed repeatedly at his phone, tried desperately to go back to another photo, then another, tried to send again, but they all were jammed stubbornly on his WhatsApp screen, with no tick to show they had been sent, and certainly no double tick to show they had been received.

Tensing up, Mkhize took stock. He was cornered – couldn't get the precious photos out, couldn't do anything more for the elephants, realised that with his shocking discovery those responsible would move heaven and earth to stop him at all costs, might target him quickly in the cross-hairs of a gunsight.

He made a decision. Not to return to his vehicle. Not to report back to those who had hired him. Instead to trek. Out of the vast compound, cutting a hole under the perimeter fence, and into the bush where they would have to hunt him, but where he might be the master, rather than any of Star's henchmen.

But they would come for him, of that he was now certain.

It was always going to be only a matter of time. Jayne Joseph had thought that for a while.

Her manager called somewhat embarrassed to say the bank were coming to collect her computer. A nervous giggle – he'd quite forgotten she had one to work from at home. They'd be round in an hour.

Over the previous weeks she had systematically copied a lot of material – gigabytes of the stuff – onto her portable terabyte drive. It was against banking rules to do that with confidential client data, and it wasn't the same as working within the bank's intranet as her office computer permitted, but it would have to do.

As copiously advised by Komal, who called by or was in touch regularly, Jayne had also been preparing for another eventuality in this strange new world.

A small white rental van had arrived at her friend's house a few doors down, was loaded up with all sorts of boxes and drove away, the bored watchers sitting in an apartment above a store across the street taking no notice.

What they did register was Jayne jogging across into the park pretty much like clockwork around midday. She normally took around forty minutes and they noted the time. One of them nipped out for a pizza, but by the time he returned his colleague was fretting.

No sign of Jayne returning breathless as normal.

They waited another half hour, thinking she might have extended her run for once, then called in.

It seemed that Jayne had simply disappeared.

Mkhize moved, fast, scurrying down and up over the dry ravines, among the bushes in the bumpy but reasonably flat, relatively treeless landscape with its wide-open grasslands.

The Veteran had instructed him a year or so before always to avoid being silhouetted as he scanned the terrain, and to evade open spaces and move along tree lines if he could, but that wasn't easy across the scruffy scrub, lumpy bush and minimal trees before him: not much cover.

When he had put a distance from the rotting herd – maybe a kilometre – he called Thandi, asking her to write down his GPS coordinates. He told her the direction in which he was fleeing, and asked for Minister Yasmin to helicopter the Sniper in to help him. He told her he might not survive otherwise, would be pursued, needed the Sniper to help, and trusted him totally.

The line was terrible, crackling, his voice fading in and out, with only one fluctuating bar on his mobile reception.

'How much danger?' she asked worriedly.

'A lot,' Mkhize replied, panting a little and still moving, as he told her what he had discovered. Told her he had the photos, but couldn't send them. 'They weren't bringing in the elephants to create a new wildlife park. They were bringing them in to kill and harvest their ivory.'

'Blood ivory,' Thandi muttered, giving him comforting reassurances. She was worried as hell, and determined to save him if she could.

The phone call – reception still poor – ended. Mkhize kept loping, constantly on the alert, looking for followers, scanning for predators – any wildlife threat – as Thandi frantically called, first Minister Yasmin, then the Sniper (who, fortunately, was in Johannesburg; getting him from even further away in Zama Zama would have been difficult, if not impossible, given the desperate time pressure).

Yasmin immediately acted, putting on notice to scramble if needed a military helicopter crew, always on standby 24/7 at Bloemspruit Air Force Base near Bloemfontein – so not too far away.

The two-person crew flew an AH-2 Rooivalk attack helicopter, a reliable and formidable beast, with a maximum speed of nearly 300 kilometres per hour. It had dual controls and was armed with a single cannon and up to sixteen long-range anti-tank guided missiles, four air-to-air missiles, and dozens of aerial rockets. The AH-2 had entered service in 1999, and was a substantial upgrade from its original design, which went back to the apartheid era. It was the product of the international arms embargo, which had forced the regime to develop an indigenous arms industry.

But this mission had to be top secret, otherwise it could still leak through the crony-riddled military. The crew had only a rough idea of the destination, were unaware of their exact target and would only be told later if they were to scramble.

Another helicopter, an Atlas Oryx transport – also developed to evade the apartheid-era arms embargo – was to collect the Sniper from Swartkop Air Force Base at Centurion, outside Johannesburg, and he had to get there pretty damn quick, Yasmin coolly instructed.

All very well, he muttered to himself, but the city's traffic was usually choked up, with regular shunts on the main road out to Centurion. He grabbed his sniper bag, checked everything and moved out as quickly as he could. He wondered whether he was still sharp enough, being a little out of practice, and certainly nothing like as agile as he had been in his youthful service during the dog days of the apartheid military. He hadn't seen any action for a while, and regular sessions at the shooting range were no substitute for the special arts of a sniper in the field.

The Sniper worried about his friend Mkhize. Never mind any rustiness – he mustn't let him down.

Irish had been kicking his heels since arriving at his hotel in Bloemfontein. He hadn't needed to show his passport, and had been given a key to his prebooked room by the driver who collected him from the airport.

He was beginning to wonder what the hell he had been brought all this way for, when Star called suddenly. No courtesies. No small talk, not even 'Hello, how are you'. Just clipped instructions. To take out a target and leave no trace. A car would pick him up in three minutes and a tracker would be there to assist him.

The tracker lived locally, doing a bit of this and a bit of that. His home was near Councillor Edwin Kubeka's, so Star tasked him with keeping a quiet eye on the councillor.

He was an Ovambo, far from his native land in northern Namibia, Ovamboland, designated a Bantustan by the apartheid government for the Ovambo people in the old South West Africa, where traditional Ovambo kingdoms had existed in precolonial and early colonial times.

His speciality was bushcraft, poaching, tracking – or all three. If there had been an opportunity, he could have been a wildlife ranger or game guard, but there wasn't. There were few jobs available in anything, anywhere locally. He had to snatch what he could.

Jayne had continued with her normal routine, running through the park, looking out for muggers and – as had become customary these past few weeks – also for watchers.

About halfway through, she darted sideways, looking back, seeing nothing suspicious, and left by a gate on the other side of the park from her home. Komal, waiting in a parked car, greeted her with a hug as she jumped in and was driven away to the new place to stay fixed by Yasmin.

When they'd planned this, Jayne had only one stipulation for the new place: superfast broadband and somewhere easy to work with her new laptop, with a new Gmail address and a VPN installed. She'd also installed a VPN in her old laptop to occasionally access her old email.

Both these new precautions should be sufficient to avoid her new location being traced, the Sniper had advised, though Jayne was never properly introduced when they spoke via WhatsApp.

As Komal pulled through the automatic gates at the new place, Jayne looked around. Modern house, large shady verandahs, leafy trees, bright shrubs in flower, lots of spiky aloes. She'd been warned by Komal to bring some workout exercises as her jogging ventures were now banned; the nearest she'd get to that sort of exercise would be walking or short-sprinting around the extensive gardens she'd caught sight of as the car parked. Jayne was relieved to see the white van already there and apparently unloaded.

She wondered how her famous relative, Helen Joseph, had coped with being the first person to be placed under 'house arrest' by the apartheid state in 1962. She'd been confined to her home overnight, unable to meet more than one other individual person at a time, unable to move about freely, virtually forced to be a non-person.

Jayne had read Helen's memoir over and over again. She would love to have met her, to have heard what it felt like.

How on a sunny Saturday morning in October 1962, Helen had been at home, garden flowers in bloom, watering the plants on her windowsill when two Special Branch officers suddenly arrived, handing her a sheaf of papers. As she read, shocked, she gradually realised that not only was she being banned but she was the first person to be placed under five-year house arrest. She was only allowed to go out to work at her office.

On Sundays and public holidays, she could not leave her home at all; on Saturdays she was confined there after 14.30, allowing her to work her normal mornings.

On weekdays, she could leave for work from 06.30 and had to be home by 18.30.

She wasn't allowed to go to normal public locations such as factories or schools.

She wasn't allowed to attend any social gatherings, defined as occasions when people had 'social intercourse with each other', meaning more than one other person at a time.

She wasn't allowed any visitors – almost the worst blow.

She had to report daily to the infamous Marshall Square police station.

She couldn't communicate with any other banned person.

And she couldn't be quoted in public. Oh, God! She remembered an article she had written as a member of the Congress Alliance on people banished to faraway places: it would have to be pulled before it went to print or the editor would be prosecuted – maybe her too.

She was alone, completely isolated. Then the abusive or

heavy-breathing phone calls began, some threatening to kill her cat, her only companion, which had featured in news reports about her confinement. Journalists were fascinated by this seemingly normal, England-bred woman, with her old-fashioned courtesies and lifestyle, plunged into a new Orwellian world.

The Special Branch also came knocking at the oddest times to monitor her compliance.

Why, flummoxed friends from outside her political circle asked when they phoned, she'd never been a communist yet had been house-arrested under the Suppression of Communism Act!

During a lunchtime break from her office as a trade union staffer, she had deliberately walked past a Congress Alliance demonstration at the City Hall bearing placards stating, 'Hands Off Our Leaders', 'She Spoke for Freedom'. Helen had defiantly raised her clenched fist, saluting the protestors. Photos captured the moment in the next day's newspapers.

She was so brave, Jayne thought, embarrassed at the comparative triviality of her own predicament.

Mkhize continued to lope. No point in running, he would collapse with tiredness. No point in walking, he would be caught.

He was sweating profusely, his dark khaki-green shirt and trousers splattered with patches of damp. Despite being pretty fit, he was tiring. Had put around ten kilometres behind him since finding the elephants over an hour ago. Listening all the time, he heard the familiar sounds of the bush. But his worry was the unfamiliar sounds of the pursuers.

Mkhize avoided water because there might be crocodiles or, even more dangerous, hippos. He looked out for buffalo or predators, especially hyenas. He watched the ground all the time for snakes, especially puff adders, lethal as they lay in the sand to catch the sun so you might step on them before you knew it. He spotted two young frolicking baboons chasing Egyptian geese guarding their eggs. But he didn't have any food, water or weapons, so he knew he was on borrowed time.

If his pursuers had one, a tracker would be spying telltale signs such as broken branches or moved grass – or 'spoor' as his ranger craft labelled them. These could be better spotted with the sun to one side, and since he had just passed high noon, that would make it a little more difficult for his pursuers. He did his best not to leave an obvious trail, but he had no time, had to cut corners.

Mkhize scurried on determinedly, recalling the old saying: 'you can run, but you can't hide.' If he had a seasoned tracker, his counter-measures would at best give him just a smidgeon of extra time. He avoided leaving any biological evidence, any blood from a scratch, certainly any faeces, or urine.

He tried his best to avoid leaving trampled or bent grass by sticking to hard, rocky surfaces – but that was rarely possible. He had to keep moving. There weren't many trees – a relief, because under trees he knew he couldn't avoid leaving snapped twigs and overturned leaves or broken cobwebs.

Didn't have time for the common deception tactic of walking backwards, so that his footprints pointed in one direction while he was moving in the opposite one, knew that a good tracker would have detected that anyway by looking at the footprints: the shortened stride and deeper imprint on the heel would have given the game away, would have revealed also gravel and dirt being dragged in the direction he was actually walking, not the direction he was trying to make his pursuers think he was walking.

Had no time to fix a leaf-covered branch around his waist, so it dragged behind him, sweeping away his footprints. Knew anyway that a well-trained tracker would probably spot the outline of the edges of the leaves being dragged along.

Mkhize understood only too well he was leaving behind a veritable map for his pursuers, but he just hoped help would be on hand, that Thandi would deliver for him. He glanced at his phone – still no reception or at best only a flickering single bar.

Jayne's new life of involuntary isolation had taken a sudden, baffling turn which she couldn't seem to do anything about.

She was helpless, both tantalisingly caught in the middle of it all yet simultaneously hovering on the edge, entranced by the police raid on Liliesleaf Farm.

It was as if she was present right there in the room, mid-afternoon, 11 July 1963, with the ANC underground high command at its secret headquarters, including Walter Sisulu, Govan Mbeki and Ahmed Kathrada.

They looked so *young*, Jayne thought.

As a cleaning van had trundled down the driveway, coming to a halt, armed security policeman suddenly burst out, not believing their luck, finding all the most wanted names police had been hunting for ages.

Jayne had repeatedly visited that very room restored in the contemporary Liliesleaf Museum, not among fields any more but surrounded by houses in the Johannesburg suburb of Rivonia, its cutting-edge technology taking her on a journey of discovery, and its special effects allowing visitors to witness Mandela's lieutenants confronted by the security police. Also, to inspect the coal bunker where a junior policeman had poked about and, to his astonishment, discovered incriminating, handwritten documents by Mandela describing 'Operation Mayibuye', a master plan to overthrow the apartheid state.

By then he had already been imprisoned on Robben Island for nine months after being betrayed while on the run, but he had never revealed either Liliesleaf or the overthrow plan hatched there. Indeed, he had sent a message to his comrades that his documents and a false passport he'd left behind should be destroyed. But they'd ignored his stricture, believing these might have some historic value: an act of disobedience that later very nearly cost him his life.

Jayne chillingly recalled how his conviction for sabotage, along with his fellow conspirators, in what became known across the world as the 'Rivonia Trial', carried a death sentence.

She'd listened to a crackly recording of Mandela's famously defiant speech delivered from the dock: 'During my lifetime I have dedicated myself to this struggle of the African people. I have fought against white domination, and I have fought against black domination. I have cherished the ideal of a democratic and free society in which all persons live together in harmony with equal opportunities. It is an ideal which I hope to live for and achieve. But if needs be, it is an ideal for which I am prepared to die.'

As it transpired, the judge – possibly aware of the international outcry and maybe domestic rioting that would have followed hanging Mandela and his fellow Liliesleaf accused – imposed life sentences. And, rather than disappearing, the accused gradually became international heroes, Mandela a global icon, their struggle ultimately triumphing.

Jayne had voraciously read everything she could about it all. How, before his arrest, and known as the 'Black Pimpernel', Mandela had toured the country on secret missions, mostly disguised as a black chauffeur with uniform and peaked cap driving his white master.

From October 1961 he was based at Lilliesleaf, masquerading as a gardener and cook, wearing blue overalls and living, as was customary then for such domestic workers, in an outbuilding, which also served as the office where he wrote his political and military strategies.

His wife, Winnie, had even visited him there with their two tiny girls, careful with her journey as she switched cars to and fro during the trips to throw off Special Branch surveillance.

Jayne watched, transfixed, as the arrests were made, wondering how on earth she could escape herself?

Suddenly she jerked awake, heart pounding, perspiring heavily in the strange bed in the strange room, mind in a whirl.

Where on earth was she?

What was happening to her?

Then she remembered.

The helicopter was ready for him, the crew having started it up and gone through all their routine checks, and the Sniper, familiar with the Oryx from decades before, ducked under the whirring rotors and jumped on board.

He strapped himself in just like the old days, putting on one of the headsets he found clipped above his seat, enabling passengers both to protect their hearing against the deafening sound and to speak to one another and the pilots.

He checked that it was properly equipped with a fifty-metre hydraulic hoist, rated for up to two personnel, specifically for use in rescue operations.

It was. No problem then for dropping him off or for picking up Mkhize – if they could get to him in time.

The Sniper remembered during training being told by a smirking instructor how the chopper had been designed and developed with the covert assistance of the French military.

That was in defiance of a United Nations Security Council resolution imposing an arms embargo. France had voted for that, but had also extracted the maximum commercial advantage on the quiet, by allowing the technicians and designers of its Puma helicopter to give advice to the South African helicopter manufacturers – totally deniable by Paris, of course, that went without saying. Even the Russians and the Chinese, overt allies of the ANC, had supplied Pretoria with military equipment on the side: money always trumped ideology.

The Oryx was a multipurpose craft, mainly used for transport and communications flights, emergency or rapid deployment, firefighting and search and rescue. It could carry up to twenty fully equipped troops, or up to six wounded personnel on stretchers with four attendants. A useful workhorse, reliable and mobile with a top speed of 300 kilometres per hour, usually cruising at around 200.

The Sniper felt comfortable – until he began thinking about being dropped on the ground. Then he would be on his own, out in the veld. His instructions to the pilot over the intercom were to scout a kopje, find a higher point from which he could survey the terrain traversed by Mkhize, see if he could spot any trackers and take them out if possible.

The plan, hastily hatched, was for the Oryx to scarper after dropping him and then to retreat, hovering back away from the chase, beyond the Sniper, just over the horizon, waiting to pick up Mkhize – if he could be spotted.

The Tracker nodded curtly to Irish, muttering, 'Follow me.'

No speaking, just following. Looking for all the telltale signs, especially for doubling back by his foe.

Irish felt out of his depth. Would have been in his element between the South Armagh hedgerows, would have led, not followed, there, breathing the sweet, cool air, would have flitted unnoticed across the damp green fields, through the farmyards without disturbing any dogs.

But here in this strange, scrawny scrub with a hot wind and a high sky, heat coming off the bare reddish-brown ground, he was an alien. So he trailed, partly resentful, partly relieved.

They moved forward relentlessly, the Tracker thin and mean out in front, eyes focused on the ground, watching for the signs he needed, the signs he recognised from the fast-moving but, he thought, tiring foe.

Irish carried his Armalite, safety catch off, ready – but wondering about the target. Usually, he knew all about them before his lethal strike, knew well in advance. But now Irish hadn't a clue, didn't even know a name, hadn't even had a photo, had been told next-to-bloody nothing; he felt uncomfortable about the motive as well. At home he was a killer in what he considered a noble cause; out here – what exactly was he?

He trudged on, sweating and wondering, keeping his head down in all respects.

*

Thandi fretted.

She had spoken to Yasmin, spoken to the Veteran, yet still felt hopeless, frustrated. What else could she do? She had suggested flying to Bloemfontein as soon as she could get a booking, simply to be nearer. But what would she do then, the Veteran asked gently? All on her own? Yasmin had also counselled against the venture.

But at least she would be in the vicinity, Thandi thought. She checked on flights, fiddled, wondered whether to go anyway, had a sense things might be coming to a head, felt she needed to be near her Isaac, just in case.

Thandi was her own woman, always had been from girlhood, often accused of being headstrong, she knew that, but still had to do what she had to do – regardless.

As Mkhize trekked on, his attention meandered to shocking ANC intra-party killings in his home province, stemming from position-jockeying within the ruling party. KwaZulu-Natal had developed a culture of blood-letting, as people competed for paid positions in local governmental and community structures.

ANC members standing in a queue in a primary school to vote for a councillor candidate were gunned down in a drive-by shooting, killing three people and injuring five other women and one man.

A prominent ANC youth figure was coming from an ANC meeting when the car he was travelling in with two other councillors was ambushed; they were all injured and he died of his injuries in a Durban hospital.

He had been a whistle-blower on one of the many dodgy multimillion-rand tenders awarded by the municipality. Yet despite scores of political murders in KwaZulu-Natal, there were few arrests and even fewer convictions.

After another attack, one woman council candidate claimed it was carried out by political enemies refusing to be 'led by a woman'.

And so it went on. Mkhize had discussed it with Thandi, and her graphic analysis still rung in his ears.

'There is almost no hope of escaping this without a real economic transformation backed by sound governance and respect for the rule of law, and we're seeing none of this in South Africa's increasingly lethal, self-serving politics,' she had said.

'Many people see the position of the councillor as an opportunity to earn a decent salary and get closer to dishing out tenders, not to serve the people,' Thandi had added. 'Any rival candidate who may be better, they try to eliminate; that's why you see so many killings.'

Mkhize glanced back behind him: nothing he could spot.

But they were there, following relentlessly, he sensed it, and was terrified, truth be told.

The Tracker had been just a boy when he'd first learned the art as an activist in the liberation movement.

He had been taught then that tracking really come of age as an important and recognised skill in the wars over Africa's late-twentieth-century decolonisation, when both state security forces and the liberation-movement guerrillas they fought deployed it to the full.

He had been taught about how the British in Kenya from 1952 to 1956 waged a counterinsurgency war against the Kenya Land and Freedom Army, popularly called Mau Mau, who rose up over the historic dispossession by white settlers of land owned by the Kikuyu people.

He was told about the brutal war by the white minority in Rhodesia in the late 1960s and 1970s against Zimbabwe freedom fighters. Zimbabwean guerrillas fighting the ruthless Selous Scouts of the Rhodesian army became renowned for their tracking skills, to which they added chameleon-like abilities for camouflage and concealment, to become almost invisible in the bush.

South Africa had adopted counterinsurgency tactics from the British. Rather than attempting to police the country's long border, they hit rebel bases – to the north in hostile Angola, with its highly proficient Cuban soldiers, and in liberated Zimbabwe too. The whole region was a theatre for proxy wars by the two superpowers, the US and the Soviet Union, during the Cold War era.

In South West Africa from the late 1960s to 1980s, guerrillas like him from SWAPO, the South West Africa People's Organisation, developed innovative anti-tracking techniques, such as boots with layers of removable soles to leave different footprints.

They put plastic bags on their feet to obscure spoor. They switched between walking with boots and bare feet. They used a cloth stuck on the end of a tree branch or stick to erase tracks. They sprinkled water on their footprints to impersonate rain and give an appearance of the prints being older.

145

The Ovambo Tracker moved forward, aware his Irish colleague was tiring behind, but confident he was catching the target ahead. Didn't know who the target was, didn't know his skin colour, and didn't want to, in case he was black like him.

But when they caught the target, then his job would be done, and it would be up to the Irishman to deal with the target. He didn't really want to know what the purpose was, suspected it was dodgy, but felt it was not his place to pass judgement.

His motive was purely the fee. When fighting alongside armed SWAPO guerrillas in the bush, the aim was clear and noble: to establish democracy in his country. But there had been no job for him in the new Namibia, so he became a tracker for hire, putting food on his family's table that way.

There had been no job for him before the liberation struggle either. He had been plucked out of poverty as a kid, where his obsession in life was hunger – not being hungry, not looking forward to one of three meals a day, but hunger, continuous aching, yearning, desperate hunger. Drinking water, hoping it would fill his empty belly when it never did. Being given a slice of white bread spread with thin gruel by a kindly neighbour who couldn't spare more than a single slice, and longing constantly for that – not every day, because that wasn't offered, remaining in a constant state of craving for food. Until recruited into SWAPO in his mid-teens, when his life really lifted off – until independence, when SWAPO took power, and he was again left to fend for himself.

He pushed on, eyes constantly weaving between the marks he sought on the ground and the terrain both ahead and alongside, not passing judgement on who was ahead, feeling older, tired in a way that he never had been when he was younger. It was simply a job for him, no longer a mission as it had been in his youthful freedom-fighter days, decades ago. Those days he could feel misty-eyed about, those days when he had felt better about himself.

How far ahead was his foe? Under two k's, he judged, and getting shorter almost by the step.

The Oryx climbed swiftly and drove forward at the same time, simultaneously upward and sideways, the Sniper enjoying the sensation, bringing back memories of swooping over the Caprivi Strip, the notorious killing ground where South African forces engaged liberation fighters, recalling the adrenaline-pumping days of his youth.

He had been serving his country, wasn't really political, knew, like all whites, he was a beneficiary of apartheid, but didn't think much about it. Had never been in the black townships ringing white cities, didn't know much about the conditions in which lived the servant majority, or even think to ask. Just accepted that was the way of life and his duty was to be a soldier.

Just as he continued to be that same soldier when the transformation came, when he had been deputed to look after Mandela as the great man walked to freedom from prison. The Sniper had never really questioned why one day he had been hunting Mandela's fighters and the next day protecting the man: just carrying out his duty.

But his current task was less clear-cut. The state — or large parts of it — had become the problem, so who he was serving had become more of a problem too.

It had begun using his sniper skills to help protect Zama Zama from rhino-poacher attacks — relatively straightforward. Then he had been drawn deeper into uncovering those responsible — more troubling, because it placed him in the position of being almost a hired gun, and he didn't like that. Serving the state — whoever ran it — had been straightforward for a trained soldier like him. Serving private interests — even ones with laudable aims — made him uncomfortable: where were the boundaries? When was he acting outside the law?

His loyalty, however, was to Mkhize, to the feisty Thandi, to the Veteran, to his cherished Elise at Zama Zama and to Yasmin — so that was straightforward. Being a passenger in an army helicopter was also reassuring, echoes of his training.

But the doubts still nagged as they surged forward, the pilot in touch with the crew of the Rooivalk attack helicopter, who remained on standby at Bloemspruit Air Force Base if needed. Hopefully not, because the Oryx planned to drop off, wait, collect and go, creating as little fuss as possible. That was Minister's Yasmin's remit. She didn't want the Rooivalk involved because it would raise the profile, might alert the bad guys.

Yet if there was a firefight, it would have to scramble and intervene of course.

*

147

To stop herself worrying while waiting at the airport for her flight, Thandi did some online reading about her husband's favourite animal, the elephant.

Zimbabwe had just sold over thirty wild baby elephants to China, condemning them to a lifetime in captivity, in clear breach of a ban on live elephant exports from both Zimbabwe and Botswana by the Convention on International Trade in Endangered Species of Wild Fauna and Flora (CITES) – and because some corrupt officials would have got kickbacks, Thandi supposed.

An elephant biologist was quoted in the story: 'These animals should be roaming in the wild with their families but, instead, they have been ripped away from their mothers for more than a year and now sold off for lifelong captivity.'

The majestic species continued to amaze her. The more facts she discovered about them, the more mind-boggling they were. Like eating around 200 kilos of food daily. Like their extraordinary trunks being able to act like suitcases, expanding and contracting as needed, dilating their nostrils to store up to nine litres of water and suck it in at huge speeds, three litres per second, and the equivalent of fifteen toilets being flushed together.

Religions elevated elephants to be sacred ancestors in many African cultures, testament to divine glory in Christian writings and in Buddhism, also revered in the Koran and Hindu culture.

Ivory from their tusks had been in use from prehistoric times in ancient Egypt, China and India, as well as ancient Greece, and the Roman empire and by early African kings. Christians had ivory figurines of crucifixions, and of the Madonna and Child, and Islamic countries had long used ivory for containers and ornamentation on weapons.

European colonists in Africa had indulged in wholesale annihilation of elephants to satisfy new urges for ivory for billiard balls, for decorative furniture veneers, for musical instruments and hilts for their swords.

Ivory was now selling at over $6,000 per kilo, and the global trade in ivory was worth about $23 billion annually – no wonder elephant poaching and the political corruption and serious crime underpinning it was so ubiquitous, she thought, learning still more about Mkhize's world of wildlife, and worrying about him even more as a result.

What could she do to help him? She had no idea. Try to be on hand,

148

nearer to wherever he was – that was about the sum of it. It didn't stop her fretting about him.

Mkhize was tiring, had been pushing himself harder and harder, but had been finding that harder and harder too.

He kept scanning 360 degrees, behind to spot anybody closing, ahead to check for rocks or crevices that might trip him and for snakes that might bite him, especially the cross-marked sand snake, hard to spot, or the rinkhals, often called a ring-necked spitting cobra, and aggressively lethal.

Mkhize was comfortable in the wild but uncomfortable in the chase. He was unarmed and sure his pursuers would be armed. He looked at his phone – the faintest of signals, the photos still stuck, nothing like enough bandwidth to transmit them – and pined after Thandi. He hoped help would come soon before they caught him, before they grabbed his phone and destroyed the precious photos of that cruel display, that evidence of elephant Armageddon.

Mkhize thought of other animals among his favourites, such as the long, spindly, incongruous, gentle, amazing giraffes, the world's tallest land mammals. Of female giraffes who stick together and form close friendships, living longer than solitary individuals, as researchers tracking their social life had found. Of how females fed in different areas from males because they are shorter and needed to browse off lower vegetation – as a result, not competing with males for food.

He thought of his mother – so stoic and cheerful. He remembered taking Thandi to see her for the first time, wishing his dad was still alive to be there too. He had parked a little away from his mother's small home in what might have been described as the village high street if you were being generous – a patchwork of little shops in rickety lean-to's and one modest supermarket. Had parked there deliberately so he could walk Thandi to his old home – two bedrooms, one living, cooking, relaxing area or room, showing her off along the way. He wanted her to see where he had come from, wanted them to see her too.

His female contemporaries, hanging about in small groups, gossiping and gawping, looked on, giving him shy smiles – not the come-on ones to which he had been accustomed on visits over the years. They stared enviously at Thandi – envious that she had captured the object of their desires.

He remembered how he had shyly introduced Thandi to his mom, noticing her eyes dampening, partly at losing him, partly with pride at the coming addition of a vivacious member to her matriarchal clan.

He remembered how nervous Thandi was before the visit, how polite she had been towards his mom.

Mkhize was engulfed by nostalgia, his concentration wandering. He thought of his father, as he had almost every day since he had passed away five years before. Thought fondly of his austere, sometimes forbidding manner – but underneath, a witty warmth.

Thought of all the bushcraft he had learned from him on their long walks in his youth, when his schoolfriends wanted to lark about and couldn't understand why Mkhize simply wanted to go off with his dad, to breathe in the clean air of the wild rather than the paraffin-cooking whiffs of the village.

They couldn't understand why he favoured the wide-open spaces, the sweep of the veld, the lure of the bush, dawn breaking in the early cold, summoning shafts of diffident light, then mid-morning blossoming out into the bright, hot sunshine of a South African winter's day – until, come late afternoon, the sun disappeared, the temperature dropping like a stone.

Mkhize thought of those halcyon days with his dad as he trudged on, his eyes filling up with emotion – annoying, that. He was glad nobody, not even Thandi, was present to witness his momentary relapse.

Abruptly, anger flared up, drove him to up his pace again. Mkhize focused, guessed he was fighting for his life, knew also that other elephants would surely find themselves victims of the conspiracy unless they could stop it, which meant first he had to get out.

He loped on, just stopping himself from stumbling down a dry ravine concealed beyond dense bushes, spotting a shy duiker leaping rapidly away, the tiny antelope characteristically porpoising in full flight – accounting for its Afrikaans name, meaning 'to dive'.

Jayne pored over still more startling material, confirming that what she seemed to have discovered in the Free State was part of a much wider criminality.

A treasure trove of leaked financial documents centring on the Democratic Republic of Congo revealed a massive laundering of $140 million of government funds, some of it being used to purchase properties in her own home city, Johannesburg – properties situated in neighbourhoods she knew well.

A Paris-based African whistle-blowers' group had obtained well over three million leaked documents from the largest bank in Central Africa, revealing a byzantine pattern of corruption and money laundering reaching right up to the top of the state, with named beneficiaries, often the relatives of top ministers and politicians, who had used their networks and control over the state bank to plunder and launder millions from government institutions.

Jayne spotted the familiar device of off-the-shelf 'shell' companies being the recipients of large dollops of funds from public institutions, with no obvious or legitimate explanations to justify these.

One aspect that puzzled her, however, was that this had all occurred despite South Africa having by international standards pretty tough regulations to curb money laundering, including via property purchases.

Clearly, the regulations weren't being fully enforced, and it also appeared to her that prosecutions were rare. It was all very well having an admirable system of financial governance on paper, but if the agencies meant to be stopping financial crime were either badly under-resourced, hobbled or simply corrupted, they could be bypassed, as had obviously been happening – and on an industrial scale.

Pádraig Murphy, panting in the heat, asked how far ahead the target was, whether he should get the Armalite ready.

The Ovambo Tracker reckoned over a kilometre, coming down bit by bit, the pace he set so relentless and so steady, but the man ahead determined, obviously knew his bushcraft.

Murphy was uneasy. Normally, his kills were well prepared, the site scouted, a hidden position located, a time chosen, an exit planned. None of that applied in this case. He was out of his comfort zone, not only in strange terrain but unable to execute the meticulous planning for which he had become renowned within the New IRA – and notorious outside it.

But he knew what he had to do. Once the target was spotted up ahead, he would pause from their yomping and prepare his Armalite, carrying it ready to lift onto his shoulder, to steady there when he stopped momentarily to fire.

He told the Tracker a range of around 300 to 500 metres would be okay for him, didn't need to be much nearer, didn't want to be much nearer, better to shoot from afar in case the target was armed. But didn't want to be much further away either.

That sort of range was comfortable for Murphy, one he was used to on kills in Northern Ireland.

He had practised during the days before at Wildealskloof Shooting Range near Bloemfontein, outdoor and accredited, quite useful sessions to check his eye was in, his rifle was ready.

He trekked on behind the Tracker, alert but bored too, thinking about the moment when he'd level his Armalite at the target, mind wondering over his almost schizophrenic stance on the criminality that underpinned the financing of his New IRA's paramilitarism and Republican politics.

There was the straight-laced side to his character, which was strict, almost moralistic and God-fearing, deprecating dishonesty and infidelity.

Then there was the expedient side, which reflected a hard-headed recognition that the war against the Brits had to be financed from some-where, and that there could be a certain honour in post–office robberies, even drug trafficking, if all was in the cause of Republicanism. He never touched drugs himself – unless you defined a pint of Guinness as a 'drug' – but was pragmatic about the revenues to his organisation flowing from its drug trade.

There was the discovery of an underground cannabis factory near his home in South Armagh. There had been a certain quirkiness about media reports, but underlying them was the reality of smuggling and crime in the region that had gone on for generations near the border and across it.

But was he part of a criminal operation now, out in the African bush? He supposed so, his motive the fee in the cause of his New IRA, therefore easily rationalised, though still disconcerting. Just a little.

The Sniper's instructions were to wound, not to kill, the crew's to pick up the guys behind Mkhize as well as to collect him if they could.

It was frustrating for the Sniper, because wounding was more exacting than killing. Not that he got the slightest pleasure from a kill – quite the contrary: he hated it. Especially in this grey world where the boundaries of what was right and wrong were so blurred, and when as a civilian he had none of the legal protection he'd enjoyed during his brief tenure as a soldier.

The Oryx swooped high over Vryburg, then veered towards the Regeneration site, where the pilot planned to turn to follow what he believed from the GPS coordinates might be Mkhize's retreat path.

His co-pilot had binoculars to his eyes, scouring the scrubby, messy terrain ahead, the helicopter high enough not to attract interest, they hoped.

The Ovambo Tracker heard the noisy bird whirring above, seeming to be coming from behind, probably from the direction of Bloemspruit Air Force Base, he thought, maybe on military manoeuvres.

It seemed far too high to worry about, though Murphy seemed unsettled, tugging irritatingly at his shirt and pointing up as if – for goodness sake – the Tracker hadn't noticed.

The helicopter continued on without pausing as the duo halted momentarily to watch, Murphy intensely allergic to the craft. It jangled memories of Brits with machine guns, long straps anchoring them to a pole in the middle, sitting legs over the edge out of open doors, pointing automatic rifles as their helicopters swooped across South Armagh, coming from the old Bessbrook army base near the Newry bypass on the main A1 Belfast–Dublin road and Belfast–Dublin railway line, and in to Crossmaglen base, where he'd often tried to shoot them down as they slowed to land.

Once he had got a hit and it lurched, smoking, to tumble onto a sports field, rotors tearing up the turf, becoming a trophy for cheering local Republicans, Murphy a hero for the day, and forever more among some.

The Oryx steamed on, seemingly uninterested, eventually to disappear over a kopje, perhaps two kilometres ahead, the Tracker estimated. He turned disdainfully to Murphy as if to gesture: 'What to worry about? Leave the worrying to me; this is my patch.'

Murphy remained sceptical and troubled. Too much of a coincidence, surely? He had noticed what seemed like military markings on the chopper. So far the walk had been pretty routine; now he was on double alert, and readied his Armalite.

Choppers, in his experience, were very bad news.

The co-pilot had spotted what he thought must be them, and now switched to search ahead for Mkhize, flying deliberately high and fast.

They searched but couldn't find him.

Then – there he was! – a lone figure, seemingly pausing, eyes searching above, turning, looking desperately, raising a hopeful thumb, perhaps, the co-pilot thought? Though he couldn't be absolutely sure, as the chopper lurched amidst the thermals, was also buffeted by the wind, which was getting up now. At least there was no mist or fog, the pilot's nightmare, the sky clear except for the habitual wispy African clouds floating well above.

'Think we found them,' the co-pilot said between the static of the intercom.'

They flew on and over a kopje ahead, convenient because they could land, sheltering well behind it to drop off the Sniper.

Mkhize wasn't a church-goer, but he almost pointed his hands upward together in prayer.

Wished that what he had just seen might involve a rescue, but couldn't be sure. No signal, no gesture, just a military copter with the country's emblem flying overhead and then tantalisingly away, its throbbing rotors encouragingly loud at one point above him, then the sound ebbing gradually, depressingly, as it vanished over the horizon, Mkhize's optimism expiring with it.

He was sure Thandi would have summoned help, sure she would have managed something with Minister Yasmin, now in a powerful security position, when before she had been operating almost freelance, hanging on inside the nest of vipers that the security forces had become under the former mendacious, mercifully deposed president.

Mkhize hoped, because he had nothing else to cling on to, that somehow he might escape. Yet was certain that if they had a decent tracker, his pursuers would catch him in time. He saw the kopje in the distance, started to think whether he should go around it. If so, which way? Or up over it. From what he could tell, it was covered in *Acacia karroo* trees, often known as sweet thorn, and useful for cover if he decided to scale the kopje.

There had been a few trees on his route so far, but mostly wild grasses, untidy scrub and scattered fountain bush, which, in full bloom, looked as if it rained flowers, but with only slender, red, tubular blooms now hanging on the small plant like little fire crackers

As Mkhize toiled, sweaty, dishevelled and troubled, his mind wandered back to the extraordinary finding that ivory poaching over decades had led to the evolution of *tuskless* elephants.

What had been a very rare genetic mutation, causing this phenomenon of 'tusklessness', had become common in some groups of African elephants subjected to persistent killing by poachers.

154

Female elephants in Gorongosa National Park in Mozambique were frequently born without tusks, which meant the regal giants had effectively been genetically re-engineered. So, Mkhize concluded, human behaviour had changed the anatomy of wild animals.

As far as he could tell, this arose out of hunting for elephants with tusks during the Mozambican civil war from 1977 to 1992, when around 90 per cent of the elephant population was slaughtered by armed forces on both sides for the revenues they needed to fund their war. Apparently, elephants who had lost their tusks were spared, and these went on to breed and pass on their tuskless characteristics to their babies.

Generations later, the same thing was visible among the 700 elephants living in the national park, but concentrated among females, seemingly for genetic differences with males, and who were therefore protected from poaching.

Mkhize could hardly process this, having read a scientific study the week before, but now his focus was on his own survival, not elephant survival.

Time dragged, sweat clung, muscles ached; Mkhize was engulfed by his loneliness and pined after Thandi, wondered about their marriage, whether they would have kids, and how they could be raised. He didn't want to be an absentee father like so many men from his village, didn't want to abandon any kids – and knew Thandi would never accept that, if indeed in her conscience-driven political life she ever found time to have kids.

The Oryx settled on the ground, its engine slowing, but not switched off, dust billowing as the pilot's voice crackled in the Sniper's headset. 'Suggest you disembark, head up the kopje, find a vantage point, I'd estimate the villains are an hour away, Mkhize much nearer.'

'Are you sure it was him?' the Sniper asked.

'Matched the image I was shown before takeoff,' the co-pilot interjected, 'pretty sure. Two behind him, tall thin black guy in front, the other shorter, white, carrying a rifle, I think.'

The pilot added: 'I'll head on and wait. Send up a flare when you are ready, and I'll be back.' They'd improvised a plan en route, but couldn't be sure of the circumstances they'd confront.

'Okay,' the Sniper muttered, wondering what the hell might happen if he wasn't successful. There didn't seem much of a back-up plan. At least his Remington PSR rifle was ready, and he had a compass in one of the multiple buttoned pockets in his khaki shirt.

He'd left behind the hard case with its special slots for different cartridges, together with precision wrenches and drives, but brought the bipod assembly, the magazines, the recoil pad and, most important, the cleaning kit, which he'd used on the flight, having had no time to clean before he left at such short notice, all bundled together with the rifle itself in a long grip-bag.

He undid his safety belt, stowed the headset back on the rail above the row of passenger seats, and made to climb down, the co-pilot having jumped out and opened the hatch for him, dust billowing.

It was like old times, tumbling out with his gear, ducking under the swirling rotors, and scampering away, still bending over, the Oryx scuttling off quickly at low altitude to wait up.

The Sniper had been left again, where all snipers always ended up, unless they were with a spotter: alone, with their own thoughts, their own insecurities, their own single-minded objective.

He quickly surveyed the kopje through his sunglasses, grateful he'd brought a hat to shade his face. About 200 metres high, he reckoned, lots of rocky outcrops, medium-sized trees, might be useful for cover as long as they didn't obscure his vision. Had to be careful of snakes basking in the hot sun, ready to be stepped upon and to snap back if they hadn't already stirred from sleeping after hearing him and slithered away.

The Sniper climbed carefully up, several dassies darting away, shy little creatures, always sniffing nervously. He thought he also saw a duiker out of the corner of his eye but couldn't be sure; he didn't think there would be many, if any, larger animals around, but you never knew what might be lurking in the shade of the acacias, out of the hot sun, which had caused him to start sweating almost immediately he began moving.

The hat was always a mixed blessing: essential for protecting his face from skin-cancerous glare, but he'd been told by his dictatorial drill sergeant in the army that you lost around 80 per cent of your body heat through your head. Had never checked that out, but always felt there must be some truth in it, for he was very hot on top.

The Sniper checked all his gear yet again: his rifle, cartridges and magazines. As well as his scope, rangefinder, bolt, bipod and moderator. All fine, enabling him smoothly to assemble his shooting machinery.

He settled down, crouching as comfortably as he could, calming and stabilising himself, loading the rifle, setting the scope magnification and focusing, so that the cross-hairs became sharp against the likely image of the targets when they came into view.

He didn't have time to perform the zeroing, but wasn't too worried. The round was chambered, a spare magazine ready – yet, he trusted, superfluous. If he needed the spare he'd be in trouble, be in a shoot-out, not a surprise shooting.

Mkhize's hopes had been dashed a while back, as the helicopter had disappeared, so he loped on methodically, gloomily but nevertheless determinedly.

Would not allow himself to lose his mojo, focused on survival, on escape with the precious photos, on shaking off the pursuers. Funny that they hadn't called in reinforcements – like their own helicopter.

Why? Maybe they wanted it to be deniable, to track and kill him on the quiet, no fuss, just to leave his body to the vultures or any hyenas and jackals about. There weren't supposed to be any big cats in the vicinity – too much human activity nearby.

Thought he might climb a bit up the kopje, its contours now clear ahead, then scramble sideways and around it to throw off the trackers if he possibly could. Just as he hadn't been sure which direction to take – left or right around it, or up and over – so they might wonder what he'd done too.

Exactly the same dilemma confronted the Tracker, who didn't seem to be sweating much – unlike himself, Irish noted – just walked fast, on and on, not complaining, not swearing at a difficult patch of scrub, just silently and relentlessly closing on their target.

Irish had thought continuously how he might handle the kill. Depended upon the circumstances, obviously. Depended upon whether he had sufficient time to see and pause and level his Armalite. Depended upon a clear sight. Upon the target not ducking among the odd tree or tall bush as Irish steadied himself. Needed an opportunity for precision shooting: wounding would be no good.

Still hadn't a clue who the guy was, what exactly it was all about, just that he was a hired gun from afar, deniable, mysterious, never to be clocked: in, kill and get out, get paid, so his New IRA could regroup and prepare for the next offensive – and he could return to being the

157

soldier he saw himself as, not the terrorist the Brits always pejoratively labelled him as.

That label always rankled. He was fighting a war to reclaim the whole of the island – to see the Ireland of his dreams reborn, united again. It was a war of liberation and he was no 'terrorist' – insulting to be grouped with the Bin Ladens.

He simmered at the very accusation. To him, the Brits were the terrorists, another of the Irish Brigade's songs epitomising his stance: 'And you dare to call me a terrorist, while you look down your gun. / When I think of all the deeds that you have done. / You have plundered many nations, divided many lands. You have terrorised our people. You rule with an iron hand. / And you brought this reign of terror to our land ...'

Sinn Féin could not claim to 'own' Republicanism, even though they acted as if they did. Even if his New IRA could not push the Brits out soon, they had to keep the flame burning for the next generation. Because there always will be a next generation so long as there was a border across Ireland.

He was not fighting for himself, now. He was fighting to keep Republicanism alive and strong, *real* Republicanism, not the *fake* one of Sinn Féin leaders like Adams and McGuinness and their successors like Mary-Lou McDonald. Once revolutionary Republicans, Sinn Féin were now constitutionalists, talking 'democracy' when there never could be democracy while Ireland remained divided.

To stop himself getting bored, Irish rehearsed all the arguments over and over again as he trudged on, struck at how hard it was to keep pace with the tall, slim man ahead who said little but had a steely purpose, which he had to admire.

Peering carefully over the top of the kopje and creeping down a bit, the Sniper had quickly found a perch, behind a large rock, a tree providing some dappled shade and camouflage.

He set up his bipod, settled his scope and crouched in position, swinging the rifle carefully in a semi-circle and then back. He would prefer, as all army snipers did, a distance of over 500 metres, and combed the terrain below for Mkhize and his pursuers.

Couldn't find them, the ground gently undulating, making it difficult. But no panic. Snipers were trained in the solace of solitude and fortitude.

Trained to settle themselves into a calm serenity. No other distracting thoughts, no worries about anything: where his relationship with Elise was going; how his boy and girl, on the threshold of adulthood, were; what his former wife was up to with her new man in the house the Sniper had fashioned during his marriage – built cupboards, put up shelves, installed a loft ladder. Nothing else intruded as he patiently searched ahead and down below.

The main problem consuming him on the flight since Yasmin had summoned him with brusque instructions, was that he had to wound rather than to kill, for that wasn't as easy. A shot to the head or the chest was more clinical, more straightforward for the sniper trade; trying only to wound was more demanding and more chancy.

Target. Trackers. Sniper. Four actors in the scene, which had settled, a stillness in the afternoon heat, any animals about lying down and sheltering from the sun if they could. Only the incessant rasping screech of cicadas disturbed the silence of the bush.

Sudden relief – the Sniper quickly buried the emotion, mustn't let it sidetrack him – he had spotted Mkhize, his Zama Zama ranger cap distinctive from above, upper frame in his gunsights, straining forward, not walking, not running, somewhere in between.

The Sniper carefully inched the rifle a notch upward to search behind Mkhize, but couldn't see the pursuers. Forget about Mkhize, don't get distracted by him, just concentrate and wait. They were out there, probably would surface in the cross-hairs of his scope sooner rather than later. Just remain patient, for patience was the opium of the sniper profession.

The kopje was a problem, the Tracker decided, as it loomed into view. Not so much because the target could go around either way or climb over it, for his tracking skills would spot which route, of that he was pretty confident.

Instead because the target might be armed, could hide up somewhere above, in a dangerous position for the two of them. He'd been assured the target wasn't armed, but you never knew. Caution had been bred into him from his teenage training days among the freedom fighters. Caution, together with utter, steely resolve and perseverance.

Caution had always been his ticket to survival during the long war of liberation in his native Namibia, then South West Africa. It was a land of

159

savanna and dry scrub, and of the Kalahari and the Namib deserts, whose undulating multi-coloured dunes had a beauty that strangers always found difficult to comprehend.

This was his own country, also rich in minerals such as uranium, vanadium, lithium, tungsten – and of course diamonds. Rich mineral resources that the European colonial powers had tussled over, that apartheid South Africa had fought for in its dirty war against freedom fighters like him for over three decades from the mid-1960s to 1990.

He walked on, Irish behind, Armalite loaded up and ready.

The Sniper had been anxious to minimise the risk of sunlight glinting off his rifle, so had to adjust his position slightly, as the sun crept around.

That was a distraction: unavoidable, however. It could be lethal to betray his position.

Suddenly, there they were.

Two figures moving almost as one: a tall black man leading, a shorter white guy just behind, could see he had a rifle of some sort, not sure what kind.

The Sniper steadied and focused, controlling his breathing and lowering his pulse rate – essential in his profession at this key moment. He settled, concentrated – then fired at the second man. Always the one behind if just a twosome – it created panic, spread confusion, went against logic that the one in front would be the main target.

Irish heard the sudden crack, felt the searing pain as one bullet, then almost immediately another, hit the top of his right arm, shattering the shoulder bone, his gun clattering suddenly down.

The Tracker turned, disorientated, then was also hit, the bullet tearing straight though one thigh, then a second bullet too.

Both men fell to the ground, hunching, writhing, trying to curb their involuntary howls of agony.

Up ahead and above, the Sniper displayed no emotion whatsoever, stayed still, searching through his scope, spotting the gun on the ground and the white bloke clutching his shoulder in agony with his left hand. Saw the black guy trying desperately to slither away.

Could easily have shot both of them again, killing them off. Didn't. Wasn't supposed to. A shame, not because he gloried in a kill. Quite the opposite: part of him was repelled at what he did. But because wounds could heal, and danger could return from these men.

160

At least for now they weren't going very far, if anywhere.

He retrieved the flare the pilot had given him and sent it skyward.

Irish couldn't believe what had happened: it wasn't supposed to be like this; he had never been hit in combat before. The image of the military helicopter flying seemingly indifferently high above an hour or so earlier flashed back into his mind.

The pain in his arm was piercing; it felt useless – he could hardly move it. What the hell had possessed him to accept this mission? Everything he had toiled for, everything he had sacrificed in his life's mission to restore the Ireland of his dreams had been shattered. Instead of fighting the Brits on his home territory, here he was in this god-forsaken place, losing everything, especially his right arm, his fighting Armalite arm.

He needed surgery – and quickly, or the arm would be permanently damaged, not simply impaired.

The Ovambo Tracker was similarly distraught, not just at the injury but at knowing deep down it was probably terminal for him – maybe not for his life but almost certainly for his ability to track, to earn a living. He was getting old anyway: now he would be redundant, now he wouldn't be able to roam the bush, to deploy his unique skills. At best he would be limping for as long as he lived – at best.

Mkhize was elated.

Just as he had almost given up hope of rescue and was assessing his options, planning for contingencies, he recognised instantly what must have happened.

Recognised the shots. Recognised the calm style. Realised his comrade the Sniper had come to save him. Gave thanks to Thandi, wanted desperately to hold her tight, began to cry for the second time that day, and tried to stop himself, for that was not the way big strong Zulu boys like him behaved.

Minister Yasmin was taking no chances over Thandi as the girl travelled once more to the Free State, this time determinedly on her own, against advice. Thandi was at once exasperating and daring – ruefully, Yasmin recognised that Thandi had much of her own stubborn self.

There had to be a back-up plan, and Yasmin asked Komal to be part of it: a late boarder, slipping into her last-minute cut-price business-class seat right in the front row, Thandi near the back of the plane, buried in her phone, oblivious.

The Veteran had encouraged Komal to go, and ensured her Makarov had been taken on ahead by the Corporal. She'd been getting her eye in again during practice sessions at a local gun club, and was a pretty good shot for someone in her early sixties.

On landing at Bram Fischer airport, Komal disembarked first, brushing by the waiting Corporal and unobtrusively retrieving a shopping bag from him as she did so, before heading out of the terminal to hang about as if waiting for a lift, the Corporal pausing, then sidling out to climb into his unmarked car.

When Thandi arrived, Yasmin had two watchers to see whether the young activist was being followed. Watchers upon likely watchers: one sipping a coffee and another standing amidst a bubble of taxi drivers holding signs for incoming passengers, except his was for a non-existent arrival.

Outside the airport entrance, Yasmin's trusty Corporal parked and waited, fending off airport security as his engine ticked over, a colleague parked nearby also with the engine running.

After her previous visit and the assassination of Jacob Kubeka, Thandi felt more secure knowing that she had back-up, yet more nervous sensing she would likely still be under surveillance by Star's hoods.

She felt self-conscious as she walked, like the other passengers, and joined a line as waiting taxis pulled up one by one. When her turn came, she jumped in, giving instructions, the driver pulling away yet coming to a screeching halt as a man walked right in front. He turned and jumped into the passenger seat, stuffing R5,000 into the driver's hand and telling him to go. Simultaneously, another man opened the rear door and clambered in next to Thandi. Both wore dark glasses, hands inside their casual jackets gripping Glock pistols.

Komal watched aghast, powerless to stop Thandi's abduction. She cocked her Makarov, crouched, both hands gripping the butt, and loosed off two shots at the rear tyres of the taxi, a BMW 320d, scruffy, scratched, looking more than a few years old.

But nothing happened. *They must be bloody run-flats*, she thought ruefully, running towards the Corporal's vehicle, jumping in as it pulled away. He wasn't happy with her, was concerned at the attention the incident would attract, the questions that would be asked.

Komal thought fast. No point in staying with the Corporal. She could be deployed more effectively elsewhere, but felt she had to disappear for a bit. She asked to be dropped off

The taxi sped off. Thandi, hearing the shots, was confused. Her two abductors turned around, mumbling angrily: 'What the hell's going on?'

Behind, her watchers cursed. But the Corporal remained unruffled, reading out the taxi number plate to his waiting colleague, with Yasmin, looped in from her ministerial office, alerting the rest of her trusted team. It was a limited circle, because she hardly trusted anybody at this relatively early stage of her tenure in charge of the country's security.

Thandi, badly shaken, tried to stay calm as the taxi's terrified driver lurched away from the airport. She reassured herself that Yasmin's team would have witnessed the incident and would be following her taxi – or so she desperately hoped.

'Where are you taking me?' she yelled, deliberately sounding angry, remembering the Veteran's dictum: 'Never let the bastards think you're cowed, even if you're sodding terrified.'

The sunglasses duo ignored her, the one in front giving directions to the driver, the one next to her on the rear seat texting something. She wondered if she should elbow him and thump the one in front, then thought the better of it: they could easily overpower her.

At least neither of them seemed to be looking for a tail, which was something of a relief. She stayed still, tried to stop herself shivering despite the heat burning down on the vehicle. During the rhino conspiracy she'd been able to operate clandestinely: nobody had known about her role under the Veteran's tutelage until right at the end, when she'd suddenly, albeit briefly, emerged into the TV spotlight.

The taxi suddenly veered into a side street and pulled to a halt under guttural instructions from the passenger in front.

She was grabbed, pulled roughly out and bundled into the back of another BMW, one of the sunglasses duo driving, the other sitting menacingly next to her in the back, his Glock pointing right at her. 'Don't move,' he growled.

Slowing down to catch a glimpse as he passed by on the main road, the Corporal gave a running commentary into his hands-free phone, instructing his mate's car behind to edge slowly into the side street and follow the BMW. He would try to do the same from further back.

*

The recoveries had been pretty straightforward for the Oryx crew. Swooping back on top of the kopje to winch up the Sniper, then down on the ground to enable Mkhize to crouch low under the rotors and scamper on board.

Forward to find the trackers, spotting them easily, neither one resisting as they were lifted up and into the cabin with Mkhize's help. He bound their limbs with tourniquets to stem the bleeding, plastering their wounds with antiseptic cream, and giving them each an injection of antibiotics. Although the irony of ending up medically assisting the two charged with eliminating him was not lost on Mkhize, he pressed on without a word.

For the entire hour-and-a-half journey back to Swartkop Air Force Base, the Sniper sat away from them, back turned, wearing a balaclava, so they couldn't see his face. In the last couple of years, on various clandestine assignments rather like this, the Sniper had never been identified. He wanted to keep it that way, the two captured men wondering who he was, what had happened, whether he was the shooter, why his face was concealed.

Minister Yasmin was both relieved and worried.

Relieved at the success of the Oryx mission, relieved the Rooivalk had not been needed, but worried at the news about Thandi. She hoped her Corporal would sort it.

The priority now was to ensure that when they landed, the two prisoners were grabbed by her own people and taken to a safe house, not processed through the normal police and prosecutorial channels, which she couldn't be at all confident of.

She wanted them out of the way, didn't want them blabbing except to her own people, didn't want their capture and whereabouts to leak back to their masters – whomever they were. Probably Star's elite, she surmised.

Komal, meanwhile, decided to freelance. But first she phoned her husband to get his take on the situation. She found the Veteran frustrated and irritable at having to subcontract his role to Thandi and her. He was not exasperated with Komal, instead with his own disability, which severely hampered his mobility, not like the old days when he had been right in the thick of the struggle.

What exactly had Komal in mind? he asked testily.

She told him.

Silence at his end. But she had become used to that, used to him brooding, especially after he had been nearly killed by the shooting a while back.

Then he snapped out of it, his voice affectionate. 'Bloody good idea. But be careful. Very careful. They could "disappear" you with no problem. They don't know who you are, would simply see you as another nuisance to be eradicated.'

He retrieved the telephone number and name she wanted, insisted she kept in close touch, and told her to keep a constant look-out for surveillance. Star had eyes everywhere on his home patch — and she was right bang in the middle of it.

CHAPTER 8

Hardly had the Veteran ended the call to Komal, still worrying about her, than his phone rang again. Yasmin.

She said a car was coming to collect him, to drive him to an address she gave in Johannesburg's northern suburbs, with instructions to approach and call a number, then to enter through the guarded gates, which would be opened for him, without delaying, without alerting prying eyes.

'There's an Irishman I want you particularly to talk to. New IRA member, apparently. I'm not familiar with the detail, but we have had intelligence on him.'

'Irishman?' the Veteran exclaimed.

'Ja, mysterious. We need to know what he's doing here, who he's working for.'

She added, almost as if in passing: 'By the way, Isaac is safe, but Thandi has been seized. Hot-headed young lady! We both know what they are like, don't we!'

The Veteran, thinking of the young Yasmin and of his spirited feminist wife, guffawed – despite also worrying and feeling guilty about their young colleague, and Komal too, right there in the lion's den.

Thandi winced, outwardly defiant but privately terrified. She'd never been grabbed like this before, was now in their hands, despite knowing help was around, but not sure what it amounted to.

The BMW had been driven into a multistorey car park in the city, and she had been pulled out, trying to kick at her captors but failing, as she was shoved roughly into the back of a Toyota Avensis. It roared away past the parked cars, down the floors, screeching, scraping walls, Thandi closing her eyes. Then it paused, the driver stuck a card in at the exit, and it was away under the lifting barrier.

Inside the multistorey, one of the Corporal's cars followed. Outside the Corporal watched, noting the furious exit, following the Toyota from a distance, the car-switching ruse not fooling him for a second.

Thandi was driven into an apparently disused warehouse, its paint peeling, its windows broken, its atmosphere dark and dank. She was grabbed, dragged out of the car, hustled to a room that had lighting but no windows, dumped unceremoniously on a chair, her hands quickly bound behind.

They started pummelling her with questions. What was she doing? Who was manipulating her? What was she up to?

Thandi said nothing whatsoever, a tactic she'd learned from the Veteran a while back. If you start talking, your interrogators can lead you on. She simply stayed stum, staring fixedly ahead – which made her interrogators even more furious.

They were getting belligerent in their utter frustration, the sly one she'd found instantly revolting beginning to run his hand over her thighs, down between them, beginning to unbutton her blouse.

It took all Thandi's willpower not to scream, instead unleashing a torrent of invective that seemed to startle even him, and kicking out at his shins. He backed off, then circled to behind, roughly sliding his hand down from her neck towards her bra strap, unclipping it, starting to push both hands around to grab her breasts.

She was powerless in her terror. They had zeroed in on her vulnerability, her self-pride, her determination never to suffer the sexual abuse targeted at so many women. They didn't have to beat her. They just had to humiliate her.

Thandi drew a deep breath as the vile specimen started gleefully to taunt her, could smell his stinking breath, feel him slimily on her bare shoulders, could feel his oily hands creeping around, taking their time, making it agonising, his mates leering in anticipation of their turn.

Then he suddenly withdrew his hands, instead crouching down from behind and to her sides so she couldn't kick, reaching round and unbuckling her belt, unzipping and starting roughly to pull down her jeans, tearing at her panties.

There was nothing she could do. Just wait for her impending violation.

167

Wait for them to pleasure themselves on her, no doubt each in turn as she was bound helpless to the chair.

Desperately trying to conceal her terror, she summoned the foulest language she possibly could, telling them all they were pathetic sexual specimens, not proper men at all, couldn't love or cherish women, could only exploit powerless women because they were weak, weak, weak.

That landed a few blows, she could tell, almost mentally pushing them back.

They had her jeans and panties right off, tossed aside, crumpled on the floor, one yanking her right ankle, the other her left one, the third unbuckling his belt, readying himself.

In her utter desperation at impending defilement, Thandi strove hard to switch her mind to another of her heroes: 'Arch', as he was affectionately known.

Archbishop Desmond Tutu, Archbishop of Cape Town from 1986, the top position in the Anglican Church of Southern Africa, previously held by whites. Forced herself to recall the conversation she'd had with Komal about him back in Johannesburg. Thandi wasn't religious – she was probably an atheist, if she bothered to categorise herself – but was nevertheless inspired by him, remembered his remarkable story.

'His non-racialism was first imprinted by another cleric – a white one – Trevor Huddleston,' explained Komal. 'Under apartheid any whites venturing into black townships were security or government. But Father, later Archbishop, Huddleston had immersed himself in townships, treated inhabitants as people not servants. Almost unheard of.'

'So that had been formative for Arch?' Thandi had asked.

'Yes, cementing a special bond between the two, black and white, but also with other religions like my own Muslim faith – rather lapsed now,' said Komal. 'Arch marched alongside imams, rabbis, priests and vicars.'

'But isn't it amazing how progressive Arch was on all forms of discrimination, not just race, but also gender and sexual orientation? Pretty unique among African clerics of his generation, surely?'

'Yes, absolutely,' Komal replied. 'He tried to persuade the Church to ordain women; he also opposed exclusion of priests from the LGBTQIA community. "All were equal members of God's family" became Arch's creed.'

'I also love his impish camaraderie,' said Thandi, smiling. 'Remember when he became prominent in global Christendom and was a regular air

168

traveller even under apartheid – when it was pretty unheard of for any black person to be on a South African flight. If looks could kill he'd have been dead a thousand times, he used to say of the white passengers as he boarded a plane in Johannesburg or Cape Town.

'He was so cheeky! When asked what you needed to win the Nobel Peace Prize, he famously replied: "A short name like Tutu, a big nose and sexy legs."'

Even in her misery, Thandi couldn't help smiling, the recollection of the irrepressible Tutu lifting her.

'Yes,' Komal smiled. 'He was inspirational, always seemed to capture the moment so perfectly. Rouse a great audience to raucous excitement, or drop to a whisper, pausing, holding everyone in the palm of his hand. He cut through to everyone, revolutionary or ruler, poor or powerful.'

'Apartheid Cabinet ministers seemed almost cowed by him, didn't they?' Thandi asked.

'Yes,' Komal replied, a twinkle in her eye. 'They'd assassinated, tortured, jailed and banned critics, but they couldn't really do that to the Archbishop of Cape Town, known across the world. He was almost invincible.'

Thandi had nodded, responding: 'For me, Desmond Tutu equalled integrity. Remember when Winnie Mandela appeared before him at the Truth and Reconciliation Commission? Arch had been a friend, but was firm about her tragic descent from brave fighter for justice and victim of police oppression, into criminal complicity in murder. He was also firm with President De Klerk, wasn't he?'

'Definitely,' said Komal. 'De Klerk had released Mandela and nego-tiated his transition to the presidency, but refused to apologise for apartheid crimes committed on his watch. He stormed angrily out of the Commission after it had heard evidence of awful, bloodcurdling atrocities by apartheid security agents.'

Komal warmed to her theme: 'Soon after Mandela became president, when new ANC MPs accepted big salary increases, Arch quipped: "The government stopped the gravy train long enough to get on it."'

Thandi laughed. 'I love the way he spoke truth to power – whether to the old apartheid rulers or to the new post-apartheid ones. They all resented him, which was why we all respected him. I was too young then, but didn't he become a sort of custodian of the "rainbow nation"? Wasn't he critical of Mandela's successors? Thabo Mbeki for his shameful HIV-AIDS denialism, then Jacob Zuma for his shameless corruption?'

'Yes,' Komal replied, 'that's always been Arch's mission.'

How, Thandi, had wondered after their conversation, could her country rediscover its moral compass as a beacon for the triumph of hope over evil, for non-racialism over apartheid? How could it learn from Desmond Tutu and strive once again to emulate his values and mission?

Then – back to the present, with a jolt. Reminiscing about Tutu had been a comforting distraction. But she was about to be grievously violated – and could do absolutely nothing at all to prevent it.

The Tracker struck a deal, would talk – but only if he and his wife were promised to be securely flown to Namibia, back to his homeland and settled in a new house.

Otherwise he would say nothing, for he knew that to do so while remaining in the Bloemfontein area would be a sentence of death for him and misery for his wife.

His request was noted and passed up to Yasmin to consider. Meanwhile he stayed tight-lipped., His wounds had been medically treated;, he didn't know what lasting injury there'd be, but was made comfortable in a decent enough bedroom he knew not where, guessed somewhere in the Johannesburg region because the journey blindfolded from the airport hadn't been that long.

Komal's rendezvous with the Free State Parks CEO had been agreed by the two women to be the Pick n Pay hypermarket in Benade Drive, in the Fichardt Park suburb of Bloemfontein.

The receptionist in the modest hotel into which she had booked herself ordered a cab and it took her there through streets that could have done with being better cleaned – there was rubbish wafting about, plastic bags especially.

Plastic bags, thought Komal, the bane of Africa, abandoned everywhere and anywhere, dusty, windblown, uncared for – and lethal for the planet. So much to do, she sighed, peering out of the cab windows until the driver dropped her off.

Hungry, she'd resolved to get some eats in the hyper, picking up first the printed version of the *Daily Maverick*. This was an innovation for the online news outlet, and the sign for both women to identify each other at their scheduled meeting place, by the rack of Pinotage bottles amidst the very wide choice of wines Pick n Pay had to offer.

170

Komal wandered about the hyper, down aisles, up others, rows and rows of them, stacks of stuff, fresh food, tinned food, household cleaning material, fresh or frozen fish, fresh or frozen meat, the lot, masses of choice.

Her husband's advice ringing in her ears, she peered around her, hardly noticing the items, searching instead for any surveillance. There didn't seem to be any, as she drifted towards where she'd first spotted the wine aisles, passing busy shoppers, normal people, not like her, not like Thandi. Wondered whether she'd been rescued, worried about her.

Komal saw a well-dressed woman younger than her with a *Daily Maverick* paper protruding almost pointedly from the metal Pick n Pay basket like Komal's, hanging over her forearm. She was browsing the row of Pinotage choices, taking a Boschendal from a shelf, examining it, putting it back. Taking a Diemersfontein, doing the same. Taking a Beyerskloof, looking it over, then repeating the exercise.

Picky, any nearby shopper might have thought, very picky.

'My husband's favourite, the Pinotage grape,' Komal announced, sidling, stopping, and looking around.

There was nobody in sight, other than a whirl of people bustling, grabbing, some in a tearing hurry, frantic, others strolling dreamily. Some were smart and tidy, others were grubby and unkempt. All races and all types of people came to Pick n Pay.

Anybody taking any interest would have seen the two women near each other on a red-wine mission, wouldn't have heard the conversation unless catching inconsequential snatches brushing by, wouldn't have had the slightest inkling about the real purpose, wouldn't even have noticed after a few minutes them gliding apart, nodding politely, if formally, to each other as strangers might, as the strangers they had been did.

Wouldn't have known that in the briefest of encounters a plan had been hatched that left both with a spring in their stride.

Murphy was frustrated, confused, bereft and angry – all at once. He'd flown 10,000 kilometres, tasked as a shooter with his trusty Armalite – all for the £100,000 fee his group desperately needed, and he'd not even fired a shot, certainly not fulfilled his assignment.

Then he had been shot himself, out of the blue – must have been from the hillock ahead of them – when he'd been assured the killing

171

was straightforward, the target probably not even armed but had to be removed. Murphy would be back in his hotel room in time for bed.

And that was supposed to be just the first of several targets.

But now he hadn't the foggiest where he was: held in captivity, bound firmly to a chair, glowering at the Veteran, who had suddenly limped into the room, resting on a walking stick.

No introductions were necessary – Murphy knew exactly who he was. Or rather who he had *been* when deputed by Mandela to fly to Northern Ireland and talk to grass-roots Republicans like Murphy who were becoming disillusioned with their own leadership.

'Hi, think we might have met at that meeting in Newry?' the Veteran said, remembering the difficult encounter with the South Armagh Brigade nearly 30 years earlier at a venue in the town on the border with the Republic.

'So?' Irish snapped back, 'what the hell am I doing *here*? What the hell are *you* doing here?'

'That's what I'd like to chat about,' the Veteran replied, smiling, being as friendly as he could. 'I was asked to come, in case we knew each other.'

'So?' Still determined to give nothing away, Murphy scowled at the Veteran suspiciously, still not really sure what to make of his sudden appearance.

The Veteran tried to put him at ease, began to chat about that time when South Africa was in transition in the early 1990s, after Mandela and his fellow trialists arrested at Rivonia in 1964 had been released.

'You guys were also in transition, weren't you?' he added, remembering the bumpy period of talks and breakdowns, of fraught negotiations over IRA bombings that abruptly curtailed its ceasefires.

'But one of the hardest things for a politician to do is to reach out to a bitter opponent in the middle of a conflict,' the Veteran asserted, ignoring Murphy's protestations about 'sell-outs'.

'I remember that's exactly what John Hume did as leader of the Social Democratic and Labour Party when he talked, in secret to Gerry Adams, Sinn Fein president, while the Troubles were still raging on the island of Ireland.'

'The SDLP were always sell-outs, counter-revolutionaries,' Murphy said angrily.

'Hang on,' replied the Veteran, 'the SDLP was, and still is, committed to the reunification of the island. But by constitutional, democratic means.'

'So? And what did the SDLP actually achieve? Sod all!' Murphy retorted.

'That's not fair,' the Veteran replied. 'The SDLP showed a lot of courage. Sinn Féin and the ANC were both parties with military wings. We had links with you, but also with the SDLP. We talked to Unionist politicians when they would talk to us. You guys will never win if you are so sectarian.'

Ploughing on, the Veteran said: 'Anyway, my point is that John Hume, like Nelson Mandela, was a real leader of substance, prepared to be bold, to lead, not just to follow whatever might be popular with his rank and file at any one time. You will remember what became known as the "Hume–Adams" talks began in strict privacy in 1988. But then they were leaked to huge criticism form Unionists, who challenged Hume about his willingness to talk to "men of violence". Some in the SDLP, including Hume's deputy, Seamus Mallon, were also critical.'

'So was I. But with our Sinn Féin leaders. That's when the sell-out began,' interjected Murphy.

The Veteran smiled, speaking quietly, assertively rather than argumentatively, trying to get Murphy to engage. 'But John Hume and Gerry Adams both showed courage which resulted in the basis of an agreed approach – the "Hume–Adams proposals".'

'Yeah, though we never saw them; they were never set out in a document. That's what made IRA volunteers like me so suspicious, so frustrated,' Murphy countered.

The Veteran, determined not to get sidetracked, was sure from similar conversations with captured prisoners in the ANC camps in the 1980s that if he could keep Murphy engaged, he might garner some confidence from him.

'But you will remember the talks focused on the idea of "self-determination for the people" of the island, both in Northern Ireland and the Republic. The key was Britain accepting that citizens on both sides of the border should democratically decide their own political future. Which meant London had to be willing to accept the possibility of a united Ireland, if that was the democratic outcome. And Sinn Féin had to accept that the outcome would be decided in the ballot box, not by the bullet.'

'Yeah, our leaders were betraying the revolution, betraying Republican traditions!' Murphy shouted.

'That's your view. But my point is different,' said the Veteran, striving to avoid confrontation with Murphy, always to be cordial. 'My point is that Hume's parliamentarianism and Adams' paramilitarism were able to find a common way forward free of violence. That was historic. And it ultimately paved the way for first the 1995 Downing Street Declaration and then the 1998 Good Friday Agreement between the British and Irish governments.'

'Both sell-out agreements,' Murphy bridled again.

'From your standpoint, maybe,' said the Veteran. 'But an end to Catholics being the victims of massive discrimination over jobs, education and housing. It ended "the Protestant state for a Protestant people" era, didn't it?'

'It did,' Murphy conceded, 'I'll give you that. But we still had the Canary Wharf bombing in 1996, when the IRA detonated a powerful truck bomb in London's Docklands, killing two people and causing over a hundred and fifty million pounds' worth of damage. I know because I planted the bomb. We sent warnings ninety minutes beforehand, but they didn't fully evacuate the area. So not our fault two people were killed, and over a hundred were injured.'

Murphy smiled for the first time at the recollection.

'Yes, I remember that well,' the Veteran reminisced, 'I was Mandela's intelligence minister in government at the time and had briefings from MI6. During the anti-apartheid struggle MI6 were spying on us! But my point is different. John Hume and Gerry Adams were talking – even while the IRA continued to bomb – and that helped end all the horror.'

Then he paused. 'I need a cup of tea. Do you want one?'

Murphy nodded, having quite enjoyed the encounter. He was a little more relaxed, though still not sure where it was leading, or why it was happening, why the Veteran had suddenly appeared.

The first one towered above a helpless Thandi, trousers and underpants below his knees, exposing himself, aroused, and with a greedy smile of anticipation.

She was petrified – but not paralysed. She had resolved to kick out, to bang her knees together, to bite if there was anything to bite, to resist. There was no way she would submit without a fight. She'd fight, resist in whatever way she could, however pointless it might prove – for she knew that in the end they could overwhelm her, knew they could penetrate her, knew they could bloody her, knew they could hurt her badly. But she was fixated on making their task as difficult as she possibly could.

It wasn't only a matter of her own dignity – there was little left of *that*, exposed as she was and so utterly vulnerable. It was also that she felt impelled to strike back against all the men who thought they could do anything they liked to women.

She tried to wrestle her ankles free, tried to bang her knees together, but couldn't. Tried to wriggle. Couldn't either. Was bound too firmly, her wrists aching, her ankles, back and legs too.

Suddenly there was a piercing ringtone, the brute clutching at a phone now protruding out of his pocket, backing away, muttering, 'Yes, boss, of course, boss.'

He killed the call, scowling at her, penis subsiding to incongruous limpness, no longer weaponised, instead pathetic. He turned his back, bare bum bulging, muttering to his colleagues in Sesotho, which she couldn't really understand.

Their mood changed abruptly.

They let go and backed away from Thandi, morose, infuriated, frustrated, and – she thought – uncertain what the hell was happening. Just as she was, unable to comprehend why she might be spared the hell that was about to be forcibly inflicted on her.

Then, to her utter bewilderment, they scarpered – the lot of them, without a word, pulling up their trousers, fastening their belts, leaving her still bound to the chair, bare from her midriff down.

She was alone, tears of relief dribbling down her face, then gnawing uncertainty setting in, still feeling acutely vulnerable, feeling ashamed, defiled, exposed.

It was impossible for her to cover herself up, to preserve her dignity.

First elation, then utter miserable desolation.

The Corporal had been fretting frantically about Thandi.

She appeared to have been taken inside an abandoned building in what must have been an old industrial park, with telltale broken windows, rusty fencing and run-down appearance. He didn't want her to be hurt and could summon his men to bust her abductors quickly enough.

Yet he also deduced that, since she had become a minor public figure, Star would be wary of hurting her, still less of killing her. It was risky, he knew, and he fretted increasingly nervously as the minutes ticked by – soon twenty, then forty, then an hour.

Just as he was reaching for his phone to call in help, the Toyota Avensis he'd tailed after the car-park switch suddenly came screeching out, wheels spinning, tyres smoking. 'Follow it!' he barked into his phone, as he edged gingerly between the disused buildings, slowing to scan them left, right and straight ahead.

Nothing, not a dicky bird.

He turned around and drove slowly back, down a couple of side alleys. Still nothing, yet he was sure he had seen her hunched between two large men on the back seat of the departing vehicle as she had been on entering. Of course she could now be in the boot, or held down on the car floor, he worried.

Then he noticed a metal door slightly ajar. He hadn't spotted it driving past just earlier, but he could see it more clearly coming the other way, opening towards him.

The Corporal killed his engine and coasted to a halt, climbing silently out. He left the driver's door open so as not to make a noise shutting it, and retrieved his Z-88 pistol, a copy of the Italian Beretta 92F and the standard service weapon of the South African military, formerly of the police service too.

He slipped off the safety catch, ready to fire, and inched forward, out of the sunlight and into the dark interior, pausing to allow his eyes to adjust.

'Tell me, what it was like in the old days? You were from Crossmaglen, weren't you?' the Veteran asked, noting Murphy was a little less brittle.

'Yes, it was like living under constant siege – helicopters flying in to land at the local military base all through the night, soldiers taking over our gardens and our football pitches, breeding real hatred for the Brits.

'The army had to rebuild its Crossmaglen security force base after we had attacked it. In April 1994, I think it was, they sent in what they said was the biggest air-mobile operation since D-day – over a thousand soldiers and thousands of tonnes of building material arriving in long lorry convoys or being flown in. During the ten weeks of construction there were five major IRA attacks with mortar bombs.' Murphy smiled at the recollection.

'In those days the IRA had its own community intelligence network in South Armagh – local farmers who would keep a constant watch for Brit soldiers or spies. Every morning and at night-time they would scour their land, beat hedges and maintain a beady eye. Unless we told them to, they would never indicate to a soldier that he'd been spotted. They would simply clock them and report back to us. We knew the ground so well, there weren't many places soldiers could use for cover. Also, we were such tight-knit communities, undercover officers just couldn't pass for locals – they'd be spotted immediately, standing out like a sore thumb.'

Murphy chortled, more relaxed about the banter with the Veteran, though still suspicious where it was leading.

Thandi had stopped trying to free herself, had wrestled with the rope binding her, wriggling and wobbling the chair. She sought to reach her clothes with her feet but couldn't, and began to hurt herself. She realised that Yasmin's people couldn't be too far away.

She had to admit defeat and sat there, lower half naked, wondering about toppling the chair over but concluding that it wouldn't really help.

So she did the next best thing, screaming 'Help! Help!'

It sounded pitiable.

So she tried to summon determination, tried again to displace her mind-set, searched for inspiration from her heroes, the Robben Islanders.

Remembered the words of Ahmed Kathrada opening the new museum on the island in September 1997, saying it was meant to express 'the triumph of the human spirit against the forces of evil; a triumph of freedom and human dignity over repression and humiliation; a triumph of wisdom and largeness of spirit against small minds and pettiness . . .'

Thought of Nelson Mandela saying on the same occasion that in the colonial and apartheid past, most people had little or no say in the depiction of their history in textbooks, libraries or research institutions: 'Our museums and the heritage sector as a whole are being restructured.' Robben Island Museum would forever remind South Africans that 'today's unity is a triumph over yesterday's division and conflict'.

She remembered also what Mandela had said on another occasion in 2001, with his characteristic frankness: 'Little did we suspect that our own people, when they got a chance, would be as corrupt as the apartheid regime. That is one of the things that has really hurt us.'

He'd identified what was happening, foreseen what could happen unless the ANC acted to stop it. And it hadn't, instead opening the door to state capture by the Former President and his buddies, the Business Brothers. And now, as a direct consequence, she was bound to a chair, awaiting her fate.

Thandi refused to be cowed, and drew strength from those struggle giants. She had once pledged to herself that she would never be beaten, never be subjugated by anyone, not even half naked and seemingly helpless as she was now.

As she tried to distract herself, she thought of her granny. She reached for another memory, one of the stories the ailing matriarch had told her, perhaps the most searing of all her reminiscences to the teenage granddaughter.

'He was so brave, so very brave, right to the very end. I remember him well from visiting the family. He was friendly, always chatted to me as an equal, not as a servant, played with the children, took the two boys for fast drives in his new car, thrilling them by screeching around sharp corners on the open road. He was a teacher and a white activist.

'Then he was arrested, tortured and sentenced to hang by the neck – the only white in the freedom struggle; over a hundred black activists were also hanged. I went with the family to the funeral, and I was told what had happened at the gallows at Pretoria Central Prison.

'How he had been escorted up the fifty steps to the hanging, a priest at his side, even though he was an atheist. The hangman was waiting for him, just another statistic among the one thousand five hundred hangings in a long hanging career.

'The hangman tied his wrists behind his back, and fixed the rope around his neck, knotting it next to one ear, then fastened a hood over his face.'

The old lady started to sob, Thandi uncertain what to do, holding her hand tight, handing her a tissue to wipe her eyes then blow her nose, before she continued.

'He started singing the freedom song "We Shall Overcome" as the hangman pulled the lever, crashing him down through the trapdoors, the rope breaking his neck, leaving a deep rope burn. They said his brain almost burst with the shock and his bowels and bladder emptied all over the floor.

'Then he was left to hang for fifteen minutes, all the blood was washed off with a hose and he was lifted into his coffin.'

By now Thandi was crying too, as she had also done listening to her granny all those years ago, crying about the memory, and also crying about herself.

She pulled herself back to the present.

'Help! Help!' she shouted again.

Her voice was too shrill, she thought, feeling embarrassed.

Silence. Nothing.

Then, what seemed like an age later, but was probably only five or ten minutes, maybe the faintest scrape.

Could be the wind.

Could be a rat.

Could be something else.

Thandi shivered – and waited.

The Corporal heard her, checked, then crept forward. He didn't want to rush, didn't want to stumble into any of her captors still there.

He heard some scratching, scuffing, rubbing, getting louder as he moved slowly forward, his Z–88 revolver gripped in both hands, pointing forward. He wished he had some other eyes and ears to cover him, and wondered what was ahead.

Pure anti-climax. He peeked around a corner – and saw the figure in the gloom, on a chair, wriggling.

Looked about for others. Was it a trap? Couldn't see anybody else. Stayed still, looking, crouching.

'Thandi,' he called quietly, 'are you alone?'

The voice startled her and she stopped twisting, listened. Had she made it up?

He said it again.

'I'm alone, tied up, they've all suddenly gone . . . they tried to rape me, I am half undressed.'

The Corporal emerged from the shadows, stepping slowly forward, still looking around in case there was a twist.

Embarrassed by her pulled–down jeans and panties, he tried to look away. He pushed them over to her and moved behind to untie her quickly. Thandi hastily pulled up her panties and jeans, and blurted out a 'thank you'. She got up stiffly, rubbing her wrists and her hips, feeling desolate at the way they had penetrated her defences – and almost her body.

She knew she shouldn't be ashamed, because she'd been the victim, but her near-violation left her vulnerable and deeply embarrassed. She

179

felt dirty, shuddering at the creepy way they'd felt her, at the gleeful way they'd contemplated raping her.

At the same time, she felt angry and determined to get the bastards.

'Thank you so much,' she said, pulling herself together, wanting to give the Corporal a peck on the cheek and a small hug.

Couldn't bring herself to, still felt so defiled, didn't want to be touched by anyone.

He seemed to sense her vulnerability, had momentarily imagined what his own wife might have felt, so kept it formal, quickly moved on, motioning her to follow.

Thandi crept out, wondering if it was a trap to catch the Corporal too.

CHAPTER 9

Star was worried. It was getting on for ten hours and he had heard nothing.

He'd only heard the girl had been captured, but they'd got nothing from her. Told them to get out, to leave her alone. Told them he didn't want her harmed on his patch. Told them she was too well known.

He was vexed by news of a shoot-out at the airport, somebody taking pot shots at his guys in their car – unheard of in his fiefdom. He had enough scandals on his hands already, local ones he could manage – make people disappear or at least button up their mouths. But hurting this girl would bring the security minister down on him like a ton of bricks, and he was getting enough aggravation from her already. He would deal with the girl in another way, get her at her home in KwaZulu-Natal – he had many allies there and he would not be implicated.

He turned his mind to the major problem confronting him. No report-back, no calls at all; he'd expected to have heard news by now of the Zulu ranger, of his elimination. Was used to his orders not only being obeyed but delivered in full.

He barked out instructions. *Find out. Get back. Soon.*

Then there was another problem: the threats against both him and his allies of corruption prosecutions – a blatant attempt to prevent them mounting a challenge to the President, he considered.

The battle within the top echelons of the ANC was hotting up and his faction had to win it or face demotion, maybe even arrest, imprisonment and (even more important) loss of income.

What Star couldn't for the life of him understand was *why* his circle was being hounded – except for factional motives, of course; he never for a moment felt any guilt at their looting.

What was wrong with senior ANC figures, including ministers, helping themselves to some of the largesse the white apartheiders had enjoyed for decades? What was wrong with ministers running businesses contracted to their own departments? This sort of 'radical economic transformation' should be the name of the game, surely?

Star resolved to double down – and at the same time to begin putting in place the extra project he now envisaged: one that would be truly seismic if it came off, as he was confident it would do.

For Komal it brought back childhood memories of crouching in the dark, dusty, noisy interior of her grandad's boot as his car trundled along bumpy tracks off the main road.

Lots of delighted shrieks from her and her small cousins, several of them, all jammed in together enjoying an adventure, to the disapproval of their parents, who nevertheless indulged their grandad in his bit of fun with them all – provided the journeys were strictly off-road, short and slow.

But that nostalgia went way back, nearly sixty years ago. Now she was cramped and curled up, aching in the Free State CEO's car boot, rushing along some main road, she knew not where, only the destination, wondering what lay in store for her, whether Yasmin would approve. Probably not – but Thandi certainly would, if she was safe. If.

Komal, nothing if not determined, remained anxious. She'd never pretended to be a hardened combatant, more backroom than front line in the struggle days, yet now had the Makarov poking into her ribs inside the raincoat she wore.

Thandi was driven on the long journey straight back to Joburg. No flight this time, no record of her departure or her destination.

As far as the airlines were concerned, she had arrived, and either stayed or disappeared. Exactly what Minister Yasmin wanted.

But as she stared out of the car window, Thandi had tears welling up in sheer relief that her Isaac had been saved. Didn't know the details. Just that he was in Joburg, and she was hoping to see him when she got there.

The personal trauma she had suffered was still haunting. She still felt unclean. She tried to shake it off, tried to make sense of what had happened to her, wondered what exactly was going on in the Free State? What was Star really up to? What would he do next?

Thandi had no answers as she tossed the conundrum round and round in her mind, occasionally distracted by scrolling on her phone. It was humming again after her captors had switched it off.

One item caught her eye as the road stretched out seemingly end-lessly, wide-open plains swishing by. Anton Lubowski, a prominent anti-apartheid activist from the 1980s, a key figure in Namibia's fight for independence, had been cruelly assassinated by the apartheid security forces in September 1989 while he was still young, only in his thirties, his daughter Nadia just nine years old.

Now about forty, Nadia had arranged an annual lecture by prominent figures to commemorate him at Stellenbosch University.

The lecturer explained how the assassination had deprived both Namibia and South Africa of a hugely talented and courageous figure, cut down so painfully a matter of weeks before the release of Nelson Mandela's mentor Walter Sisulu and fellow ANC leadership comrades in October 1989, so that he neither witnessed nor participated in the defeat of apartheid.

During that four-year process, Thandi read, from Mandela's release to his being elected president, more people had been killed by the apartheid state and its proxies than at any time during the previous four decades.

The lecturer asserted that too many people took for granted that Mandela had walked free from prison, took for granted that apartheid had eventually been vanquished, but reminded everyone that the struggle was long and bitter, taking nearly one hundred years from the days when, under British colonial rule, the roots of apartheid were established.

Protests to stop whites-only Springbok rugby tours from 1969 to the early 1980s provoked fierce anger, especially in Britain, New Zealand and Australia, with one British activist branded in the South African media 'Public Enemy Number One'. Demands for international trade, economic and arms sanctions were fiercely resisted, prominent anti-apartheid activists assassinated.

Sadly, Thandi reflected, those who fought for great causes, from slavery abolitionists to suffragettes and anti-apartheid campaigners, seemed always to be unpopular at the very time they most needed support – only to be glorified, some even sanctified, once they had triumphed.

Mandela may have been feted in Washington and London after his release, but the majority in the British Parliament and the US Congress – and their governments of the day – opposed him and the ANC's freedom struggle for almost the entire period he was imprisoned, Margaret Thatcher notoriously denouncing him as a 'terrorist'.

Thandi was determined to awaken her generation of 'born frees' – young people like herself who had never lived under apartheid. But she knew only too well, because she was part of it, that South Africa was now involved in another struggle – to free itself from corruption and cronyism.

She looked out of the window, Johannesburg's tallest buildings appearing on the horizon, the Hillbrow telecom tower above them all.

Soon she hoped to be reunited with Mkhize. Elated at the prospect, Thandi also began to shiver at the flashback horror of her near-violation and how he would respond when, *if,* she told him all about it.

Piet van der Merwe's partner, Peggy, was engrossed in the description of a holiday she fancied – an all-inclusive luxury voyage combined with enticing-looking experiences at Victoria Falls and a Big Five safari.

It wasn't cheap, but then her newish man had just received a fat fee for a project she hadn't quizzed him about because he'd advised her not to do so.

When he'd said that, she'd been irritated initially, then accepted when he'd told her they might be able to go to about R60,000 each for a holiday.

She examined the small print – what was included, what wasn't – because the biggest attraction was the twelve-night luxury cruise from Cape Town to Port Elizabeth, Maputo, Durban and back to Cape Town.

Then the doorbell brought her back down to earth, frowning, for she wasn't expecting anybody.

She made for the front door, warily looking through the peephole for any threat. Curious: a black woman with a toddler in her arms? Peggy opened it gingerly, noting that the woman, quite slim with an attractive face, looked uncomfortable.

'Sorry,' she stammered, 'is Mr Van der Merwe in please, madam?'

'No, he's out,' Peggy replied rather brusquely, adding in a softer tone, 'Can I help?'

The woman looked embarrassed, the little boy, quite a pleasant chirpy face, maybe of mixed race, Peggy surmised.

'My name is Jo-Jo. I used to work for Mr Van der Merwe, caring for his wife,' she said, looking down shyly at her worn-out sandals, adding 'He was a good man.'

'Oh, is there a problem?' Peggy said a little tersely, checking herself.

'Well, yes, I need to speak to him.' She stood there, expectantly, the little boy getting restless, wanting to be put down.

There was something about the toddler Peggy couldn't quite place: was it the way he smiled? 'Can I have your cellphone number please?' she asked. 'I'll get a pen and paper.'

Jo-Jo wrote it down, looking dejected, almost as if she might cry. 'But I had hoped to see him. Can we wait, please?'

Peggy felt sorry for her but was peeved at being disturbed. 'All right, then,' she said reluctantly, 'come around to the back door, your boy can play in the garden.'

She didn't want her white neighbours to start gossiping, for the nearby houses were full of nosy and bored retirees.

Murphy found himself enjoying the argument with the Veteran: they had much in common in their hinterlands, even if so much divided them now.

The Veteran was chatting about how he had joined first the ANC, out of frustration and desperation, after the government had banned it and the movement had gone underground. He had been recruited to its armed wing, MK.

'So that's me. How did you get involved?' the Veteran asked almost casually, trying to draw Murphy in.

'I started feeling uneasy with the Provisional IRA in the early 1990s, when the people at the top seemed to me more concerned with furthering their own agenda than they were with following a real Republican agenda.

'When Provo leaders like Gerry Adams and Martin McGuinness called me a "dissident", to me it was a badge of honour. What mattered more than anything to me was the continuation of the armed struggle itself, and those two leaders were stopping us doing that.'

The car stopped, the CEO jumping out and unlocking the imposing gates to Regeneration Park. The bored security staff had been alerted to her arrival – a routine visit, nothing to bother their real boss about, for the CEO was back and forth all the time.

They had Mkhize's GPS coordinates and drove to the spot where he'd photographed the grotesquely lifeless elephant carcasses. Komal was now out of the boot and in the passenger seat.

Nothing to be seen. They double-checked the GPS coordinates, but their positioning was correct. Still nothing.

Komal had her Makarov ready, safety catch off, and the CEO her rifle. They walked about, searching, perplexed, cicadas in a frenzy, the bush otherwise eerily still.

Then Komal spotted some fresh vehicle tracks. Seemed to be thick tyres, heavily indented, like a tractor – maybe a digger?

Suddenly she realised.

Soil on the surface of an area the size of a couple of rugby pitches was freshly turned over, maybe had been dug, for there were fresh tyre tracks.

The two women looked at each other, hardly saying a word, not needing even to confer about their next step: get out – and fast. Komal quickly climbed back into the boot for her uneasy return trip.

Murphy described himself as a 'traditional Republican'.

An odd label, thought the Veteran. As the two talked, Murphy seemed more to him like a 'fundamentalist Republican'. And their faction had never advanced the cause of Irish reunification in a way the sophisticated Gerry Adams/Martin McGuinness strategy undoubtedly had.

'Surely we all have to agree, the Irish border has become invisible partly because of Adams/McGuinness, because of the Good Friday Agreement and the end of the IRA's military campaign?' the Veteran asked.

'But the north and south are not one country!' said Murphy.

'Okay, but look at the practicalities,' the Veteran countered. 'To all intents and purposes the island of Ireland is becoming one entity, despite the two separate jurisdictions. The border is completely open and almost non-existent today, isn't it? Tens of thousands of people live on one side and work on the other. Farms straddle it. Often you've no idea which jurisdiction you're in along its length, with its multiple crossing points. Surely that's a massive advance from the years of armed security and watchtowers straddling the border?'

'Yes, of course,' Murphy conceded, irritated now, 'but we are still not one country, are we? And that is what Republicans have sacrificed so much for.'

The Veteran continued: 'But companies trade without restriction over the border. People cross the border in both directions to go to schools and colleges and hospitals, or to get treatment from doctors and pick up prescriptions. There are common standards over food safety and farming, shared cancer care and blood transfusions, shared gas and electricity supplies.'

Murphy gave a supercilious sneer: 'Sinn Féin's acceptance of the consent principle was a major departure from our entire history as Republicans. They have sold us out.'

The Veteran, smiling – which infuriated Murphy even more – continued: 'Instead of your impossibilism, for the first time in the history of the IRA there is a practical, achievable route to Irish reunification through the Good Friday Agreement. Yes, of course it rests upon democratic consent. And rightly so. You have to persuade enough Unionists to your point of view, not continue trying to bomb and shoot them into accepting your stance over their future.

'Yours is an absolutist, purist Republicanism,' the Veteran continued. 'It's also a failed Republicanism and in my view always will be.'

Then he was even blunter. 'Your politics is like the fundamentalism of the global Islamist groups like al-Qaeda or ISIS: sole inheritors of the "creed", the ones who pronounce who is a pure believer and who is an infidel who must be beheaded, including other Muslims but of the Shia rather than their own Sunni faith.'

That riled Murphy. 'Don't you dare compare me with zealots like ISIS!' he fulminated.

'But the Brits are still running the show,' Murphy went on. 'MI5 are still headquartered outside Belfast. Their huge new building was built in 2007 – the very same year when your beloved Sinn Féin went into bed with Ian Paisley's Democratic Unionists in the British-negotiated puppet self-government at Stormont.'

The Veteran shook his head, resigned at what was becoming a pointless dialogue of the deaf. He knew full well that Murphy's IRA splinter group was small and isolated in Republican-supporting communities. That it enjoyed nil support on Capitol Hill, where US Congress members, backed by the large and influential Irish-American community, had granted Sinn Féin leaders Gerry Adams and Martin McGuinness the quasi-hero status of freedom fighters from the 1980s onwards.

The Veteran knew too, from his days as an intelligence minister under presidents Mandela and Mbeki, that the New IRA, like other 'dissident' Republican groups, was also heavily infiltrated by British and Irish intelligence agents – and infested with criminality, including drug trafficking, to fund their activity.

187

That also, however, they came from a long trajectory of Irish Republicanism going back to the 1860s, with deep-seated fears of 'sell-out' and 'betrayal'. That for those factions, Irish Republicanism was always 'unfinished business'.

What would actually constitute 'finished business' for these groups, the Veteran wondered, staring at Murphy, who was slumped, smirking, in the chair to which he was bound? For them, conflict and 'the struggle' – either with the Brits or with each other – seemed to be an end in itself.

It was a shame, because the guy was intelligent, politically quite well-read and might even have good traits, given half a chance. The Veteran had witnessed, during the liberation struggle, activists of a similar ilk to Murphy in the ANC's armed wing.

But he was tiring. Turning to limp out on his stick, he called ominously over his shoulder: 'I'll be back.'

Irish remained slumped, his rage tempered only just a little by the residual awe in which, at least before this encounter, he had long held the Veteran for his legendary role in the ANC's underground campaign.

The Veteran limped back from confronting Murphy, feeling completely washed up, slumping on a sofa, short of breath, perspiring heavily.

He could just imagine Komal scolding him, saying, 'You cannot keep doing these things in the way you used to! Delegate to me, to Thandi, to others. Keep your powder dry. Preserve your energy so you can deploy your abilities better. Stop trying to micromanage everything.'

But after a snack followed by a snooze, he hobbled back into the room, intending deliberately to needle Murphy into making a revelation.

'Call yourself a revolutionary and you end up as a shooter for a corrupt elite,' he chided.

Murphy bridled, his temper rising. 'I am supporting the group which wants "radical economic transformation", not you sell-outs!' he shouted.

Aah, thought the Veteran, confirmation of what he suspected, even though Irish didn't seem to notice. It was the slogan of Star, the Former President and their corrupt but large ANC faction.

'The problem with sectarian guys like you,' the Veteran chided, 'is it's always the individuals or groups nearest to you politically that become your enemy, rather than your real opponents. It's a problem, especially on the left of politics.'

'The problem with sell-outs like you,' Irish bristled, 'is you get co-opted into a new establishment and forget your roots.'

The Veteran ignored him. 'Let me give you a history lesson,' he said instead, deliberately adopting a patronising tone.

'Sod off,' Irish replied, but the Veteran ignored him and started to talk anyway. Irish would simply have to hear him out, even while trying not to listen.

'Under apartheid, government and big business was run by whites only for whites only. But when Mandela and our ANC leadership began negotiating a transition from apartheid, they were fearful white businesses and the vital skills they had monopolised would flee abroad and investors would be frightened off.

'So we struck a compromise for the sake of a peaceful and economically stable transition. A black majority to run the government through democratic election, but the white minority still to run the economy.'

'That's my point!' Irish countered. 'A pact with the devil!' He'd been provoked to engage, to the Veteran's quiet satisfaction.

'What was the alternative?' replied the Veteran. 'How could we have done anything else? South Africa was on a knife-edge, the economy crashing. A revolutionary strategy by the ANC would have triggered a horrendous civil war, flight of wealth, financial calamity and political turmoil.'

'So you caved in!' Irish smirked.

The Veteran pretended not to notice: 'Just look what happened in Mozambique and Angola – civil wars for decades, peppered with landmines, infrastructure destroyed, economic chaos. Those were non-negotiated transformations. If we had followed suit, there would have been violence and mayhem. We had rising, irresistible people power. But they had the army, the security forces of a brutal state. They also had the global centres of finance and investment behind them.'

The Veteran could sense Irish was listening closely now, even if refusing to look at him. 'Leninist insurrections have not had a happy outcome; in the old Soviet Union, China or Latin America, one-party state dictatorship, economic failure and rampant corruption.'

Murphy was silent, couldn't think of a rejoinder.

So the Veteran appeared to offer an olive branch. 'We have a new black business elite, even some black billionaires, and a large and growing new black middle class. But we haven't stopped inequality increasing as it has throughout the world.'

The Veteran paused, inviting for a response, Irish still looking resolutely at the wall, not at him.

Silence. The seductive lure of silence, deliberately deployed.

Irish gave in first, muttering: 'So you admit it! You haven't delivered for the masses!'

'Not true!' the Veteran replied. 'We have abolished apartheid. We have greater protection of human rights than any other constitution in the world. Black school attendance has doubled, black university students are up tenfold. Millions more have housing, electricity, running water.'

'So what?!' Irish barked back.

The Veteran had him. 'So what? So what! All your revolutionary rhetoric and you are blinded to the betterment in people's lives. Nothing like enough, of course. But still much, much better for millions.'

He paused, then went for the jugular. 'As for *you*! Your paymasters are the new corrupt elite, aren't they? The preachers of "radical economic transformation" – for themselves *alone*. A leftist slogan opportunistically grabbed to justify their rampant looting, repeatedly used by Star as they call him.'

The Veteran let that hang for a moment. Then said ruthlessly: 'Your paymasters are gangsters robbing the people to enrich themselves and you're their gun-for-hire! Star's very own Irishman. What a bold Republican revolutionary you are!'

It was as if Irish had had a red–hot poker thrust into his underbelly. He exploded with foul invective.

But never once denied the charge, noted the Veteran. Mission accomplished. Job done.

Saying nothing, he got up and shuffled out again, leaving Irish to stew. He never came back, was driven home to rest, called Yasmin on the way to confirm what Irish had admitted. Wondered and worried about Komal, didn't like being the passive partner confined to barracks, yearned after the action.

The car was still on its way when his phone rang, with Komal's number flickering in the encroaching gloom of the evening. He grabbed it hungrily, listening intently.

She was safe, on her way home, with lots to report.

Utter relief for the Veteran, who felt tears welling, emotion engulfing him – he must be getting past it, too old for this sort of thing, becoming a softie.

It was one thing over three decades ago despatching enthusiastic young cadres over the borders, sometimes going with them, sometimes losing them to waiting security forces. It was quite another subcontracting danger to those women closest to him: his wife, whom he loved; his protégé, whom he cherished. Both had to carry on the struggle in ways he couldn't, seemingly a never-ending battle.

The Veteran closed his eyes for the remainder of the journey home.

Minister Yasmin took the call from Komal, listening carefully, saying little, reflecting hard.

'Sure you were in the right spot?'

'Absolutely.'

'So they must have buried the carcasses?'

'Must have.'

'And the tusks will be on the move, maybe out of the country already?' Yasmin asked rhetorically, thinking hard about the usual route – out of South Africa, probably for this size of tusk consignment on board a ship disguised as some other consignment, but maybe in smaller batches by air, to China for processing and export, mostly to the rest of Asia.

And not much she could do about it now. Too bloody late.

CHAPTER 10

Van der Merwe was taking no chances after being outed the last time during the rhino conspiracy.

Most uncomfortable it had been, meant he'd had to lie low for a while, let out his Johannesburg house and move in with Peggy in Pretoria. It was very convenient that they'd found each other; blissful, in fact.

Just one matter that needed explaining. He'd arrived back, giving Peggy a big hug and a smoochy kiss, only to find she was gesticulating over her shoulder at Jo-Jo and the boy, as if to say, 'What the hell's this all about, then?'

He went over to them, Peggy watching like a hawk as he picked up the toddler and hugged him affectionately, warmly greeting Jo-Jo.

'They are friends from my old home,' Van der Merwe called over his shoulder. 'I'll explain later.'

Which he would do after they had left, Jo-Jo meanwhile confiding all in a rush and embarrassed that she was finding it hard to cope. Caring for the child meant she couldn't get a full-time job and needed additional support from him.

Even though he had long known he would have to spill the beans to Peggy at some point, Van der Merwe had dreaded having the conversation, feared she might throw him out in disgrace.

But to his immense relief, although shocked, she didn't berate him, was matter-of-fact about it all, seemed instinctively to empathise – as long as nothing like that ever happened again, or he would be out on his ear.

His secret would remain with her alone. It was their past apart, and they were the future together, needed each other as they grew older in pragmatic mutual dependence.

*

Bob Richards took the WhatsApp call from the Veteran early – very early as pre-arranged, because at that time of the year South Africa was two hours ahead.

It was 05.45 and dark outside, would be for a while yet as London slowly came to life. Cleaners and refuse workers had long been out, and in an hour, alarms for metropolis office workers would begin ringing; they would come tumbling out of bed, straight into showers, grabbing coffees, shoving snacks down their throats, rushing for trains, underground or overground, cramming like sardines into commuter carriages, sweaty in summer, breathy in winter, women with blokes pressed right up against them, mostly inadvertently, sometimes not.

An early riser always, Richards had a routine. A glass of pure aloe juice sweetened with a dose of pure cranberry – otherwise hard to drink raw – but always his first liquid upon waking up; it was expensive but, he believed, a big boost to his immune system. Then a cup of organic rooibos; he never poured boiling water into it, first letting the kettle settle a bit, enabling the caffeine-free tea to infuse for at least five minutes to get the full value of the antioxidants.

He didn't drink coffee, didn't get that kick to start the day like millions, maybe billions, of other caffeine addicts. Tried to get into the local gym for however long he had, sometimes only ten minutes, sometimes a full hour; in his fifties he wasn't a gym hero but tried to keep as fit as he could in between the red wine and the real ale.

He took the call at the agreed time: 06.00 London, 08.00 Joburg.

It was the Veteran's number on his screen, but it wasn't the Veteran.

'Hi,' Komal said, 'sorry, he's struggling a bit this morning – sometimes happens when his injury is sharp as he wakes up. He had a bad night, as is often the case these days, but he won't be long.'

She filled Richards in on Jayne Joseph, on the Free State developments, updated him on Thandi, gave him a taster on what had happened to Isaac, said he had a request.

Richards' interest quickened. He loved a bit of adrenaline-injecting action, making a difference where he could – which in recent years seemed to have been on his old anti-apartheid stamping ground, South Africa.

His parents, prominent British Anti-Apartheid Movement figures, had sadly passed recently, one after the other. They had been inseparable, his dad expiring soon after his mum died. They'd been compatriots of the Veteran and Richards had sort of taken on their mantle.

193

Komal continued to brief Richards, and he was impressed. He hadn't had much of an opportunity to get to know her but was broadly aware of her own anti-apartheid hinterland and her journalistic professionalism, though she was younger than the Veteran, nearer to his own age, he surmised.

'Here is the old codger, better late than never,' she said playfully, handing over the phone.

'Can't get the wives these days,' the Veteran announced, chortling, Richards hearing Komal playfully chiding him in the background.

'Watch yourself, comrade!' Richards replied, always enjoying the sometimes deliberately provocative, politically incorrect, banter in which the Veteran specialised but was never serious about. Had either of them meant it they would have been unceremoniously ejected from their marriages by their wives.

They quickly got down to business, the Veteran briefing him on what he wanted the MP to do. If he wouldn't mind.

Of course not, Richards replied, would be delighted. The news was in its way as startling as what he'd first exposed under parliamentary privilege, information fed to him by the Veteran or Thandi.

There was also, the Veteran explained, a possible second or third instalment, as there was a money-laundering side to the conspiracy they were trying to unravel.

And, Richards was shocked to hear, Thandi had been abducted, but they had found her, she was safe now. He remembered meeting the impressive, intense and vibrant young woman.

In his own mind he wasn't the villain, the media's manufacture of a mafioso chief of a gangster state. He was 'Star' – the name his followers and friends had given him since his youthful days of footballing prowess.

A box-to-box midfielder, shielding and supporting his defenders one minute, driving through the next. Playing one-twos to leave opponents frozen, bewildered by his vision, 360 degrees, eyes continuously swivelling, uncannily aware of players to either side, behind, forward. A little dink over an opponent allowing a striker to dart through into space, collect his perfectly timed pass and create havoc.

He only very rarely scored himself but was the conductor-in-chief of the team, revered for both his sporting ingenuity and his never-give-up willpower.

Some of that industry he'd brought to his political career, but not the artistry. Some of that strategic vision he'd brought too, but not the care, always helping teammates out if they'd made an error or been caught by an opponent.

These times, he'd become the captain, not the comrade, feared rather than liked, attracting fierce loyalty from acolytes for only what it brought them.

Star had evolved from midfield maestro to consummate commander, enriching not just himself and his family but also his supporters, some of the closest around him evolving in tandem to become his enforcers.

But they too didn't for a moment consider themselves malevolent or selfish. They were the people acting for the people by utilising their power to stay in power. Because they had been chosen by the people, they had to enforce the people's will as they defined it for themselves.

'Radical economic transformation' they chanted. And all fiercely believed they were the repositories of the ANC faith. Critics called them 'gangsters', but gangsters weren't ever elected like *they* had been. Never mind the way they used the dark arts to stay in power and entrench that by spreading largesse and position to their followers, some in desperate circumstances after the transformation.

One day freedom fighters with minimal remuneration but mutual support, next day MP or councillor with status and salary, their extended families looking for sustenance and reward. But there were too many mouths to feed, jobs to find. So they kept taking advantage of their new roles to get maximum handouts and leg-ups.

All these clever blacks and moany whites simply didn't understand, Star ruefully reflected. But, no matter, it had always been him against the odds, hadn't it? Wasn't that the *real* story of his life? Had to look after himself first and foremost – because nobody else would or ever had.

Bob Richards stood to speak, clearly and slowly, in the Grand Committee Room, which was up the stone steps and to the side within Westminster Hall.

On the main floor below was a public exhibition commemorating the suffragettes. One of them, Emily Wilding-Davison, had a plaque in her memory on the wall alongside the Chapel of St Mary Undercroft crypt, off Westminster Hall. There, in a protest for votes for women, she had locked herself inside a cupboard on census night 1911, her

195

census form recording her postal address as 'Found hiding in crypt of Westminster Hall.'

Richards, when escorting visitors from his parliamentary constituency or friends around Parliament, always asked the police officer up the stairs from Westminster Hall near St Stephen's entrance to unlock the door to the chapel, so he could show them the plaque that had been installed after pressure from Tony Benn, who'd nailed his own plaque to a wall but been rebuffed by the parliamentary authorities as defacing a World Heritage Site.

He had secured an adjournment debate, during which MPs are allowed to raise any issue, a row of journalists he had pre-briefed unusually in attendance: normally, the stenographers for the official report on Parliament's proceedings, Hansard, were the only ones joining any MPs participating in debates. But, after his previous explosive interventions, the media had been immediately interested once alerted by Richards.

The speech he had emailed to reporters, strictly embargoed until he sat down after delivering it. The text had been drafted by Jayne and Thandi, Komal with her journalist skills sub-editing it, and the Veteran checking it over.

Richards began by explaining the context: rampant corruption and cronyism organised by the premier of the Free State, the ripping off of virtually every public contract, the violence underpinning it. He attributed the shooting of Councillor Edwin Kubeka and the murder of Jacob Kubeka directly to Star's henchmen, knowing that this could be quoted in the South African and UK media without any legal comeback, as he was speaking under parliamentary privilege.

Then he came to the even more dramatic part.

He had the digital photos Mkhize had taken of the elephant herd, horrifically spread-eagled, tusks removed, splayed on their sides, with signs of scavengers, one with vultures already pecking away ravenously.

These he had pre-released to the media, along with the embargoed text of his speech, explaining the location and the context.

'So what brave activists have discovered, risking their own lives, is a grotesque and heartless conspiracy.

'First to get a twenty-five-million-pound government grant to build a wildlife park at Vryburg, a small, poverty-stricken town in one of South

Africa's poorest provinces, with massive unemployment, which would have created over a hundred new jobs, most for local people, many trained with new skills.

'Then to spend just a fraction of that taxpayers' money on this project, bringing in a herd of elephants. And, most brazen of all, perhaps, to organise a poacher attack to poison the elephants with cyanide, killing them all and stealing their tusks to be smuggled out and sold, at an extra profit. The great bulk of the public grant hasn't been spent and probably never will be. My activist sources have been investigating this and when they are in a position to provide more evidence of their findings, I will reveal these if I can secure another debate to do so.'

Then he issued a public invitation to the media: go to Vryburg Regeneration Park, look for freshly dug earth at the GPS coordinates he cited, excavate and, as sure as day follows night, you will find the elephant carcasses.

Bob Richards paused, letting what he'd said so explosively settle in, Radio 702 and eNCA television news in South Africa were carrying the live British parliamentary feed, and social media was beginning to buzz, one of Star's aides frantically alerting him.

Star, though livid at the revelations in London, couldn't really care less. He'd been threatened with prosecution, vilified in the local media, attacked by opposition politicians, so this was water off a duck's back.

His gravy train continued unabated, his Free State fiefdom undiminished, his power within the ruling ANC unaffected.

He could summon up ANC cronies from his party faction to demonstrate in his support, to toyi-toyi in the celebratory ANC resistance dance, chanting his name defiantly at the world.

Star had been untouchable and felt he always would be. The MP in London – what was his name? – had made accusations before, was loved by the media; some said had helped narrowly defeat his friend, the Former President, at that shock ANC conference, thrusting him out of power, replaced by his deputy, who was Star's avowed enemy, who was causing all manner of problems, and who had to be defeated.

He instructed his people to use social media aggressively to target the MP as a white colonial puppet, to signal his own defiance at 'external interference' in the country's affairs – never mind that this was precisely the phrase, precisely the accusation, levelled by apartheid's rulers

197

at international campaigns against apartheid spearheaded by ANC president-in-exile Oliver Tambo.

Star wasn't going to take any nonsense from this figure from afar, even though the South African media were already covering it wall-to-wall.

Bugger them all.

Star stood proud against the world, advocating, like his friend the Former President, 'radical economic transformation' – a rousing phrase to the faithful and the poor. Left-wing sounding too. But in practice a slogan for taxpayer theft and corruption, 'radical economic transformation indeed' for a new corrupt black elite to replace the old white corrupt apartheid elite: radical self-enrichment, more like.

The only difference being the new elite was much more shamelessly blatant about corruption, whereas the old one had been more cleverly covert.

However, there now needed to be another plan for the next, already organised and imminent elephant consignment, and Piet van der Merwe was alerted to execute one.

News editors in London and New York, forewarned about Bob Richards' revelations, asked their South African correspondents to report as soon as possible.

The Economist sent one of its senior journalists, the daughter of a 1960s anti-apartheid activist, on the next flight from London to Johannesburg, and then to Vryburg, for an investigative feature.

The *New York Times* also alerted their freelance correspondent in southern Africa. So did the *Wall Street Journal* and the *Washington Post*. The *Financial Times* news editor asked its Johannesburg-resident correspondent to follow up, as did the *Guardian* and the *Times* theirs. The international media pack began to chase each other to be first to a new angle on the story.

It had all the makings of a big one. Elephant extinction, poaching, international crime, political corruption. Quite a potent mixture.

Jayne, meanwhile, had been burrowing away in hiding, missing her long runs in the park but making use of the ample garden for several fast walks daily.

For most of her time she was glued to her computer screen, delving into what she had found, trying to join up the dots of a complex picture, trying to find out exactly what was happening with all the suspicious transactions she had uncovered.

It seemed pretty clear at one level. Public money granted for a project in a small Free State town. That same public money then diverted to go chasing around the international financial networks and then appearing to be funnelled back into the country – but what after that?

'Follow the money' was the old mantra. But now it was 'follow the digital trail'. So she tried to do so, but her head was hurting, even with Murray Bergstein's helpful tuition.

Start at the beginning, she told herself. Go step by step. Would have preferred to be online still, directly into the bank's server, but had pretty well all the data she needed. There were some nagging, important gaps, however.

She pondered. Her colleague at work, the one who she suspected fancied her but had never made an advance, the one who had smuggled her the note with the Veteran's number. Komal could contact him, for she had his number.

Jayne went to work, typing out a picture of what had happened with the bank-transaction information she already hand, and explaining the gaps her friend might be able to fill in.

The second elephant herd had been long procured, and was loaded up in the same transporter as the first one, but the destination had been changed.

Van der Merwe in no time had been directed to another area in the Free State, also under Star's control. After the revelations in London, no pretence any more to SANParks about the purpose, no charade about creating a safari park. His escorting rangers were this time handpicked from Star's patch.

The herd was restless, though sedated from the journey, the Matriarch especially agitated, as if full of foreboding, stumbling out trumpeting, ears flapping angrily, peering around suspiciously, the rest of the herd also unsettled, the young bulls raring for a fight.

Hennie Strijdom was only too aware that, hippos and buffalo excepted, African elephants killed more people than any other large land-based mammal, around 500 annually.

He knew their habits, knew the difference between a charge that was bluffing and one that was attacking. The former was a deterrent to a threat, typically with ears fanned out, swinging from side to side, legs pivoting from one to the other, trunk not pinned up and under the body, but instead swaying side to side or hanging down below.

On the other hand, Strijdom knew only too well, if an elephant's charge was for real, that would be evident by its ears pinned back on its head, the trunk tucked up underneath. That was the time to run – if possible, zig-zag to confuse.

Facing such danger, it was important to give them plenty of space – while constantly on the alert for bulls once they had reached adulthood, especially during their annual musth, when their hormonal churns and testosterone surges made them especially aggressive, even more impossible to control.

From which, if cornered, escape was most unlikely and, if caught by an attack-charge, Strijdom knew elephants used their tusks to gore humans, throw them and crush them, stomping until dead. He didn't scare easily, but he found himself shivering anxiously.

As the transporters came to a halt, Strijdom recognised the symptoms of an elephant herd in trauma and therefore especially dangerous. The plan had been to dart them with cyanide licks, like the other herd, but this situation was too dangerous for that. The herd was about to obliterate all their captors.

So he activated a fall-back plan. Tranquillise them with poisoned arrows, then hack off their tusks with machetes and axes, but taking no pleasure in the gory outcome.

Even Strijdom had to concede it was bloody beyond belief as he and his men repeatedly slashed at the half-sedated animals, who screeched in pain, writhing, his men taking turns hacking the blood-soaked elephants on their backs and hind legs as they lay helplessly on the ground. When some of them attempted to stand up, their faces, legs and trunks were viciously lacerated.

But for Strijdom there was no space for sentimentality. Job to do, job done, as they methodically hacked the tusks off, sticking them in bags, taking them away.

On such missions, he prided himself on a clinical lack of emotion. But as he looked back at the tuskless, twitching, bleeding mess of once-regal giants strewn and splayed around, Hennie Strijdom almost felt ashamed.

Almost.

*

All Thandi's forebodings were reinforced. She had turned down the President's request to become an MP because she wasn't convinced she could be an independent spirit within the faction-ridden ANC.

Now investigative journalists had reported that, since the President had come to power, pledging to eradicate the rampant corruption and cronyism under his predecessor, the pace of corruption had not slowed substantially.

New power-station contracts had been awarded, not to the best tender but to a Russian-backed foreign one prepared to pay back-handers. A local black-owned company, which had refused bribe overtures from the energy minister's departmental director-general and his daughter, had been cut out despite offering the best value, greenest option. So much for the ANC's policy of black economic empowerment.

Meanwhile, the health minister had been forced to resign because of contracts handed to a family company. And so it went on: the President, clearly well-intentioned, couldn't control his gravy-train-addicted ministers and officials because they still wielded enormous power within the ANC's ruling elite.

Thandi, complaining ruefully to Mkhize, shook her head in despair – though doubly determined to fight on. She'd been reading an inspirational book on Oliver Tambo, ANC president-in-Exile while Mandela and the rest of the movement's leadership was on Robben Island.

Tambo – now he was a leader to look up to.

But was it that the anti-apartheid struggle had spawned exceptional figures thrown up in exceptional circumstances? And that once it was over, people had reverted to type, with the same frailties as leaders and citizens the world over?

She thought again of people of her age who knew nothing of the struggle, nothing of the history that had given them new opportunities barred under apartheid. All they seemed interested in was materialism – mobile phones, the latest fashions, the hottest celebrity, going clubbing, finding a boy or a girl.

Thandi sighed, thought again wistfully of her late granny, thought of Jayne's relative Helen Joseph, hoped she was treading in their footsteps.

It seemed to her such a very, very long walk to freedom.

An almost comical scene. A male rhino was chomping away on a nicely thick patch of green grass – 'having his lunch', Mkhize explained to enthralled guests in the Land Cruiser – when the resident elephant herd, three of them to the fore, rumbled up to enjoy a bit of chomping on the lush pickings themselves.

At first the rhino, head down, took no notice – lunch first, intruders later – then as the three got closer, he turned and padded towards them, the three followed by the other dozen or so elephants hastily backing away from the advance of the solitary rhino, dehorned in protection against poachers.

A few trumpeted as if in protest, then they regrouped, as if to say, 'We're not going to be bossed around by this cheeky guy,' and advanced again.

The scene repeated itself, the rhino munching, apparently uninterested in the advancing giants, then suddenly turning, raising its head and trundling back toward them as they hurriedly retreated again.

'You can see who's boss!' Mkhize laughed. 'Maybe only a hippo would also be able to force a herd to back off like that.'

The crude felling of the second elephant herd provoked bitter anger in conservation circles, and some media attention from journalists wearied by yet another outrage in the gangster state.

Minister Yasmin chalked it up on her lengthening list against Star's gang, but decided not to prioritise it. Bigger fish to fry, she pragmatically, though uncomfortably concluded.

What puzzled Jayne time and again was why internationally respected banks would open bank accounts for shell entities registered in a free-trade zone such as Ras al-Khaimah, whose primary attraction was as a highly secretive offshore jurisdiction.

What were they doing this for? Shell companies, with their ownership anonymity, were generally classic vehicles for money laundering and other illicit financial activity, moving illicit funds from one part of the world to another to facilitate mafia crime, terrorist activity and looting.

As for the others – the so-called professional enablers – they also were deeply complicit.

Auditors did soft audits for fat fees and lavish hospitality, some of them among the Big Four global auditing firms. Yet that contravened all their professional obligations and the regulations under which they operated. Surely these auditors themselves were the criminals too, even if by default?

Consultants did fancy reports to gloss over thieving realities, again receiving fat fees. Were these consultancy corporates themselves the criminals too, even if by default?

Lawyers helped set up the shell companies and facilitated the purchase and sale of properties: again, such activity could not have happened without them. Surely these lawyers themselves were the criminals too, even if by default?

Finally, estate agents were conduits for property investments and disposals, supposedly regulated to prevent money laundering but in fact allowing a blind eye to be turned. Surely these estate agents were themselves the criminals too, even if by default?

Although most of this shady practice was quite legal, Jayne found it repugnant – a seamy side of global corporates that presented themselves as businesses with high standards.

Nevertheless, she was starting to get a clearer picture about what had happened and was developing thoughts on policy needed to block this sort of thing in the future.

'So what to do about all this?' Komal asked.

'The answer has to be to clean up the global financial system from top to bottom,' Jayne replied. 'Starting with governments. Unless they take a strong lead, unless they coordinate and cooperate across national boundaries, criminals and terrorists will continue to get around the law by relocating themselves and their stolen funds and assets to more weakly policed or lightly regulated places such as Dubai, Hong Kong and the Caribbean tax havens.'

'Many criminals also relocate to countries without extradition agreements in place. As far as I can see, governments – including in Britain and the US – only pay lip service to curbing financial crime without actually doing so.'

'All of the corporates culpable – banks like HSBC, consultants like Bain, accountants like KPMG, lawyers like Hogan Lovells – are either London-headquartered or London-located, and the same is true of New York. China is culpable, since Hong Kong is a money-launderers' paradise. The United Arab Emirates also, with Dubai heaven for looters. India as well, guilty of turning a flagrant blind eye to the Business Brothers who live there.'

Komal, paused, taking all this in. 'But to open a bank account or

203

legitimately move money, you and I, and the average, honest citizen on a modest or medium income, have to run an obstacle race, with all sorts of compliance procedures and requirements. It's a pain in the ass. But somehow these same banks give a nod to global criminals.'

Jayne nodded ruefully: 'But money launderers don't carry around banknotes in suitcases as they once did. Funds moved across the world today leave a digital footprint. And I know that banks possess the technological and financial clout necessary to stop all this and track down the looted money. But they simply don't do that.'

'So, what should we be demanding?' Komal asked.

'Well, I have started to write down my own agenda for change,' Jayne replied somewhat tentatively: this was new territory for her.

'What, you mean now you are a poacher-turned-gamekeeper!' Komal cackled cheekily.

'Yes, suppose so . . .' Jayne looked sheepish.

'We have to try and stop criminals hiding behind complex layers of shell companies to conceal who's really owning them. That means doing something new. Banks and all the auditors, consultancies and lawyers should be required by law to share otherwise confidential client information between them. That certainly didn't happen over the Former President and his mates, the Business Brothers. It isn't happening with Star either.'

'Okay, but how would that actually happen?' Komal asked.

'There have been big advances in technology,' Jayne responded immediately, 'so it's much easier than ever to collate, to store and to share data. Yet that hasn't happened. So the financial criminals make hay. The banks, the regulated auditors, consultancies and lawyers don't share information – either among themselves, or with each other, or across their professional borders.'

'But I don't understand,' Komal interjected. 'Surely bankers and all these professionals should be the first line of defence when it comes to corruption?'

'Yes, they should. But they aren't,' said Jayne. 'Although some sharing of information already occurs, it is pretty ineffectual. Us bankers always hide behind so-called client confidentiality. But frankly, that's become an excuse. They could so easily share useful data and intelligence on a confidential basis with regulators and enforcement agencies.'

She paused as the two women grabbed a glass of water each.

'A main culprit is what we in BSBC called "passporting".' Jayne paused again, this time having noticed Komal's brow furrowing.

'What I mean by that,' she added, 'is the way criminals gain access to a financial institution's multinational network through a country that is much less regulated, such as Dubai or Hong Kong for instance.'

She stopped again. 'Are you with me?'

Komal replying 'Think so.'

'Okay, let me explain it another way. "Passporting" allows criminals to gain access to a financial institution's multinational network through a much less regulated part of the world. And when it is exposed, they claim ignorance about what goes on in their own branches operating in jurisdictions in their global networks where anti–money-laundering policies and procedures are not nearly as rigorous, or where there are opaque banking and corporate structures. And once into these global banking networks, criminals are able to move, hide and invest their stolen gains in complicated or hidden offshore trust accounts.'

Jayne continued: 'These banks are global. They cannot be allowed to get away with saying, "Nothing to do with me," if a swindler opens an account in Johannesburg and thereby opens the door to the money going to, say, Dubai or Hong Kong. They are global institutions, with each branch digitally interconnected.'

'What about penalties, then?' Komal asked

'I have been thinking a lot about this in the last week,' Jayne said carefully, 'and I think banks and these other professional corporates I have mentioned should face additional sanctions if they are found to be assisting or waving through money launderers. Licences should be immediately stripped from them if they fail to meet anti–money-laundering standards. There have to be new regulations to ensure personal responsibility by financial executives. At the moment, it's the whole corporate rather than each manager held to account. That has to change so that they get sanctioned.'

Komal listened hard. 'What sort of sanctions?' she asked.

'Permission for offenders to work for what is known as a regulated entity (like a bank) should be withdrawn. There should be fines and perhaps even prison for the most serious offences. This would force managers to take a much more proactive role in combatting financial crime and corruption, especially over state procurement, where taxpayers' money is at stake.'

'But surely it is no good just South Africa or just Britain or just any other country doing this?' Komal asked. 'Has to be every country, surely?'

'Absolutely,' Jayne replied enthusiastically, her eyes bright. 'The buck stops with *every government*. Either they adopt these standards together or they sink together. For instance, extradition agreements are another weak point. It is important that money laundering and other types of financial crime are extraditable offences and that the guilty are extradited.'

'Quite a list of demands!' Komal exclaimed, full of admiration. 'Now the question is, what do we do about them?'

Star was a proud man.

Maybe he hadn't suffered the privations of the Rivonia heroes, sentenced to spend the prime of their lives in prison, and in a way he resented them, always praised when he was always pilloried. Maybe he hadn't been subjected to the torture or the beatings of those revered in the freedom struggle. But he'd had his own dose of apartheid police-state brutality.

He remembered several months spent in Ramkraal Prison during the state of emergency that followed the 1976 Soweto school student uprising. It was an old building first built in 1893, and conditions weren't good. Nor were his interrogators. One had forced him to put his own faeces in his mouth, which he had to swallow. For weeks afterwards, he had shuddered at the smell, the taste, the indignity, the degradation. It was his own private dread, resurfacing periodically in early-hours nightmares.

Even now, the episode would spring back to haunt him, reinforce his anger, reinforce his self-justification at the role he played. It was his time to eat properly, to enjoy the comforts once the prerogative of the corrupt apartheid elite. He didn't think of himself as corrupt or venal, any more than they had. It was his entitlement, just as they had thought it was theirs. It was his time, just as it had been theirs.

He hadn't respected the laws of the apartheid era, which imprisoned his people in every way imaginable, from their lower classification at birth all the way through life: what schools they couldn't go to, what levels of skills and education they couldn't attain, what hospitals they couldn't enter, the nicer neighbourhoods they couldn't live in, or the nicer city parks they couldn't enter, except if caring for a white toddler as a domestic worker for their mistress.

He'd got used to defying the law, so for him doing so now in the post-apartheid era came naturally. No matter that they were ANC-made laws, not apartheid state-made laws. No matter that in the Free State he made the laws himself as premier.

If laws didn't suit him, he didn't obey them, thought nothing of that. Never thought he was doing wrong. This was his time, and he was helping himself liberally in his time on his terms, respecting what he chose to, not what others told him to, certainly not the President, whom he despised with a not-so-hidden venom – and was determined to bring down, one way or the other.

Komal's pertinent question to Jayne had made her think.

'You mentioned the key role of governments,' she'd observed. 'From what you have uncovered along with Bernstein, isn't the truth that they haven't really lifted a finger to block the money launderers who use London as well as Hong Kong, Dubai as well as New York, Delhi as well as the Caribbean tax havens, Moscow as well as Beijing, Gibraltar as well as Mauritius?'

Jayne nodded. Everywhere, she thought.

'Isn't it true that presidents and prime ministers talk the good talk but never walk the walk?' Komal asked.

When Komal opened the front door, Thandi asked immediately to see her first, didn't want to chat to the Veteran until afterwards.

They sat down in the kitchen together, Komal indicating to the Veteran to wait.

Thandi, eyes moistening, poured out her heart while Komal listened, hardly saying anything, giving her a hug, allowing her to ventilate, getting her to go through the detail of the ugly, multiple assaults, the near-rapes, prodding gently, saying that if she'd been through that herself she'd be feeling exactly the same: both ashamed and unclean – which, although ridiculous *objectively*, was normal for women in that predicament or worse – and bitterly angry.

The two women remained huddled, the Veteran in the next room troubled, wondering what the hell was going on, feeling excluded, blaming his disability.

Then Komal reached for a piece of paper, something she'd printed off: 'I want you to read this, please. It's beautiful, searing, terrible and lovely all at once. It may help.'

'It's by a friend of ours who passed just a year or so ago: Hugh Lewin, struggle activist and political prisoner, who served seven years in Pretoria between 1964 and 1971. He wrote a moving memoir about the experience, called *Bandiet*. You should read it.

'Hugh said of his poem "Touch", and I've copied the text: "It's very emotional because the poem reminds me of so many aspects of what it was like being in prison: the violence, cruelty and brutality. Reading it remains an intense experience for me because the memories it evokes are still very strong."'

Komal handed over the paper and Thandi began reading:

When I get out
I'm going to ask someone
to touch me
very gently please
and slowly,
touch me
I want
to learn again
how life feels.

I've not been touched
for seven years
for seven years
I've been untouched
out of touch
and I've learnt
to know now
the meaning of
untouchable.

Untouched — not quite
I can count the things
that have touched me

One: fists
At the beginning
fierce mad fists
beating beating

till I remember
screaming
don't touch me
please don't touch me

Two: paws
The first four years of paws
every day
patting paws, searching
– arms up, shoes off
legs apart –

prodding paws, systematic
heavy, indifferent
probing away
all privacy.

I don't want fists and paws
I want
to want to be touched
again
and to touch
I want to feel alive
again
I want to say
when I get out
Here I am
please touch me.

Thandi stared at Komal, sobbing heart-wrenchingly.

She hadn't cried like that since her Granny had died, the Veteran hearing her and wondering what on earth was going on.

The two women hugged, long and tenderly: 'Show the poem to Isaac when you first see him, Thandi, and, whatever you do – don't bottle it up. Tell him everything, especially about the shame bit, about feeling dirty – then let him touch you, let him cherish and nurture you.'

*

The Veteran was relieved to see her safe again, and received a clipped explanation, was especially troubled about the gang-rape attempt, told her it was his fault, how he felt intensely guilty about having sent her on the mission in the first place.

'Don't be silly,' Thandi replied

He'd noticed immediately by the way she walked determinedly into his sitting room that she was in no mood for small talk or her usual pleasantries about his health.

She seemed distracted, almost detached, not her usual bubbly self, wasn't willing describe her ordeal, didn't want to explain exactly what had happened to her, seemed to have displaced the trauma – or been too ashamed to talk about it, or had already done so with Komal. The Veteran would find out later.

Not a good sign, he thought. Bury that sort of thing and it came back to bite you in unexpected ways, might even affect her marriage if she bottled it up.

'What the hell is happening to our country? Is all lost?' she blurted out. 'Are all our efforts, the risks to our lives, the threats we have faced, for nothing?'

She paused expectantly, face taut.

The Veteran sat back on his sofa, upper back painful; he must have slept awkwardly or something. He spoke slowly, trying to lower the temperature.

'What's on your mind, Thandi?'

'Look at the local election results,' she said impatiently. 'Despite massive unemployment, despite massive gender-based violence, despite basic education and health collapsing, despite growing hunger and mental distress, barely a quarter of eligible South Africans chose to vote this week!

'The vast majority either didn't register, or registered but then didn't vote. There were tens of millions of no-voters, most young, black and poor. It's like returning to minority rule!' accused Thandi.

'The terrible voter turnout seems to be because people think if they voted it would just encourage the gangsters who run municipal and city government!'

'The ANC is not even meeting the basic needs of most citizens as it is required under the constitution,' she blurted out. 'The country is plagued by violence and human-rights abuses, the poor suffering the most, subjected also to daily police violence, as well as widespread social violence, against women and gays, lesbians and other LGBTQIA people.'

The Veteran nodded sympathetically: 'Agreed.'

But his assent just seemed to irritate her. 'It's all linked to the ANC's utter disintegration from an organisation of freedom fighters into one just looking after itself in government at all levels.'

'True,' the Veteran replied, nodding.

'Okay but what the hell are we doing about it, then?' Thandi asked pointedly. 'Lawlessness, violence, political assassinations by warring ANC factions, unrelenting attacks on railway lines, stealing of ammunition from police stations, random sabotage against energy resources – all on top of an economic crisis, job losses, low growth and extensive hunger.'

'Again, can't disagree with you.'

Thandi was in full flow. 'Self-styled "struggle veterans", many with criminal records, even held three leading government figures hostage. These lawbreakers, as well as those responsible for law enforcement, are directly linked to the ANC. Instead of the rule of law, lawbreaking is almost a daily fact of life.'

The Veteran interrupted, nodding. 'An especially bad sign was the way that a very senior police chief was assassinated in the Western Cape because he was trying to block the leakage of weapons and munitions from the police to gangsters and criminals. And the Western Cape is supposedly the Shangri-la of the country.'

But instead of taking that as an endorsement of her views, Thandi seemed almost to take offence.

'Yes, yes. But it's much worse than that. Although the President says all the right things, like trying to stop acts of corruption and patronage, he seems completely unable to deliver anything, completely failing to bring those responsible, some at the very top of the ANC, to justice,' she said accusingly.

'It's no good just having constitutional rights on paper. They have to be upheld and that isn't happening. Political gangsters can do what they like. If those at the top, locally, provincially or nationally, can get away with murder, then why can't we? That seems the common view from the woman on the street.'

The Veteran had never seen Thandi looking so miserable.

'Things are falling apart in South Africa today,' she added disconsolately. 'All we have done seems to be for nothing, that's what Isaac keeps telling me – and he has his ear to the ground much better than us politicos.'

'Yes, can't disagree with anything you say, except the very last bit,' the Veteran responded gently.

He knew his gutsy young comrade only too well. Confront her and he'd lose her trust. Also, he'd seen too many young militants burn themselves out with their sheer intensity and hyper-activism, then become disillusioned. He was worried this might happen to Thandi.

'You have done amazing things, Thandi. To stop bad people, stop them destroying the legacy of Oliver and Adelaide Tambo, of Nelson Mandela, of Albertina and Walter Sisulu, of Ahmed Kathrada, of Chris Hani, of Govan Mbeki, of Lillian Ngoyi, of so many other heroes.'

The Veteran paused to give emphasis to his next point, noting he had her full attention.

'You stand on the shoulders of these giants, Thandi. They struggled and sacrificed so much over long, bitterly hard decades. And they never gave up until victory was theirs. But the torch always gets passed to successor generations to take the struggle to a new level, to meet new challenges, to defeat those trying to undermine it.'

She nodded. 'Suppose so,' she said soberly, 'just that there seems so much to do, so few to do it.'

'Very true,' the Veteran replied gently. 'Always has been, throughout history, always will be, change always driven by a small minority. And it is too easy to forget about, or become cynical about, our history.'

'Quite a peroration!' Thandi was smiling now, seemed uplifted.

'Yes, sorry!' He smiled too, pausing, 'but we have no choice. We have got to reclaim those values of morality, integrity, social justice and equal opportunities that inspired Mandela, Tambo and hundreds of thousands of anti-apartheid activists.'

Thandi nodded, but seemed far away now, the Veteran noted, so he added, 'But remember too, Thandi, that African proverb: "If you want to travel fast, travel alone. If you want to travel far, travel together." You cannot do everything on your own. Staying power, working collectively is what matters.'

Komal presciently poked her head round the door.

'Come on, you guys, time for a drink! And I mean wine, not juice. Red or white, Thandi?'

'He's got no time for such bourgeois frivolity! The struggle continues!'

Thandi paused, cackling with laughter. 'But *I* do. Red wine for me, please – better have a large one to recover from the battering he's inflicted on me.'

She smiled impishly, Komal conspiratorially. The Veteran, relieved that Thandi seemed to have come out of her shell, pretended to shake his head in mock-disapproval.

'Clever blacks.' That was the phrase he'd appropriated from his ally-in-chief, the Former President.

And Star had noted quite few of them rising up the ladder in his own fiefdom, the Free State ANC.

If it had been used by a white, it would have been racist, but used by a Basotho about his own people it was seen as arrogant and disparaging, typical of the man used to getting his own way

Too many of them, asking awkward questions, gaining popularity, challenging his grip on power. Eloquent, in their early thirties, they worked for the likes of Absa, Sanlam, Distell, some of the main corporates. They'd gained MBA degrees from places like Pretoria University's Gordon Institute of Business Science, attended its campus in Johannesburg's Illovo suburb, were bright, with professional lifestyles, part of the fast-growing black middle class.

Star didn't like them. In fact, he despised them. They hadn't been brought up in poverty like him. Their education was post-apartheid, their opportunities – always denied to him – were many. Because of the struggle, because of what he and his generation had sacrificed. And now they had the effrontery to turn on him? Bastards.

They would have to be sorted. Expelled, probably – to begin with, at least. And worse if that didn't work.

As for that young woman ... (What was her name? Thandi-something? Matjeke?)

'Clever black-in-chief' she was proving to be, and infuriatingly persistent. He hadn't bothered about her when she first appeared in the spotlight, even when she was implicated in the demise of the Former President. Had clocked her then, but forgotten her – until she turned up mucking around in his own backyard.

Now she was top of the list of 'clever blacks' to be dealt with. Permanently. But he couldn't afford that to happen in Bloemfontein: he, would immediately be blamed, and would have the Pauli van Wyks,

Ferial Haffajees, the Bongani Bingwas, Pieter Louis-Myburghs and all the other stuck-up, self-important media meddlers tramping all over him. What did they call themselves? 'Investigative journalists'? More like 'counter-revolutionaries', or 'white monopoly capital' agents. But in their wake would doubtless come meddling opposition politicians.

Matjeke could be – would be – dealt with in quite another way, in her backyard. Safer for him that way.

Star's hijack plan was even more audacious than the ambitious scheme to relocate thirty rhinos by Boeing 747.

Could Van der Merwe's team somehow get control of the aircraft or force it to land so that poachers could pounce, shoot or dart the rhinos and hack out their precious horns?

The two men were careful never to meet in person, always communicating by encrypted means or through intermediaries, for instance over cash payments.

Star had discovered details of a plan to move the animals 3,000 kilometres north up the African continent by jumbo jet.

It followed a similar successful move of the 1.5-tonne rhinos from a game reserve in South Africa to be rehomed in Rwanda after a forty-hour journey over 3,000 kilometres. The purpose was to spread white rhinos across the continent in safe habitats and prevent them from being pushed to the brink of extinction by poachers.

Van der Merwe looked into what had to be done. It was a huge logistical operation. Sixty tonnes of animals, crates and feed to transport. The rhinos first had to be quarantined ahead of the move in a temporary enclosure for two months. When it came to the journey, they couldn't be fully sedated, because if completely prone and lying down, their sternums could be injured.

Instead, they would have to be partly drugged to stay calm and stable, though still able to stand, able to maintain normal bodily functions and remain placid during the flight, to avoid the nightmare of going on the rampage in the airliner. The logistical hurdles seemed formidable, but it had been done before and so presumably could be done again.

But how to safely intercept and grab them during the journey, Van der Merwe wondered. On the Rwanda trip, there had been official police escorts before and after the flight, so it was unlikely he could organise the hijack on the ground. It had to be in the air.

Who among his contacts could possibly accomplish that? Strijdom might have some ideas. For Star wasn't interested in problems, just solutions. That's the way he always was. Gave orders. Expected them to be delivered. Never mind the difficulties or dangers.

So far Van der Merwe had managed to do that. But this was something else entirely.

They had collected his passport and bags from the Bloemfontein hotel room, but not his Armalite case, which was redundant, his favoured possession lying out somewhere in the bush, if it hadn't already been purloined by someone.

Murphy was put on a British Airways flight at OR Tambo International Airport direct to London by Minister Yasmin's officers. During the ten-hour overnight trip, he dozed fitfully – depressed, he thought, really for the first time in his life.

He went over the entrails of his mission. Had he made any mistakes? No, he didn't think so. Wasn't his fault that an unknown sniper had been deployed. Could he have been the tall, silent, mysterious figure in a balaclava on board the chopper? Probably, he thought.

He hadn't even been fully briefed on why they were tracking Mkhize, why he had to kill him. In fact, he hadn't actually been told anything about the context, or the reason. Had been treated very poorly – especially badly for a proud Irish soldier like him.

Murphy finally fell asleep, dreaming of being loose again in the hills of South Armagh, heading to see his woman, soaking up the damp greenery, immersed in the history of his fighting tradition, thankful he had at least escaped that godforsaken dry, hot, bare terrain in which he had been so badly humiliated. The Brits had certainly never managed that in his native Ireland.

He woke to the sound of breakfast being served, the cabin lights back on, some snoring around him. Just over an hour later the Airbus landed at the vast Heathrow Terminal 5. It seemed to take ages taxiing to dock at one of the 133 air bridges winched out from one of the many piers attached to the main building.

The bleary-eyed passengers jumped up immediately, jostling to retrieve their overhead cabin luggage. One helped him, just as he'd done so on departure, because Murphy's right arm was in a sling, pretty useless and painful if moved. He followed the queue out, heading for the shuttle that would transport them all to arrivals.

215

Murphy stepped through the gap after business class, left in front of first class, stumbling out of the airliner with the other passengers.

But two men standing immediately to one side stepped forward, grabbed him firmly and hustled him to the left, through a hatch, down some steps and into one of two cars, indicator lights flashing, parked engines idling on the tarmac.

Dawn was breaking in the grey drizzle, and Murphy shivered as he looked up at the giant plane shimmering, its lights beaming through the cabin portholes, baggage already being unloaded via a lift and onto a truck with a flashing red light.

He spent the rest of the day in a cubicle somewhere in the vast Terminal 5 building, unshaven, tired and frustrated, being interrogated by MI5 officers. There wasn't much to tell them, because they seemed to know quite a bit already about where he had gone in South Africa and what he had not done. Must have been briefed by the South Africans who'd grabbed him. Exactly who the South Africans were, he wasn't sure, initially thinking it was military–intelligence officers, but disoriented by the entrance of the Veteran.

Finally, his luggage having been grabbed from a baggage reclaim carousel by someone, Murphy was escorted through a departure gate, in front of other passengers peering curiously at him, and put on a flight to Belfast, wondering if he would be detained there too.

But, curiously, he wasn't. Just ignored, shoulder aching, arm still pretty useless, as he walked out of George Best airport through the modest line of shops, eateries and coffee bars to a taxi rank.

Good old Belfast drizzle. A little chilly after all the sun, but nice to be home, where he felt more in control. He was driven to the house in West Belfast where he would report. All the way, he scanned anxiously behind but could spot none of the telltale signs of a tailing vehicle

Despite being in pain, Murphy began to relax at last.

The intruder normally moved in the shady circles of ANC criminality in KwaZulu-Natal, where he lived.

But this time his order came from on high, originating from the Free State. His target was the young woman in Richards Bay.

Didn't really know why, didn't know anything about her, except she was a serious troublemaker apparently, just orders to take her out – and seemed a pretty straightforward job, like he'd done often enough.

Case the apartment, check she was inside that night, then shimmy up the fire escape, grab onto the waste pipe and prise open the bathroom window, conveniently ajar to catch what little coolness there was after the humid heat of the day.

He crept inside.

Then all hell had broken loose for him.

Silhouetted from behind against the slivers of moonlight illuminating the darkness of their marital apartment were the three figures.

Mkhize's muscled frame, Thandi's trim curves – she standing small but strong alongside her husband, the intruder on the floor writhing in agony, pleading in terror. Terror, not just of them but of the threat from a boss who never ever brooked failure – and failure loomed, buffeting him.

Mkhize had just kicked the intruder in the testicles, Thandi still had her Makarov levelled at him, gripping it steady in both hands. The intruder had no idea what might happen to him next.

'One last time – who sent you?' Thandi barked, the same question yet again, and it was her he feared most. Her steely calm was unnerving. Mkhize's short, sharp brutality he understood. But she bred absolute and total fear in him, well beyond the punching and kicking he'd endured.

The intruder hadn't come across anything like her in his murky male world, beginning as a township tsotsi and graduating to a hired gun for the boss. He'd never imagined anyone could match the boss for sheer unadulterated terror. But now that person stood above him. She would kill him, of that he had no doubt.

Survival mode kicked in.

'If I tell you, then what will happen to me?' the intruder asked haltingly, the words dribbling out of his mouth.

'We will let you go,' Mkhize replied evenly.

'But only after we've searched you and taken what we need – any keys, ID.' Thandi interjected quickly, Mkhize glancing at her, their eyes meeting with mutual understanding.

'Empty your pockets, take off your shirt,' Mkhize said, 'and no tricks!'

Thandi blurted, 'Now, who's your boss?'

The intruder, looking straight at her as if he was transfixed, muttered a name, noting in surprise she wasn't startled. Instead, satisfied, she was nodding.

Mkhize motioned at him to remove his trousers and hand them over, quickly searching the pockets. Two sets of keys, one tagged with a car-registration number, the other presumably for a door, together with a phone and an ID card – useful for Yasmin to trace him.

Mkhize wondered briefly whether to try and hold him, and whispered quickly to Thandi while keeping his eyes firmly on the man.

'Maybe Yasmin could try to turn him, use him as a state witness?' she whispered back, her Makarov levelled firmly at the intruder.

'Too dangerous for us,' Mkhize replied. 'We have no means of doing that – how on earth could we hold him securely and then deliver him to her? We can't trust the local police.'

Taking no chances, he gestured to the intruder: 'Pull yourself back-wards along the floor. Don't try any funny stuff or I'll kick you again in the same place. Except this time even harder.' Watching the man like a hawk, he motioned Thandi to open their front door.

The intruder inched awkwardly backwards on his hands and backside, his pain obviously unbearable, Thandi's pistol still pointing at him.

Then he tumbled slowly backwards down the stairs and through the entrance, Mkhize following and slamming the door shut.

The intruder limped painfully away into the night, humiliated without his trousers and above all paranoid, not just by what had happened to him but by what he feared would be the consequences of his failure.

A week later his blotched, bullet-riddled body would be found on waste land, nibbled at by rats.

When Mkhize returned to their apartment, Thandi clung to him, unable to stop herself shaking.

Although they tried, neither could get back to sleep and early in the morning they called Minister Yasmin, telling her they had the man's things and that there would also be DNA on his trousers.

Yasmin arranged for it all to be collected. She wasn't surprised that the intruder had been sent by Star – though the contacts in his phone might be useful.

She would also arrange for a proper security alarm to be fitted to their apartment – not one supplied by a private alarm company but one that, if triggered, would alert her own trusted team.

Afterwards, Yasmin and the Veteran had a long heart-to-heart about Thandi's new vulnerability, and what, if anything, could be done to protect her, the Veteran especially frustrated that his own disability meant there was probably nothing he could do. He had got her into this predicament and there was little he could do to shield her.

For the young woman had told them both in no uncertain terms that she would not be intimidated. If anything, the attack seemed to have made her even more determined.

It was rather neatly done, Minister Yasmin reflected afterwards, a nice bit of work the Sniper had conceived for her.

And she'd been able to pay his IT company – quite properly, though she was careful not to spread the news of the project beyond a select and trusted few.

Through her he'd consulted the Australian police technical expert who'd found a way to install a Trojan horse app in an underworld social-media network thought by the criminals using it to be secure for their own messages.

The Sniper, with their help, designed his own equivalent network, with his own Trojan horse app, able to decrypt messages on it for officers in a special new unit attached to Minister's Yasmin's office, who would read these 24/7.

Yasmin had found a paid informant within Star's circle, who started handing out Android phones with the app installed to his colleagues. One of the phones was given to a delighted Star himself, the only irritant being that he already had three phones, two of them burners.

His inner circle began using the network and, thinking it was unique to them, did not hide or encrypt their messages, soon providing a gold-mine to Yasmin's team, though she disciplined herself not to intervene over messages about protection rackets, petty crime, beatings and even killings, actions Star or his henchmen had ordered through the network, labelled Naamloos.

Yasmin was biding her time. She hoped her instinct was sound, because it was mighty exasperating knowing full well what Star's criminal gang was up to but not intervening for fear of compromising something bigger, hopefully much bigger.

For Star, it was time to act – and decisively.

Not the rhino-hijack idea any more. The logistics of that seemed too risky, even for him – and anyway, he'd thought of something else

219

hugely more important even than getting more millions from the rhino horns.

Almost every week there were new reports of imminent arrests high up in the ANC, individuals everyone knew had been, and still were, aboard the looters' gravy train.

The media were now speculating he might be next. Bloody outrageous! A man of his stature! A man of the people, no less! He was furious.

There was only one thing that could put a stop to all this nonsense.

High stakes, very high stakes – yes, of course. But he'd sensed for a while that the moment of truth was coming.

Returning home was not like usual for Pádraig Murphy.

He didn't expect a hero's greeting, to which he had grown accustomed over the years after successful kills. But he didn't expect the suspicion either. It made him angry. He had a status among the dissident groups in the Republican movement, was admired, sometimes jealously envied, for his paramilitary record. Trusted too.

Suddenly all that was being junked. It seemed they didn't believe him when he explained that he had returned without the £100,000. Didn't believe him that he had been effectively ambushed. Didn't even bother about his injury. Just that he had failed to carry out a task as instructed by the leadership.

What was even worse, there was a hint in their questions that he might have betrayed them, might have the cash stashed away somewhere, because it was always understood that he would be paid in large anonymous bundles of notes, not electronically, where a digital financial trail would be left. They didn't like the fact that he had spent the best part of a day with the hated MI5 either.

Betraying the IRA? *Him*? After all he had done? The very suggestion was woundingly offensive.

Murphy felt bitter facing the men he had thought were his comrades, had risked a great deal for, were in a common clandestine cause, had the solidarity of conspirators up against everyone else.

Then, in the early hours of the morning, tired and angry, there were sudden smiles all round. Apologies, too, for doubting him. They would drive him straight home to Armagh, well, to his woman, for he had no home as such.

There were no hands shaken; the mood was too fractured, too tense for that. But there were a few pats on the shoulder, a few greetings in Gaelic. Then he was ushered into the back of a scruffy vehicle, couldn't see what kind, too dark for that.

But Murphy never made it to see his woman.

Instead, he died, shot in the back of the head. The man grabbing him – though very calculatingly not shooting him – was an undercover MI5 officer, the one who had questioned him most aggressively, most persistently.

Murphy's last, bitterly desperate thoughts had been about the Veteran, and whether he might indeed have been correct after all.

No IRA funeral for him, no men in balaclavas and camouflage fatigues marching, Armalites loaded, held upright against their shoulders, fired over his grave. No hearse led by sombre Republican leaders, honouring him. No streets lined with sympathisers. No piper, while the coffin, draped in the Irish flag, was lowered into his grave. No recognition for the Republican soldier-hero he'd once been.

Murphy was dumped by the side of a little-used but accessible road, one of the many that criss-cross the border.

A call to radio stations in both jurisdictions ensured that his execution made the main evening news bulletins. Those in the Republican movement would know who he was, and, in any case, they could rely on 'security sources' to brief the media.

When it became known that someone of Murphy's standing had received a visit from the 'Nutting Squad' it would do wonders for discipline within the organisation.

Murphy had paid the price of failure and, in truth, he would have expected to end up in a ditch, hands tied behind his back with a bin bag covering his head. God knows, he'd done it to others often enough.

His woman would be bereft and wear black for months to come. His elderly South Armagh parents would want to know if he had received the last rites. As it happened, the priest who usually obliged was on a retreat in the west of Ireland at the material time.

But they wouldn't tell the family that.

They were thoughtful that way.

Naamloos had thrown up another matter bugging Minister Yasmin.

Star was plotting to resurrect the massive nuclear deal with Russia, pushed hard by the deposed Former President, who was widely believed to be getting a multimillion-rand kickback. The R1-trillion, 9,600 MW deal would be a mega-expensive drain on taxpayers when the country had abundant, cheaper renewable energy resources.

But Star also seemed to be plotting with the Deputy President, and Yasmin hadn't been able to find out what the Deputy President, not at all reliable, had really been up to during an extended five-week leave of absence in Russia, or about the unconfirmed reports of people sent on saboteur training sessions there.

Van der Merwe arranged to see Strijdom again. The two accomplices needed to talk in person, and couldn't possibly risk conversing over a phone.

They were comfortable with each other, especially after the Vryburg operation. Mission accomplished for Van der Merwe, who had got his cut, and satisfaction for Strijdom, who had been paid as promised.

But where exactly to meet? Both men were paranoid about CCTV cameras. Both Joburg and Pretoria were peppered with them. Hundreds of thousands of cameras had sprung up throughout the suburbs, complementing ones in the city centres, in shopping malls and on streets.

Cameras recorded when you left home, when you got to work, when you slipped out for a surreptitious smoke. If you called in sick, they recorded you out and about. If you called home to say you were working late, they observed you leaving your workplace and ducking into a lover's apartment block.

Effectively, these CCTV camera networks were an alternative intelligence network to the police – and concentrated among a few companies. Privacy campaigners protested at infringements of human rights and privacy – the right to meet who you want, to go where you please, to travel about without a digital record of your movements on a company server somewhere.

Not that either Van der Merwe or Strijdom had ever troubled themselves about civil liberties. The two men were pretty contemptuous of such matters and of the activists who campaigned about them. But they were worried about new software enabling hours of video footage to be analysed to locate individuals or their cars within seconds. Worried about the capacity to track people through facial-recognition technology, and their vehicles through digital number-plate recognition. Worried about

222

video feeds also capable of picking up sounds within range of the camera, including their secret conversations. Worried about artificial intelligence enabling powerful video-analytics software and adding to the potency of this ubiquitous urban surveillance.

No more searches, with dog-tired, bloodshot eyes, of videotape spread over days (or, if you were very lucky, hours). Anyone could now be located immediately within an ocean of video recordings tracking their movements.

When Strijdom had researched all this online, he had realised just how omnipresent digital surveillance had become, making it virtually impossible for anyone to prevent their movements from being recorded.

He thought maybe they could meet within the fifty-five-hectare Johannesburg Zoo, a vast sprawling complex with plenty of spaces in the open, away from prying digital eyes. Perhaps behind the gorilla sculpture on Centenary Lawn, where there was a discreet bench, but only early morning on a weekday, because the zoo got very crowded at weekends? But CCTV cameras were probably there too.

Then Strijdom remembered. The Wilds, in Joburg's Houghton suburb. Used to be a no-go area because of muggers but had been rehabilitated by volunteers, undergrowth cleared, plant life restored, footpaths and hiking trails opened up, devotedly maintained by community volunteers, several of whom had created sculpted owls, bush babies, monkeys and antelope to attract nature enthusiasts and tourists, and encourage a sense of safe adventure among those who might still be wary of the area's past reputation for crime.

They'd turned it into something of a wildlife haven of running water-falls and fountains in the bustling city, a place where people could walk on the kopje or stroll around relaxing and enjoying, instead of worrying about mugging or car-jacking on the streets.

But when he suggested this rendezvous to Van der Merwe, the lean Afrikaner was sceptical. 'Don't worry, it's very different now,' Strijdom reassured him, 'I've even taken girlfriends there, some nice private spots for a bit of *gevry* – and not just snogging, occasionally more!' He gave a leering laugh.

'Okay,' Van der Merwe reluctantly assented.

The irony of two arch-conspirators of high crime worrying about minor street crime seemed lost on them.

*

Jayne felt she might have cracked it – at last.

Her banker friend in BSBC had taken a huge risk for her sake. Promised to meet her somewhere safe, maybe his apartment, where he lived alone and they could engage in private, he'd suggested tentatively.

Komal, who'd quietly made contact on Jayne's behalf, wasn't too keen on that – not so much on security grounds, rather because a young woman surreptitiously accepting an older man's invitation into his home when she was an office subordinate could easily be misinterpreted, even manipulated.

But there seemed no alternative. So she picked Jayne up from the safe house and first drove past the venue to check for any surveillance – there was none she could spot, having looked for the telltale signs the Veteran had advised her of.

With Jayne wearing a wig to transform her appearance, the two women went to reception, where a bored-looking Somali called up and got the okay for the two to take the lift to the fifth floor.

It was a penthouse flat – not opulent but very comfortable, fashionably furnished, with a large balcony. Seemed spotless and ultra-tidy – maybe to impress Jayne, Komal thought suspiciously.

But the banker couldn't have behaved more respectfully. Obviously flustered at Jayne's appearance, and a little disconcerted at her polite refusal to explain where she was now living, he was punctiliously solicitous and quickly showed them into his study.

It was the very opposite of the Veteran's jumble of untidy documents, Komal noted. Not a paper, let alone piles of them, lying around. Just a pristine desk with a smart PC on loan from the office to enable him to work from home, as Jayne had initially done. With full access to the bank's intranet, as she'd initially been allowed.

Inviting Jayne to sit on his ergonomic chair, he drew up another chair and began uploading. Soon the two were engrossed, Komal having little idea what their banker-speak actually meant. So many acronyms, so much jargon; it offended her journalistic love of clarity, sounded to her like techno-financial gibberish.

Komal went to the living room, scanning his books, starting to dip into one. She was so engrossed that she hardly noticed time slipping by until Jayne came in flushed with excitement, clutching a memory stick the banker had given her.

*

224

They each felt so relieved, such a load off their shoulders.

A world away in The Wilds, in the middle of the bustling city, but not of it. Just a pop-up library at the entrance and a mobile Craft Coffee van. No honking cars, no flurry, no hurry. No smog, no hustling street vendors streaking between cars belching at traffic lights. No beggars. No cameras.

Instead, Mother Nature reincarnated in an urban jungle. Lush trees and bush, aloes coming into glorious reddish bloom, a waft of sapphire, wild flowers, sixteen hectares of indigenous vegetation on the sides of two rocky kopjes, with foot trails, hikes and natural waterfalls, buck, and a giraffe appearing suddenly on walkabouts.

Van der Merwe spotted Strijdom up ahead, bulkily fit, on a wonderfully paved path made of stones, heading up a kopje as they'd arranged for their clandestine rendezvous. Apparently, the winding paths had been laid for Joburgers' enjoyment by prisoners from the notorious Johannesburg jail known as The Fort. He'd also found out by chance that, during the 1980s, MK cadres used to meet there to conspire and confide, away from the apartheid security forces. The irony of the comparison with these two modern conspirators was not lost on Van der Merwe.

Hennie Strijdom looked at the shrubs and trees in The Wilds, buried in his personal history, remembering – with some pride – his own role in some of South Africa's most heartless and vicious apartheid years.

The two started chatting as they strolled along, just another pair of walkers among all the others.

'You know many of the worst apartheid atrocities were under President F. W. de Klerk,' Strijdom remarked, 'during those four years between Mandela walking from ten thousand days spent in prison to freedom, and being elected president in April 1994.'

'But didn't De Klerk deny all knowledge?' Van der Merwe responded.

'Yes – unbelievable!' Strijdom exclaimed. 'He always denied everything that the state "third force" agencies, or the state's covert assassination squads, were up to. But ministers set us up and signed off our operations. Their strategy was try to cling on to power at the same time as negotiating a transition to democracy. They were talking to Mandela at the same time as killing his grass-roots activists.'

'Weren't you part of all that?' Van der Merwe asked.

225

'Yes, not just at Vlakplaas but also in Stratcom – remember that? Also known as Strategic Communications?'

Van der Merwe nodded. 'Don't remember much about it, not like Vlakplaas, which I helped with supplies.'

'Stratcom was a state-orchestrated and -funded agency,' Strijdom explained. 'We conducted a sort of psychological warfare: intimidation. Some low-grade stuff like vandalising property and threatening phone calls. Higher-grade stuff like secret arms caches. One of our tasks was to spread disinformation to discredit Winnie Mandela. A sort of character assassination against the likes of her.

'Another was to target individuals investigating or blowing the whistle on state crimes, by smearing them with fake and doctored intelligence dossiers and fictitious misinformation, which we fed to media platforms. We deliberately jumbled fact and fiction, we pushed out lies.

'Stratcom was about annihilating opponents. We were trained to permanently neutralise – ideas or people or institutions – on behalf of the government of the day, using unlimited state resources to do so. We became sadists hunting for the opponents of our masters, getting up to all sorts of things to terrorise anti-apartheid activists. We used chemicals to neuter contraception. Used HIV-infected blood. Emptied a laxative into the instant coffee of trade unionists. Poured tear-gas powder into air-conditioning systems. Used illegal firearms and linked up with criminals or actually became criminals ourselves. They talk about corruption today – and it is bloody awful – but we were corrupt ourselves, and monsters too, when I think what we did.'

Van der Merwe had a sudden flashback, his mouth creasing into an ugly smile. 'Remember also that programme you guys ran for the Defence Force? What was it called? Something like "the Aversion Project"? The one for gay soldiers?'

Strijdom nodded at the memory, feeling awkward – his latest girlfriend had a gay brother who seemed a decent enough guy. 'Yes,' he said, 'I certainly do. The project to identify gay conscripts and give them the "full treatment", to try and cure their homosexuality by electric shocks and the like. Don't think it ever worked, mind you, but it certainly discouraged them!'

The two veteran apartheid agents meandered along, planning the assignment ahead, Strijdom take-it-or-leave-it about his lucrative fee, paid in cash the usual way. In advance. And soon. It was quickly agreed.

More details would follow. Meanwhile, would he scout the venue, find a suitable vantage point?

Minister Yasmin wasn't easily stunned, but the intelligence sent her cold with shock.

Naamloos had picked up something that justified all her instincts to ignore the smaller stuff and keep waiting for a big one before pouncing.

And this didn't come much bigger.

In her inimitable manner, she didn't suddenly issue a warning and act fast, instead starting to think, coolly, clinically, calculating the odds of different strategies. The immense rewards that might come from taking a risk – an extreme risk – but one where the political and security rewards would be greater, much greater.

Yasmin pondered hard for nearly twenty minutes, then made her decision.

The intelligence had to be hugged close or it would leak to the bad guys through the operatives still well placed in the country's security system. Also, for the same reason, she couldn't deploy the usual security networks at her disposal, couldn't even alert the President's protection guys.

Time to call in both the Sniper and Thandi.

And to seek a one-to-one with the President. On a matter as seismic as this, she had to have his buy-in. But only in strict confidence – not even his head of office or personal security chief could know. Couldn't proceed on her chosen high-risk course otherwise.

In this situation only the President could be trusted. Nobody else.

Back in the safe house, Jayne quickly inserted the memory stick into her laptop and began to work.

It had started to make sense – a sort of sense.

Christ, these criminals had been well advised, she thought. The global corporates delivering soft audits turning a blind eye to duplicity; consultant reports peppered with detail to gloss over fake business plans; internationally reputed law firms setting up shell companies to conceal the Svengali behind them all in Dubai, Hong Kong, Caribbean offshore tax havens.

Much of that she had gleaned already, but at last she had the makings of a full picture. More importantly, the beginnings of a real digital trail showing what had happened to the Vryburg money. And even more important than that, where it all led: to the figure hiding behind it.

She might actually have him nailed at last.

Jayne burrowed away, not noticing the hours slipping by, only the twinges in her back, the cramp on her shoulders as she defied all the advice to take regular breaks from crouching over her keyboard.

She had to ensure the proof was watertight, so she could nail him.

Her meeting with the President wasn't in his office in the Union Buildings atop Meintjieskop, overlooking Pretoria.

Instead, Yasmin had asked to meet him alone at his official residence, which Mandela had renamed from its old title Libertas to Mahlamba Ndlopfu, meaning 'New Dawn' to symbolise the Africanisation of the house, to bind it to the whole population, not just the white minority. The flat white building, designed Cape-Dutch style following the farmers who had first settled in the Cape centuries before, was built to honour its colonial heritage, to honour ancestors of the white minority, its name Libertas denoting freedom – for those white settlers, that was.

At Yasmin's specific request, the President joined her to stroll in the lush, spacious gardens. She didn't want any eavesdroppers; even his security team left them alone.

Despite the immense pressure he was under, the President was convivial and courteous, listening intently. When she explained her plan, he stood and stared at her. Time froze for a moment. She could almost hear his mind whirring.

'A big risk,' he said slowly. 'For me personally, of course, a very big risk. But also for the future of the country.'

Yasmin said nothing, just let him follow his train of thought, speak his mind. She knew from long years of comradeship that was how he was with people he could trust.

'But a much bigger risk to alert the enemy, that's what you are saying, aren't you?' the President asked, looking at her.

She nodded sombrely.

'Better to flush them out? And if we succeed, we can move to isolate them? Crush them? Because they will be so discredited even their allies will disown them?'

Yasmin nodded again. She didn't need to tell him that she had calculated the odds, assessed the conundrum, inside out and upside down. He knew that, knew her of old, trusted her completely.

They wandered through the gardens in the late-afternoon sun, evening

228

drawing in. So tranquil, so gorgeous – and so utterly at odds with the horror that would arise and the chaos that would result if the choice they were contemplating backfired.

The President placed his arm around her shoulders – not invading her personal space, just in a gesture of affection.

'You have my agreement,' he said. 'Let's go for broke.'

For the first time since she had been shown in for the appointment, Yasmin smiled. Not out of pleasure, but out of respect for the courage he was displaying, wondering how he would sleep over the next couple of weeks, knowing she wouldn't sleep very well, if at all.

On her shoulders, already cramped with tension, she carried an immense burden.

CHAPTER 11

Jayne briefed the Veteran, Komal listening intently at his side after they'd driven to the safe house in response to her excited call.

'Great work!' he said. 'How the hell you've managed to decipher that lot, I've no bloody idea.'

She looked pleased.

'But no rest for the wicked!' he grinned, 'I'd like you to write it all out, explaining what you have uncovered. Keep it simple. Tell a story. Ensure it can be understood, because you are an expert – most people reading or listening won't be. Do it as a speech, as if you were explaining it to an audience yourself.'

'I've never delivered a speech!' Jayne exclaimed.

'Don't worry about that. Komal was a professional journalist – she will happily sub-edit it.'

'Oh I will, will I, dear?' Komal winked mischievously at Jayne.

'Okay – okay!' the Veteran held up his hands in mock apology. 'I will ask Komal very nicely if she will sub it.'

'That's better – course I will,' she said.

'And I will look it over myself to ensure it's clear, with the right impact,' the Veteran said, adding, 'always watch out for these journalists, never can trust the buggers.'

Jayne was never quite sure what to make of their banter, so she stayed quiet, smiling nervously as the two laughed at each other, before she headed off to start work again.

Bob Richards had also been biding his time to say what he had to say.

Apparently not anything like as explosively sensational as his revelations over the poisoned elephants, which had even put him in the unusual position of getting double-page spreads with Mkhize's photos in the tabloid newspapers. The *Daily Mirror* excepted, he was used to being panned, not praised by tabloids such as the *Daily Mail*, *Sun* and *Express*, which had all had a right go at him over supporting Extinction Rebellion protests.

He had been tipped off by the Veteran that something more would be coming soon, and began preliminary enquiries as to when he might get a slot to speak in the Commons.

For Hennie Strijdom it may have seen better days but still retained prestige, albeit somewhat tired, in Johannesburg's city centre, as a sort of heritage trophy to past commercial glory.

It was where all the main business deals were done in the gold-rush city – the metropolis on the edge of the world's largest known gold deposit, first officially designated open for prospecting in 1886 by British colonial rulers, although gold had been informally traded and worked there over earlier centuries.

Founded in 1887 by Cecil John Rhodes at the outset of the frantic tumble for gold, the six-storey Rand Club (built in 1904) harked back to the era of British mining magnates. It had a handsome entrance hall and majestic staircase beneath a spectacular stained-glass dome, as well as an amply stocked gunroom and an outstanding library. At its huge mahogany-panelled Main Bar, the longest in Africa, beer was still served in tankards. Striking miners had attacked the club in 1913 and its defence led to fierce street fighting, the scars still visible on the facade.

Intrigued, approvingly intrigued, Hennie Strijdom wandered into the members-only club during the hours open to the public and looked it over, noting the hunting trophies adorning one wall above stuffed otters and partridges in glass cases, paintings of Lord Nelson, the Battle of Trafalgar and a Second World War RAF fighter plane, a whiff of Kipling and Churchill, a gentleman's club from Pall Mall displaced into what was once Britain's Highveld frontier, where the wars for mineral riches against the Boers were plotted.

However, he was much more interested in viewing the entrance and the building's situation. Once a hive for the surrounding centre of commercial activity, it was now something of an oligarch's throwback in a bustle of downtown street vendors, spaza shops, jumbled taxi ranks and hustling hawkers, the large corporates having long evacuated to plush Sandton or new business hubs even further away from the old city centre. Where once the neighbourhood was white and opulent, now it was black and poor, old office buildings disused, windows cracked and dirty, some spaces squatted.

Strijdom looked around, walked about, slipped away outside to glance upward for possible viewing points, climbed staircases in buildings he could access, spent several hours thoroughly casing the joint – and eventually chose his spot, as much for its clear sight down onto the Rand Club's entrance as for a speedy getaway.

He would return once more before the day of his mission for a final check, wondering what it would all look like in years to come when plans were completed to rejuvenate and gentrify this rundown old commercial centre.

Hennie Strijdom was never casual about a reconnaissance, always meticulous, always ultra-careful, didn't like spontaneity, wanted to make a plan that would be robust if the unexpected popped up – as it invariably did.

Jayne tried her best to place an explanation around following the looted money, tried to untangle the detail of the digital trail, tried to jettison banker-speak, tried to drop the jargon, imagined herself as her illustrious relative Helen Joseph, delivering a speech to an audience that didn't understand the mysteries of her financial world.

But it was tough. She'd never done anything like this before. She'd written reports for bosses – yes, plenty of them. But all within their financial realm, all of them knowing the in-language, all experts in her profession. Lots of shorthand assumed. Lots of technicalities taken for granted. Lots of terminology in common.

She'd been charged with writing in what the Veteran had termed 'clear-speak' – and she wasn't used to that, thinking about it for the very first time, realising her financial-techno sphere was a chasm away from that of the average well-informed citizen, grasping that she had to imagine she was talking to that citizen, had to put herself in the position of that citizen.

Jayne began tapping away on her computer, her shoulders now aching with cramp and tension again.

*

Minister Yasmin had arranged for Thandi to be enrolled as a cleaner at the Rand Club, and she wrapped a scarf around her head and neck, wore baggy, unkempt trousers, steadfastly looking down as she walked about, adopting the reticent mode of a worker at the bottom of the food chain – such a contrast to her usual manner, head held high and proud.

It was early morning, two hours before breakfast was served at seven, when Thandi arrived through the staff entrance to join other cleaners, speaking mostly in her first language, isiXhosa, uttering only a little stumbling English. There was an air of excitement at the official visitor due mid-morning, and quite an occasion was expected.

Getting straight down to work, avoiding gossip and deflecting curiosity about her, Thandi found her back soon ached from all the bending and scrubbing, reminding her of the relative comfort of her life – for her cleaner colleagues a daily grind, for her just a one-off, thankfully.

Polishing in the Rhodes Room, she peered up, noting one of the walls with an imposing bookcase of important-looking volumes, another with a fireplace, grandfather clock and a huge full-length portrait of Cecil John Rhodes, its caption reading: 'Cecil Rhodes is remembered for his enormous contribution to the development of Southern Africa.'

Not at all how Thandi viewed the old imperialist, the one who had established the roots of apartheid over half a century before it was formally institutionalised, ensured blacks could not walk on the pavements of the city, only on the streets, had also barred brilliant Cape Coloured fast bowler Krom Hendricks from representing his country on its first-ever cricket tour of England in 1894 because he wasn't white.

The place was fascinating to Thandi as she hoovered the thick carpets, wiped the wood panelling on the walls, cleaned the Romanesque columns, dusted the glass-fronted bookshelves, wiped the plush leather sofas.

It was a tapestry of past and present, of colonial supremacy with genuflections to the new democracy: tall portraits of Nelson Mandela and the Queen on the first floor; in the entrance hall a bust of Chief Albert Luthuli, former president of the African National Congress; nearby a small statue of Paul Kruger, president of the independent South African Republic and famed Afrikaner leader in the war against the British beginning in 1899 – a war primarily for control of the gold and diamond wealth of the country in the hands of the British since the 1870s. In the billiard room, she noted the stuffed heads of antelope, springbok and kudu, jutting out from the walls, their horns pristine, almost defiant, she thought.

Tired and aching by the time her early cleaning shift had ended, she stayed on unobtrusively, first in the domestic-worker quarters long after the other early workers had departed, biding her time and waiting for her next allotted task, her first one already having been accomplished when dawn was just breaking, guests still sleeping and catering staff only just arriving.

Thandi carefully let the Sniper into the building and saw him slip through the sliding iron gate and into the 106-year-old wood-panelled lift, watching pensively as it winched and whined its way upward. There was nobody else about.

The veld fire raged through Zama Zama, smoke choking the air above the safari park, everyone – rangers, cleaners, cooks, guests – out trying to beat down the flames with damp sacks.

The sun almost disappeared in the dark pall hanging overhead, and insects flushed out by the burning heat were gobbled up by soaring and swooping birds.

Poachers had deliberately lit the fire to flush out the animals, which scampered blindly out of harm's reach, but then found the fire beating them – and the arsonists – back too.

Across the country, the climate emergency was triggering fires in the veld. Extreme weather events were making the environment drier, with more heat waves predicted, along with longer periods of drought as temperatures increased.

Mkhize was only too familiar with the usual causes: lack of firebreaks; people burning rubbish dumps; people making fires while waiting for taxis on the side of road and then leaving the fires burning; discarded cigarette butts; electricity lines not properly maintained, leading to wires touching and sparking in high winds.

Then there was the tradition of certain farmers to burn mountain veld, aiming to regenerate vegetation. But those fires were often not properly controlled and on windy days could run completely out of control into neighbouring farms, degrading the veld by damaging the roots of the grass and removing tonnes of carbon from the soil.

But this one in Zama Zama was man-made to order, and the wanton damage to the game reserve – which had survived poacher assaults, droughts and torrential rain – was grievous.

It was only saved by the bravery of Isaac Mkhize and his ranger team, as they somehow managed to corral the raging flames, mercifully helped by a sudden ebbing of the fierce wind. Later, they discovered two charred bodies – poachers from a local village – amidst the blackened, smoking devastation, surrounded by the sadly severed stumps of trees and bushes, their once-green leaves crumbling to ash.

Sometimes even Mkhize despaired at nature's ferocity unleashed by wanton human behaviour. As he gloomily surveyed the habitat carnage, his thoughts turned to Thandi, wondered how she would fare on her latest mission, whether she would ever have time to bear the children he craved.

The suave-suited former diplomat had retired from the Foreign Office a while back after a distinguished career, including serving as the prime minister's special representative in the hotspots of Baghdad and Kabul.

At his retirement do, he made a witty, self-deprecating but also self-praising speech, gently poking fun at himself and the mandarins above and alongside him.

Afterwards, he walked wistfully from the grand nineteenth-century building in King Charles Street, its rich decoration meant to impress foreign visitors and remind them of Britain's then imperial power and Victorian grandeur.

Wistfully because he'd enjoyed his diplomatic career and had once been right at the centre. As Principal Private Secretary to the Foreign Secretary, he'd been a key policy adviser and gatekeeper, briefing 10 Downing Street and on first-name terms with prime ministers.

But he was not one for nostalgia, not least as he'd moved seamlessly a month later into a new job as BSBC's corporate relations director. Although having had no banking experience, his global expertise was ideal for such a position in a global bank. His new office in a shiny sky-scraper in Canary Wharf was no match for the Foreign Office, of course, but prestigious enough to befit a man of his status.

Resolving or managing problems had exercised him throughout his diplomatic career, and one confronted him right now in his new role. It was the way in which a backbench MP popped up periodically in the House of Commons with well-sourced speeches fingering BSBC as being highly complicit in South Africa's tawdry tale of state capture and, especially, money laundering.

So well-sourced, he'd been advised, that the MP must be the recipient of insider information from their bank.

235

So damaging, he was only too aware, that BSBC's reputation was being shredded, just at a time when it was in trouble for money-laundering allegations in Latin America. US Treasury officials were investigating, and were threatening to withdraw the bank's US licence. A consequence so deadly for the bank that nothing must be permitted to reinforce it. Nothing. Certainly no meddling MP or whining whistle-blower.

He issued a fresh instruction the public-affairs firm contracted by BSBC to monitor Parliament and to open doors in Whitehall: keep a watchful eye on Bob Richards, especially for any forthcoming slots he had secured for adjournment debates.

Then he instructed the Johannesburg office to seal the leak and hunt down the whistle-blower.

Komal's journalistic skills had been invaluable in turning Jayne's presentable draft into something much clearer and sharper for the impact it deserved and for the Veteran to have a final look at.

This he had done, and then had emailed the draft securely to Bob Richards. The MP had been alerted in advance so he could secure a slot to deliver the speech, enabling the results of Jayne's dogged research to be revealed to a global audience.

Richards began looking at it in his office on the fifth floor of Portcullis House, the other side of Westminster Bridge Road from the Palace of Westminster, overlooking the River Thames, constructed from 1992, said to be the most expensive in Britain, not least for its bomb-proof foundations erected over Westminster Underground Station.

Richards had come to expect arresting drafts from the Veteran, and this one was certainly no disappointment. The clarity with which it explained the complicity of international corporates in the Vryburg scandal was startling even to someone, like him, familiar with South Africa's debilitating state-capture outrage. Also provided was a detailed letter to the prime minister.

He began some minor tweaking, impressed at how oven-ready the draft was for him to deliver.

Several mornings later, Richards rose again in the Westminster Hall chamber, and spoke for close on twenty minutes, in a coruscating indictment of the complicity of international banks, auditors, accountants, consultants and lawyers in the rip-off of a poor rural village in the Free

236

State, again naming Star as the chief conspirator, as he had over the ele-phant massacre.

But his main focus was on the responsibility of governments.

'None of this would have happened without governments either turn-ing a blind eye to money laundering or waving it though. These are the key culprits.

'The United Arab Emirates has permitted Dubai to become a money-laundering haven, China likewise over Hong Kong. India, where the Business Brothers who looted so shamelessly under the previous President, has sheltered them and enabled at least one of its partially state-owned banks to be a conduit for money laundering. The UK has allowed its Overseas Territories in the Caribbean to advertise as offshore tax havens, stuffed with shell companies concealing their true owners. Banks like HSBC, Standard Chartered and Baroda should already have surrendered the digital trails revealing where the Business Brothers and the Former President's family laundered their money.

'The corporates and lawyers that set up shell companies, mainly in Hong Kong, Dubai and the Caribbean, must also provide full details of their own connivance in the looting and money laundering.'

'Global professional services companies have access to client data, and it is high time they established robust compliance policies and procedures to recognise and prevent money laundering.

'Banks must start sharing client information with each other, with other corporates and with state enforcement agencies, instead of hiding behind the veil of "client confidentiality", which has become a charter for money laundering.

'This tawdry story began with the head of a provincial government in South Africa – known as "Star" – blatantly stealing public money intended to build a safari park employing many jobless and poverty-stricken locals. Then laundering it out through BSBC Bank to its branches in Hong Kong and Dubai. Then commissioning lawyers and accountants to set up shell companies – whose real or beneficial owner is in fact Star – and move the money around the international financial networks so that it is very difficult to trace.

'Instead of investing the five hundred million rands, or twenty-five million pounds in sterling, of government money through Vryburg Regeneration's account, most of it was transferred to a company in the United Arab Emirates called Frontway Limited, registered in

Ras al-Khaimah, which attracts highly secretive offshore companies. However, Frontway also has an account with BSBC.

'Once the Vryburg funds were in Dubai, they transferred over four hundred and eighty million rands of it through another two shell companies, into another BSBC account for another UAE company called Precise Investments. After which it was transmitted into Broadway Trading through an account in the State Bank of India. Then back into South Africa.'

'Fortunately, brave investigative activists and a bank whistle-blower have got to the bottom of this, and I have written to the prime minister describing in great detail what happened and how. And it's no good if the PM says, "Nothing to do with me what happens in a faraway country," for it certainly is. He and other heads of government condemn money laundering, then allow it to happen, including through London-headquartered or -based global corporates.

'The victims are always the jobless and the poor. It's time the bankers, the consultants, the auditors, the accountants, the lawyers and the estate agents became the victims of a concerted international drive by governments to stop and prosecute the money launderers.'

On the top floor of the Rand Club, the Sniper eased his way out to head up onto the roof, to a position he had carefully sought after a recce two days earlier, a spot from where, concealed, he could see across a wide span to the buildings across the street, searching for the gunman, especially for several key positions he might have used himself, had that been his task.

He quickly assembled and checked his rifle, then crouched, settling down to wait. Six hours, not that long. Not like those weary nights when he had been protecting the rhinos in Zama Zama. A relatively civil hour as the sounds of the awakening city encroached.

His mind wandered wistfully to how, almost matter-of-factly, Elise had suddenly suggested during a telephone call that he move into her bedroom next time he visited. He had imagined a tantalising smile and glint in her eyes.

She'd taken him completely by surprise – pleasurable, intoxicating surprise. He'd yearned for that, but learned not to expect it in case it never materialised. Now it had, or would next time he arrived in Zama Zama.

Abruptly he blanked out the stirring sensation, the anticipation, and forced himself to focus. He couldn't afford to be distracted.

The Sniper hadn't spotted any telltale movement opposite, complicated, though, by the position of the club in Loveday Street, at the corner of Fox Street. The assailant could conceivably be off Fox rather than somewhere across Loveday, and the Sniper started to worry he might miss him.

He thought about the irony of protecting the president-to-be walking from his prison gates more than a quarter of a century ago, and now the sitting president. Time coming full circle.

But at least, like that first time, he was working for the state – or rather that part of it loyal to the President. Not quite as neat and tidy this time for a man of military training such as the Sniper but somewhat tidier than some of the missions he had carried out in recent times, when he'd felt awkward about his deployment, gaining comfort only by knowing he was with the good guys, no question his enemies were the bad ones. But wondering for how long he could continue this sort of thing, his knee hurting a little, the odd bone creaking a bit – though at least the rifle still rock steady in his hands.

He looked around constantly and waited, feeling immense responsibility. If the assassin succeeded, all hell would break loose in the country. Just like it would have done when he was there on 11 February 1990, helping to ensure that Mandela walked peacefully to his own and his people's freedom.

Minister Yasmin was a worrier, and never more so than now.

She'd taken the calculated risk and it was on her shoulders, fair and square. She'd deliberately decided to endanger the President's life, and had been fretting about that ever since he'd agreed.

The odds had been assessed, she'd computed all the possibilities she could think of – and each time, it came down to the same conclusion: go for broke. Checkmate the enemy or they would return again and again. Sort them once and for all.

But still she worried, couldn't sleep, dozed, then woke startled again.

The crunch moment was getting ominously nearer.

The President's limousine departed exactly on time from his official Mahlamba Ndlopfu residence in the Bryntirion Estate, overlooking the capital, Pretoria, the driver taking his place within the motorcade of escorting police motorcycles and security vehicles.

He was driven among the cluster of buildings – the presidential guest house, the Deputy President's house, called OR Tambo House, past the beautifully laid flower beds, shrubs and trees, away to the side fifteen tennis courts, a nine-hole presidential golf course and a helipad.

The British prime minister, on an official visit, had been very envious of the sumptuous estate, with its perimeter security system of 200 CCTV cameras, four gatehouses and some eight kilometres of fencing festooned with anti-climb motion-detection devices.

The President felt secure in Bryntirion. He was a cautious man, manoeuvring carefully to outwit his powerful factional opponents within the ANC but moving far too slowly and frustratingly for his supporters, who yearned for decisive leadership and rapid, radical change to place South Africa back on the Mandela road, away from the dismal decade of looting and cronyism that had all but bankrupted and crippled the country. He was a strategist, plotting his moves like a chess master, remorselessly checkmating his enemies. But that took time and cunning, for he was never someone for grand gestures that fell flat.

But this time he was worried. He found it it hard to take another look at his speech to the business community, hard to make those final revisions and tweaks to the text as was his wont. This irritated his media staff, who had released the speech in advance, embargoed to the time of delivery.

The birds were tweeting, the jacaranda blooms bright, as his car swept past the gate to a salute from the guards and began making its way down through and out of the city. Soon he was passing the looming Voortrekker Monument away to his right off the N1 highway to Johannesburg. Later he caught sight of Kyalami motor-racing circuit, reminding him of the annual nine-hour race he had followed as a fan.

This journey, however, was fraught, the conversation with his wife earlier still fresh in his mind. She had begged him not to go. 'Why take the risk? Why?' she kept pleading, tears rolling down her cheeks.

'Because I have to,' he kept replying, 'it's my duty. We have to confront the enemy at some point, I cannot keep ducking sideways when they move against me.'

The armoured BMW 7 Series swished along, gobbling up the kilometres amidst half a dozen security vehicles, blue lights flashing, that constituted his motorcade, with police motorcyclists leading the way. Usually he worked sitting in the back, a burly armed security officer in the front passenger seat. The longer the journey, the more work, the more official documents he devoured – just as well he wasn't like former British Prime Minister Tony Blair, who suffered from car sickness if he ever tried to do that, and instead worked on the phone.

The President sat in the back, thinking not of his speech but what might happen immediately beforehand.

The Sniper watched and waited, constantly combing the view in front of him, trying to put himself in the assassin's place.

Where would *he* go? Try to imagine yourself in the other person's skin. Try to think as if it was *you*. What would you do? Where position yourself? Both for an attack and, equally important, a safe exit?

The Sniper scanned constantly, worrying about whether he was still up for this. He'd been there for hours already, was growing tired and also impatient. What was this escapade about anyway? To stop a President from being attacked – a President who was well-intentioned, yes, but frustratingly slow in doing what had to be done to get the country up and functioning properly again after more than a decade of looting. Meanwhile, too many of the bad guys were still up to no good.

'Pull your bloody self together,' he muttered to himself. 'Focus. Concentrate.'

Below him, Loveday Street had come alive, a veritable sea of vendors, hawkers, people doing this and that, cars hooting, cars parking, a buzz of chatter wafting upward toward him.

Then he thought a caught a glimpse. Just a tiny one. Maybe a glint of sunlight striking a metal object? Wasn't sure. Couldn't see it again, but clocked the point anyway to keep a beady eye on it. At an open window, but if anyone was really there, they were well hidden.

Not a bad choice of spot, however, dark inside and quite handy for a shot at the club's front entrance. Had to assume the shooter was a pro, couldn't rely on anything else.

Strijdom had crept into position, set himself up; helpful that the locality had been in decline, buildings dishevelled, many unoccupied, others squatted, a jumble of peeling paintwork, broken windows, and no maintenance. But crucially for him very few people about on the upper floors of what seemed once to have been a prime office, dating back a hundred years, probably more he reckoned.

It had been a relief to find his chosen spot the same as when he'd first found it, nobody in sight, dusty and empty.

Strijdom set up his rifle for the shots needed. He'd never considered himself a long distance shooter like professional snipers were, even killing over several kilometres. His expertise was in much shorter distances, like this one.

Relieved that there didn't appear to be much extra security about with an hour to the allotted time, Strijdom began to relax – not to lose concentration, on the contrary to be able to focus upon his principal task and not to have to worry about external security factors.

Come to think of it, wasn't it rather odd that the place wasn't already buzzing with thickset grim looking men in shades with obvious bulges where guns were carried? The thought flashed through his mind then passed. Some of them must be inside the club; the President never arrived anywhere without boots on the ground ready and waiting for him, able to receive the team of protection officers who travelled with him.

There was, however, obvious movement. Lots of men, just the very occasional woman, arriving for the speech, chattering to each other, a sense of anticipation, people in the street, clearly unaware of the imminent VIP visit, beginning to notice something was afoot.

Also the arrival of television teams, setting up, reporters ready to commentate live to camera, mobile vans with satellite dishes on top to send back live coverage.

Then Strijdom did notice something. A couple of the guys with shades emerging from the building, having a look around. Safe to assume there might be more inside.

Shouldn't be a problem.

Ready now, he waited.

The Sniper remained locked on and locked in to the emerging scene in front of him.

No more fleeting thoughts about Elise's thrilling invitation, or the anticipation it had provoked in him. No more nagging worries about the proprieties around his role in the past, though certainly not now.

Just a relentless, steely focus on his job. To save a president, no less. A huge responsibility on him; he had never failed during his anti-poaching missions, but they paled into insignificance compared with the weight upon him now.

242

His eyes continued to rove, sweeping in a semi-circle in front of him, always coming back to the glint that may or may not have been of any significance.

The Sniper's role was always solitary. Everything resting on his shoulders. No support or back-up. Succeed or fail. All down to him.

He was used to that, had been trained from his young days into the responsibility, a heavy one, but also not something he could ever allow himself to be consumed with worry over. Get dragged down that side alley and you started failing from the moment you did so. Couldn't afford to do that, and never had. Wasn't going to be dragged down now, this his biggest-ever test, to save his president – not from something that might or might not happen, like when he was a safety precaution in 1990 over Mandela, but something that would certainly happen and it was all down to him to stop it.

His knees were nagging but his concentration was total, finger near the trigger, scope set, all lined up for the cross-hairs to get the enemy in them. Then boom.

The Sniper waited. Patience was his second name – maybe his first – on an assignment such as this. Patience was about winning, impatience losing, and losing was unthinkable.

When he'd first taken office, the President had seen himself as a man of the people. He would appear unexpectedly on a beachfront or in a shopping centre to chat with startled passers-by. He had wanted to be different from his predecessor. He hadn't much cared for all the cavalcade razzmatazz, but had learned to live with it, reluctantly accepted the advice of his security people.

As per Minister Yasmin's instructions, the President's motorcade suddenly stopped in a Johannesburg side road. It was a residential area, with not many people about, so there were only a few curious stares.

His protection officer, staring about constantly, got out and opened his door, heavy and armour-plated like the windows, very difficult to swing back to close if leaning down on a slope as it was now, very difficult to swing open if leaning up a slope.

The President stepped out, speech in folder to hand, guided by the protection team now all around him to one of the MPVs – also armoured – in the motorcade. He climbed in, feeling strange, never having been in one before, with most of his team confused but obedient nevertheless.

One of his protection officers – bulky like him, sort of looked like him – climbed into his limo, sat in his place, also feeling strange.

Ready, the motorcade set off, bang on time, just Johannesburg's clogged, belching traffic, often gridlocked, between him and his appointment.

He felt awkward, the armoured jacket underneath his shirt uncomfortable, his armpits growing moist despite the air conditioning. But Yasmin had insisted that it was absolutely necessary to wear it.

Star watched SABC news, only half listening to the reporter talking from in front of the Rand Club, previewing the President's speech on the future of an ailing economy from a briefing by his press team.

Journalists always pontificating, blah-blah-blah, Star thought, sometimes libellous stuff about him, though not today.

Media? He hated them, those reporters on the *Daily Maverick* the very worst, always one fabricated accusation after another. One reporter had even had the effrontery to pen a book about him. Full of stuff. Made him furious. Not so much with the journalist – just trash like the rest. No, with his sources, some of them so well-informed that they must have been, or even still were, very close to his innermost circle. Why he hardly trusted anybody any more. Him against the world, so he could change the world – sod the lot of his enemies, to hell with any fickle two-faced so-called friends.

He would have the last laugh when he took over the country. Star on the soccer pitch, star he would also be on the presidential pitch – if all went to plan, and today was crucial.

He sat in front of the TV screen, hardly watching, fiddling with his phone, especially the encrypted apps, vital to him they were, praising to heaven the information from the staffer in the President's office on his payroll, because her mom and dad needed full-time care and that was expensive.

Yasmin watched from her office, tense, stomach knotted, desperately hoping her high-stakes judgement and her amateur team would pay off.

This was the biggest risk she'd ever taken. Caution was her middle name, yet she'd thrown caution to the wind. Gone for broke. Put the most important person in the country in danger in order to smoke out his enemy.

She waited, fidgeting with her phone, hoping to hell that she'd made the right decision, knowing it was too late — far, far too late — to have second thoughts now.

Strijdom knew that from the moment the presidential cavalcade arrived, there'd be no time for second thoughts. Just clinical shooting.

He'd studied the videos on YouTube, knew the formation, the pattern of arrival, where the President's limo would be among the MPVs, their blue lights flashing.

The welcome party walked out into the sun, surrounded by the shades, all of them scanning constantly, around, up and down, more of them than he'd first spotted. Didn't matter to him, really. What mattered was a clean shot, or, even better, multiple shots — and then a quick getaway.

Unable to concentrate on the crisply printed speech in double-spaced sixteen-point Arial font, the President, sitting awkwardly in the unfamiliar seat of the back-up vehicle, felt the armoured vest underneath his crisp white shirt rubbing itchily. He knew he was entering a trap that might mean he'd lose everything: his life, and with it the country handed over on a plate to his arch-enemy — to be ransacked again.

He'd crafted the messages to his business audience, mostly white and of a certain age. He needed them on board with their connections to the City of London and their old-boy networks. Needed their buy-in to get foreign investors back, needed their buy-in to stop the white business-talent exodus to London and elsewhere in the world.

He was normally a cool customer, unfazed by pressure, plots and the twenty-four-hour media pandemonium that came with the territory, always tried to focus on what mattered, cocking a deaf ear to the 'noise' as he described it to his team, always nervous on his behalf.

But this was different. Why the hell had he agreed to it?

The President thought again of the conversation with Yasmin. He trusted her implicitly, trusted her with his life — literally — a cool customer and a worrier with a huge conscience. One for the sidelight, not the limelight, worth her weight in gold — not many like her in his life.

Hoped to God she was right this time. Or else it was curtains for him, for the tens of millions who'd voted for him, and for the country.

*

The Sniper noticed the text from Yasmin: 'ETA 2 minutes', kept roving in front of him, waiting, always a cat-and-mouse game of waiting, never ever break cover first, always try to out-wait the assailant, dangerous, of course, especially in this case, because waiting a millisecond too long could spell failure and death for the target.

But shooting prematurely could expose his position, make him the target and leave the assassin free to go about his sinister work.

Inside the Rand Club, guests had made their way from mingling over pre-event drinks in the bar to be seated. Outside, the welcome party had emerged: officers of the club, the city mayor and the Gauteng provincial premier, waiting expectantly.

The protection officers on the ground, eyes roving behind their shades, readied, watched the growing crowd surging forward, expectant but not sure what was happening, except something different, something interesting.

Strijdom, sensing the moment was coming, primed himself.

Around the corner came the helmeted motorcycle outriders, followed almost immediately by the flashing blue lights on the MPVs. The excited crowd, smartphones ready for photos, fell silent as the cavalcade came to a stop.

Although pre-rehearsed and on a routine, it all seemed pretty chaotic, vehicle doors opening, shades swivelling, people gawping, welcome party smiling and moving forward.

The protection officer climbed out of the limousine, looked swiftly around, then opened the back door. The bulky figure emerged and waved, smiling, the welcome party hesitating momentarily, appearing confused.

Strijdom seized his moment, what he'd planned for, squeezed off two shots, always aimed for the chest – more target area than the head – saw him stagger, heard the screams, faces stricken with horror, as the target fell to the ground, excitable commentators on live television relaying the story.

Then – something wrong? Strijdom caught a glimpse from the corner of his eye of another, much more familiar, bulky figure emerge from an MPV behind, smiling stiffly, hands extended, crowd turning.

Confused, Strijdom broke all the rules of cover – had never done that before – and rose a little to get a better sight of what the hell was going on. He swung his rifle around, trying to line up the second figure in his cross-hairs, maybe unleash more shots.

At that moment, the Sniper had him. He fired off several bullets, saw them hit the shooter somewhere in his upper torso, wasn't sure exactly where, the opportunity only split-second, the image too mixed, saw him lurch a little backward, then disappear.

Down below, the dummy president rose shakily, thanking his lucky stars for the armoured vest, relieved for both himself and his boss, to whom he waved a nervous thumbs-up.

The President saw him, was veering over out of concern, then was suddenly enveloped by his protection team, guns drawn, hustling him into the building and to an area off the main entrance corridor to pause, take stock and regroup before his speech. The crowd outside was stunned, aghast, reporters beginning to speculate, television and radio chatting, news coverage extended, their stories shifting instantly, herd-like, from the President's economic message to the dramatic attempt on his life.

Consternation outside the Rand Club, the media excitedly reporting the attempted assassination, Yasmin glued to the eNCA television channel, tears of relief welling up inside her, phone ringing, the President on the line, thanking her, wishing her all the best in tracking down those responsible.

In one sense, the world had been lifted right off her shoulders, where it had sat for ages.

In another, the battle had only just begun,

The Sniper swiftly but methodically stowed away his rifle, checked he'd left no trace, slid back into the building, found Thandi beckoning towards one of the guest rooms, vacant, left ready for him.

She followed him in, looking away, embarrassed, as he undressed and changed into a suit hanging in the wardrobe, one he hadn't worn for years – no need, wasn't in that sort of business environment. It felt tighter than when he'd last put it on, as Thandi grabbed the clothes he'd taken off, stuffing them into a black plastic bin bag, lifting the gun case too, surprised it was so light. She gave him a little hug, hadn't ever shown that sort of affection to him, and left with hardly a word, looking tense and determined, making her way swiftly down the stairs and out through the staff quarters, as a cleaner unnoticed amidst the chaos in front.

*

247

An interval later, the Sniper slipped gingerly out of the room, called the lift and headed down to join the guests awaiting the President, trying to dispel both the extreme tension and the huge stress that had enveloped him over the previous hours and more, wondering again whether he was really up to this sort of thing any longer.

He found an excited hubbub down below, a chaotic, confused concern. He stood as unobtrusively as he could, then followed the crowd to the dining room, searched for his allocated place on the guest list – under a pseudonym, of course – and sat down, nodding, hardly in time to stand up again and clap in the President, the place buzzing with excitable gossip and speculation.

Later on, after hearing the speech and the questions that followed, gulping down his food, only half-sipping at a glass of wine, waving away the waiter replenishments that kept coming, making small talk like he'd also not had to do for ages, until the other table guests began ignoring him as rather boring, the Sniper would meander out into the street with everyone else.

And nobody would notice him in the throng.

Star had watched the live coverage, transfixed, his frustration growing to fury.

He made a call – clipped, never did small talk. 'What the fok happened?'

'Don't know, boss, trying to find out,' came the nervous reply from one of his coterie.

Strijdom exited as best he could, the pain searing and worsening, blood seeping, aware of the consternation he had unleashed, confused at how and why the shots had hit him. The shooter must have been waiting for him, must have known of his task: there must have been a leak.

He'd never been hit so directly before. Suffered near-misses, once been grazed by a Kalash, but had never taken bullets mangling his flesh and insides, wasn't sure how badly but suspected the worst.

An odd, confusing sensation for him. He'd always felt he was omnipotent – not out of foolhardy schoolboy bravado but because he was the ultimate pro, always preparing as fastidiously for his exit as for his task. Staying safe was always top of his list, even above mission success, though until now there'd never been a conflict between those two objectives.

Clutching his gun case, he stumbled downstairs, through corridors, out of doors and into others, worried at the bloodstains he was leaving.

These would mean his DNA could be captured – and that, as far as he knew, had also not happened before.

He heard shouts below; it seemed people were already in the building, one starting up the stairs. He saw the lift moving to the ground floor, clicked his Beretta safety catch off and peered down the stairwell. He fired at a figure clambering up, managing to hit him.

His planned exit through a connecting corridor to another building was still a few floors down.

But the pain was getting unbearable, and he began to think about a discreet hospital clinic he'd earmarked a while back, just in case. He'd have to get there pretty bloody quick.

Thandi's instructions from Yasmin had been crystal clear.

Just disappear out the back. Nobody would take the slightest notice of yet another black domestic worker carrying a load on her back, especially when all the action was at the front of the Rand Club.

Meandering through the streets for around half an hour, she hailed a minibus taxi, squeezing in among all the other passengers.

She would eventually walk to the Sniper's block of flats, report in at the front desk as he'd prearranged, and make her way to his apartment, ostensibly as his cleaner. There she would deposit his stuff and switch on his TV to follow the breathless breaking news, after an hour returning his key and heading off.

The President's security detail felt acutely embarrassed at their failure to prevent an attack but thanked their lucky stars for the mystery figure who had saved their principal. They had joked with him when he first took office that their task was not really to save *him* but to get the one who attacked him.

Some stayed nervily with him in the Rand Club, others joined the hunt for the shooter.

They thought they'd identified his sniper spot, started swarming into the building, half-empty and, only part-functioning, with at least a semi-working lift, it seemed.

Consternation: one of them downed by a shot from above, the others having to take cover and inch their way upward; the guy seemed still to be there. They had to catch him if they could.

*

249

Strijdom managed to get to the connecting corridor on the fourth floor, sliding through and out of view from his pursuers relentlessly climbing up the block.

He reckoned he might just have lost them, certainly hoped so, because as the seconds tripped by, he seemed to be getting weaker.

As he peered anxiously behind him, a thought flashed into his mind of his place in Sea Point and the woman who'd jumped at the chance to join him there – just as they always did. Thought her pretty nice, was looking forward to spending time with her; maybe she'd be the one to settle down with – you never knew. Hadn't happened so far, but then, he hadn't really wanted it to, had he?

Maybe he was going soft? But the thought persisted as he lurched on, getting nearer to the rendezvous point with Van der Merwe. What a trooper the guy was, would certainly need him now for the getaway they'd planned.

The protection officers sweated and heaved their way up the floors, scouring above and to the sides, guns levelled in front, two hands gripping them, determined not to lose another colleague, determined to get their foe, to redeem themselves – partially, at least.

The wheezing, scraping lift carrying a couple of them reached the top, and they stepped gingerly out, sunglasses in their pockets, eyes swivelling in the half light.

Nothing. He'd gone. No sign of him from their colleagues continuing to climb either.

Waiting in the multistorey car park, Van der Merwe's phone had gone viral with alerts about the attack on the President.

Good for Strijdom! The guy was such a pro. Never failed – though it wasn't at all clear what exactly had happened, or whether the President was dead. The reporting seemed blurred on the detail. Then it was followed by even more confused news flashes about another attack, not on the President, maybe on his assailant?

Just as well, if so, that Star had put into place a Plan B – or rather a consequential Plan B. Star thought of everything.

Van der Merwe hunched over his steering wheel, engine ticking over, air con on, and waited, didn't like being so close to the action – that had never been his way, always in the shadows, never on the front line, that was for others.

Then he saw the lurching figure, clutching his gun case. Jesus! He was leaving a trail of blood, would probably bring some of it into his own car, worried not so much about the mess but about the DNA implicating *him*.

Strijdom grabbed at the back door, levering it open, slumped inside, hauling his case in too as Van der Merwe stuck the car into gear and gunned the engine, peering about for any followers, or anybody taking any notice. Didn't seem to be anything untoward he could spot.

The car sped down and round the corners onto the lower levels, ticket in the barrier, lifting and out onto the street, heard sirens wailing in the distance.

'How are you?' he grunted, 'Doesn't look very clever.'

'No, man, Strijdom wheezed. 'How long to go?'

'Couple of minutes, traffic permitting.'

'I'm bad,' Strijdom grunted. 'Just get me to my car and I'm away to get treated.'

Van der Merwe drove fast, looking constantly for a tail, but couldn't see one, didn't think his fellow conspirator was going to last, had to offload him soon, worried about blood on his car's back seat, thinking as he always did about himself first, worried about CCTV clocking his car registration.

He screeched into another multistorey car park and pulled up alongside Strijdom's car, helping him out, slinging the gun case in the boot, worrying that the man seemed to be weakening, seeming dazed, never ever seen him like that.

But no time to hang around. Van der Merwe drove off as quickly but as decently as he could, putting a distance between them before he halted at the ticket machine.

Feeling faint and dizzy, gripping the steering wheel to steady himself, Strijdom started his engine, ready to reverse out of the parking bay.

Then oblivion.

Strijdom's car exploded and he, with it, was blown to smithereens. A car bomb of the kind that had assassinated anti-apartheid activists in the previous era, like the one that nearly killed Albie Sachs, instead leaving him badly maimed with only one arm, lucky to escape alive, stumbling bloody and burned out of the vehicle.

Van der Merwe, leaving through the barrier, heard it. Didn't feel much. Sorry about the guy, yes of course – he'd been good to work with, was

251

impressive, even personable in a chippy, arrogant sort of way. But Star's last-minute instructions had been crystal clear. Leave no loose ends.

So he hadn't. And his bonus awaited. Just wondered what would happen to that million rand deposited with Strijdom in advance. Such a waste. Shame he couldn't get his hands on it.

CHAPTER 12

Thandi made her way to the safe house, attracting no interest, just another black domestic worker arriving at a gated property in the comfortable neighbourhood. She changed back into her normal clothes, discovering Jayne and Komal still glued to the television news channels, the story having evolved since the lunchtime drama.

She was still shaking, and both women embraced her without knowing about her exact role, making her feel better.

Minister Yasmin's office had indicated that she was advancing her investigation, hints were dropped about an 'assassination coup', news that encouraged reporters to speculate about a wider plot.

Yasmin had meanwhile found Naamloos a veritable treasure trove, the messages harvested, the phone calls too. A live video from a drone hovering above the vicinity and clocked by nobody – as advised by the Sniper and covertly arranged by her Corporal – had captured the scene, though not either of the shooters.

For a prosecutor, it was pretty well all gold dust.

From her government office, Yasmin was driven a short distance through Pretoria to see the relatively new chief of the National Prosecuting Authority, a formidable woman drafted in by the President, coming with an excellent reputation built at the International Criminal Court in The Hague.

She had been tasked to clean up the NPA – still stuffed with officials allocated by the Former President to pervert investigations and spare his bent cronies – and make early arrests of the gravy-trainers. After the past decade of looting, there had been a public clamour to see the culprits in 'orange overalls', as prison garb was known.

Yasmin asked that the two women take a walk in the building's rudimentary garden, didn't want to risk being bugged, and updated her on the evidence she'd uncovered. The NPA chief probed expertly, was concerned about only one point that would be revealed in court – namely, the deliberate risk taken with the President's life, which meant Yasmin would probably be called as a witness and the defence's legal team would try to attack her, using all the ploys top advocates had been using to delay and undermine bringing to justice the looters, including the Former President himself.

The NPA chief, who'd aged noticeably even in the short year or so in post, assigned her very best assistant to supervise the case, asked Yasmin to do the same, and the two bade farewell, both bearing heavy responsibilities to meticulously prepare for the prosecution.

For there were too many cases of corrupt politicians hiring expensive lawyers from opulent offices to run rings around prosecutors, advancing technical objections, spotting loopholes, using fancy legal footwork.

Star followed the news, then heard the rumour first from his source in the President's private office. They were coming for him, were confident about the case against him.

He needed to summon up his cronies to demonstrate if necessary. Former 'veterans' they called themselves, the bunch that always turned out to order and defend the Former President by protesting when he was dragged to court, as if they were somehow standing up for the true ANC of Mandela, Tambo and Sisulu.

Safely back in Zama Zama, the Sniper and Elise had snuggled up intimately in bed together, discovering each other, and then lying back, beginning to talk.

'Was it you who killed the President's assassin?' she asked impishly.

He smiled, having expected the question and having rehearsed his answer. 'Thought you might ask me that! But, my lovely Elise, as you know almost better than anybody from my role fighting poachers in your own game reserve, I have pledged never to discuss it with anyone not directly involved.'

'Even me!'

'Even you!'

She smiled pensively, giving him a hug, her breasts firm against his back, her arms tight around him. 'I understand, of course I do. And I'm proud of what you did, even though you cannot admit to it. But now we are properly together, I must ask you to discuss with me beforehand if you are ever asked to undertake another dangerous mission.'

The Sniper unwound her arms, turned over, and held her close.

'I promise,' he replied.

But, although he didn't say so, he felt his days as a sniper might well be numbered anyway.

Elise's thoughts turned to the rhinos grazing peacefully outside, dehorned to protect them, something she'd resisted doing until persuaded by a persistent Mkhize that it was essential for their own survival. She wondered, however, whether her elephant herd would be safe. She was determined not to have their tusks removed, but would that be needed to protect them?

Such a crying shame that these two noble species might have to lose their natural, foraging, fighting, imposing protuberances in this way.

Although Yasmin's meeting with the head of the NPA had been productive, she remained concerned at the timescale, because bringing the crooked politicians and officials serving the Former President to court was taking far too long – years and years, delays from legal manoeuvres by defence law-yers seemingly endless, legal costs to the taxpayer mounting exponentially.

For Star that simply wasn't good enough, Yasmin concluded. He was not only corrupt but a real danger to national security. Things had to happen much more quickly, and she decided to do something not in her normal, cautious, stickler-for-procedure nature.

She would arrange for a few selected journalists to be briefed, but only strictly off the record, that the police had 'digital evidence' of Star's culpability for both the attempt on the President's life and the massacre of the two elephant herds.

The phrase 'digital evidence' was not to be elaborated upon, but it was explosive enough to produce the headlines and stories she wanted without tipping off the gangster himself as to its exact nature.

There was a risk in doing this – of course there was. The NPA wouldn't like it, and the President would be worried.

But Yasmin had never put pleasing people, even friends and colleagues, at the head of her agenda. Getting results occupied that top spot.

*

Jayne got a cryptic message via a letter delivered to her flat and picked up by her neighbour friend, who'd opened it at her request.

Phone the South African CEO of BSBC immediately.

She did so using the new burner phone provided by Komal, and had a brusque conversation, which he said was being recorded.

The only way the confidential information contained in Bob Richards' explosive parliamentary speeches could have been obtained was via her. She was, therefore, being sacked with immediate effect. Furthermore, the mortgage the bank had provided, enabling her to move from her own home in Cape Town and buy a new flat in Johannesburg, was being immediately revoked. She'd therefore have to repay it in full.

'But I will have to sell the flat to do that,' she replied.

'Understood,' he said drily, added that a letter would be delivered shortly confirming all that and making it clear that, since she'd acted in breach of her employment obligations, the bank reserved the right to take legal action against her.

Whether it did so would depend upon how she acted in future.

'So you are censoring me from revealing the outrageous looting and corruption at Vryburg, then?' replied Jayne.

She was stunned but still defiant

'Not "censoring" you at all. Simply requiring your compliance with the duty to client confidentiality you swore to uphold when you joined BSBC,' he said evenly.

Jayne got the impression he was almost embarrassed. Almost. For she'd been something of a protégée to him, and he'd been pretty decent to her.

She paused, the moment of silence hanging uneasily between them, thinking carefully about how she might end the conversation, something she'd rehearsed with the Veteran before making the call.

'Well, I have enjoyed working for BSBC. Up until recently. Personally, you have treated me well. Up until recently. But please be clear that if I am asked to testify in public, I will tell the truth. That is a higher obligation than anything I signed up to with the bank. I certainly did not sign up to covering up corruption, and if you want to take action against me, that is what I will tell any court hearing.'

The CEO didn't respond, ended the call formally, privately admiring her pluckiness but never admitting to that, knowing his next call to the ex-diplomat in London, in his corporate relations skyscraper office, would be as difficult, bearing unwelcome news as he would have to: the girl simply wouldn't be intimidated, and the risk of the bank taking legal action against her was huge.

When his informant had warned that they were preparing a prosecution, Star had begun to regroup, to talk directly to his closest circle, some summoned to see him, others receiving messages through his cell-like network. All in person, not by phone, encrypted or otherwise.

But then a fresh blow. The headlines in certain media outlets left him completely flummoxed – and that was an entirely new experience for Star. Indeed, he was alarmed by the precision of the reports which appeared almost simultaneously in the *Daily Maverick*, *News24* and the London *Guardian*.

The '*digital evidence*' phrase jumped right out at him, left him reeling, almost as if from a physical blow.

Digital evidence? Linking him directly to the assassination attempt? Indeed, as the very orchestrator of it, right in the frame for attempted state murder?

It was one thing having regular allegations about corruption, state capture – run-of-the-mill stuff. It didn't much bother him, happened all the time, never was any follow-up action by the state authorities, who seemed impotent when it came to him.

But had to admit to being badly rattled by this obviously carefully orchestrated briefing from somewhere on high. It left him unable to sleep properly. Round and round it went in his mind: *how?*

He needed also to activate his failsafe Plan B, the one he'd long held in reserve, to protect his back, buy time and advance his cause. Was confident he'd win out in the longer term, for his enemy, the President, had badly disappointed voters and loyalists, dashing hopes, been too indecisive, hadn't shown the steel or produced the results he'd promised.

Nothing seemed to work in the country any more. Power cuts regular and persistent, water cuts growing, all the consequence of years of corruption and maintenance neglect by incompetent cronies of the Former President and his mates, the Business Brothers, who'd looted and bribed their way throughout the state infrastructure and administration, leaving it almost paralysed from top to bottom.

The mail never arrived, municipal government never delivered, the police took bribes, were lazy and incompetent. So people established their own parallel networks. Private mail couriers blossomed for the businesses and individuals who could afford them. Private security empires expanded, patrolling homes and responding to burglar alarms where police should have been. Well-intentioned community vigilantes began establishing local order in former townships. Volunteers ran soup kitchens or food-banks. Charities set up and funded schools to give hope to black youngsters trapped in despair by failing at hopeless state schools. And so it went on.

Under apartheid, the state was a jobs gravy train for the white, mostly Afrikaner, minority. Under the ANC it had been stuffed with incompetent cronies, becoming worse than useless. And the President, who'd been elected by the Party and then the people to sort out the mess, seemed completely unable to do so.

Disillusionment was deep and widespread, not just among white, Indian, coloured and middle-class urban black voters supporting other parties or burgeoning numbers of independents, but among the poor base of the ANC, who'd demonstrated their utter dissatisfaction by simply refusing to vote.

Crushing setbacks in the latest local election results showed that the President would be a sitting duck when the Party came to decide whether to re-nominate him at its elective conference.

That would be his moment, Star was certain – and his plans were already well advanced, his coffers to bribe delegates already full, where his people had not already been positioned to be those very delegates.

But, meanwhile, he was indeed spooked, pondering long and hard what to do.

After her boss – *former* boss now, she grimaced – had cut the phone call, Jayne walked out into the safe-house garden, mind racing, emotions surging.

Although the stress had subsided in one important way: no more danger to her life, it seemed, not even the sort of threats and intimidation she'd got used to living with when first a fugitive.

But a different sort of stress, which would now keep her awake in the small hours: what would be her future after she had self-destructed her career?

It was one thing to be commended for acting out of principle, for 'doing the right thing'. That was all very nice, but she had to pay her bills – and they were not inconsiderable, as she'd got used to a banker's lifestyle.

She had first been elated at the impact of her role, exhilarated by Thandi's vivacity and Komal's wise counsel, felt herself changing as a person, eyes opened to a new world of moral imperatives to activism, politics and struggle.

In the time that followed, all that subsided, and she was left disoriented. Though she was still in touch with both women, they had moved on and she'd been stranded in limbo, not quite sure how she could contribute to making the world a better place but not wanting to return to her old world, where earning money was the primary motivation.

She'd also been startled by the treatment of whistle-blowers, who were hounded by their former employers and threatened by their adversaries – and that despite promises by the President that wrongdoers would be rounded up and they would be championed and protected.

A former senior partner of a global management consultancy had found himself in exactly that predicament after going public about its deep complicity in the state capture, corruption and looting by the Former President.

Offered no protection against criminal threats by the looters, and frightened by the murder of another whistle-blower, he'd even felt it necessary to leave the country for England, a pariah when he should have been one of the heroes the President had lauded.

Jayne began feeling depressed at the stranded halfway house of her situation, then promptly jerked herself back, thinking again of Helen Joseph, who had endured such privation, shown such courage and fortitude, and of the inspiring end to her memoir where she had quoted the US Freedom Riders' song: 'Deep in my heart, I do believe, that we shall overcome one day.'

She reflected hard, still feeling desperately lonely, hoped she could be even half as strong as Helen had been.

The jacarandas were in full bloom, falling petals all over the city's street verges and in the lush gardens of the Bryntirion ministerial estate as Yasmin and the President strolled around in the late-afternoon sun, a cool breeze keeping them comfortable.

She'd brought the Veteran with her because the President wanted a debrief, and the two men knew each other from the early 1990s, during the four years of negotiation after Nelson Mandela's release from prison.

Their stroll took an hour or so, the President relaxed, waving greetings

259

to the gardeners, those who'd served back when Mandela took over remembering fondly how he'd always stopped to chat to each one, knew their names, asked about their children or grandchildren. A real 'people's president', Mandela had been; this one was more like him than the others in between, they gossiped.

First on her agenda was an uncomfortable one for the President, who had personally chosen all his close staff and advisers. One of them close to him was an informer.

He was shocked, unsettled, then brusquely muttered to Yasmin: 'Please smoke out the culprit for dismissal.' He'd never liked doing that sort of thing himself.

There were a number of details Yasmin wouldn't disclose, even to the President, which irked him momentarily, before letting it pass because he trusted her totally.

Like how the media stories about Star's responsibility had come to appear, about which she raised an eyebrow and shrugged.

Like who her shooter was: didn't he deserve a special commendation of some sort, or at least a personal thanks?

'No, Yasmin insisted, 'his identity will always remain secret. But I can tell you that three very brave women helped out in crucial ways.' She named Thandi, Komal and Jayne, explaining their different roles. How Thandi had been captured and nearly raped.

'Thandi! Again the saviour!' the President exclaimed. 'The young talent I asked to stand for Parliament – and she turned me down!' He smiled wistfully. 'Doesn't happen that often to presidents.'

'Feisty free spirit, she is,' the Veteran interjected. 'Wish we had more like her.'

'Yes, yes,' the President retorted impatiently, 'but why couldn't she have joined me?'

'Because,' said the Veteran cheekily, 'she is the very antidote to that Katy Perry lyric – you know the one? – words to the effect if you stand for nothing, you fall for everything.'

Noting the President wincing, the Veteran moved on quickly. 'And don't overlook Jayne. She was crucial in exposing the money laundering. But no bank will now employ her. Nor has she been given any protection, is suffering from threats and intimidation.'

'Tell me more about her?' the President asked. After hearing a concise explanation, he stopped walking, looked thoughtful, staring out over the

260

city below, the sun beginning to set, the sky starting to turn a mixture of orange, pink and purple-red, below street and building lights starting to twinkle.

'We could do with an expert like her, a banker-insider, working within the Treasury, but reporting directly to me. Will you ask her for me, please? I don't want to call her myself unless she would be agreeable in principle.'

'Of course,' said the Veteran, promising to find out.

Then he paused and added as an afterthought: 'By the way, what on earth persuaded you to risk your life like that when Yasmin suggested it?'

This time it was Yasmin who winced, the President gazing into the distance, then speaking deliberately. 'Well, I thought long and hard, because it was pretty mad.'

He paused, smiling. 'But a wise older person once said this to me: "An opportunity of a lifetime has to be taken within the lifetime of the opportunity."'

Some privately analysed it as the signs of an impending insurrection, though without enough concrete evidence to join the dots.

Electricity pylons crippled, mobile phone masts downed, railway tracks buckled, heists from companies too afraid to report them, stones through the windows of the Constitutional Court.

Not vandalism, but precision sabotage: too little to attract media attention, too effective to be ignored.

Must have been schooled, Minister Yasmin thought. Was that what the intelligence whispers reaching her were about? Whispers of apparatchik cronies despatched to Russia for training as saboteurs, all younger guys, the MK vets too old for that sort of thing now.

They'd lost their ticket to loot – the presidency. They were being hunted by the judiciary. They were subjected to remorseless coverage by investigative media.

So, bypass all that apparatus of white monopoly capital, all that liberal rule-of-law stuff, including a gridlocked multi-party political system and the much-vaunted constitution, and go for broke – confident that the state security system was so weak and compromised it wouldn't be able to resist, confident that the populace was now so disaffected they wouldn't defend a system that didn't defend them.

261

The saboteurs would never admit to planning insurrection, but Yasmin worried there might be no other word for it.

As Mkhize guided the Zama Zama guests, sundowners were served by his sidekick Steve Brown, who'd taken orders before their departure for the late-afternoon drive in the Land Cruiser.

Some Cokes and Pepsis, most beers and white wine, a few gin and tonics, all prepared by Brown – slices of lemon even cut for the G&Ts – and stowed with ice cubes in a cooler box.

After viewing the game – enthralled by a leopard, ambling unexpectedly on the track in front of them, seemingly unconcerned as they slowed alongside, until it disappeared into the long grass – they'd pulled up astride a hill overlooking the game reserve, the sky bursting out into layers of red-purple and yellow-orange.

Mkhize was reminiscing about his wildlife escapades, the guests sipping and chattering, when one asked him earnestly: 'Remind me again of that killer fact about elephant deaths you mentioned?'

'Burned into my psyche,' said Mkhize.

He paused, the guests still and attentive now.

'One is slaughtered every fifteen minutes – nearly one hundred each and every day.'

Star had told nobody. Not his staff. Not even his wife. Certainly not his children, now well into adulthood, comfortable in the life he'd helped make for them, but anxious to distance themselves from the burgeoning negativity of his reputation.

The night was pitch black as, telephone switched off, he borrowed his PA's small Renault Clio and drove to his bolt-hole, a small home in an outer Bloemfontein suburb, registered to the same name as his false passport and purchased with laundered money looted from provincial budgets, letting himself into the garage and pressing the remote to shut the door again.

Inside the house, always kept neat and tidy by its cleaner, who also had no idea its real owner was Star, he quickly assembled a disguise retrieved from a locked suitcase so that he closely resembled the passport photo.

Pulling down the ladder attached to the inside of the loft's small door recessed into the ceiling, he found another couple of locked suitcases, one with clothes and other personal items, the other with bundles of rands – many of them – together with credit and debit cards also in the name of the passport. Amazing what could be possible to circumvent bank-identity, proof-of-address and other regulations, when you had the resources and know-how.

Then Star drove to Lanseria Airport on the outskirts of Johannesburg where a private Learjet 35, with a range of over 5,000 kilometres, awaited him, engines running, the pilot having already gone through all the usual pre-flight checks and preparations.

Having boarded smoothly, Star flew straight to Dubai, where he also had a home, though had never even seen or lived in it.

Upon landing, he stepped out freely, as if through a curtain, from air-conditioned comfort to stiflingly dry heat.

There, safe from arrest or extradition, to plot and plan for a triumphant return – or so he hoped.

EPILOGUE

Thandi wasn't a rugby girl; Mkhize wasn't a rugby boy – soccer was his game, and she occasionally half-watched matches on TV with him while fiddling on social media.

But here she was, ecstatically cheering in the sometimes unsafe township, almost a suburb now, alongside Richards Bay, the crowd swelling as the game went on: black and white, young and old, men and women, gathering in front of a big screen.

Beforehand, the Springboks had been written off, especially because their opponents England had unexpectedly pulverised the mighty All Blacks in the semi-finals. But with victory seeming possible, shoppers and gym-users flooded in, Thandi among them, nearby fast-food queues disappearing.

She joined black spectators singing 'Shosholoza', a regular at sporting events, its haunting lyrics once chanted by black gold miners swinging their pickaxes deep underground for white bosses.

Fifty years earlier the whites-only Springboks had been hammered by British anti-apartheid protesters who disrupted their matches – their rugby supremo Danie Craven insisting 'there will be a black Springbok over my dead body'. Yet here was a multiracial Springbok team under a black captain, Siya Kolisi, crushing the favourites, England.

The captain's journey from utter township poverty to the summit of world rugby typified Thandi's amazing, infuriating, frustrating, roller-coaster of a country. Married to a white woman, he was born a year after Mandela had walked out of prison, and a few years before Thandi herself.

She'd begun watching the match with Isaac almost dutifully, expecting to slip off to do some shopping. Then she became enthralled as a black

Springbok winger – another plucked from poverty into rugby – caught a high ball and lunged past hapless England defenders, scoring the thrilling first try against the team that only days before had vanquished the omnipotent New Zealand.

She didn't really understand the complex rules but saw her country winning the collision battle, bullying and breaking the English forward pack.

But Thandi still couldn't believe they might win. Yet – and despite the apartheid legacy of inequality and destitution, which still thwarted sporting opportunity – they were showing much greater resilience, seeming to want to win more than the English team who, as youngsters, had never even thought about where their next meal was coming from.

Hers was a team mostly of giant white Afrikaner farmers, used to eating well, combined with blacks from deprived townships where food was painfully scarce.

Watching them singing the national anthem with common purpose before the match had brought more tears to Thandi's eyes. The white players raucously sung the Xhosa and Zulu verses of 'Nkosi Sikelel' iAfrika', the black players with gusto the Afrikaans and English verses.

She'd noted that the day before the World Cup final, the country's international credit rating was downgraded to negative, the murder rate stood at nearly sixty daily, rapes at 120 daily, and crime remained rampant.

Yet somehow rugby, once the emblem of apartheid on the sports field, became a unifier. Whites who had never before ventured into townships rose to their feet chanting their Xhosa captain's name, and for the next eighty minutes didn't sit down, singing and toyi-toyiing.

Then – Thandi could hardly believe it – the titanic match was over, and her Springboks were crowned Rugby World Cup champions. *Her* Springboks? Granny Matjeke would never have imagined that, telling the young Thandi with a whimsical smile how she, and every single South African who wasn't white, used to cheer any and every visiting team, never the all-white apartheid Springboks, wanting them to be beaten, wanting even the tiniest blow struck against white supremacy, even its symbol on the rugby pitch.

Chanting and dancing in the crowd after the match, Thandi hugged her beaming Isaac, thinking about what had happened to them both in the previous months, how her country could so enticingly optimise, almost simultaneously, the extremes of joy and despair, of evil and good, of greed and generosity, of selfishness and selflessness, of obscene wealth and abject destitution.

Maybe they were still the special country of Mandela and Tambo and Tutu after all. Maybe they were still an extraordinary people. Maybe they could still pull together and achieve their dreams.

But maybe also she still had to fight hard for that – and to keep fighting, to keep being a campaigning activist as the Veteran had always counselled.

GLOSSARY

bakkie	pick-up truck
bandiet	'bandit' or 'hoodlum', but also derogatory slang for political prisoners
braaivleis	barbecue
gevry	snogging
kopje	small hill
Naamloos	anonymous
spaza shop	informal convenience store, widespread in South African townships
stywe pap	stiff, almost starchy white porridge eaten with savoury dishes
toyi-toyi	a chanting, shuffling crouching dance associated with the resistance to apartheid
tsotsi	young male gangster
veld	open bush terrain, or fields

ACKNOWLEDGEMENTS

A number of busy people have helped me with this novel, for which I am extremely grateful, though only I am responsible for the final text.

Ronnie Kasrils gave invaluable comments and suggested important alterations; he might even recognise one of the principal characters.

Luthando Dziba, one of South Africa's top wildlife conservationists, gave significant input and advice on the wildlife parts.

Amina Frense also suggested corrections and spotted errors; again, she too might even recognise one of the principal characters on whom she gave me some background.

Zohra Ebrahim and Fiona Lloyd gave some helpful steers, and I am grateful to Fiona for permission to include 'Touch', the profoundly moving poem by her late partner and our family friend, Hugh Lewin, contained in his book, *Bandiet Out of Jail*.

Dennis Godfrey and Marisa McGlinchey commented insightfully upon the Irish dimension, Marisa's book *Unfinished Business* an invaluable source on the character Pádraig Murphy.

My wife, Elizabeth Haywood, has been an enormous support, reading the draft forensically, making important points, suggesting corrections.

I have relied upon my own oral and written evidence in November 2019 to the Judicial Commission of Inquiry into Allegations of State Capture, chaired by Deputy Chief Justice Raymond Zondo, and on that subsequently given by Paul Holden, who with Andrew Feinstein has been hugely impressive in unpicking the tangled web of money laundering and corruption in South Africa after Jacob Zuma became president in 2009.

The inspirational Thula Thula Game Reserve near Richards Bay,

KwaZulu-Natal, which I visited with Elizabeth in 2015, provides a real-life backdrop to some of the story.

Pieter-Louis Myburgh's fine book *Gangster State* was an important reference.

I am also grateful to Sarah and Kate Beal of Muswell Press, and Fiona Brownlee too, for pressing me to write this, for their publishing expertise and enthusiasm, for Sarah's skilful first edit, as well as to Kate Quarry and Alfred LeMaitre for both their forensic copy-editing.

Gower, South Wales, June 2022

SOURCES

Among the books and publications I relied upon during my research are the following:

Lawrence Anthony, *The Elephant Whisperer* (London, Sidgwick & Jackson, 2009)

Megan Emmett and Sean Pattrick, *Game Ranger in Your Backpack* (Pretoria, Briza Publications, 2014)

Dan Freeman, *Elephants: The Vanishing Giants* (London, Hamlyn, 1980)

Toby Harnden, *'Bandit Country': The IRA and South Armagh* (London, Coronet, 1999)

Helen Joseph, *Tomorrow's Sun* (London, Hutchinson, 1966)

Hugh Lewin, *Bandiet Out of Jail* (Cape Town, Random House, 2002)

Françoise Malby-Anthony, *An Elephant in My Kitchen* (London, Sidgwick & Jackson, 2018)

Marisa McGlinchey, *Unfinished Business: The Politics of 'Dissident' Irish Republicanism* (Manchester University Press, 2019)

Pieter-Louis Myburgh, *Gangster State: Unravelling Ace Magashule's Web of Capture* (Cape Town, Penguin, 2019).

Sharon Pincott, *Elephant Dawn: The Inspirational Story of Thirteen Years Living with Elephants in the African Wilderness* (Johannesburg, Jacana, 2016)

Rachel Love Nuwer, *Poached: Inside the Dark World of Wildlife Trafficking* (London, Scribe, 2018)

Ronald Orenstein, *Ivory, Horn and Blood* (Toronto, Firefly, 2013)

Jacques Pauw, *The President's Keepers: Those Keeping Zuma in Power and Out of Prison* (Cape Town, Tafelberg, 2018)

Julian Rademeyer, *Killing for Profit: Exposing the Illegal Rhino Horn Trade* (Cape Town, Zebra Press, 2012)

Daphne Sheldrick, *An African Love Story: Love, Life and Elephants* (London, Viking, 2012)

Christopher Vandome and Alex Vines, *Tackling Illegal Wildlife Trade in Africa: Economic Incentives and Approaches* (London, Chatham House 2018)

Athol Williams, *Deep Collusion* (Cape Town, Tafelberg, 2022)

Investigative articles in the *Daily Maverick* and online articles in the *Guardian* were also very useful.

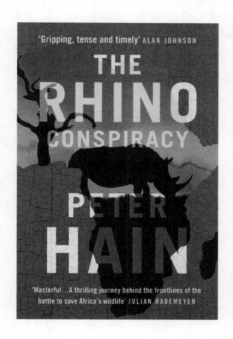

'Gripping, tense and timely' ALAN JOHNSON

THE
RHINO
CONSPIRACY

PETER
HAIN

'Masterful...A thrilling journey behind the frontlines of the
battle to save Africa's wildlife' JULIAN RADEMEYER

Available in paperback

ABOUT THE AUTHOR

Peter Hain was born in South Africa. His parents were forced into exile, in the UK, in 1966. He led the Anti-Apartheid Movement and the Anti-Nazi League during the 1970s and '80s. Hain was the Labour MP for Neath 1991–2015 and a senior minister for 12 years in Tony Blair and Gordon Brown's governments. He chaired the UN Security Council, and negotiated international Treaties curbing nuclear proliferation and banning the trade in blood diamonds. He is a member of the House of Lords.

Hain has written or edited twenty-one books – including *Mandela* (2010), memoirs *Outside In* (2012) and most recently *Pretoria Boy* (2021). His thriller, *The Rhino Conspiracy*, was published to great acclaim in 2020.